D0838286

FORBIDDEN EMBRACE

Jason tightened his embrace, crushing Desirée's soft body to the length of his own, deepening the kiss. Desirée felt as if the breath were being sucked out from her lungs, the marrow from her bones. Her legs gave way beneath her, and she would have sagged to the ground like a limp rag doll had Jason not swept her up in his powerful arms and carried her off the verandah to a spot beneath a huge oak tree, laying her gently on the new spring grass.

Desirée looked up at him, still dazed by the passionate kiss. She saw him smiling down at her, a warm glow in his misty-green eyes. Then, as he lay down beside her and enfolded her in his arms, her heart raced with anticipation.

"Desirée, my only desire. I have waited a lifetime for you."

But Desirée didn't hear his words. A roaring had filled her ears, and she blindly clung to him, afraid she would drown in the new sensation he was arousing in her.

Rebel Heart

Lauren Wilde

ZEBRA BOOKS
KENSINGTON PUBLISHING CORP.

ZEBRA BOOKS

are published by

Kensington Publishing Corp.
475 Park Avenue South
New York, NY 10016

First printing: March 1986

Printed in the United States of America

For Denise, my daughter and good friend, with love.

Prologue

The boy stood at the edge of the swamp. Greyish-green tendrils of fog rose from the murky water, swirling and ebbing around him, giving both him and the swamp an eerie, ghostly appearance. For several long minutes, he stood as still and silent as the giant cypress trees behind him, his gaze locked in intense concentration on something in the distance.

A strange hush fell over the swamp. Not a leaf stirred; not a creature moved. The swamp and all of its inhabitants watched with breathless anticipation to see what this human, one who was as much a part of this dark, mysterious world as themselves, would do next. Even the cypress trees, the ancient sentinels that had guarded this forbidding marshland since the beginning of time, seemed to be watching—waiting.

Finally, the boy walked slowly from the shadows of the swamp and stepped into the sun-washed clearing, his movements surprisingly graceful, for at thirteen, he was at that awkward age when most boys, whose bones were growing faster than the rest of them, were clumsy. In the glaring sunlight and clothed only in a pair of tattered, knee-length pants, he looked to be nothing but bone and bronzed skin. But despite his lankiness, the promise of the magnificent specimen of manhood he was a destined to become was there. Already, he was taller than his contemporaries. His shoulders were broader, and the muscles that would eventually fill out his big frame were strong and sinewy.

Once again, he stood, his eyes still glued on the magnificent plantation house in the distance. From here, he could barely see the three chimneys that jutted from the roof of the mansion, his view being obstructed by the tall, massive oaks that surrounded it. But he didn't have to see it to know what it looked like. He had already committed every towering white pillar, every window, every brick to memory. To him, Whispering Oaks was the most beautiful plantation in all of Louisiana.

Whispering Oaks. The name had been derived from the thick Spanish moss that hung from the huge oak trees, rather than the trees themselves; moss that was so long it trailed the ground in some places, fluttering in the gentle breeze and making a soft, muted sound that resembled whispering. Yes, the boy thought with a smile of approval, even he couldn't have named the plantation more appropriately.

His eyes drifted to one side of the mansion where he knew that the plantation office, the summer house, and the *garconnier*—the bachelor quarters—stood. To the back were the kitchens and, off to the opposite side, the stables and blacksmith shop. Behind all of this, screened discreetly by a row of trees, was the long row of whitewashed cottages—the slaves' quarters—and, at the very rear, the huge brick factory, where the sugar was refined. And surrounding all of this man-made magnificence, stretching for miles and miles around, were the sugarcane fields, the green stalks reaching to the sky in search of the warm June sun, their tassels waving in the gentle breeze.

As his eyes again swept admiringly over the lush fields and impressive buildings, he once again renewed his vow to see his dream come true, a dream that had been born the day he had seen Whispering Oaks for the first time three years ago. Someday, he would own a plantation as magnificent and beautiful as this one.

Just how a poor swamp Cajun was going to accomplish such a feat he hadn't figured out yet. But that didn't discourage him. Each visit to the plantation, an almost ritualistic weekly affair, had made him all the more determined, so that by now his dream was a fierce obsession. Someday, somehow, he would have his own Whispering Oaks.

His eyes dropped to the grounds below the huge moss-draped trees, sweeping over the broad expanse of neatly clipped lawn, the rose garden, whose flowers were blooming in a rainbow of colors, and the hedges of gardenias, azaleas, and camellias that lined the long circular driveway. The look on his face was one of anticipation as he searched the area for *her*.

He had discovered her a year ago, this girl-child who drew him to this place as much as the land and the magnificent mansion that stood on it. His first glimpse of her had filled him with fear, for instead of riding a sedate pony, as he would have expected of a young girl, she was mounted on a full-grown, spirited mare. As she had come tearing down the driveway at breakneck speed, the horse's hooves throwing clods of dirt behind it, his breath had caught in his throat, his heart racing, terrified she would fall from her lofty perch on the horse. It was an animal that he thought was certainly too much for such a small child to handle. But as she had veered sharply, jumping the hedge by the driveway with all of the skill and expertise of a born equestrian, his fear had turned to

9

utter amazement and then admiration.

Since that time, he had seen her almost every visit he had made. She was racing her horse across the open clearing, the sun playing over and picking up the reddish highlights of her long chestnut hair as it trailed behind her. Several times, she had laughed, a clear tinkling sound that had been a delight to his ears and sent his spirits soaring. He was fascinated with her. To him, she was a fairy princess: beautiful, elusive, half wild. And now, he came to catch a glimpse of her as much as to view the beauties of the plantation, and somehow, in a way which he couldn't explain or didn't fully understand, she, too, had become a part of his dream.

His heart raced in anticipation as his eyes anxiously continued to search for her, and then, not seeing her, his spirits plummeted. Was he to be cheated of the sight of her again today? On the few occasions he had missed her, he had left feeling a keen disappointment, a discontentment that had not left him until he had feasted his eyes on her the next time he visited.

Finally, he saw her in the distance, riding down the path that led from the stables and joined the circular drive at the front of the plantation house. His face broke into a wide smile as he watched her, and then, seeing the three boys and the girl who rode behind her, he scowled, resenting their intrusion into what he felt was something private and special between him and this girl.

As they cantered down the driveway, he stepped back into the shadows of the swamp and stood, scrutinizing the intruders. Judging from their size, the boys, two dark-haired and one golden-headed, appeared to be about his age. Behind them rode an even younger girl, her small pony struggling to keep up with the pace the horses had set.

10

Suddenly, the girl riding at the head of the column veered her horse sharply and broke away from the others, galloping straight toward the swamp where he stood, her long chestnut hair whipping around her face.

"Desirée! Come back here!" the older, dark-haired boy called. "You know you're not supposed to ride near the swamps."

But the girl ignored the boy's command and only spurred her horse harder, her gay laughter ringing in the crystal-clear morning air.

"Desirée! You're going to get your hide tanned for this!" the boy called, then, seeing his threat had no effect on her, spurred his own horse in pursuit, the others following.

As the whole group rode toward him, the Cajun stepped even further back into the shadows of the swamp, knowing that it wouldn't be wise to be caught trespassing on this land. He crouched behind a low palmetto and watched as the girl sped toward him, feeling that same thrill he always felt when he saw her racing across the clearing. Then his eyes narrowed, spying a hole in the ground some burrowing animal had made, a hole that was right in the path of the girl's horse.

His heart leaped in his throat with fear for her, and then, stepping from the concealing shadows, he ran into the clearing, yelling, "Watch out!"

His warning came a split-second too late. The mare's hoof caught in the hole, tripping her, and the girl went flying through the air to land with a loud thud on the hard ground.

The Cajun boy tore to her side, barely managing to sidestep the horse as it raced past him. Kneeling beside the girl sprawled on her back on the ground, he asked in an anxious voice, "Are you hurt?"

Desirée's senses were spinning. She looked up and, through her blurred vision, saw a head covered with dark, unruly hair and a strange bronzed face. "What happened?" she asked in a dazed voice.

Pointing to the deep burrow in the ground, the boy answered, "Your horse stepped in that hole and tripped. I tried to warn you, but I was too late."

Desirée sat up, the boy supporting her shoulders as she did so, and peered at the hole. Then looking up into the boy's face above her, she caught her breath. What strange, beautiful eyes, she thought. Why, they're the same greyish-green color as the morning mist that rose from the swamp.

As Desirée continued to stare in amazement at those misty-green eyes, the boy asked, "Does it hurt anywhere?"

Suddenly, Desirée became aware of her humiliating position on the ground and of her riding companions galloping rapidly up to them. She was acutely embarrassed by falling off her horse, and her pride stung worse than her little bottom that had taken the brunt of her fall. Fighting back tears of shame, she ignored the boy's question and struggled to her feet, brushing furiously at the dirt on her riding habit. In her haste to regain her dignity, she lost her balance. The Cajun boy reached to support her.

"Take your filthy hands off her!" the golden-haired boy yelled furiously as he jumped from his saddle.

Desirée and the Cajun boy both turned in surprise. But before either of them could say anything, the blond-headed boy pushed the Cajun away, saying angrily, "Get away from her, you swamp rat!"

"Stop it, Beau," Desirée said, stepping between the two boys. "What's wrong with you?"

"Get away from him, Desirée!" Beau commanded. "Don't you know what he is? He's one of those

12

swamp rats, one of those wild Cajuns."

Desirée looked back at the strange boy, for the first time seeing all of him. Dressed in his tattered pants, with his black hair hanging about his bronzed face, and his eyes, now darkened to a deep emerald green and flashing with anger, he did look like some fierce, half-naked savage. And then, she remembered that his hands and voice had been gentle with her. But how could that be? A savage couldn't be gentle.

She was still pondering this strange paradox when the others rode up. The two boys dismounted quickly, the older asking, "What happened, Desirée?"

Desirée turned to her brother and started to answer. "My horse—"

"He spooked her horse, Thad," Beau interrupted, pointing to the Cajun.

Thad whirled, glaring at the accused boy.

"I did not!" the Cajun said in an angry voice.

"You did too!" Beau spat. "I heard you yelling."

"I was yelling to warn—"

"See?" Beau interjected. "I told you he was yelling. *Mon Dieu*! Desirée could have been killed."

"What are you doing snooping around here, anyway?" Thad asked.

"I wasn't snooping. I was just looking."

"Looking for trouble, you mean," Beau said hotly. "Come on, Thad, Armond, let's teach this trouble-maker a lesson."

As the two girls watched in horror, the three boys flew at the stranger. A minute later, the four boys were rolling on the ground, fists flying and legs thrashing. But the aggressors soon learned they had bitten off more than they could chew. The wiry Cajun was as slippery as an eel and as strong as a ox. The boys were having a hard time getting in a clear blow, and even when they did, it seemed to have no effect on their fierce adversary.

The little girl on the pony started crying, sobbing, "Oh, Desirée, stop them! Someone is going to get killed!"

Desirée looked down at the tangled, thrashing mass of bodies. With the dust raised from their rolling on the ground, it was hard to tell who was who. Suddenly, the wiry Cajun emerged from the bottom of the heap and, in a lightning flash, was on his feet. He loomed over the other boys still sprawled on the ground, a thin line of blood trickling down one corner of his mouth over his chin. There he stood, his eyes glittering dangerously, and he crouched, waiting for the three boys to come to their feet and rush him again.

Seeing her opportunity, Desirée took advantage of the brief lull in the fight. She rushed between the Cajun and the three boys struggling to their feet. Facing her riding companions, her black eyes flashing with anger, she screamed, "Stop it! All of you!"

"Get out of the way, Desirée," Thad said, gasping for breath, his right eye swollen and already discolored.

"*Non!*" Desirée snapped. "I will not get out of your way! This time you're going to listen to *me*. That boy didn't spook my horse. He was yelling to warn me about the hole." She pointed to the burrow, saying, "That hole. The hole my horse tripped on."

Thad and Armond looked at the large hole. Their eyes widened with surprise.

"That doesn't matter anymore," Beau said angrily, swiping his bleeding nose with the back of his hand. "We've still got a score to settle with this swamp rat. Come on, let's get him!"

But Thad had no desire to tangle with the wild, wiry Cajun again. He knew now that the boy was

14

more than a match for the three of them. Casting him a look of grudging admiration, he said, "No, leave him alone, Beau. You heard what Desirée said. He didn't spook her horse."

"But he's trespassing," Beau objected. "Are you going to let him get away with that?"

"He isn't hurting anything," Thad said, turning away. "Now, come on. Let's get out of here."

Beau watched sullenly as Desirée and the two boys mounted their horses. He glanced across at the Cajun, still crouched and waiting.

"You still gonna throw me off, golden boy?" the Cajun taunted softly. "Or do you only fight when the odds are three to one?"

Beau glared at the Cajun, wishing that Thad and Armond hadn't backed down. He would have dearly loved to put this scum in his place, send him running back to the swamp where he belonged. But then, he saw the determined glint in the boy's strange eyes and realized that this one would never turn tail and run, no matter what the odds. The realization only made him hate the Cajun more.

"Come on, Beau," Thad called. "Leave him alone. This is *my* father's land. So what do you care if he's trespassing or not?"

Beau was glad for the out Thad had given him. He was hotheaded, but he wasn't a fool, and there was no way that he was going to take on the dangerous Cajun by himself. "If you say so, *mon ami*," he replied. Giving the Cajun one last heated look, he turned and walked to his horse.

Once Beau mounted, the group rode off across the clearing and away from the swamp, the boys anxious to leave the scene of their humiliation. But before they turned into the shell driveway, Desirée reined in and swung her horse about.

15

She looked back and saw the Cajun boy still standing there, proud and defiant, his strange green eyes still glittering with anger. With the swamp as a backdrop, he looked as wild and dangerous as the dark, mysterious land that had bred him. A shiver of fear ran through Desirée.

And then, across the clearing, their eyes met and locked.

"Desirée! Come on!" Thad called.

But Desirée couldn't move for the life of her. Those disturbing, misty-green eyes seemed to be holding her, drawing her to him.

At that minute, with a wisdom that far surpassed her years, Desirée knew that their destinies were somehow linked. She knew, without a shadow of a doubt, that their paths would cross again and somehow merge into one. Fate had decreed it.

"Desirée! If you don't come this instant, I'm going to tell Mammy Lou, and she'll tan your bottom!"

Her brother's threat broke the strange spell. Desirée whirled her horse, calling, "I'm coming!"

But as she galloped toward the others, Desirée couldn't resist the urge to look back at the boy once more. She glanced over her shoulder, but he had disappeared, fading away into the dark, mysterious fog-shrouded swamp that claimed him as one of its own.

Chapter 1

"Desirée! Desirée!"

Desirée turned and looked at Jeanne Marie in amazement as she rushed into her bedroom. *Mon Dieu!* What had gotten into her shy, retiring cousin? Usually, she was so quiet that you never even knew that she was around. And now, to come running into her room, yelling like that? If *Tante* Josephine heard her, there would be hell to pay.

"Lawsy, Miss Jeanne Marie," Mammy Lou said. "What are you so excited about?"

Jeanne Marie was startled, not realizing that Desirée's mammy was with her. She looked at the old Negress. She was as broad as she was tall, her skin so black it shone with a bluish luster. Dressed in her grey uniform, with its starched, immaculately white apron, and her woolly hair tied in a neat, snowy-white turban, she looked very stern and very forbidding to Jeanne Marie.

Jeanne Marie stammered, "I'm—I'm sorry, Mammy Lou. I—I didn't mean to scream to like

17

that." She flushed. *"Mon Dieu!* I must have sounded like one of those fishwives down on the docks in New Orleans."

As Jeanne Marie's dark eyes watched her apprehensively, Mammy Lou frowned. What was wrong with the pretty little gal, anyway? Always scared of her own shadow. It's that strict Creole mother of hers, Mammy thought, shaking her head in disapproval. Always harping at the girl about behaving like a lady, making her so nervous. Lawsy, a little bit of enthusiasm was just natural in a young girl. It didn't mean she wasn't a lady, just because she let herself go every now and then. Now, her baby was just as much a lady as Jeanne Marie, but she wasn't any shrinking violet.

"Oh, for heaven's sake, Jeanne Marie," Desirée said in an exasperated voice. "Stop apologizing and tell me what you're so excited about."

Mammy chuckled to herself. Nope, she thought, there certainly wasn't anything shy about her baby. If truth be known, the girl was just a little too spirited. Trying to raise her had been a formidable task for the old woman.

"I'll—I'll tell you later," Jean Marie answered, eyeing Mammy Lou nervously.

"Don't be silly," Desirée snapped. "And stop looking at Mammy Lou like that. You know she's not a tattletale like your mammy, always running to your mother and telling her everything we say." Desirée flounced on her tall canopied bed, her petticoats swirling about her legs, saying, "Now, tell me what you're so excited about."

"Well, it's really not all that exciting," Jeanne Marie said, trying to play down her impetuous out-

18

burst. "I just wanted to tell you to hurry and finish dressing, so you can come down to the ball."

"Why? Has the dancing started already?"

"*Non.*"

"Then, why should I hurry?"

Jeanne Marie flushed, giving her normally ivory skin a becoming rosy flush. She's so pretty, Desirée thought, with her dark hair and dainty features and soft brown eyes. But why does she have to be so painfully shy?

"Come on, Jeanne Marie," Desirée coaxed. "Tell me what's going on before I die of curiosity."

"Well, it's just that—that Armond brought another officer home with him for the ball tonight."

"Someone we know?"

"*Non.* I think Armond said he was from South Carolina."

Desirée came off the bed with a cry of delight. "I know! He's handsome and you're anxious to meet him."

Jeanne Marie blushed an even deeper shade of red.

"Oh, Jeanne Marie, stop looking so embarrassed," Desirée chided. "I'm glad you're finally interested in someone. Why, you should have had a beau of your own years ago."

Jeanne Marie flushed again, this time with shame. What her cousin said was true. She was almost nineteen and should have a steady beau by now. Why, in a few more years, she'd be a *vieille fille*, a spinster. But the young men had never flocked around her like they had her beautiful, spirited cousin. Desirée seemed to draw them like bees to honey. Why, if she hadn't shared her coming out with Desirée, none of

19

the young gentlemen would have even come to their box at the French Opera House, and she would have been disgraced in the eyes of the Creoles. Jeanne Marie had often wondered if that was why her mother had insisted that Desirée be introduced into society along with her, for she usually disapproved of her cousin, saying Desirée was wild and a bad influence on her.

"I'm afraid the young men aren't attracted to me," Jeanne Marie muttered. "I'm not beautiful like you are."

"*Mon Dieu!*" Desirée snapped. "Now, you really are being silly. Why, you're a lovely girl. The only reason the men don't act interested is because you're so quiet and shy. Why, you won't even talk to them."

"But I never know what to talk about," Jeanne Marie objected.

"Why, you can talk about anything. Anything that interests them. Ask them about their plantations, their race horses, the war."

"*Non*, I couldn't do that! *Maman* says a lady shouldn't talk about the war. It's vulgar."

"Oh, for heaven's sake, Jeanne Marie. The war is the *only* thing the men talk about nowadays. If you want to take part in the conversation, then you have to talk about it. Honestly," Desirée said in a disgusted voice, flouncing away to stand before the floor-length mirror where Mammy Lou waited with her ballgown, "they're like a bunch of little boys with a new toy, always talking about their grand plans for how they're going to whip the Yankees, and practicing marching in their gaudy red and yellow uniforms."

"Why, Desirée, everyone thinks the Avegno Zouaves look very dashing in their handsome uniforms."

"Well, I don't! I think it's ridiculous for grown men to go walking around in baggy pants that look like oversized bloomers. And as if that's not bad enough, they have to wear those silly tasseled fezzes. They look more like they're dressed to go to the Mardi Gras than to war."

Jeanne Marie watched as Desirée lifted her arms for Mammy Lou to slip her ballgown over her head. The movement caused Desirée's breasts to strain at the soft material of her camisole. Jeanne Marie averted her eyes in embarrassment, for her cousin was much more full busted than she. In fact, Desirée was much more curvaceous all over, despite the fact that she was several inches taller than Jeanne Marie.

As Desirée emerged from the yards and yards of blue silk, she continued: *"Oui,* the men are like little boys playing games. Why, this war has been going on for over a year now, and nothing has happened but a few little skirmishes."

"There was that big battle at Manasses," Jeanne Marie pointed out.

"Yes, but it was months and months ago. Besides, I wish that battle had never even happened."

"Never happened?" Jeanne Marie asked in a shocked voice. *"Mon Dieu!* How can you say that? It was a big victory for the South."

Desirée whirled to face her cousin, saying, "I'm just as patriotic as anyone else in the South. But if that battle had never happened, Beau and Thad wouldn't have gone rushing off to join General Beauregard's army, and they'd still be here in Louisiana."

21

Mammy Lou, who had been buttoning the back of Desirée's dress when she whirled away, said in exasperation, "Lawsy, child, will you be still? I'm never gonna get you dressed if you don't stop all that flitting around."

"I'm sorry, Mammy," Desirée said, turning her back to Mammy.

"But Desirée," Jeanne Marie said, "you know the only reason Thad and Beau went is because General Beauregard is a native son of New Orleans and another Creole."

"*Non*, that's not the only reason," Desirée replied hotly. "They went because they were scared to death the war would end before they could get into the fighting. You know how they are. Both of them. Jumping into every fight they can find."

Jeanne Marie looked at Desirée thoughtfully, then said, "It's Beau you're really angry with, isn't it?"

Desirée turned, saying, "I'm not angry with him. I'm just—just provoked." Tears glittered in her black, velvety eyes. "Oh, Jeanne Marie, if Beau hadn't gone rushing off like that, we'd be married by now. Do you realize our wedding should have taken place six weeks ago?"

"But there's a war going on," Jeanne Marie argued.

"I know that!" Desirée snapped, then said in a bitter voice, "But he could have joined one of the volunteer companies here in Louisiana, like Armond did. Then we could have still been married." Desirée walked to the canopied bed and sat down on it. "Oh, Jeanne Marie," she cried. "Sometimes I don't even think Beau loves me."

22

Jeanne Marie rushed to the bed and sat beside her cousin, saying with surprising spirit, *"Non,* Desirée! Don't talk so foolish. You know Beau idolizes you. Why, he worships the ground you walk on. And you're not being fair to him. You know he planned on being back before the wedding. Why, no one ever dreamed the war would last this long."

"Oui, I know," Desirée admitted, staring down at her hands in her lap. "He thought he would only be gone a few months." She looked up at her cousin. "But that's just what I've been saying. This war has been going for a year now, and we're no closer to beating the Yankees than we ever were. At this rate, there's no telling how long Beau might be gone."

Desirée rose, walked dejectedly to the vanity, and sat down on the stool before it. Jeanne Marie watched as Mammy Lou combed her long, chestnut tresses and then arranged her hair so it hung in long curls at the back of her head. Once again she admired Desirée's beauty. Her cousin had inherited her creamy, flawless complexion, her dark, expressive eyes, and her aristocratic features from her Creole mother, along with the intriguing mole that sat off to one side of her pretty mouth. But the color of her hair was her legacy from her Scots-Irish father. Jeanne Marie shook her head, thinking that with the hot blood of those three nationalities running through her veins, it was no wonder Desirée had such a fiery temperament.

But, at that minute, Desirée didn't look a bit fiery. Jeanne Marie had never seen her looking so sad and dispirited, and because she loved Desirée like the sister she had never had, Jeanne Marie's heart went out to her. She wished there was something she could

23

say to comfort her cousin.

Desirée glanced up into the mirror and saw the look on Jeanne Marie's face. She looks as miserable as I feel, she thought, then felt a pang of regret for distressing her cousin.

"Oh, don't pay any attention to me," Desirée said. "I don't know what's wrong with me lately. It's just that I'm so—so—"

"So what?" Jeanne Marie coaxed.

"Oh, I don't know. So—so tense and fidgety." Desirée frowned, then added, "I guess I'm just worried about Beau, that's all."

Mammy Lou, who had been listening to everything, thought it was more than worry about Beau that was bothering her baby. At twenty, Desirée was ripe and ready to become a woman in its fullest sense, her body aching for a fulfillment that, in her innocence, she didn't understand. Yes, she was ready for physical love, and the man who should have initiated her into those delights by now had run off to war, leaving her to deal with strange longings.

While Mammy Lou wasn't at all surprised to know Desirée was sexually frustrated, her criticism of Beau had surprised the old woman, for she had thought Desirée completely blind to the faults of her betrothed. Unlike all of the mothers with marriageable daughters who thought Beau, with his wealth, his golden good looks, and his polished charm, was the best catch in all of Louisiana, Mammy Lou had never been impressed with the young Creole. To her, Beau was just like so many of the sons of these wealthy planters: irresponsible and spoiled, too busy gratifying their own needs to settle down. Mammy Lou had

24

always hoped for better for her baby: a real man.

Jeanne Marie watched Desirée while she rubbed crushed rose petals over her cheeks to give them more color, saying thoughtfully, "Maybe you feel that way because you've been cooped up for so long. It must be hard not to be able to go to any of the parties or balls because your betrothed isn't here to escort you. I'm glad you decided to come to the ball tonight, even though *Maman* said—" Jeanne Marie flushed, realizing she had blundered.

Desirée laughed, saying, "Oh, don't look so horrified, Jeanne Marie. I know your mother doesn't approve of my coming to Terre Doux for the dance tonight. I can just imagine what she said. But then, your mother doesn't approve of anything I do. So what difference does it make? She's never liked me."

"*Non*, Desirée. It's not that my *maman* doesn't like you personally. It's just that—"

"Now, don't start that old business about your mother being Creole and disapproving of me because I'm '*a la Louisiane*, half French and half American," Desirée interjected in a firm voice. "And don't say it's because I'm wild either, because I'm not! I don't do anything the other girls don't do, Creoles included." Desirée turned back to the mirror and smoothed her hair saying, "*Non*, your mother just doesn't like me, that's all."

Jeanne Marie frowned. She couldn't argue with Desirée's words because she feared they were true. She had never understood why her mother was so critical of Desirée. True, her mother did come from one of the older, stubbornly French families that looked down on all Americans, thinking them crude and brash and much below them. But somehow, her mother's disapproval seemed more personal, almost vindictive. And Desirée wasn't wild either, despite what her mother said. Like so many other of the *jeunes filles*, she was just lively and spirited. Except . . . Jeanne Marie's frown deepened. Except for that business of riding all over the country in the middle of the night—all alone. Thank God her mother didn't know about that. She doubted if even Mammy Lou knew, which surprised her, for the old woman seemed to have an uncanny way of knowing everything. No, only she and Armond knew of Desirée's wild midnight rides, and although they had both tried to discourage her, pointing out how dangerous it was, Desirée still continued them.

"Jeanne Marie? Are you listening to me?" Desirée asked.

"What?" Jeanne Marie asked, startled from her musings.

"I said, I think it's a silly rule anyway. Why should I stay at home, like some cloistered nun, just because Beau isn't here to escort me? Besides, this ball is different. After all, it's not like I'm galivanting around, going to all kinds of parties and balls. I'm part of the family."

"*Oui*, that's what Papa said," Jeanne Marie answered. "He said, since you're his niece, you'd be one of the hostesses and not a guest. Besides, he said he didn't see any reason why Armond couldn't take you to some of the balls. Many of the girls who are betrothed are being escorted by their brothers and cousins."

Desirée smiled. How like her uncle to defend her to his wife. Uncle Paul had always been exceptionally kind to her, as if he were trying to make up to her for the way his wife treated her. But then, as the daughter of his only sibling, she expected it was only natural he would be protective of her, since she was his only living blood relative, other than Thad and his children.

"See?" Desirée said, her dark eyes taking on their usual sparkle. "Even your papa thinks it's a silly rule. Why, all I'm going to do is dance. What harm could that be?"

Desirée twirled about the room several times, pretending that she was dancing, her hooped skirt swaying gracefully. Then abruptly, she stopped, a devilish smile crossing her lips. "*Non.* Maybe, I'll do more than dance," she said in a defiant voice. "Maybe, I'll flirt with some of the young gentlemen, too."

"Desirée! You wouldn't!" Jeanne Marie said in a shocked voice.

"Well, maybe just a little," Desirée conceded. Then she laughed, saying, "But don't worry, Jeanne Marie. I promise I won't flirt with your beau."

Jeanne Marie flushed, saying, "Oh, he's not my beau. I haven't even met him yet. I just saw him coming in the door with Armond."

"Well, once he sees you, he will be," Desirée said. Catching Jeanne Marie's hand and pulling her to her feet, she turned to Mammy Lou, saying, "How do we look, Mammy?"

Mammy looked at the two girls. Jeanne Marie was dressed in a light pink confection that accented her daintiness and made her look like a little doll. Desirée's ballgown was a blue silk, the low-cut bodice molding her high, full breasts and tiny waist to

27

perfection. The neckline was enhanced with a spray of darker blue silk flowers. Another spray of silk flowers cascaded down the entire length of one side of the full-hooped skirt.

"You're both as pretty as a picture," Mammy Lou answered in all sincerity. "Those young gentlemen's eyes are going to pop right out of their heads when they see you two li'l gals."

Desirée looked at her mammy, feeling a surge of love welling up in her for the old woman who had raised her and her brother. It had been Mammy Lou who had gently and lovingly rocked them on her broad lap, comforting them and nursing their little hurts. It had been Mammy Lou who had scolded and punished them when they did wrong. It had been Mammy Lou who had guided them, with all the love and patience she could summon, and it had been Mammy Lou who had fought back the Angel of Death when she and her brother had thrashed in delirium with the dreaded yellow fever, the same disease that had taken her mother's life. But even if her mother had not died when she was a child, Desirée would have loved this old Negress more than the woman who had birthed her, for her mother had been a shallow, frivolous woman, more interested in her balls and parties than her children, often leaving them on the plantation with their black mammy for months at a time, while she pursued the gay social life in New Orleans.

Desirée stepped forward and fiercely hugged the big woman, saying in an emotion-choked voice, "I love you, Mammy Lou."

Mammy Lou's black eyes glittered with tears. She

loved both of the children she had raised, but this spirited girl had a special place in her heart. "I love you, too, honey lamb," she said, hugging Desirée back. Then she stepped away, saying, "But you're going to muss your pretty dress hugging this old woman. Now, you two li'l gals go and have yourselves a good time."

Desirée smiled, saying, "We will, Mammy." She turned to Jeanne Marie, catching her hand and leading her to the doorway, saying, "Come on, Jeanne Marie. I can hardly wait to see this mysterious young man you've been telling me about. To get your attention he must be something very special."

Chapter 2

Desirée and Jeanne Marie stood poised on the middle of the wide spiraling staircase. From there, they could look down into the huge ballroom that sat to one side of the foyer below them. Hundreds of candles flickered on huge crystal chandeliers, sending prisms of light which danced across the huge room where the crowd of men and women already stood, chatting and waiting patiently for the music to begin.

Desirée's dark eyes swept over the crowd. The women were dressed in every color of the rainbow and every hue in between, the jewels on their throats and in their hair glittering in the candlelight. The men wore their colorful Zouave uniforms or elegant evening wear. On a raised dais, at one end of the room, the musicians, slaves that had been trained to use musical instruments, sat and waited, their black faces beaming with pride as they displayed the new scarlet tunics and white pants for this special occasion. Once the ball began, their music would fill the

30

huge room and drift out the french doors and windows into the galleries and spacious lawns beyond. Then when the dancing began, the whole ballroom would be turned into a giant kaleidoscope of flashing, whirling colors.

"I don't see Armond and his friend anywhere," Jeanne Marie said to Desirée. "Do you?"

Desirée scanned the milling crowd below them, and then, as if an invisible hand had reached out and turned her head, directing her attention to the corner of the ballroom right below them, she saw him.

There was no doubt in Desirée's mind that this was the man Jeanne Marie had told her about. His commanding presence seemed to fill the whole room, crowding out every one else with his vitality. He towered over the shorter Creoles standing around him, the striking breadth of his shoulders straining at the butternut flock coat he wore, as if they would burst from the confining material any minute. Desirée frowned, wondering if it was the well-tailored uniform he wore that made him stand out among the other men. Up against him, the Creoles, dressed in their gaudy Zouave uniforms with their baggy trousers, seemed somehow less manly, almost effeminate. Her eyes drifted over him, noting the broad expanse of his chest, the trim waist circled with a yellow sash, the lean hips, and long sinewy legs. No, she decided, it wasn't the uniform that made this man seem so much more masculine. His strong sexuality and compelling virility came from something much deeper than his clothing or even his magnificent physique. It stemmed from the very roots of his being.

Her eyes darted back up to his face, anxious to see

31

more of this man who radiated masculinity like a fire did heat waves. His dark head was tilted downward as he talked to his companions, but Desirée, from her viewpoint on the stairs, could tell that he was clean shaven, and long sideburns on his face accenting his strong jawline and the rugged planes of his face. His skin tone was dark, but unlike the Creoles around him, it was more bronzed than swarthy. Desirée wished he would look up so she could see more of the tall, darkly handsome stranger's face.

And then, as if sensing her wish, the man did glance up, and Desirée's breath caught in her throat. Greyish-green eyes stared up at her, looking at her with such intensity that she felt pinned to the spot.

A strange feeling of déjà vu swept over Desirée. She'd seen those eyes somewhere before. But where? Her mind struggled to remember, but her subconscious stubbornly refused to give up the memory, holding it like some well-guarded, precious secret.

"Desirée," Jeanne Marie whispered. "That's him. The man I was telling you about. But *Mon Dieu!* Look at the way he's staring at you."

Desirée was very much aware of those disturbing misty-green eyes on her, slowly sweeping down the entire length of her body. She was accustomed to the bold looks of the hot-blooded Creoles, but none had been this bold. His eyes seemed to be stripping her of every vestige of clothing. A warmth swept over her, from the tips of her toes to the top of her head, a flush that stemmed from something more than just embarrassment.

Desirée's pride came to her defense. She stiffened with indignation, her black eyes flashing. How dare he, she thought angrily. How dare he look at me like that!

And then as his eyes rose and locked on hers, Desirée felt that strange feeling of déjà vu again. He seemed to be peering into the very depths of her soul, drawing it out, slowly draining her of her resistance, her very being itself. A weak feeling washed over her. She clutched the banister beside her for support. What dark, mysterious power does he hold over me that he can make me feel this way? Never had she felt so exposed, so vulnerable, so threatened. This man is dangerous, she thought, her heart racing in fear.

"Desirée?" Jeanne Marie asked in an alarmed voice. "What's wrong? You're so pale. Are you ill?"

Desirée jerked her eyes from the stranger's, breaking the strange spell, and said in a dazed voice, "What?"

"I said, are you ill?"

Desirée quickly glanced down at the man, seeing him still watching her intently. But that intense, penetrating look had gone from his eyes. Suddenly, she felt foolish. What in the world was wrong with her, entertaining such fantasies? Why, no man could hold someone in his power by sheer eye contact alone. And besides, what hold could this man have over her?

Feeling reassured, she answered, *"Non,* I'm not ill. I just felt—a little light-headed there for a minute."

"Are you feeling better now? Do you want to go back upstairs and lie down?"

"Non, I'm fine now," Desirée answered, taking a step down the stairs. "Come on, Jeanne Marie. Let's hurry. The dancing will begin soon."

As Desirée and Jean Marie descended the stairs,

33

Armond looked up, and seeing them, smiled and called, "Jeanne Marie, Desirée! Come over here. I want you to meet someone."

As the girls walked toward Armond and the stranger, Desirée was aware of the man still watching her. Deliberately, she avoided looking into his eyes, still shaken by the strange sensations she had felt on the stairs. Instead, she concentrated on her cousin's face, thinking how attractive Armond was with his dark hair and eyes and dapper mustache.

"Jason," Armond said when the girls had come to a stop before them, "I'd like you to meet my sister, Jeanne Marie, and our cousin from New Orleans, Desirée McAllister." Turning to the girls, he said, "This is Captain Jason Montgomery, recently arrived from Charleston."

"My pleasure, ladies," Jason drawled with a deep, baritone voice, bowing slightly.

"Jason has been sent down here by the War Department to study our harbor defenses," Armond informed the two girls.

"Oh?" Jeanne Marie responded with a shy smile, and then, remembering what Desirée had told her, asked, "And will you be making any suggestions on how to further fortify New Orleans?"

"No, I'm afraid not, Miss Corbeau," Jason answered. "I'm here to study your fortifications in hopes of obtaining ideas on how to strengthen Charleston's defenses. Since our two cities are so similar, both harbors located on rivers, guarded by forts, and surrounded by swamps and marshes, the army feels Charleston might be wise to follow the example set by New Orleans."

34

Desirée, still determined not to look into the man's eyes again, had focused on Jason's mouth instead. But her discomforture only grew, for his mouth, while strong, had a sensuality about it that disturbed her almost as much as his eyes had. She jerked her eyes away and stared at a point just over his shoulder.

"Then the War Department considers our defenses adequate?" Jeanne Marie asked, feeling more confident.

"More than adequate," Jason replied.

"And you, captain?" Desirée asked, finally gathering enough courage to join in the conversation. "What do you think of our defenses?"

Jason looked at her, and once again Desirée was aware of those misty-green eyes on her. A sudden warmth suffused her.

"Frankly, I'm impressed, Miss McAllister," Jason replied. "With Forts Jackson and St. Phillips guarding the river downstream, aided by the four vessels of the Confederate Navy, two of the State of Louisiana, and six of the River Defense Fleet, including the ram, *Manasses*, I'd say it would be impossible for an enemy fleet to sail up the Mississippi and attack New Orleans."

"And even if a Yankee fleet could manage to get past the forts and navy, they'd never manage to get past the cables," Armond pointed out.

"Ah, yes, the cables," Jason replied in a thoughtful voice. "How clever of you Louisianans. No one else would think of stringing heavy cables across the river to keep the enemy from sailing up it."

Several other officers, overhearing the conversation, had drifted closer, curious to see what this stranger thought of their defenses. One of the officers asked, "Then the cables have been repaired?"

Jason's eyes darted to the man, his dark eyebrows arching in surprise. "Oh? Was there some problem?"

"Why, yes," the man answered. "I heard that the raft that the cables were attached to had been damaged during the recent flood, and the cables had snapped, leaving almost a third of the river open."

Jason turned to Armond, asking, "Is this true?"

Armond flushed, wishing the man had kept his mouth shut. His commander hadn't wanted the War Department to know about the weakened defenses, thinking the cables would be replaced soon enough. "Partly," Armond answered, shooting a heated look toward the man who had let the secret slip out. "The cables did snap, but the river *isn't* open. We've temporarily strung chains across that section, just until current from the spring floods slows down and we can replace the cables."

"What size chains?" Jason asked.

"One inch," Armond answered.

So, Jason thought, one third of the river was protected with one inch chains instead of two and a half inch cables. And he bet he knew just what part of the river those chains lay in. This was just the break he'd been waiting for, the chink in the enemy's armor. Damn, he wished he was meeting that courier tonight instead of tomorrow night. If Captain Farragut was going to move his fleet upriver, he'd better do it fast, before those cables were replaced.

Aware of Armond's dark eyes on him, Jason said smoothly, "Well, that should certainly be adequate. I shouldn't think any ship could break a chain that

36

size."

"That's what we thought," Armond replied, relieved that the captain was in agreement.

At that minute, the music began. Jason glanced at Desirée, and for one terrifying moment, she thought he was going to ask her to dance. Then, when he turned and led Jeanne Marie onto the ballroom floor, Desirée sighed in relief. Thank goodness, he had remembered his manners and asked his hostess to dance first. Jeanne Marie would have been very hurt, especially since she had shown an interest in him. Besides, Desirée didn't want to dance with the captain. If his look alone could unnerve her, how much more disturbing would it be to be held in his arms?

Armond led Desirée onto the ballroom floor. For a few minutes, they danced in silence, just enjoying the music and the swaying movements of the lilting waltz. Then, catching a glimpse of Jason's whirling Jeanne Marie across the ballroom, Desirée asked, "How well do you know Captain Montgomery, Armond?"

"Not well. As I said, he just arrived in New Orleans a few days ago." He looked at Desirée thoughtfully, then said, "Why do you ask?"

"Because I think Jeanne Marie is interested in him."

"Jeanne Marie is interested in Captain Montgomery?" Armond asked in an astonished voice.

"Yes. Why do you act so surprised? After all, the captain is a very attractive man."

"It's not that. It's just that Jeanne Marie is so shy and the captain is so . . ." His voice trailed off.

"So what?"

Armond frowned, then said, "I started to say

37

intense. But that would be putting it much too simply. From what I've seen, the captain appears to be a very complex man. On the surface, he seems to be as polished and as socially tractable as the rest of us. Yet, just below the surface, I sense a wild quality, a strength that bends to no authority, no adversity. Let's just say that Jason is too much man for a woman like Jeanne Marie to handle. I don't think she would feel comfortable with him."

Desirée frowned, wondering if that was why the captain had appeared so much more virile and masculine than the others, because he was *too* much man.

"*Non ma petite*, don't frown so. I'm sure Jeanne Marie will realize the captain is not for her. And as for Jason, I don't think we will have to worry about his pursuing her." He gave Desirée a penetrating look, saying, "It seems to me he was much more attracted to you."

Desirée's color rose. "Nonsense, Armond. You're just imagining things."

Armond chuckled, saying, "*Non*, I was not imagining things. I saw the way he looked at you. I'm afraid Jason is going to be in for a big disappointment when he discovers you've already been claimed." He paused, then said, "By the way, have you heard from Beau recently?"

"*Non*. But we had a letter from Thad last week."

"And what did your brother have to say?"

"That he was bored. That nothing had even happened yet, except for one small skirmish."

Armond chuckled, saying, "And after all of the boasting he and Beau did about how they were going to whip the Yankees before we here in Louisiana even got a shot at them? *Non*, I was afraid those two were in for a big disappointment when they discovered that soldiering wasn't all excitement and thrills but often just tedious, hard work."

"Is that why you didn't go with them? Because you knew it wasn't going to be all that exciting?"

"*Non*, that wasn't the reason. I don't crave excitement like those two do. I'm afraid I'm just a simple planter at heart."

"But you joined a company of volunteers, too," Desirée pointed out.

"*Oui*," Armond agreed, then added, "but not for the same reason Beau and Thad joined up. Eventually my company will be called up, and when we are, I will fight as fiercely as any other loyal southerner. But until then, I'm content to stay here in Louisiana and help my father with Terre Doux."

Yes, Desirée thought, Armond had never been as restless as Beau and Thad. He had always been more serious minded, more settled. And she could understand how he felt about Terre Doux. Like her, his roots were sunk deep into the Louisiana mud. He had a profound love for the land. She felt the same way about Whispering Oaks. Except Whispering Oaks was no longer her home, she remembered glumly.

"Ah, *petite*, why such a sad look?" Armond asked.

"I was just thinking about Whispering Oaks."

"*Oui*, that is sad." Armond frowned, saying, "I could never understand why your father insisted on selling it."

"He said that after my mother died there, it was too full of unhappy memories. But I think it was more than that, Armond. I think it reminded him too much

39

of his guilt. You see, he insisted my mother go to Whispering Oaks that summer instead of keeping her in New Orleans with him, as she begged him to do. I think he felt like he had sent her to her death, that if she had stayed with him in the city, she might not have even been stricken. He wasn't."

"*Mon Dieu*, Desirée! It's ridiculous to blame himself. Ordinarily, sending her away from New Orleans was the best thing to do. How was he to know that year the yellow jack would be so bad it would spread all over Louisiana, instead of confining itself to the city, as it usually did. Why, the epidemic of fifty-three was the worst in Louisiana's history. The death toll rose to over forty-thousand."

"I know," Desirée answered. "But the point is, despite all reasoning, my father still blamed himself. And I will have to admit, he seems happier in New Orleans with his cotton brokerage. Certainly much happier than he was at Whispering Oaks after my mother died. I suppose that's all that's important."

And what about your happiness, *petite*? Armond thought angrily. Is it not important, too? He had always thought Desirée's father selfish when he sold his plantation without any thought to his children. Whispering Oaks was their birthright. It should have been theirs some day, just as Terre Doux would be his and Jeanne Marie's.

The dance ended, and as Desirée and Armond walked from the ballroom floor, Desirée sighed and said, "*Eh bien*, at least I have one thing to be thankful for. Thank God, *Oncle* Paul bought it and it's still in the family. And he promised me he would never sell it."

Yes, Armond thought, his father was a true Creole, believing firmly in *le nom de la famille*, all for the family. He stopped and looked down at Desirée, saying in a quiet voice, "Nor shall I ever sell Whispering Oaks, *ma petite*."

"You promise, Armond?" Desirée asked, her eyes shining with relief.

"I promise, Desirée," Armond replied in a firm voice. "Whispering Oaks shall never leave the family."

Desirée threw her arms around Armond and kissed him on the cheek, crying softly, *"Merci*, Armond. Thank you so much."

Armond grinned, saying, "Could I do any less for my favorite female cousin?"

Desirée laughed, saying, "Favorite? I'm your only female cousin."

"Oui, but if I had a hundred, you'd still be my favorite."

Desirée knew Armond wasn't just being gracious. He meant every word. She, Thad, Jeanne Marie, and Armond had always been close. Growing up on neighboring plantations, with hardly a day going by that they weren't in each other's company, they were more like brothers and sisters than cousins.

The ball continued, and Desirée was claimed for every dance. Most of her partners had once been old swains, for Desirée, with her high spirit and stunning beauty, had been one of the most sought-after belles in Louisiana. But none of the men overstepped themselves; the only hint of their regret that she was Beau's betrothed was the look of longing that came into their eyes when they thought no one was watching.

As Desirée whirled about the ballroom, she glanced

41

about the room for Captain Montgomery, wondering where he had disappeared to, and why he hadn't asked her to dance. She should be glad, she told herself firmly. He's much too dangerous, with his bold eyes and magnetic masculinity. But as the evening progressed, Desirée's disappointment only grew, until she found herself actually vexed. Where had he disappeared to? Had he become bored with the dance and left?

But Jason hadn't left the ball. Nor had he forgotten Desirée. After the first dance with Jeanne Marie, he had retired to a corner of the room. There, screened by a large potted palm, he had stood and watched Desirée as she danced, content for the time being in just feasting his eyes on her.

One of the first things Jason had done when he had returned to Louisiana was to visit Whispering Oaks. He had been shocked when he had seen it. The plantation had been completely deserted, the beautiful mansion and its surrounding buildings falling into disrepair and almost swallowed up by the tangle of voracious vines and shrubs that had grown at random. The sight had made him heartsick.

Then he had looked at the fields, seeing no sign of neglect there. Already, the tender green shoots of the sugarcane that had been planted the previous fall were lifting their heads to the warm sun, and there wasn't a weed in sight.

What had happened? Had the plantation been sold? And if so, why? And why didn't the new owners live on it? And what had happened to the people who had once lived there?

It had been the last question that had disturbed

Jason the most. What had happened to *her*, the child he had been so fascinated with, the fairy princess of his youth?

He had never been able to forget her. Even after he had gone north, her memory had clung tenaciously in his mind. He had only to close his eyes and he could see her racing across the clearing on her horse, her chestnut hair trailing behind her, her laughter ringing in the air.

As he had grown into manhood, he had rebuked himself as a fool, telling himself that he was behaving more like a silly, emotional adolescent than a full-grown, reasonable adult. But still, in the shadows of his mind, the memory of her had lingered, haunting him.

He had left Whispering Oaks that day feeling strangely empty, fearing he was doomed to be forever haunted by the memory of her. And then when he had seen her standing on the stairway, his heart had leaped to his throat. Not for a second had he doubted that this enchanting, beautiful woman was she, the fairy princess of his youth. And fast on the heels of his recognition had come a new profound realization. He loved her. He had loved her from the minute he had laid eyes on her years ago, had perhaps loved her since the beginning of time, and always would. That was the reason he had carried her in his memory all those years.

And now, he stood watching her whirling around the ballroom. The fascinating, winsome child had grown into a beautiful, desirable woman. And Jason was no longer a boy. He was a man, with a man's desires. He wanted her as he had never wanted any other woman in his life. Long ago, fate had decreed her as his love. Now, it was up to him to make her his woman.

When the dance ended, Jason stepped from behind the palm and walked across the ballroom, his eyes never veering from his destination as he weaved his way through the crowd. When he stood behind her, he said, "May I have this dance, Miss McAllister?"

Desirée recognized that rich, baritone voice. She whirled, intending to refuse, still irritated that he had ignored her for so long. But the words never reached her lips, for once she looked into those misty-green eyes, she was powerless.

Jason took Desirée in his arms and whirled her onto the dance floor. For a moment, Desirée danced as if in a daze, totally unaware of the music and the dancing couples around her. She seemed to be locked with this man in some strange vacuum that defied time and space.

And then, as awareness slowly returned, Desirée became acutely conscious of even more disturbing sensations: Jason's hands, one holding hers, the other at the small of her back, seemed to be burning her. She could feel the heat radiating from him and smell his heady, masculine scent, a scent that left her feeling strangely light-headed. Beneath her hand, she could feel the corded muscles of his broad shoulders. Suddenly, she found it hard to breathe. His overpowering masculinity seemed to be smothering her.

"Captain Montgomery," Desirée said in a breathless voice, "you're holding me much too close."

Jason laughed, and Desirée caught the flash of white teeth against his bronzed skin. "That's impossible, with these hoops you ladies insist upon wearing," Jason said. His voice lowered to an even deeper timbre. "But believe me, if I could, I *would* hold you closer—much closer."

Desirée flushed, both from his bold words and from the effect of his deep, husky voice on her. *Mon Dieu*, she thought wildly, he *is* dangerous! I have to get away from him.

Abruptly Desirée stopped dancing, saying, "I'd prefer not to dance, captain. It's—it's much too hot in here for all of this activity."

Jason realized he shouldn't have said what he had. Desirée was a well-bred young lady, accustomed to being wooed with soft words and glowing compliments. No doubt his frank admission had shocked her tender sensibilities. He would have to watch himself, move slower. But damn, it was going to be hard to do. After holding her soft body in his arms, smelling her intoxicating scent, and all the while acutely aware of her full breasts rising and falling just inches from his chest and of that enticing little mole that sat beside her mouth just begging to be kissed, he was about to burst for want of her.

"I think I shall retire to the ladies' room and lie down and rest for awhile," Desirée said, starting to turn away.

But Jason had no intention of letting her get away from him. "Nonsense," he said in a decisive voice. "What you need is some fresh air."

To Desirée's horror, he caught her arm in a firm grip and swept her out a nearby french door to the verandah outside. For a brief minute, Desirée thought to struggle, then realized it would only serve to draw attention to her.

Once they were standing on the gallery, she whirled, her dark eyes flashing with indignation. "How dare you, captain! We shouldn't be out here alone."

"But we're not alone," Jason countered, motioning down the long porch. "There are other couples out here."

Desirée glanced over her shoulder, seeing the vague, shadowy silhouettes in the distance. And judging from how close they stood to each other, they were engaged couples or those who were in the advanced stages of courting. The couples only served to remind Desirée precisely why she shouldn't be out here with this man. She was betrothed to another, and if anyone had seen her stepping out here with this virtual stranger, her reputation would be ruined.

"Are you afraid of me?" Jason asked in a quiet voice.

Desirée's head snapped around. His eyes locked on hers. At that minute with those shimmering green eyes watching her so intently, she was afraid, and not for her reputation. No, it was for herself that she feared; that, and this man's spellbinding magnetism.

Frantically, Desirée tore her eyes away from his. Then she noticed his smile. Was he mocking her, taunting her? Never one to refuse a dare, her fierce pride rose to the surface. She'd be damned if she'd run from this man like some frightened animal. "Of course, I'm not afraid of you!" she snapped. "It's just that—"

"I'm glad you're not afraid of me," Jason interjected with a soft voice, taking her arm again. "I would never want that."

46

His words and the soothing tone of his voice momentarily disarmed Desirée. Numbly she allowed herself to be led to a secluded, darkened corner of the verandah. And then, realizing where they stood, she glanced nervously back at the other couples. From here, she could barely see them. Surely, at this distance, they wouldn't recognize her. No, she wouldn't run. First, she'd put this—this rake in his place!

She opened her mouth, fully intending to give Jason a dressing down he'd never forget. But before she could say a word, Jason, still curious to know why she had left Whispering Oaks, asked, "Have you lived in New Orleans all your life?"

Desirée was stunned. She had assumed the bold captain had brought her out here with seduction on his mind. His casual question confused her. She looked at him warily, saying, "No, I moved there about nine years ago."

"And where did you live before that?"

"On a plantation near here."

"And why did you move?"

Desirée frowned, wondering at the strangeness of his questions. "My mother died of yellow fever and—" She hesitated, reluctant to tell this man of her father's strange guilt.

"And what?" Jason prompted.

"And my father decided he no longer wanted to be a planter," Desirée answered in a rush of words.

"And what happened to the plantation?"

If Desirée had thought Jason's personal questions strange, she was totally baffled by this one. Why should this stranger care about what had happened to Whispering Oaks? "He sold it to my uncle. Why do

47

you ask?" she questioned in a suspicious voice.

Jason shrugged and leaned his broad shoulder against one of the towering columns behind him. "Just curious."

Desirée resented his curiosity, and his strange questions had somehow disturbed her. "I hardly see what business it is of yours where I live."

"I'm sorry, Desirée," Jason replied softly. "I didn't mean to pry. I only wanted to know more about you."

Desirée's breath caught in her throat when Jason spoke her name with his soft, southern drawl. Tingles ran up her spine, almost as if he had reached out and caressed her. "Captain Montgomery," she replied indignantly, "I don't recall giving you permission to address me by my first name."

Jason chuckled, a low rumbling coming from deep in his chest; a sound that played havoc on Desirée's already befuddled senses. He pushed himself away from the pillar and stepped toward her, saying, "Oh, come now, Desirée. We both know that once a man and woman have been introduced, it's perfectly permissible to use first names."

"But I don't want you to call me by my first name!"

Jason stepped closer, and Desirée once again felt herself being smothered by his compelling virility. She tried to step back from him, but her legs refused to obey her brain's command. She stood rooted to the spot, as if caught in some invisible trap, and watched as his hands rose to cup her face.

Raising her face, Jason said in a whisper-soft voice. "Why don't you want me to say your name? It's a beautiful name, almost as beautiful as the woman it belongs to." His eyes roamed over her face hungrily as his voice dropped to an even huskier whisper. "Desirée. Desirable woman. Yes, so beautiful a name, so appropriate for you."

At the sound of his voice, a warm curl formed in the pit of Desirée's stomach, and as Jason's lips softly brushed hers, that curl spiraled outward.

Jason dropped featherlike kisses across Desirée's face, stopping to nibble at that enticing mole beside her mouth before his lips burnt a blazing trail across her cheek and up the long column of her throat. Moving up to her delicate earlobe, he bit it ever so gently, then muttered with a tortured groan, "God, Desirée. Do you have any idea of just how desirable you are? What you do to me?"

A delicious shiver ran up Desirée's spine at Jason's words and at the feel of his tongue lazily circling her ear. Suddenly, her legs seemed too weak to support her. She swayed, and Jason encircled her with his strong arms, pulling her to him, his mouth capturing hers.

Jason's brain warned him to go slow, but with Desirée's soft breasts pressing against his chest, her intoxicating scent in his nostrils, her lips so soft, so inviting, so moist, he couldn't get enough of her. His tongue brushed across her lips, then over her teeth, before probing, demanding entrance, so that he could taste the honeyed sweetness beyond. And when Desirée opened to him, his heart raced wildly as he crushed her to him, molding her soft body to his long hard one.

Desirée's senses were whirling as Jason's warm tongue caressed and then swirled around her own. She clung to him as if her life depended upon it, and then tentatively kissed him back, barely hearing Jason's groan of pleasure. As his fingers slipped beneath the material of her bodice to caress her breast, she moaned and moved even closer.

And then through her dulled senses, Desirée became aware of a draft on the back of her legs. Suddenly, she realized he was holding her so close the back of her hooped skirt was tilted upward. And his hand was on her breast! A vision of Beau with his golden hair and blue eyes flashed through her mind. *Mon Dieu!* What was she doing, standing there and letting this man kiss her, touch her so intimately?

Frantically Desirée tore her mouth free and struggled from Jason's arms. She backed away, her dark eyes flashing. "How dare you!" she cried indignantly. "How dare you kiss me like that, touch me so intimately!"

Jason's own senses were still reeling from the heated kiss. His breath was ragged as he said, "I'm sorry, Desirée. I didn't mean to get so carried away. But when I'm around you, it's hard to keep my emotions under control." He smiled derisively, adding, "If not impossible."

He stepped closer and Desirée stumbled back from him, hissing, "Don't touch me!"

Jason frowned. Why was she acting so indignant? True, he had gotten carried away with his passion, but she had responded to him, pressing her soft body closer, her own tongue dancing around his and driving him almost wild. Was that it? Desirée was a well-bred young lady. Had her own passion shocked her? Was she ashamed of herself?

50

Jason said in a gentle voice, "Desirée, there's no reason to be ashamed of what happened between us. It's only natural that two people—"

"Me ashamed?" Desirée interjected in a furious voice. "*Non!* You're the one who should be ashamed. Trying to seduce a betrothed woman."

Desirée's last words were like a dash of cold water on Jason's heated senses. For a minute, he stood in shocked silence, then asked in a measured voice, "What did you say?"

"I said I'm betrothed, and you, captain, are no gentleman!"

A slow anger rose in Jason. Desirée was his. What man dared to claim what was his, dared to defy destiny itself? "Who? Who's the man?" he hissed.

"No one you know!" Desirée spat.

In two swift strides, Jason caught Desirée's arm and dragged her forward to him. His eyes flashed angrily. "Dammit, Desirée! Answer me! What's his name?"

What in the world was wrong with him? Why, from the way he's acting, you'd think *he* was her betrothed, that *he* was the one who had been wronged.

Jason shook Desirée roughly, demanding, "Answer me!"

"Beau!" Desirée muttered, her heart racing with fear. "Beau Fourier."

Beau, Jason thought, his anger turning to cold fury. Oh yes, he remembered the golden boy. And Desirée had chosen that weakling, that coward to be her future husband? No! Over his dead body. Desirée belonged to him, and no man, particularly not that one, was going to take her away from him.

"Where is he?" Jason asked in a low, menacing voice.

Before Desirée had been afraid of Jason's overwhelming masculinity and of her own strange attraction to him. Now, she was terrified of the man himself. When she had said Beau's name, the look in his eyes had been absolutely murderous. "He's with General Beaureguard's army," Desirée answered, for the first time glad Beau wasn't in Louisiana. The way this wild man was acting, she wouldn't be surprised if he challenged Beau to a duel, and there was no doubt in her mind which of the two would be the victor. She shivered.

So, Jason thought, the golden boy had rushed off to join General Beaureguard, undoubtedly hoping some of the illustrious general's glory would rub off on him. And what would happen when he got a taste of battle, when he discovered that war wasn't all glory and excitement? Why, he'd run, like all the glory seekers, like all the cowards.

"Please, captain," Desirée said in a terrified voice, "let me go. You're hurting me."

For the first time, Jason realized he was taking his anger at Beau out on Desirée. He released her, and Desirée stepped back, rubbing her arms where Jason's fingers had bitten into them, watching him warily.

Jason looked down at her, still disbelieving that she would choose a weakling like Beau for a husband. No, Desirée was too much woman for a man like him. Did she really love him? He remembered the way she had kissed him back. Could a woman like Desirée respond like that to one man when she really and truly loved another?

"Do you love him?" Jason asked.

"*Mon Dieu!* Of course I love him. I wouldn't be betrothed to him if I didn't."

But Jason still wasn't convinced. Maybe she just thought she loved Beau. He had seen more than one hasty betrothal where the woman, caught up in the emotionalism of her beau going off to war, had agreed to wait for his return. "No, I mean do you really love him? With all your heart and soul. With every fiber of your being."

Every fiber of her being? Desirée thought. What in God's name was he talking about? And how dare he question her like this, probing into something as personal as her feelings for Beau. "That's none of your business, captain."

Jason's eyes narrowed as he stepped closer, and he said, "Oh, but it is my business, Desirée. I *have* to know."

"*Non!* Stay away from me!" Desirée cried in a shrill voice. "If you touch me again, I'll scream!"

Desirée's shrill voice and threat reminded Jason where he was. He glanced quickly over his shoulder at the other couples in the distance, aware for the first time of the precarious position into which he had put himself. You damned fool! You got so caught up with Desirée, you completely forgot why you're here: to ferret out the weaknesses of the enemy's defenses. And if she should start screaming, undoubtedly Armond would challenge you to a duel. And that's all you'd need, drawing unnecessary attention to yourself. If they should ever get curious about you, start investigating and find out those papers from the War

53

Department are forgeries, your whole mission would be ruined, to say nothing of your life. Fool! Crazy damed fool! Now you've got to get yourself out of this mess.

Jason smiled and said in a smooth voice, "I'm sorry, Desirée. I didn't realize that you were betrothed and I was out of line. I'm afraid it came as a great disappointment to me. But I shouldn't have gotten so angry. I apologize for my unseemly behavior."

Desirée was totally dumbfounded by Jason's abrupt change of behavior. Just a minute ago, he was acting like a wild man, and now, like a perfect gentleman. She stared at him in disbelief.

"I never meant to insult you or compromise you in any way."

Compromise. The word reminded Desirée of her own precarious position. Why, she didn't dare tell anyone what had happened here tonight between her and this man. To do so would bring about her own ruin. Besides, if he hadn't known she was betrothed, she really couldn't blame him all that much for kissing her. But, she had never been kissed *that* way before. No, that wasn't true. Once, she had allowed Beau to kiss her like that. But Beau's kiss had never aroused her, excited her as this man's had. She flushed, filled with shame that she could respond so wantonly to a man she didn't even love, hardly even knew. What in the world had possessed her?

"Desirée?" Jason asked softly. "Will you accept my apology?"

Desirée, still occupied with her perplexing thoughts, was startled by Jason's voice. Glancing up, she saw him watching her intently, looking every inch the perfect gentleman. Eyeing him warily, Desirée replied, "*Oui*, captain. I accept."

"And I hope, despite what happened here tonight, we can still be friends?"

Desirée wasn't too sure about that. She didn't trust herself around this disturbing man. But certainly, now that he knew she was betrothed, he would keep his distance. "*Oui*, captain."

"I think under the circumstances, we'd best not be seen entering the ballroom together," Jason said.

Desirée nodded in agreement.

Jason gave Desirée one long, lingering look, and then his lips curved into a slow, sensual smile. "Good night, Desirée," he said softly.

Desirée stood, rooted to the spot, and watched as Jason stepped off the verandah and strode across the wide lawn. Even after he had disappeared from view, swallowed up by the darkness, she stood, her senses once again reeling from Jason's warm look and his devastating smile.

Chapter 3

The dew still sat on the grass, glittering like diamonds in the sunlight, when Desirée mounted her horse and rode away from Terre Doux early the next morning.

After Jason had left her the night before, Desirée had not returned to the dance. Instead, she had retired to her room, feeling too shaken by the encounter and her own body's treachery to face anyone. After giving Mammy Lou the excuse of having a headache, she had tossed and turned for the better part of the night, her mind reeling in confusion, her body aching strangely.

And now, she raced down the driveway, across the fields, recklessly jumping her horse over hedges and any obstacle that kept her from her destination: Whispering Oaks. There, she could find solace. There, she could think.

She tore down the treelined road that led to the plantation drive, barely ducking a low-hanging limb. A branch on the limb caught the net that held her long chestnut hair at the back of her head, ripping it from her. But Desirée paid no attention, too intent on reaching Whispering Oaks to care that her hair was flying in every direction.

But just before she reached the shell driveway that led up to the plantation house, she veered sharply, heading toward the swamp instead. And when she had reached the edge of the marshy land, she reined in and sat on her horse, staring out at the shadowy, mysterious world that was part water, part land, and part in between.

What drew her here? Since she was a child, she seemed to be fascinated with this swamp. Was it the dark, brooding beauty that attracted her? Or was it because of its danger, a forbidden territory for her, and therefore all the more alluring? No, it was something much more than that. There were swamps all over Louisiana, but only this one drew her to it, and only in this particular spot. It was as if she were seeking something. But what?

She gazed out over the swamp, watching, waiting as she had done so many times in the past. As always, she saw nothing unusual. Her eyes dropped to the surface of the murky water, seeing the greyish-green mist that hung over it. A faint glimmer of recollection teased at the back of her mind. She struggled to capture it, but it slipped away from her, as elusive as the mist itself.

Frustrated, she looked up at the towering cypress trees, as if seeking the answer there. But the ancient sentinels stood silent, brooding, devulging nothing. Feeling that same disappointment she always felt, she turned her horse and headed once again for Whispering Oaks.

The once wide driveway was thick with underbrush, in some places a mere pathway. Desirée's mare had to pick her way through the low palmettos, ferns, and tangled vines that had crept up from the swamp, which seemed determined to take back the land that had once belonged to it. Not until she reached the oak trees that surrounded the mansion did the underbrush give way. Here the grass grew, the tender, new shoots seeking the warmth of the April sun.

Desirée rode beneath a giant oak and raised her head, seeing the long festoons of Spanish moss waving in the gentle breeze. She cocked her head and listened. Yes, she thought with a smile, they're talking to me, welcoming me back.

She dismounted and walked through the trees, feeling a serenity surrounding her, then filling her. She stopped beneath one old oak and looked up at its massive branches. This was the tree that the blue jays had always built their nest in every spring. Were they still here? And then catching a flash of blue against the dark green leaves, her heart filled with gladness. Thank goodness, Whispering Oaks hadn't been completely forsaken. The jays still made it their home.

She turned and then froze in her tracks, seeing Jason sitting on a magnificent black stallion a short distance away. She watched silently as he rode up to her, noticing that this morning he wore a white shirt and dark pants instead of the butternut uniform he had worn the night before. Strangely, the simple clothing seemed to emphasize his masculinity, the shirt straining at his broad shoulders and open at the neckline, revealing a dark mat of curls, the skin-tight pants molding the sinewy muscles of his thighs.

But Desirée wasn't as disturbed by the sight of his

blatant masculinity as she was by the fact that he was at Whispering Oaks, that he was invading on her own, very private domain. When he stopped before her, she said in a resentful voice, "What are you doing here?"

"I was out riding and spied this place, then came to investigate. I didn't mean to intrude. Do you want me to leave?"

Jason held his breath, fervently hoping she wouldn't ask him to leave. When he had seen her riding up the road by the swamp, with her long chestnut hair whipping about her face and shoulders, he had thought his memory had come back to haunt him once again. But now that he knew she was no vision from his past but honest-to-God flesh and blood, he didn't want to leave and doubted if he could if she asked him to.

Desirée looked up at Jason who waited patiently for her answer. Suddenly, she felt very foolish. What right did she have to ask him to leave? Whispering Oaks didn't belong to her anymore. "No, that's not necessary," she answered.

Jason breathed a silent sigh of relief, then dismounted. He stood for a minute, looking about the plantation, then said, "This used to be your home?"

"Yes."

Jason walked a few steps away, then stood silently scanning the deserted mansion. He turned to Desirée, saying in a soft voice, "It must have been very beautiful."

Desirée looked about her, seeing the underbrush that was taking over the once spacious lawn, the weed-choked driveway, the tangled vines and overgrown bushes that seemed to be smothering the mansion. Her gaze settled on one towering column where the

59

paint was chipped and peeling. Tears came to her eyes. "Yes," she answered. "It used to be very beautiful."

Jason saw the pain in Desirée's eyes. He longed to take her in his arms and tell her that he shared her pain, but he knew he couldn't reveal their childhood meeting, not without exposing himself as an imposter and Yankee spy. Instead, he simply said, "I'm sorry."

Desirée looked at him in surprise, knowing somehow that he knew exactly how she felt and that in some strange way he shared it with her. She studied him closer. Today he didn't look as wild and dangerous as he had last night. Nor did he look to be the polite gentleman. No, standing there with his eyes filled with compassion, she felt as though he was an old friend, one with whom she could share any secret, any confidence.

"Do you think we could go inside?" Jason asked. "I'd like to see it. That is, if you don't mind," he added.

"No, I don't mind. But I think it's locked."

"Come on," he said, taking her arm gently. "Let's see."

When they stood on the wide gallery before the massive oak door, Jason tried the doorknob. "See," Desirée said. "I told you it was locked."

Jason leaned over and looked down the long length of the verandah, saying, "Come on. I think I know how we can get in." Catching Desirée's hand, he led her to the french door at the one end and, taking a penknife from his pocket, jimmied the lock. Seeing the shocked look on Desirée's face, he chuckled, saying, "Don't worry, Desirée. I'm not a professional thief."

Jason opened the french door, and they stepped into the room, the heavy smell of dust and stale air almost choking them. Desirée looked about the empty room, seeing the light from the french door playing over the fine dust particles their movements had stirred. She looked up and saw the cobwebs that covered the beautiful chandeliers that dangled from the high ceiling.

"It looks so empty without the furniture and the draperies," she said sadly, her words echoing in the huge room. "And it's so dirty."

Jason's eyes darted about the room. How often in the past had he longed to see the inside of this mansion. And now, seeing it, he wasn't in the least disappointed. "No, Desirée, you're looking at it from the wrong perspective. Furniture is only a dressing. The house is still here, just as beautiful, its walls just as strong as ever. Oh true, it's got a bit of dust on it, but that's only on the surface." He bent and brushed his hand across the layer of dust on the floor, saying, "Look at that shine, Desirée. Why, the wood looks as if it's just been waxed."

Desirée looked down at the floor, the wood shining with a warm, reddish-brown luster. She had never before noticed how beautiful the floors were. Except for the ballroom, they had been covered with rugs. Why had they covered the beautiful wood?

She looked about the room, for the first time seeing the beauty of the house itself: the stately walls and the towering ceiling with its heavy swirls of stucco. Then her eyes caught on the wide molding surrounding a doorway. She walked to it and scratched at the peeling paint, seeing the beautiful wood beneath. She fingered the molding lovingly, realizing she had never

61

even noticed the delicate design that had been carved into it. Like the floors, its beauty had been covered.

She turned and looked at the wide windows and french doors. Without the heavy draperies, the whole room was drenched with sunlight, giving it a spacious, airy look. Yes, she thought, that too had been a mistake. Why build windows to let the light in, then turn around and keep it out?

"Which room was this?" Jason asked.

"The dining room."

"Can we look at the rest of it?"

"*Oui*," Desirée answered, as anxious as he to explore, realizing that she, too, was seeing it for the first time.

They stepped into the foyer. Seeing the wide, twin staircases that spiraled up to the second floor, looking like a giant horseshoe, Jason's breath caught. He scanned the long row of windows that sat at the top of the staircase and then stared at the huge chandelier dangling from the ceiling, its delicate prisms catching the sunlight, despite the dust that covered it. He glanced down at the floor and frowned, then knelt on one knee and again wiped the dust away. He looked up at Desirée, saying in an almost awed voice, "Do you realize this is solid marble?"

Desirée looked down at the green and grey swirls, seeing that, too, for the first time. A slow anger filled her.

Jason rose and looked around the foyer, saying in a hushed voice, "It must have been beautiful."

"It was," Desirée answered. "But it could have been much more beautiful."

"What do you mean?"

"Oh, Jason, you were right when you said furnishings are just a dressing, but in this case they were a shroud. The way my parents furnished this house, they didn't enhance its natural beauty; they hid it. They covered the floors with carpets, the windows with heavy drapes, and then crowded so much furniture into the rooms that you couldn't see the walls. I had always thought it was so beautiful, but I had no idea of how just how beautiful it could have been."

"Yes," Jason agreed. "I could never understand why people built homes in the Greek revival style, hoping to get that light, airy look, and then turned around and destroyed the very effect they were looking for."

"*Oui*," Desirée said in an angry voice. "That's exactly what they did. They destroyed it, or tried to. Come on," Desirée said, whirling around and heading for the salon. "I want to see what other mistakes they made."

As Jason and Desirée walked from room to room, Desirée saw them, not as they had been, but as they should have been. And when they stepped back into the gallery an hour later and Jason pulled the french door closed behind them, Desirée felt a sadness even more powerful than she had felt on her other visits. She had always loved this beautiful mansion, along with everything else in Whispering Oaks. It had broken her heart to see it falling into disrepair. But now, she felt that an even deeper injustice had been done to the stately building, one that she fervently wished she could correct.

Her eyes drifted to one of the towering columns, its paint cracked and peeling. Would anyone ever live here again? Certainly not Armond, for he loved his home at Terre Doux as much as she loved this one at

Whispering Oaks. Jeanne Marie perhaps? No, if she ever did marry she would probably marry a planter who had his own plantation.

She walked to the column and lovingly traced the deep furrows carved there with her fingers. Would no one ever look at these columns, watching in fascination as their color changed to a dusky rose in the sunset or see them in the moonlight, glowing with a life of their own. Would no one's laughter ring through this beautiful building's halls again, or tears splash on its floors? Would it never again know the patter of children's feet or the firm step of its master? Was it doomed to stand here forever, empty and silent, forsaken by all, a building with no soul?

Tears welled in Desirée's eyes and trickled down her cheeks. Seeing them, Jason gently pulled her into his arms, cradling her, and Desirée allowed herself to be comforted, somehow sensing that this man didn't just understand her anguish but shared it.

Jason rocked her gently, his cheek brushing her hair tenderly as she cried softly, her head burrowed in his wide chest. "Ssh, love, don't cry," Jason whispered. "All is not lost. Someday Whispering Oaks will be your home again."

Desirée lifted her head, saying in a choked voice, "But how?"

At that point Jason didn't know how. He only knew that he and Desirée were destined for each other and that in some way fate intended Whispering Oaks to be part of their destiny. "Just take my word for it. Trust me."

And at that minute, Desirée did trust him. Looking up into those misty-green eyes, she had the strangest feeling that she had come home, and not to Whispering Oaks. She had a profound sense of belonging in this man's strong arms, arms that circled her protectively, keeping the world at bay. Never had she felt so safe and secure.

Her eyes drifted over his face and then locked on his mouth. She remembered how these sensuous lips had felt on her own, and suddenly, she wanted to feel them again. She lifted her head, her lips parting in silent invitation, and Jason didn't disappoint her.

His lips were warm and mobile as he placed soft feathery kisses on hers, then nibbled at the corner of her mouth, his tongue flickering with sensual promise. Desirée shivered, turning her mouth, begging for more, but Jason's lips left her mouth to explore the intriguing mole beside it and then moved across her cheeks to her eyelids.

The feel of Jason's tongue brushing her eyelashes was more than Desirée could bear. A moan escaped her throat. She caught his head, tangling her fingers in the soft curls at the nape of his neck, bringing his lips back to her own. And when his mouth covered hers, she tasted the salt of her own tears as his tongue explored her lips, then her mouth.

Jason tightened his embrace, crushing Desirée's soft body to the length of his own, deepening the kiss. And Desirée felt as if the breath were being sucked from her lungs, the marrow from her bones. Her legs gave way beneath her, and she would have sagged to the ground like a limp ragdoll had Jason not swept her up in his powerful arms and carried her off the verandah to a spot beneath a huge oak tree, laying her gently on the new spring grass.

Desirée looked up at him kneeling over her, still dazed by his passionate kiss. She saw him smiling down at her, a warm glow in his eyes. But what was he doing up there? And then, as he lay down beside her and once again enfolded her in his arms, her heart raced with anticipation.

Jason covered Desirée's face and throat with fiery kisses, one arm cradling her, his free hand stroking her arms, the sides of her breast, her hip, her thigh, and then, sweeping upward in one long sensuous caress, rose to cup her breast, his thumb brushing the tender, aching nipple through her clothes. Desirée clung to him, feeling as if every nerve ending in her body was tingling. And then, when she felt his warm hand slip beneath her riding jacket and blouse, she sucked in her breath at the feel of his fingers against her bare skin.

Jason captured her mouth once more, his tongue stroking and caressing in unison with his fingers teasing the hardened bud on her breast. Desirée lay lost in a sea of pure sensation, the world spinning around her.

Jason's mouth left hers and nibbled at her delicate earlobe, and he whispered, "Desirée, I've waited a lifetime for you."

But Desirée didn't hear his words. A roaring had filled her ears. Blindly, she clutched him, fearing she would drown in all these new sensations.

Jason's lips and tongue traced the wildly beating pulse down Desirée's throat and then moved across the soft rise of her breasts. For a minute, he allowed his eyes to feast on her full, creamy breasts, rising and falling in quick succession under her transparent chemise, and then, impatient to taste her there, he quickly unbuttoned the flimsy garment, pushing it aside, his mouth following his hands.

When Desirée felt Jason's warm lips nibbling, his tongue swirling around the sensitive peak, the heat that suffused her body seemed to flood to the core of her womanhood, leaving her aching and throbbing. Instinctively, she arched her hips, seeking in some way to assuage the almost painful sensation. When Jason shifted his weight, his thigh nestled between hers, she felt him pressing against her lower abdomen, hard and throbbing, seemingly scorching her through their layers of clothing. For a second, a tingle of fear ran through her, for that blatant proof of his arousal seemed enormous and very threatening. And then that fear quickly fled, giving way to the exquisite sensations Jason's lips and tongue were invoking at her breasts.

Desirée was quivering all over, her breath coming in short gasps, when Jason finally lifted his head and gazed down into her passion-dulled eyes. "You see, Desirée," he whispered, his own breath ragged with need. "You don't really love Beau. We were destined for each other. You and me."

Mentioning Beau's name was Jason's undoing. Through her dulled senses, Desirée saw the flash of her betrothed, his eyes boring into her, condemning her. And then, she became aware of her bared breasts, her skirts pushed up to her hips, and of Jason's hand on her thigh. Guilt and shame rose in her, followed quickly by sheer horror at what she had allowed to happen.

With a strength she didn't know she had, she pushed away from him and jumped quickly to her feet.

She stood over him, tears of shame and anger glittering in her eyes, clutching her bodice closed with her hands. "You rake! You unspeakable bastard! *Mon Dieu!* And to think I trusted you. Thought you my friend."

Jason came to his feet in one fluid movement. "Desirée," he said, reaching for her, "listen to me."

"Non!" Desirée screamed, backing away. "Don't touch me! Don't you ever come near me again!"

She turned and ran to her horse, fumbling with the buttons on her chemise and blouse, tears streaming down her face. Catching the horse's reins, she quickly led her to the mounting block that sat next to the driveway and mounted. Shooting Jason a look of pure loathing, she whirled her horse and galloped away.

Jason watched her as she recklessly rode across the open fields, then called, "Desirée! Stop fighting it! You can't change destiny!"

Chapter 4

Desirée's ride to Whispering Oaks earlier that morning was tame compared to her ride back to Terre Doux and away from Jason. She rode as if all the demons in hell were after her, her horse's hooves kicking up the loose dirt and leaving a thick cloud of showering clods in their wake.

As she rode across the fields, approaching Terre Doux, the slaves hoeing the rows watched wide-eyed with disbelief as she sped toward them, her long hair whipping about her and her skirts flapping about her legs. And then, when she was almost upon them, the slaves dropped their hoes and scattered in every direction as Desirée's horse jumped the wagon sitting in the field.

Entering the plantation grounds from the rear, she raced past the huge brick sugar factory and the whitewashed slave's cabins, recklessly jumping another hedge before she came to a screeching halt in front of the stable, the mare rearing and pawing the air in fright.

Then, without even waiting for the astonished stable hand who was running to help her dismount, she jumped from the saddle and ran across the yard, half stumbling, tears streaming down her face. She tore around the huge water cistern that sat at the back of the plantation house, then up the backstairs to the upper gallery. She jerked open the french doors and bolted into her room, and then, seeing Mammy Lou standing there with an armful of dirty clothes, she came to an abrupt halt.

Mammy Lou dropped the clothing on the floor, saying in a shocked voice, "Lawsy, child! What's wrong with you? Tearing in here like the devil himself is after you."

Desirée was stunned speechless. The last person she had wanted to run into was her old mammy.

Mammy's dark eyes narrowed. She waddled to Desirée and slowly circled her, saying, "What's your hair doing down like that? And how did those grass stains get on your skirt?" She picked a twig from Desirée's tangled hair. "And what's this twig doing in your hair? What happened child?"

Desirée wasn't about to tell Mammy the truth. Why, the old woman would be ashamed of her, even more ashamed than she was herself. "I—I fell off my horse."

"Fell off your horse?" Mammy Lou asked in an astonished voice. "Lawsy, child, are you hurt?" the big, black woman asked, her eyes filling with concern, her hands quickly running over Desirée's arms, checking for broken bones.

"No, I wasn't hurt."

"Then how come you've been crying?"

"Because—because I was so—so mad!" Desirée cried, her black eyes flashing with renewed anger.

"You sure you ain't hurt?"

"I'm sure, Mammy. Believe me, I'm all right."

"Well, you may not be hurt, but I'm not so sure you're all right. First, that headache last night, and now falling off your horse. Why, I can't ever remember you falling off your horse, not even when you was a li'l child."

That teasing glimmer in the back of Desirée's mind reappeared at Mammy's last words. She held her breath, concentrating with all her power, determined it wouldn't elude her this time.

"Lawsy, child! What's wrong with you. You're as white as a sheet."

Instantly, the glimmer was gone, disappearing like a puff of smoke. Frustrated, Desirée snapped, "Oh, Mammy Lou, will you shut up!"

Mammy Lou's head snapped back as if she had been slapped. Then she said in a stern voice, "Now I know you're sick! You ain't *never* talked to your old mammy like that."

"Oh, Mammy Lou," Desirée cried, feeling even more ashamed. "I'm sorry. I didn't mean to say that." Fresh tears glittered in her eyes. "I don't know what's wrong with me."

Mammy Lou enfolded Desirée in her huge arms, crooning, "There, there, honey lamb. Don't you go worrying your pretty head about that. When you're feeling poorly, it's just natural you're short tempered. But your old mammy will have you feeling fit as a fiddle in no time at all."

"Yes, Mammy Lou," Desirée muttered. But she

71

knew, this time, Mammy Lou wasn't going to be able to make her feel better. No one could take away her shame.

"Now, let's get you out of those dirty clothes and into a nightgown," Mammy Lou said, stripping Desirée's riding jacket from her.

But as Mammy Lou started unbuttoning Desirée's blouse, a horrifying thought came to Desirée. Remembering only too well Jason's hands and mouth on her breasts, she was terrified that Mammy Lou might see some evidence of what had happened. Brushing the old woman's hands aside, she said, "I'll take care of this, Mammy. Why don't you get my gown?"

Quickly, Desirée turned her back on Mammy Lou and started undressing. For a minute, Mammy Lou watched her with a puzzled frown on her face. She'd been dressing and undressing this little gal all her life, and here she was, standing with her back to her as if she were ashamed for her old mammy to see her nakedness. Mammy Lou shook her head. Yes, her baby must be sick. She wasn't acting at all like herself.

While Mammy Lou was getting her nightgown from her armoire, Desirée looked down anxiously at her breasts. No, she thought, they don't look any different. But they certainly felt different. They were still aching, them and that—that other place.

Mammy Lou slipped Desirée's gown on and helped her into bed. After Mammy Lou left, Desirée lay in the big canopied bed, feeling miserable. She had never felt so ashamed of herself. She was glad Mammy Lou had decided she was sick. It gave her an excuse to stay in her room. This way, she wouldn't have to face *him* again, for apparently Jason hadn't just come for the ball, but for a visit, too. That cad! Desirée thought, whipping up her anger at him again, for somehow placing all the blame on him helped to assuage her guilt and shame.

Mammy Lou walked back in the room with that waddling gait that was so much a part of her. Handing a cup to Desirée, she said, "Here, honey lamb, this will make you feel better."

"What is it?" Desirée asked, taking the cup.

"Something to help you sleep."

Yes, Desirée thought, that's what I want to do. Sleep. Then I can escape the shameful memory of what happened.

Desirée took the cup and gratefully drank the warm, bitter liquid. But long after Mammy had tucked her in, darkened the room, and left, Desirée lay awake, staring at the canopy above her, her mind reeling in confusion.

How could she have let Jason kiss her and do all of those other indecent things? She blushed in remembrance. It was bad enough that she had succumbed to the handsome captain in the first place, but she was promised to Beau, making it doubly shameful. And she loved Beau with all of her heart. Ever since they were children, they had both known that someday they would marry.

It was *his* fault, Desirée thought, once again whipping up her anger at Jason. Why, all of that talk about being friends was just a trap. All the time he was luring her into feeling safe and secure with him, he still had seduction on his mind. Oh, she could forgive him the night before, because he didn't know

73

she was betrothed. But he knew it today. The man had no honor at all.

And what was all that crazy talk about destiny? Was the man mad? Whoever heard of anything so foolish?

Drowsily, Desirée rolled to her side, the tisane Mammy had given her finally taking effect. I'll go back to New Orleans tomorrow, she thought. That way, I'll never have to lay eyes on him again.

Reassured that she would be safe from Jason's dark, compelling attraction by putting a safe distance between them, Desirée yawned and closed her eyes, escaping into oblivion.

When Desirée awakened, it was dark outside. She looked sleepily at the candle on the table beside her, wondering what had awakened her. Seeing Jeanne Marie about to slip out the door, she called, "Jeanne Marie?"

Jeanne Marie turned, then said, "Oh, I'm sorry, Desirée. I didn't mean to wake you up. I only meant to see if you needed anything."

"That's all right, Jeanne Marie," Desirée answered, sitting up. "I'm not sleepy anymore. Come on in."

Jeanne Marie closed the door behind her and walked over to Desirée's bed. Sitting on the side of it, she asked, "How do you feel?"

"I'm fine now. All I needed was some sleep. I didn't rest very well last night."

"*Oui*, I missed you at the dance and went looking for you. Mammy Lou told me you had a headache and had gone to bed."

Desirée looked across at her cousin, a new guilt rising up in her. Jeanne Marie had been interested in Jason. Had she unwittingly lured him away from her? Desirée didn't think she could live with any more guilt. She had to know if Jeanne Marie was still attracted to him. But how? She didn't want to be too obvious about it.

"Did you enjoy the dance?" Desirée asked. "Did Captain Montgomery ask you to dance very many times?"

"*Non*, just that once," Jeanne Marie answered. "And I'm glad he didn't ask me again."

"But why not? I thought you were attracted to him."

"I was, but—oh, Desirée," Jeanne Marie said in an earnest voice, "I hope you don't think I'm being flighty, but I don't think the captain is for me. It's true, he's very handsome, but—"

"But what?" Desirée prompted.

"But he—he frightens me. He's too—too—"

Too dangerous? Too much man? And no wonder shy little Jeanne Marie had been frightened of Jason. He *was* dangerous, as she had learned only too well. "I think I know what you mean."

"Oh? Did he frighten you, too?"

"*Oui*," Desirée admitted, wishing that she had listened to her instincts and kept her distance. If she had left Whispering Oaks the minute she discovered he was there, then maybe she wouldn't be feeling so miserable right now.

"*Eh bien*, we don't have to worry about him anymore," Jeanne Marie said. "He's gone."

75

Desirée's heart rose to her throat. "Gone? Gone where? Back to New Orleans?"

"*Non*, back to Charleston. He said his business was finished here, and he was going back to his regiment."

Desirée felt a sudden, overwhelming disappointment filling her, so powerful she felt as if her life had been sucked from her.

"*Mon Dieu*, Desirée! What's wrong? You look terrible."

"I don't think I'm feeling quite as well as I thought," Desirée answered in a dazed voice. Lying back down, she muttered, "I think I will go back to sleep."

Jeanne Marie rose from the bed, saying in a worried voice, "Do you want me to get Mammy Lou for you?"

"*Non*, all I want to do is sleep," Desirée answered, wishing that Jeanne Marie would leave so she could be alone and think.

Jeanne Marie hesitated, then said, "All right, if you say so." She walked to the door, then stopped and turned, a concerned look on her face. "I hope you feel better in the morning."

"I'm sure I will," Desirée muttered absently.

After Jeanne Marie had left, Desirée lay in bed trying to cope with her tumultuous emotions over the news of Jason's departure. I'll never see him again, she thought. He's gone. Walked right out of my life. But isn't that what you want? Didn't you want to put a safe distance between you and him? You should be glad he did it for you.

But Desirée wasn't glad. She only felt a strange emptiness, an emptiness that made her earlier miseries seem meaningless.

Perversely, she dwelled on all of their encounters, as if by etching the memories in her mind she could keep Jason from leaving her. It was a mistake. With the memory of his lovemaking that morning still so vivid in her mind, her body was soon aching all over, aching for the fulfillment that Jason's torrid kisses and tantalizing caresses had promised but not assuaged.

For hours, Desirée tossed and turned, her breasts aching, her loins throbbing. "Damn him!" she muttered, pounding the pillow next to her. "How dare he walk into my life, totally disrupt it, and then walk out again!"

She tossed the covers off and flew from the bed, pacing the floor like a caged animal. Then abruptly, she stopped, a gleam coming to her eye. She knew what she needed. A ride. A ride in the night air and solitude always soothed her, calmed her.

Quickly, she stripped off her gown and slipped into her pantaloons and chemise, then her blouse and riding skirt. Sitting on the bed, she pulled on her socks and riding boots and then walked to the vanity, combing her hair and tying it back with a ribbon. She picked up her riding jacket, then tossed it aside.

She opened the french doors and peered down the darkened gallery. Seeing no one about, she hurried through it and crept down the stairs at the back of the plantation house, then darted for the stable.

As usual the stable was deserted at this late hour of the night. Without hesitation, Desirée sought out her mare, saddled her, and led her outside to the mounting block. A minute later, she was in the saddle and walking the horse over the wide lawn of Terre Doux, deliberately avoiding the shell driveway for fear the noise of the horse's hooves on it would alert someone.

When she reached the road, she stopped. She glanced down the road in the direction that she usually rode, toward Whispering Oaks. But she didn't want to go there tonight. It was the memory of what had happened there that morning that she was trying to exorcise. Turning the horse in the opposite direction, she called, "Go girl!"

Desirée raced down the road, feeling that same exhilaration she always felt with the cool night breeze on her face and whipping her hair around her, the trees on the roadside rushing past her. She looked up and saw the clouds scuttling across the dark sky, the moon dipping in and out behind them and alternately bathing the landscape in moonlight, then shadows, giving it an eerie effect.

When she came to a fork in the road, Desirée veered from the main road, taking instead the smaller one that followed the bayou, a road that Desirée knew would be completely deserted at this time of the night. For a long distance, she galloped down the road and then, as it narrowed even more, slowed to a canter and finally, a sedate walk.

Her eyes darted about the dense undergrowth all around her, then looked up at the huge trees looming over her which looked like giant, black wings. She nervously eyed the Spanish moss hanging from the trees, fluttering in the breeze and looking ghostly in the darkness. The scent of magnolias and night-blooming jasmine filled the air, so heavy it was almost suffocating. Desirée shivered and reined in. Suddenly, she was frightened. It seemed as if everything was closing in her: the trees, the darkness, the eerie silence. She was just about to turn her horse and flee from this place that seemed to be filled with an almost palpable menace when the moon came from beneath the clouds, and momentarily everything was cast in a soft white light.

In that moment, Desirée spied a horse standing in the underbrush to one side of the road. Long after the moon had dipped behind another cloud and the road had been thrown in darkness again, Desirée stared in disbelief. She had recognized that stallion. It was Jason's horse.

But how could that be? Jason had left, gone back to Charleston. Or had he?

She peered into the darkness and then, as the moon reappeared, tingeing the landscape with a soft light, she saw Jason standing in the distance at the bank of the bayou and looking downstream.

What was he doing down there? And what was he looking at?

Her curiosity aroused, Desirée dismounted and tied her reins to a lowhanging limb. Then she crept cautiously through the underbrush, being very careful to make no noise. She crouched behind a low palmetto and peered down the winding bayou in the direction Jason was gazing.

And then she saw what he was watching so intently: A man, standing in a pirogue, was poling his way down the bayou to where Jason stood.

What was going on? And who was the man? She crouched lower, watching, listening.

The pirogue grounded on the bank with a whisper-soft noise. The man laid his pole down and stepped from the log canoe, saying, "Evening, Cap'n Steele. Did you think I wasn't coming?"

"No," Jason answered. "I knew you'd be here, sooner or later."

Jason handed the man an oilskin pouch, saying, "Well, here it is, the last dispatch. I think Captain Farragut will find everything he needs in there: the placement of the gun batteries at Forts Jackson and St. Phillips, the auxiliary ships present and their gunpower, everything. But I think he's going to be particularly interested in the placement of those chains in the river."

"Chains?" the man asked. "You mean cables, don't you, cap'n?"

"No, one third of the river is barred with chains, not cables."

"Well, I'll be damned," the man muttered. Then, looking at Jason with admiration, he said, "I'll have to hand it to you, Cap'n Steele. For an army man, you're pretty smart."

Jason chuckled at the sailor's oblique compliment.

"But what if we still can't get through, cap'n? What if General Butler has to march overland?"

"Through ninety miles of swamp?" Jason asked in a horrified voice. "I hope to God not. But just in case he does, I've included everything I could find out about the McGehee and Chalmette line of batteries below New Orleans, too."

The sailor nodded, then said, "What you gonna do now, cap'n?"

"My orders were to lay low after I turned in my last dispatch and see what happened. If we're successful in taking New Orleans, I'm to join General Butler after he occupies the city. If not, I'm to make my way back north."

"Well, cap'n, I sure as hell hope we're successful. If we ain't and those Johnny Rebs figure out where we got all of this information, your life won't be worth a plug nickle. Hell, they'll have every Johnny Reb in the South looking for you."

",I can take care of myself," Jason replied in a calm voice.

The sailor eyed Jason thoughtfully. More than once, he had noticed Jason's catlike walk, reminding him of the cougars that roamed this swampland. Yes, not only was the captain one of the most intelligent and quick-witted men he'd ever known, but he had an animal's instinct for survival, too. Nope, the Johnny Rebs would never catch him.

Desirée had listened to the whole exchange in fascinated horror. Jason was one of those hated Yankees? Why, he hadn't been sent here by the War Department but by the Union to spy on them. And the Union Navy was going to attack the forts guarding the Mississippi and New Orleans? *Mon Dieu!* She had to get away from here and warn them!

"Well, cap'n," the sailor said, holding out his hand. "I guess this is the last time we'll be seeing each other. It's been a pleasure working with you, sir." He grinned, saying, "And if you ever should decide to transfer to the navy, I'd be proud to serve under you."

Jason held out his hand and then froze, hearing the neigh of a horse.

"What's that?" the sailor asked, looking about apprehensively.

But before he even had the words out of his mouth,

81

Jason had whirled and darted into the underbrush, his movements so swift the sailor stood blinking in stunned disbelief before he finally came to his senses and ran after him.

In her haste, Desirée had lunged suddenly from the underbrush and frightened her horse. The animal had reared, neighed, and pulled its reins free, running a few yards away into a nearby bog. Frantically, Desirée had pulled the horse from the bog and was still struggling to mount when Jason ran up behind her and jerked her down.

Whirling her around, his eyes widened in surprise. "Desirée!"

"*Oui*, Desirée, Captain *Steele*," Desirée spat, her eyes flashing with anger.

Jason's eyes narrowed. "Then you heard?"

"*Oui*. Everything! Coming into our homes, accepting our hospitality, pretending to be our friend, when all the time you were spying on us, while all the time you were nothing but a filthy Yankee spy!"

The sailor had run up during Desirée's outburst and now stood beside them. "We gotta do something, cap'n," he said in a low, menacing voice. "We can't have her blabbing her mouth."

"Desirée isn't going to tell anyone anything," Jason said in a steely voice, giving Desirée a hard look.

"I mean it, cap'n. We can't take any chances. Too much is at stake." He reached for his knife at his belt, saying, "We have to get rid of her. If you like, cap'n, I'll do it, being as you know her and all."

Jason whirled, placing himself between Desirée and the sailor. "I said, I'd take care of it," he ground out.

The sailor saw the dangerous gleam in Jason's eyes and backed away a step.

"Your job is to get those dispatches back to Captain Farragut as fast as you can," Jason said in a firm voice. "I'll take care of things on this end. Now get going!" Jason barked.

"Aye, cap'n," the sailor answered, feeling a shiver of fear run down his spine. He backed away nervously, then swung about and tore off through the underbrush to his pirogue.

In the meanwhile, Desirée had been slowly backing toward her horse. Jason whirled and caught her wrist, jerking her to him. Desirée gasped, her heart racing in fear at the furious look in his eyes.

"What the hell are you doing out here in the middle of the night?" Jason asked in an angry voice.

"Riding. I like to ride at night," Desirée answered nervously.

Jason glared down at her. She had put him in a hell of a position. He didn't dare let her go. He knew Desirée. She'd run and tell everything. But what in the hell was he going to do with her? Killing her, as the sailor had wanted to do, was out of the question, although right now, he longed to throttle her. No, he'd have to take her someplace, someplace where she'd be safe and yet not be able to escape and tell what she knew until after the battle had taken place.

Desirée was jerking at her arm, saying in a pleading voice, "Let me go, Jason, or whatever your name is. Please, let me go. I won't tell anyone. I promise."

Jason gave a short harsh laugh, saying, "Do you really think I'm that crazy. Like hell you won't tell anyone!"

Desirée had been frightened of Jason before, but never like this. The night she had told him she was betrothed, he had been angry, but now he was furious, and a furious Jason was an awesome sight.

Jason wheeled and walked to Desirée's horse, almost jerking Desirée's arm out of its socket as he dragged her behind him. He scowled down at the mare's legs, half covered with mud. "Where in the hell have you been riding? In the swamps?"

"No. My—my horse ran into that bog over there," Desirée said in a small voice, pointing to the nearby bog.

Jason stood for a minute, a thoughtful look on his face. And then he smiled, a smile that looked absolutely diabolical to Desirée. He slapped the horse hard on its flank, and the mare, already frightened, bolted and galloped off down the road.

"What are you doing?" Desirée asked as she watched the horse disappear in the darkness.

"Hopefully starting a sequence of events that will explain your disappearance."

Desirée swallowed hard before she asked nervously, "My disappearance?"

"Yes, your disappearance. That horse will go back to the stable, and when they find it in the morning and discover you missing, they'll go looking for you."

Desirée's eyes lit up with hope.

Seeing her look, Jason shook his head, saying, "No, Desirée. They won't come looking here. With all that mud on your mare's legs, they'll think you wandered into the swamp in the dark and got thrown. That's where they'll look for you."

"But when they don't find me, they'll go looking

84

elsewhere," Desirée pointed out.

"And by that time, we'll be long gone."

"They'll keep looking," Desirée insisted.

"Yes, for awhile. But when they don't find you and no one has seen hide nor hair of you, they'll go back to their first assumption. In the dark, you rode into the swamps by mistake and got thrown. Then, you wandered off in a daze and stepped into quicksand, got eaten by an alligator, or just got hopelessly lost. The fact that they never find your body wouldn't prove anything. How often have you heard of a man wandering off into the swamps and never being seen again?"

Desirée shivered, knowing that what he said was true.

Jason pulled Desirée toward his stallion. "What are you going to do with me?" Desirée asked in a terrified voice.

"I haven't decided yet."

He shoved her toward his horse, saying, "Get on."

Desirée hung back. With a muttered oath, Jason swooped her up and tossed her into the saddle. And then, with a speed that astonished her, he mounted behind her.

Desirée looked down at her legs stretched across the horse's broad back and saw her skirts riding up almost to her thighs. She pushed at them frantically, saying, "I can't ride this way."

Jason shook his head in disbelief at her words, then chuckled, saying, "I'll never be able to understand women. I should think, at this point, your modesty would be the least of your worries."

With that, he spurred his horse, and the stallion galloped off down the dark, lonely road, the trees

85

rushing past them. Desirée hung on to the saddlehorn for dear life, trying to ignore the muscular arms around her and determined she wouldn't touch any more of this hated Yankee than she had to.

But as they rode, Desirée discovered that she had more immediate worries than what Jason was going to do with her. The night air had taken on a decided nip, and it rushed against her face, chest, and up her exposed legs. She was beginning to feel chilled to the bone. Adding to her misery was her unaccustomed position on the saddle. She had never ridden astride before, and with only her thin pantaloons to protect her, the insides of her legs were beginning to feel chafed. *Mon Dieu*, she thought, how do men stand riding in this position with *that* between their legs? Then she flushed at the thought.

"You're shivering, Desirée," Jason said. "Lean back so you can absorb some of my heat."

"Non!" Desirée cried, deliberately pulling herself even further up in the saddle, an act that made her wince with pain, for it only increased the pressure on her chafed thighs.

"You stubborn little mule," Jason muttered, taking the reins in one hand and jerking her back to him with his other arm.

Desirée struggled, but all was in vain. The arm locked around her was like a band of steel. Finally, she sat rigid, only too aware of Jason's warmth surrounding her.

"Now, isn't that better?" Jason asked, his warm breath fanning her neck.

"Non! I would rather die of pneumonia than be anywhere near you!"

Jason chuckled, the sound even more disturbing to Desirée because, with her back locked against his hard chest, she could feel the rumbling as well as hear it. "You're just all defiance, aren't you?" Jason asked. "Oh, Desirée, what am I going to do with you?"

Desirée wondered at the question. Was he teasing her or was he serious?

An hour later, they were still riding down that dark, deserted road, and Desirée had discovered that she had a whole new set of miseries to deal with. With Jason's arm still locked around her, she was much too aware of him. She could feel the hard muscles of his chest pressing against her back, his warm breath fanning her neck. With every gait the horse took, her thighs brushed against his, and his arm brushed against her breasts. She began to feel that aching again, in places it was indecent to ache, and now, she was feeling uncomfortably warm. To make matters worse, Jason's masculine scent was surrounding her, blotting out even the smell of the magnolias and jasmine and making her feel strangely giddy.

When Jason finally slowed the horse, and the stallion trotted into a small clearing beside the road, Desirée almost cried with relief. She had no idea what he planned to do with her, but anything was better than the torture she had gone through the past hour.

Jason walked the horse through the clearing to an old shack sitting by the side of the sleepy bayou. Hastily thrown together with half timber and half palmetto leaves, Desirée recognized it as a deserted trapper's hut. "We're not going to stay here?" she asked in a shocked voice.

"It's better than nothing. At least it will keep the night dew off."

Jason dismounted, tied his horse to a tree, and then lifted Desirée from the saddle. As he carried her toward the shack in his strong arms, Desirée snapped, "I can walk!"

"I doubt it," Jason replied. "After riding that horse astride for three hours, I doubt if you can even stand."

Desirée flushed, wondering how he had guessed the condition of her thighs.

Jason kicked open the door of the hut, bent as he carried her through the low doorway, and then sat her on her feet. Desirée glanced around the darkness fearfully, hoping that some wild animal hadn't claimed the hut as its lair. She was aware of Jason's fumbling in his pocket, but when he flicked the match head with his thumb and the light flared, Desirée jumped in surprise.

Jason lifted the match and then, spying something on the ground, walked to it and picked it up. Desirée watched while he transferred the flame from the match to the candle snub and then lifted it.

Desirée's eyes darted wildly around the room, half expecting a bobcat or black bear to lurch from the shadows. And then, something did come flying at her. She shrieked and ducked, looking up to see Jason watching her with an amused smile on his face.

"What was that?" she asked in a weak voice.

"A bat."

"A bat?" Desirée asked in a horrified voice. "There're bats in here?"

"Yes. They probably hole up in those palmetto leaves."

Desirée had seen bats flying out of the oak trees at Whispering Oaks at night. "But I thought bats are night creatures. What's *it* doing in here at this time of night?"

Jason shrugged, still looking about the shack. "Maybe it took the night off."

Desirée shot him a disgusted look, then glanced around the hut. There wasn't much to see. In one corner sat a crate. Apparently, this had served as the trapper's cabinet, for she could see some old tin plates and cups and a rusty frying pan. At the opposite corner was a small rope bed, covered with Spanish moss. Beside the two old, moth-eaten blankets hanging over one end of the bed, that was it.

Jason walked to the crate and picked up a tin plate. Dribbling a few drops of hot wax on it, he pressed the candle in the wax and then sat it down on the crate. Then he walked to the bed and picked up the blankets, shaking them out. Dust flew everywhere.

Desirée watched as he stared down at the rope bed thoughtfully. "If you think I'm going to sleep in *that* you're crazy," she snapped. "I'd rather sleep on the ground."

"I'm afraid, for once, I have to agree with you. It looks like the mice beat us to it."

Us? Desirée thought in horror. She had meant *she* wasn't going to sleep in it. Had he thought to sleep with her? Desirée's eyes narrowed. What was he planning? Was he still thinking seduction? *Non!* She'd scratch his eyes out if he tried anything with her. He might kill her, but she'd be damned if she let him lure her into that trap again.

Desirée watched warily as Jason walked toward her,

carrying the two blankets. He dropped one blanket on the ground and then spread the other one out. Rising he said, "Sit down, Desirée."

Desirée's eyes darted to the blanket and then back up to Jason. *"Non!"*

Jason's eyes flashed dangerously. "Dammit, I'm not going to stand here arguing with you. We've only got a few hours till daylight, and I don't intend to spend it arguing." He caught her arm and forced her down, saying, "Now sit!"

Desirée watched as Jason sat beside her and pulled off his boots and socks, tossing them to the side. "Take off your boots, Desirée."

Desirée shot him a defiant look and opened her mouth. "Don't bother!" Jason snapped. I know what you're going to say. *Non!"* He jerked Desirée's legs from beneath her, slipping his hands under her skirt and pulling off her boot, then her sock.

But when he reached for the second boot, Desirée scrambled back. The feel of Jason's fingers sliding down her leg had totally unnerved her. *"Non!* I'll do it."

When Desirée had removed her boot and sock, Jason tore a strip from the second blanket and tied their ankles together.

"What are you doing?" Desirée asked.

"I'm tying you to me so you won't get any crazy ideas about running off in the middle of the night."

She would be tied to him the rest of the night? *"Non!* I'd rather be tied someplace else."

"Where? That bed?"

Desirée looked at the bed with horror, remembering what Jason had said about the mice. "I thought not,"

90

Jason said, seeing her look. "And since I'm the only other solid thing around here, it's going to be me."

Jason pushed Desirée down and lay beside her, flipping the second blanket over them. Desirée lay beside him, her body rigid, acutely aware of their legs tied together.

"And don't get any ideas about untying that blanket either," Jason said in a firm voice. "Let me warn you, I'm a very light sleeper. Now, you'd better get some sleep. It will be daylight in a few hours."

Sleep? With mice and bats in the room, and tied to a wild man? Why, I won't close my eyes for a minute, Desirée thought.

And Desirée didn't fall asleep for a good while. Long after Jason's deep, rhythmic breathing filled the air around her, she lay awake, her heart pounding in her ears. But it wasn't fear of the mice or bats that kept her awake, or even the fear that Jason might try something. No, it was the feel of Jason's long muscular leg pressing against hers, seemingly scalding her right through their layers of clothing, that kept her awake so long. That and other disturbingly sensual memories.

Chapter 5

When Desirée opened her eyes the next morning, she found herself staring up at the sunlight peeking through the palmetto leaves above her. Still half asleep, she looked around the light-dabbled hut with dazed eyes. Then, remembering where she was, she flew to her knees, glancing about her.

Jason was not in the shack. Where had he gone? Desirée wondered. Had he left her locked in this hut? But that would be ridiculous. With one end covered with palmetto leaves, she could easily escape. Then maybe he had just abandoned her, thinking she'd never find her way back to the plantation. Desirée smiled smugly. But he was wrong. She knew exactly where she was.

Then, hearing a soft neigh outside, all of Desirée's hopes fled. No, she thought. He wouldn't leave without his horse. He must be somewhere outside.

Desirée rose and walked to the palm leaves that

formed one wall of the hut. Much to her disgust, she couldn't see a thing through the thick, fanlike leaves. Then, spying a shaft of sunlight near the ground, she knelt and bent over, peering outside.

Jason was nowhere to be seen, but she could see his stallion behind a thick copse of trees. At least, she could see the animal's head. She wondered if she could make a quick dash for it. Once she was on that horse, there would be no way Jason could stop her.

"Looking for something?" a voice said from behind her.

Desirée froze, recognizing that deep male voice. Then, realizing her undignified position on the ground, with her bottom stuck up in the air, she scampered to her feet, sputtering, "I was—was just wondering where you were."

Jason's green eyes were shimmering with amusement. With that guilty look on her face, he had no doubt what she had been doing. Planning her escape, obviously. And damned if she hadn't been a delightful sight, with her soft, delectable little bottom sticking up like that.

"I've been outside, cooking our breakfast," Jason informed her.

"Breakfast?" Desirée asked in surprise.

"Yes. But if you want it, you'll have to step outside. I don't serve breakfast in bed." Jason's eyes flicked the the rumpled blankets on the ground.

Desirée flushed. How dare he remind her that she had spent the night with him—tied to him no less!

With all the dignity she could summon, Desirée marched out of the hut and over to the small campfire burning under a huge magnolia tree. Jason picked up a tin plate and handed it to her.

Desirée looked down at it, her nose wrinkling with distaste, as she said in a disgusted voice, "Fish? For breakfast?"

"I'm sorry I can't offer you ham and eggs," Jason said sarcastically. "I wasn't planning on entertaining a guest."

Before Desirée could think of a snappy retort, Jason thrust a tin cup in her hands. She looked down at it, saying, "Then where did you get the coffee?"

"From my saddlebags," Jason answered, motioning to the leather pouches laying on the ground nearby.

Desirée's eyes darted to the spot Jason had pointed to, seeing not only the stuffed saddlebags but also a clean blanket and oilskin, all stamped with CSA.

Seeing the look of surprise on her face, Jason said, "I didn't say I didn't come prepared, only that I wasn't prepared for a guest. I'd planned on living off the land, so I only brought along the essentials."

"Then you don't think the attack on New Orleans will be successful?" Desirée asked in a hopeful voice. "You've prepared to make your way back north?"

Jason's eyes flashed dangerously. "No, I didn't prepare myself for running. I'd intended to spend a week or so out in the countryside, until Captain Farragut had time to make his move. No sense in sitting around New Orleans and taking the chance of my real identity being discovered."

"And just what is your real identity, sir?" Desirée asked, her anger at this Yankee spy rising to the surface again.

"Captain Jason Steele, United States Army, at your service, m'lady," Jason ground out.

94

Desirée's dark eyes flashed. "And do you think being an officer in the Union Army makes your spying on us any more honorable? *Non!* You're nothing but a thief. Why, all of your provisions, even this cup," she said, waving the cup at him, the coffee spilling over the sides, "is Confederate Army issue, stolen property!"

"For your information, I didn't ask for this mission. I was ordered to do it. And you're damned right that's stolen property. I'd be a damned fool to run around here with *Union* Army supplies."

"And the uniform? Do you still have it?" Desirée asked indignantly, feeling that the uniform of her beloved South had been desecrated by this Yankee.

"Yes, I do," Jason replied. "It might come in handy again."

So, Desirée thought, he wasn't all that confident that the Union would be successful in capturing New Orleans after all. The realization comforted her, but only for a minute. She'd feel much better about the impending battle if the South had been forewarned. Damn! Why hadn't she been more careful last night?

She glanced across at Jason, sitting on a fallen limb and eating his breakfast. But all is not lost, Desirée thought. I'll find some way to escape. He's got to let his guard down sometime. And when he does, I'll be ready to make my move. I just have to be patient and wait for the right opportunity.

When they were finished eating, Jason started packing everything away, including the two old blankets and tin plates and cups from the trapper's hut, rolling them up in his oilskin. As he bent to pick everything up, Desirée noticed the wicked-looking

95

knife he had strapped to his lean waist. He hadn't been wearing a knife last night, she remembered. She shivered.

Jason stood, his bedroll tucked under one arm, his saddlebag thrown over his broad shoulder. Taking her arm with his free hand, he said, "Come on. Let's get moving."

Desirée started for the horse, but Jason pulled her back, saying, "No, this way."

Desirée glanced back at the horse in confusion and then realized that the animal wasn't saddled and waiting as she had thought, but tethered in a small clearing beside the bayou.

When Jason led her down a path in the opposite direction and under a big willow tree by the bayou, Desirée spied the pirogue in the murky water beside them and realized that that was what he was leading her to. "Where did you find that?" she asked.

"Hidden in the undergrowth farther downstream. It took me awhile this morning to find it. But I knew the trapper would be back this winter and would need his pirogue."

Suddenly, Desirée was terrified. Remembering the knife strapped to his waist and the sailor's threat the night before, she feared that Jason planned to take her down the bayou, kill her, and then hide her body. "Are you going to kill me?" she asked in a weak voice, her legs trembling badly.

"No, Desirée, I'm *not* going to kill you, although I'll admit I seriously considered throttling you last night."

"Then where are you taking me?"

"To someplace where you'll be safe, and yet, not

able to escape and tell what you know. Now, get in."

"But we can't go wandering down the bayou. All of Louisiana is laced with thousands of these small streams, winding and crisscrossing swamps with each other. We'll get lost. Why don't we take the road?"

"Because where I'm taking you can't be reached by road."

"Where *are* you taking me?" Desirée asked, her apprehension rising once more to the surface.

"If you must know, into the swamps."

Desirée's knees buckled. *Mon Dieu!* The man was mad! "*Non!* You're insane! No one goes out into the swamps, much less a Yankee. They're dangerous. Treacherous! You'll get lost for sure. We'll *both* die out there!"

"No, Desirée, I won't get lost. I know the bayous and swamps around here like the back of my hand. And all the other waterways around here, including the Mississippi. That, plus my familiarity with New Orleans, was why I was chosen for this mission."

"But—but how do you know that?"

"I was born here in Louisiana and spent half my life here."

At his revelation, Desirée's eyes flashed with a renewed anger. "Why—why, you're worse than a spy. You're a turncoat. You're a born Southerner who's turned traitor!"

"I said half my life, Desirée. The other half I spent in the North."

"And when the war came, you sided with them— the Yankees!" Desirée said, her voice full of contempt.

Jason scowled. The decision to fight on the North's

side hadn't been an easy one for him. He had been as torn as the country itself. A large part of him was still southern. Like the giant cypress trees in the swamps that had once been his home, his roots sank deep in the Louisiana mud. And yet, he had known in his heart that the North was right. As Lincoln had said, "A house divided against itself cannot stand." It was Jason's firm conviction, that only by keeping the two parts of the country together, forming one strong whole, the nation could survive. He didn't fight for the North. He fought for the Union.

"I have my reasons for fighting on the Union side, Desirée. Good reasons. I happen to believe they're right."

"Right?" Desirée shrieked. "Why, the North—"

Jason caught Desirée's arm in a bone-crushing grip, interjecting in a steely voice, "I'm not going to stand here arguing politics with you, or waste my time trying to explain my convictions. This war will be fought, but not by you and me—and not here! Now, get into that pirogue!"

Desirée looked up at Jason. With his eyes glittering with anger and his mouth a firm, determined slash across his face, he looked very dangerous. On trembling legs, she walked to the pirogue and stepped in, then sat down on the small seat at the opposite end of it.

She watched mutely while Jason placed his saddlebags and bedroll in the middle of the crude canoe. Then he picked up the pole and shoved the pirogue into the murky waters of the bayou, ducking his head to avoid a low-hanging branch as the canoe slid from beneath the willow tree. As they entered the main channel of the bayou, a new terror came over Desirée. The small, crude canoe didn't look exactly safe to her. What if it should sink? There were alligators and poisonous snakes in these waters!

"Are you sure this thing is safe?" she asked in a frightened voice.

Jason chuckled, replying, "This is probably the sturdiest boat in the whole world, Desirée. It's made from a hollowed-out cypress log. Why, it probably wouldn't rot in a hundred years. And yet it's not heavy either, at least not in the water. Cypress wood, despite its toughness, has an amazing buoyancy. That's why we Cajuns claim one of these pirogues can float on a heavy dew."

"Cajun?" Desirée asked in an astonished voice. "You're Cajun?"

"Yes, half of me, is. Like you, I'm half French."

No wonder he dares to go into the dangerous bayous and swamps, Desirée thought. That half land, half water country was Cajun territory, just as New Orleans was Creole. Yes, if he was part Cajun, he undoubtedly did know all of the waterways, and he wouldn't get lost. But she would. Even if she managed to escape him, she'd have no idea of how to get back to New Orleans. And if she didn't get back to New Orleans to warn them of the Union threat, it would be all this man's fault.

Desirée sat in the pirogue glaring at Jason. Before she had been afraid of him because of his overpowering attraction, had been angry at him because he had made her betray both herself and Beau with his sensuous advances. But now she hated him. Yes, this Yankee spy, this turncoat was her enemy.

Non! I won't let him get the best of me, Desirée thought furiously, her dark eyes darting around her. I won't get lost. I'll memorize every turn, every twist we make.

But as Jason poled their way down one sluggish, winding bayou, then down another twisting stream, and then another, Desirée became more and more disorientated. The murky water twisted and turned, widened and narrowed. In some places, the stream was so narrow the thick trees on either bank stretched across it, darkening it and making it look like a deep tunnel. At those times, Desirée would peer anxiously into the dense underbrush all around them, terrified that at any minute some wild animal would come lurching out at them or, even worse, some snake curled in the thick branches would resent their intrusion and strike.

At yet another place, the bayou seemed to completely disappear. Desirée watched in disbelief as Jason poled them into what looked like a solid wall of tall reeds, expecting to hear the crunching sound as the pirogue grounded. As they glided through a sea of cattails, she glanced down and saw that only an inch or two of water lay beneath them. And then suddenly, the bayou widened again. Desirée looked back, utterly amazed. No wonder the Cajuns say these pirogues can float on a heavy dew.

By the time they stopped for lunch, Desirée knew she was completely and hopelessly lost. While Jason occupied himself building a fire, she stood on the banks of the bayou and with a heavy heart, stared off in the direction from where they had come, knowing that escape would be pointless, even dangerous.

And then Desirée's eyes caught a glimpse of something fluttering in the breeze above the trees where the bayou twisted and disappeared. Her heart raced with excitement, for she had recognized that proud flag with its starred, crossed bars and the pelican flag that flew beneath it. She knew that right around the bend was a vessel of the River Defense Fleet that patrolled these bayous, and it was coming this way.

Then remembering Jason, she glanced over her shoulder, fearing he, too, had seen the flags. But seeing that he had disappeared into the thick brush behind them in search of firewood, her eyes darted back to the bayou where the small steamboat was slowly chugging its way around the bend.

All is not lost after all, Desirée thought, her spirits soaring. She had only to wait until the boat was close enough so she could be seen and could call for help.

The next few minutes seemed like a lifetime to Desirée. She watched anxiously as the steamboat seemed to inch forward, her own nerves crawling with impatience. And then, when she judged the boat to be finally close enough, she opened her mouth to call.

But Desirée never uttered a word. A band of steel closed around her chest just below her breasts. But it wasn't Jason's arm around her that stopped Desirée from calling. It was the feel of the knife that he held at her back with his other hand that silenced her.

"Don't try it, Desirée," Jason warned in a low, menacing voice against her ear.

Desirée's heart raced in terror. Beads of perspiration broke out on her forehead. Jason held his breath, praying to God that Desirée would heed his warning, for he knew he could never sink his knife into her sweet, soft flesh. Even if it meant failure of his mission and his own death, he could never do anything to harm her, much less kill her. He could only hope that she was frightened enough not to call his bluff.

When he felt Desirée trembling with fear, Jason relaxed the bone-crushing grip around her lower chest. Desirée sucked in a deep breath of fresh air. Still holding her tightly against him, Jason whispered in her ear, "When they pass, smile and wave at them. We're only a young Cajun couple seeking a place of solitude for our lover's tryst."

Desirée could feel the cold metal of the knife pressing between her shoulder blades. When the boat passed, she did as Jason had ordered her to do. Raising her arm, she waved and smiled, and then jumped as Jason called a greeting in French, his Cajun accent so thick she couldn't even understand him.

A voice from the steamboat answered him in that same Cajun French. And then, as the steamboat chugged down the bayou, farther and farther away, the only sound was the steady swish, swish, swish of the paddles.

It wasn't until the patrol boat had disappeared from view that Jason finally withdrew the knife and released Desirée. She whirled on him, her dark eyes flashing. "I hate you!" she spat. "Do you hear? I hate you!" Then she threw herself down on the mossy ground and cried bitter tears.

Jason watched while Desirée sat on the ground and cried, feeling as if his heart would break. He longed to take her in his arms and comfort her, tell her he could never hurt her, but he knew it wouldn't make any difference to her. Desirée was just as fiercely loyal to the southern cause as he was the Union one. She had felt honor-bound to warn her people. She didn't cry because she was angry with him but because she had failed. And he wasn't angry with her because she had tried, either. He would have been disappointed in her if she hadn't.

For a brief moment, he wondered if he were wrong in his belief that Desirée and he were meant for each other. If their destinies were meant to be joined, then why were so many obstacles being thrown between them? It was bad enough that she thought she loved another. But now, because of this war, they were enemies, too. But then he remembered that the gods of fate were often perverse. They may have promised her to him, but they had never promised to make it easy for him to claim her. No, Jason thought with renewed determination, he wouldn't give up. No man or no damned war was going to keep them apart!

That afternoon Desirée was resigned to her position as Jason's prisoner. She knew she had lost her chance to escape and warn New Orleans. And Jason had been correct. Her outburst and tears *had* stemmed more from anger at herself than him. She had failed because she had let her fear override her duty. And now, knowing that there was nothing else she could do, she stopped worrying about her escape and for the first time noticed the beauty all around her.

Because he didn't want to risk the chance of running into another patrol boat, Jason had taken them deep into the bayou country where the streams were too narrow and shallow for the steamboats. Here

103

the world was strangely silent, and everything seemed to move in slow motion.

Desirée looked about this strange new world in wonder. Was it her imagination or were the colors really magnified? The huge trees all around them seemed greener, the Spanish moss that hung from them greyer, the lotus blossoms that floated in the water on foot-wide pads yellower. All the colors of the flowers seemed more vivid, the tree orchids pinker, the flowers on the trumpet vines redder, the spiderlilies whiter, the wild irises bluer. Even the water had changed from the yellowish, murky color to a brilliant, shimmering green as it reflected the trees around them.

Feeling a lassitude creeping over her, Desirée leaned back in the pirogue and let her hand trail, noticing that the bayou seemed to have no current. Then she smiled, remembering that the first French who had come to this land had called the bayous the "sleeping waters" for that reason. She lifted her head and watched the fleecy clouds, driven by the gentle gulf breezes, drifting across the deep blue sky.

And then suddenly, the land dipped below sea level, and they were in a great cypress swamp. Desirée sat up and watched in breathless awe as they floated past the huge tupelo gum trees, the massive water willows, and the giant, ancient cypresses, whose branches were festooned with Spanish moss, ethereal and haunting, some so long it trailed in the water. She looked up at one huge cypress, seeing its cones and feathery leaves, then the delicate tree orchids that covered the entire top of the tree. As they weaved their way around the huge, swollen bases of the old cypresses and past their peculiar knees that jutted from the swamp, Desirée noticed that in places the water was covered with duckweed, giving it a slimy appearance, and in others it was a dark tea color from rotting bark and fallen limbs. As she gazed at this silent, mysterious, hauntingly beautiful land around her, Desirée felt as if the world had stopped turning, that time, itself, stood still. A vast sense of peace, a serenity like she had never known, filled her as the swamp cast its strange spell on her.

For here was a world that had changed little, if any, since the beginning of time. Isolated by its forbidding terrain, it was a land virtually undisturbed by civilization. It was Eden before the fall of Adam and Eve, before mankind knew of anger, hatred, jealousy, greed, war. There was no place in this tranquil liquid land for man's cares and worries, for the ugliness he had brought into the world. With its overwhelming peacefulness and its haunting beauty, the swamp lulled and soothed, stripping man of his anger, his frustrations, his cares, making them seem insignificant and meaningless. And Desirée was not immune to its tranquilizing, almost hypnotic power.

As Jason watched Desirée, he could almost see the anger and tension leaving her. He knew what was happening. The same thing that had happened to him before was happening to him now. The swamp was casting its spell over both of them.

When Desirée looked up at him and smiled, Jason's spirits lifted with hope. Maybe the gods had decided to be kind to him after all, he thought. And maybe by the time they had to leave this mysterious, wondrous land, he would have convinced her that their destinies lay together.

The land lifted, and once more they floated down a sleepy stream. Then suddenly, there was an airlessness about the bayou, as if the world had suddenly stopped breathing. The stillness became eerie. Not a leaf stirred. The silence lay around them like a thick blanket, while a strange haze covered the sky.

Jason scanned the heavens, saying, "There's a storm coming. We'd better get out of the water."

Desirée looked around her in disbelief. She hadn't seen any clouds. A minute later, the sun was blotted out, throwing the bayou in darkness. In the distance, a jagged white flash of lightning lit the darkened sky. And then, Desirée heard the patter of raindrops on the leaves of the trees above them.

After Jason had grounded the pirogue and helped Desirée from it, he pulled the crude canoe farther up on the bank and, picking up his saddlebag and bedroll, quickly scanned the area. Pointing off into the distance, he said, "That big palmetto there looks like it would give the best protection. Come on."

But before Jason got the words out of his mouth, the storm was upon them, stunning Desirée with its suddenness and its ferocity. The wind lashed the trees around them with a vengeance, twisting the Spanish moss first one way than the other. Lightning flashed a jagged streak across the sky, then forked and forked again, briefly illuminating the whole area in a blinding white light. Thunder rolled and crashed all around them, and then, the rain came in torrents.

Jason flung his saddlebag over his shoulder and took Desirée's hand, pulling her after him as he dashed across the small clearing. But before they reached the protection of the palmetto, they were drenched to the skin by the driving rain.

Desirée started to scamper under the protective leaves, but Jason held her back, saying, "No, let me look first. Better to get wet than bitten by a cottonmouth."

Desirée shivered in revulsion while Jason carefully lifted the huge leaves and looked under them. Then tossing his saddlebag and bedroll under them, he caught Desirée's arm and pulled her under the palm with him.

Although the palmetto was larger than most, it was so low Desirée and Jason had to sit in a hunching position under it. With the wind lashing the palm wildly around them, the leaves looked like giant hands that seemed bent on beating them to death, slapping at their faces, arms, and legs. But despite the thrashing leaves, Desirée was glad to be beneath the shelter where it was relatively dry. She felt much safer there, with Jason's strong arm protectively around her, than out in that angry storm. As the raging storm built to its crescendo, Desirée watched it with disbelief. It seemed impossible that this was the same bayou that had been so still and peaceful just minutes before. The wind howled through the trees, twisting the branches and moss in every direction, as pieces of branches and greyish moss flew everywhere. Added to the noise of the howling wind was the deafening rolls of thunder and the loud crashes of lightning. The strong smell of ozone filled the air. The bayou itself, which only minutes before had been placid, its surface as smooth as glass, was now solid white with white-caps as the water was thrashed by the wind. Desirée jumped as yet another ear-splitting crash rent the air around them, then gasped as the jagged, white-hot bolt struck a huge oak tree across the bayou. The whole top of the tree came tumbling down, crashing through the lower limbs, its Spanish moss ignited by the tremendous heat and bursting into multiple flames. And then it hit the ground with a loud thud, shaking the ground with the impact of its fall, the fires immediately extinguished by the driving rain.

Desirée shivered at the violence around her. Jason tightened his arm around her, saying, "Are you cold or afraid of the storm?"

"A little of both," Desirée admitted, glad for the heat that radiated from his big body and the security of his powerful arms around her.

And then, just as suddenly as it came, the storm was gone. As Jason helped Desirée from beneath the palmetto, she looked around her in disbelief. The bayou had returned to its former serenity. Not a leaf stirred, the only sound the dripping of water from the trees. Even the water on the bayou was perfectly still. The only evidence of the recent violence that had occurred here was the broken branches, pieces of moss, and the petals from hundreds of flowers that littered the ground.

Desirée bent and picked up a huge magnolia blossom that had been torn from its tree. Unbelievably, the creamy petals were still intact. Absently, she lifted it to her nose to smell its heavenly scent, gazing about her in dazed wonder.

Jason looked around, saying, "We might as well camp here for the night."

"So early?" Desirée asked in surprise.

108

"Yes. It's going to take me awhile to find dry firewood." Then, looking at Desirée's soaked garments, he frowned and said, "You'd better get out of those wet clothes before you get chilled."

"But I don't have any dry clothes to put on."

"You can wrap up in a blanket until your clothes dry out. Thank God, I wrapped my bedroll in my oilskin this morning, so everything in there should be dry."

Desirée watched as Jason fished his bedroll and saddlebags from beneath the palmetto, then untied the small rope around the bedroll. Wrap up in a blanket? Walk around here with only a blanket to hide her nakedness?

"*Non*, I'm not cold," Desirée lied, for the only thing that hadn't returned to the bayou was its warmth. There was a decided chill in the air.

"Desirée, we can't take any chances of you catching swamp fever," Jason said in a firm voice. "We're a good two days from civilization and the nearest doctor. Now don't argue."

Was that what caused swamp fever? Desirée wondered. A chill? Well, who knows. Even the doctors didn't know what caused these strange fevers that plagued this marshy country. But she did know she didn't want to take any risks of catching the dreaded fever. And certainly, once things had warmed up again, her clothes would dry out quickly.

"All right," she said reluctantly.

"I'll go and look for firewood while you're changing. Don't do too much wandering around and watch where you step. The storm probably stirred up snakes."

Desirée shivered, looking about her fearfully as Jason strolled off into the thick underbrush. Picking up the blanket, she walked behind the palmetto they had hidden under, watching the ground carefully. Quickly, she stripped off her wet blouse and skirt, dropping them over the palm to dry. She looked down at the chemise and pantaloons, thinking for a minute she could at least keep them on. But seeing the way the thin, wet material was clinging to every curve of her body, hiding absolutely nothing from view, she decided against it. Stripping off her chemise, she tossed it over the palm. Getting the pantaloons off over her boots proved to be a chore, but Desirée was determined she wasn't going to stand around barefoot for one minute. Finally managing to get them off, she tossed them at the back of the palm where they couldn't be seen by Jason.

She looked down at herself, thinking how ridiculou she looked stark naked with only her boots on. Quickly, she wrapped the blanket around her and walked back into the clearing.

She was perched on a small log, a log she had carefully examined before she sat on it, when Jason returned carrying an armload of firewood. Jason glanced at Desirée, clutching the blanket around her, grateful that, for once, she hadn't argued with him. Then, suddenly very aware that she was naked beneath the blanket, Jason felt his heat rise and jerked his eyes away from her.

He knelt on the ground and arranged the kindling, cursing himself. All afternoon long, he had been acutely aware of her, but he had promised himself that he would move more slowly with her. He wanted to gain her trust, give her time to get to know him personally, convince her that he wasn't her enemy before he attempted to make love to her again. But this afternoon, when he had sat with his arm around her under the palmetto, it had been all he could do to keep from crushing her sweet body to his and kissing her until she was breathless. And now, tormented by visions of her nakedness under that blanket, his loins ached and throbbed. Tonight was going to be sheer hell.

Jason rose and stripped off his wet shirt. Tossing it over a nearby bush, he knelt once again and started breaking the longer branches into small pieces. Desirée sat on the log, her eyes glued to the rippling muscles on Jason's broad back as he snapped the branches as if they were mere twigs. Having grown up on a plantation, she was accustomed to seeing the naked chests and backs of the male slaves as they toiled in the fields. But there was a sensuousness about the way Jason's powerful muscles moved beneath his bronzed skin that left her feeling strangely weak and giddy.

When he rose and turned, Desirée's breath caught at the sight of his bronzed chest with its dark mat of curls, hair that tapered down his taut abdomen and disappeared at his belt. And then her eyes darted lower. In the skin tight pants, with the damp material clinging to his muscular thighs, his maleness was clearly outlined in bold relief. Remembering what *that* had felt like against her abdomen that day at Whispering Oaks, her mouth turned dry and her heart raced. A warm flush washed over her, a heat that had nothing to do with embarrassment. She guiltily jerked her eyes away to stare dumbly at the pile of firewood behind him.

Darkness fell with a suddenness on the bayou, and the land that had been strangly silent all day came alive with the sounds of crickets and bull frogs. The great horned owls hooted in their deep bass voices, the screech owls in their high-pitched ones. Out in the bayou, a fish splashed, and somewhere in the distance, a bull alligator roared, the air reverberating with the spine-tingling sound.

Desirée watched silently as Jason gathered Spanish moss and lay it on the ground by the fire. Armful after armful was tossed down, until a soft pad at least four inches thick covered the damp ground. And then as he lay a blanket over it to form one big pallet, Desirée's eyes widened, and her heart thudded in her chest.

"I'd prefer to have my pallet on the other side of the fire," Desirée said in a weak voice.

Jason rose, saying, "I don't think that would be a good idea, with all those wild animals running around. I had thought to put you between me and the fire."

Desirée had been aware of the increased activity in the dark underbrush all around them as the night prowlers came out in search of food. She had seen the flying squirrels leaping from one limb to another in the trees above them, a bat darting from the Spanish moss to catch a flying insect, and caught a glimpse of a possum as he scurried from one bush to another, his long ratlike tail dragging the ground behind him. Even now, the bushes all around them were rustling. What other animals were out there? Were there any black bears around? Cougars?

112

Her eyes flew fearfully to the branches above her. She half expected to see a flash of gold as a big cat leaped from one limb to another, or a pair of feline eyes glittering in the firelight as he crouched above her. A shiver went through her.

It seemed she had a choice between taking her chances with the wild animals roaming around out there in the dark or this rugged human animal who had been arousing strange and bewildering feelings in her all evening. Then she remembered that Jason hadn't tried anything the night before. And, at least, tonight she wouldn't be tied to him. But she would feel much safer if she weren't naked under the blanket.

Desirée was aware of Jason who waited for her answer. "All right," she answered. "But first I'm going to put on my clothes."

Clutching her blanket, she walked across the small clearing to the palmetto where her clothing was drying, hoping she looked dignified and not as ridiculous as she felt. She hesitated, seeing that the palm was in total darkness. Aware of Jason's eyes on her, she gathered her courage and walked to the palmetto, her eyes nervously searching the darkness around her.

To her disappointment, she found her skirt and blouse were still wet. She fingered the slightly damp chemise and pantaloons. She knew that the thin material held nothing from view, but just having them on would make her feel more secure. At least, she wouldn't be totally naked.

Once she was dressed in the flimsy garments, muttering oaths as she struggled to get the pantaloons on over her boots, she wrapped the blanket around

113

her tightly again, hoping Jason wouldn't realize that she was only in her underwear. She glanced at him as she walked back across the clearing, grateful that he was occupied with the fire and had his back to her. Quickly, she lay down, wrapping the blanket tightly around her.

Jason rose, walked to his side of the pallet, and sat down. After taking off his boots and socks and placing them to the side, he picked up his blanket, tossed it over him, and lay down.

Desirée rolled quickly to her side, facing the fire with her back to Jason. She stared at the flickering firelight, acutely aware of Jason behind her and her racing heart. Then she heard Jason chuckling softly. A tingle ran down her spine at the almost sensuous sound.

"Do you always wear your boots to bed, Desirée?" Jason asked in an amused voice.

Desirée glanced down and saw the toes of her boots peeking from underneath the blanket. Feeling ridiculous, she sat up and quickly stripped the boots off, then her socks, tossing them aside. She lay down once more, refusing to even give Jason a quick glance, but she was very aware of those misty-green eyes on her.

She lay listening to the night noises, wishing that she wasn't so aware of Jason's heat, of his heady scent drifting across the small distance that separated them. *Mon Dieu*, was this to be another night like last night? Was she doomed to lie half the night again, tormented by those peculiar longings?

A hair-raising scream rent the night air, and Desirée bolted up, her heart racing, her eyes darting about the darkness in terror. A sudden, eerie hush fell over

114

the bayou, as if every living creature were listening, preparing itself for flight. The abrupt silence was even more unnerving.

"There's nothing to be afraid of, Desirée," Jason said in a voice that sounded strangely husky to Desirée's ears. "The cougar's not anywhere near us."

And then, as if in agreement with Jason, the night creatures went back to their business, the noises sounding even louder after the strange silence.

Desirée looked across at Jason sitting beside her. Her breath caught as she saw his eyes locked on her breasts, the soft mounds rising and falling in quick breaths from her fright. She could feel those misty-green eyes devouring her. And then, to her horror, she felt her nipples swelling and hardening, as if it were Jason's hands and not his eyes that were caressing them. Cover yourself, her mind screamed. But her hands refused to obey the command.

And then, as Jason lifted his head and those smoldering green eyes locked on hers, Desirée felt as if the tension had been suddenly sucked from her body to be replaced with a strange languidness. With a will of their own, her arms raised, not to cover her breasts, but to curl around Jason's broad shoulders, a soft animallike moan escaping her lips as he gathered her in his arms and lay her back down, following her to the soft, mossy pallet.

"Desirée, Desirée," Jason muttered against her lips as he placed soft, tender kisses on them. His warm mouth brushed her cheek before he bathed her temples, her forehead, her eyelids, her nose with feathery kisses. Then, spying the mole beside her mouth from the corner of his eye, his lips moved to that enticing

115

beauty mark, drawn like a bee to honey.

Desirée felt Jason's lips nibbling there, his tongue flickering like a fiery dart. She whimpered, moving closer, and then gasped as her throbbing breasts brushed the crisp dark curls on Jason's naked chest through the thin material of her chemise, hearing Jason's breath catch as he, too, felt the sensuous caress.

Jason's tongue grazed Desirée's lips with the lightness of a butterfly's wing before it slid across her teeth and then, as her lips parted, darted inside, exploring every inch of her honeyed sweetness before sliding, then swirling around hers. Desirée kissed him back, at first tentatively, then hungrily, feeling more than hearing Jason's groan of pleasure.

A small moan of protest came from Desirée's throat as Jason's mouth moved away. But then, as his warm tongue traced the pounding pulse down her throat, Desirée's heart raced with anticipation.

As Jason's slender fingers unbuttoned her chemise, he kissed every inch of exposed skin as he slowly descended, and Desirée thought she would scream with frustration. Then, when he pushed the flimsy garment aside and his warm hand cupped one soft mound, she rolled her head side to side, thinking she couldn't stand any more of this delicious teasing. Her nipples were aching, feeling as if they would burst for want of his mouth on them. She cupped the back of his head and arched her back in a silent, urgent plea.

As his teeth gently raked one throbbing peak before his tongue rolled it, Desirée cried out in a half-strangled voice, "Jason!" She felt as if a fiery dart had shot straight to the core of her womanhood,

116

leaving it burning in its wake as a warm wetness flooded from her.

Desirée saw Jason's face above her, his eyes darkened with passion, an almost anguished look on his face. "Desirée," Jason said in a ragged voice, "if you're going to stop me, do it now. I can't take anymore. We've got to go all the way or stop right here."

Jason held his breath, seriously doubting that he could stop at this point. Every muscle in his big body was crying for release.

But Desirée was too aroused to even consider stopping. Her blood felt as if it were liquid fire. Her loins ached. She knew that only Jason could put out that fire, ease that ache.

"No, don't stop," she whispered, once again cupping his head and pulling it forward, this time offering her lips.

A feeling of sheer joy shot through Jason. With a small cry of exhilaration, his lips captured hers in a deep, fierce, passionate kiss that sent both of their senses reeling.

There was no turning back now. Desirée's hands roamed hungrily over Jason's broad shoulders and back, reveling in the feel of those powerful muscles under her fingertips. But soon, even that was drowned out by sheer sensation as Jason's hands caressed and fondled her, his lips and tongue devouring the sweetness of her lips and skin. She wasn't even aware when he slipped off her pantaloons and hastily stripped off his pants.

But when his fingers brushed the insides of her thighs before tangling in the soft curls between her

117

legs, awareness suddenly returned. And then feeling his hand cup her there, in that most intimate of all spots, she closed her legs instinctively, saying, *"Non!"*

"Let me touch you," Jason murmured in a husky voice against her ear.

Non! It's indecent! Desirée thought to say, but before the words reached her lips, Jason's tongue was teasing her ear, and his fingers were already working their magic. But, for once, Desirée was oblivious to Jason's tantalizing tongue, for it seemed as if every nerve ending in her body had suddenly shifted to her loins as his fingers parted the soft, aching lips, sliding over the wetness there, seeking and finding the throbbing bud, then circling and stroking sensuously.

"Mon Dieu!" Desirée whispered as a whole new barrage of sensations attacked her senses. She felt as if her body had turned into a flaming torch, searing her clear down to the soles of her feet. Her muscles tensed in anticipation. And then, the sweet ripples began, growing to delicious undulations, leaving her limp, her breath coming in gasps.

She was still floating on a warm, rosy cloud when Jason rose over her, parting her thighs. Deliberately, he had held back his own passion, wanting this first time for her to be as beautiful as he knew it would be for him. But he couldn't hold back any longer. His whole body was quivering with need, every muscle demanding release.

He entered her slowly, tentatively searching for the barrier that he knew was there, and then finding it, he hesitated. He had hoped he would not have to hurt her, but now, feeling her tightness, he feared there was

118

no way he could culminate this lovemaking without doing so. And for Jason there was no turning back. He felt as if he would burst if he didn't find release soon. Sliding his hands under her soft buttocks, he lifted her, pressing his hot, rigid maleness against the membrane and then, feeling it give, plunged in.

Desirée cried out as sudden tears came to her eyes, and Jason felt as if his heart had been wrenched in two at the sound. He held her, his hands soothing her as he whispered endearments and kissed the tears from her eyes. Then, feeling her tight warmth surrounding him, his big body broke out in a sheen of perspiration as he fought desperately for control, every muscle trembling with effort.

Once the splitting pain was replaced with a dull ache, Desirée became aware of Jason inside her, hot and throbbing, feeling enormous and filling her completely. And then, as her muscles began to relax and Jason began to move slowly inside her, even more exciting and wondrous sensations began. An intense feeling of anticipation filled her as every nerve in her body came alive. Instinctively she moved with him, faster and faster, straining, seeking something that she knew nothing of. Then, as Jason's hot mouth crashed down on hers in a fierce, demanding kiss, she spiraled upward. She held her breath, every muscle in her body taut with expectation, the tension growing until she felt she would burst from her skin. Suddenly, Jason stiffened, his groan of ecstasy filling her ears, and slowly the strange tension left her as she drifted back down to earth.

Jason lay with his head buried in the soft crook of Desirée's neck, his breath coming in ragged gasps.

119

When his breathing returned to normal, he raised his head and looked down at Desirée. Smoothing back her damp hair, he kissed her tenderly on the forehead, her eyes, then on her mouth, before lifting his head and again gazing down at her.

Desirée looked up with dazed eyes and saw Jason's face above her. How beautiful his eyes are, she thought, with their strange color and thick dark lashes. She raised her hand and brushed a lock of dark hair from his forehead, then traced his strong jawline with one finger. Jason caught her hand and turned his head, kissing the palm softly. A strange warm feeling stirred in Desirée, a feeling that had nothing to do with desire. She frowned, briefly puzzled, before her eyelids drifted down in exhaustion.

Jason rolled to his side and gently placed Desirée's head on his shoulder. His hands caressed her back and shoulders absently as he lay thinking.

He knew she hadn't reached her fulfillment, and he felt a keen disappointment that she hadn't. Reason told him that as an untutored virgin it would be too much to expect her to experience total ecstasy her first time, but Jason had wanted that for her. For him, it had been the most exhilarating, most exciting experience he had ever felt, and he had wanted her to share it.

He looked down at her, wondering what her reaction would be when she awakened in the morning and remembered what had happened. In the cold light of day, would she regret it? Would she turn on him again? He had claimed her body, but he knew she was still a long way from being completely his.

Jason reached for the blanket and tossed it over

them. He lay for a long while staring up at the dark sky, his arm curled about Desirée's shoulders. He groaned softly, thinking the gods of fate weren't going to make it easy for him.

Chapter 6

When Desirée woke up the next morning, everything that had happened the night before came rushing back. *Mon Dieu*, she thought in horror. She had let Jason make love to her again, and this time, reason had not returned soon enough to save her from disaster. She had given her virginity, her bride's gift, to that Yankee. What's more, she had done so willingly. What in the world had possessed her?

Did he hold some dark, mysterious hold over her? He had only to touch her to melt her resistance, to destroy her will. She couldn't stay with him. Her body betrayed her at every turn. She had to get away!

Desirée sat up, looking frantically around the small clearing for Jason, but he was nowhere in sight. Her eyes scanned the bayou's edge and froze on the empty pirogue. Without a moment's hesitation, she threw off the blanket, jumped to her feet, and hurriedly dressed.

Still buttoning her bodice, she rushed to the bobbing canoe, then bent and struggled with the knot in the rope where Jason had tied it to a fallen log. Cursing under her breath, she jerked on the rope, fearing that Jason would return before she could escape. The knot only tightened.

Then she heard it: a slight rustling in the underbrush beside her. She looked up, expecting to see Jason. What she saw made her blood run cold.

A seven-foot alligator lumbered toward her, its beady eyes glittering in anticipation and its mouth frozen in that perpetual alligator grin. As it approached, an overpowering musky smell reached Desirée's nostrils, a stench that marked it as a male of the species. Desirée rose and then stood rooted to the spot, her scream of terror dying in her throat as the muscles contracted in fear. Paralyzed, she watched as it opened its huge jaws, and found herself staring at the awesome pink gaping hole that was its mouth, its sharp teeth gleaming in the sunlight.

Jason was just a blur in her peripheral vision as he flew from the underbrush, yelling, "Get back!" Desirée was shoved out of the way so roughly, she stumbled and fell, the fall knocking the breath from her.

She looked up to see Jason had placed himself between her and the alligator. The reptile wasn't in the least perturbed. One victim was as good as the other.

The alligator lunged at Jason, moving with an amazing speed for such a large, cumbersome creature. Jason jumped out of the way as the powerful jaws snapped shut. Only when Desirée saw the long rip in Jason's pants did she realize how close the alligator had come to taking off one of Jason's legs. The realization left her weak.

Slowly, Jason backed away to the edge of the bayou. The alligator followed, its beady, protruding eyes glittering with deadly intent. Again it lunged, its massive jaws open. Again Jason jumped away to the sound of that huge vise snapping shut. This time, Jason was left standing in knee-deep water. To Desirée's horror, on the third strike, Jason slipped on the muddy bayou bottom and tumbled backward into the sluggish stream. The alligator slid into the bayou after him.

Jason disappeared from Desirée's view, swimming to the bottom of the bayou. The alligator followed him to the murky depths. A moment later, they shot to the surface, Jason on the alligator's back, his arm around the reptile's thick neck and arching it back. The alligator twisted and turned, its powerful tail thrashing wildly and throwing water everywhere. Then they both disappeared beneath the surface of the bayou again.

Desirée scampered to her feet and watched from the side of the stream, desperately peering into the murky water, but she could see nothing of the man and the reptile. She jumped as the alligator's tail briefly emerged, flashing and twisting in the sunlight, before it disappeared again with a loud clap as it hit the water. For a moment, the only sign of the struggle between the two at the bayou's depths was the boiling of the muddy water, and then, even it disappeared.

Desirée stared at the bayou. Not a ripple could be seen. She strained her eyes, trying to see through the muddy water, then gasped when she saw the red stain slowly floating to the surface.

Terrified, she sank to her knees, not knowing if the blood came from Jason or the alligator. A strange hush fell over the bayou, as if all its creatures were waiting with bated breaths to see which had won the death struggle. The minute that passed seemed a lifetime to Desirée. Tears welled in her eyes. A hard lump formed in her throat.

Suddenly, a figure shot to the surface, and Desirée startled in fright. A sob of relief escaped her throat as Jason's dark head emerged. Wearily, he waded from the marshy stream, the muddy water cascading from him. The sun flashed on the hunting knife he held in his hand, the blade still stained with the alligator's blood.

Jason towered over Desirée, where she still knelt at the edge of the bayou, the water dripping from his clothes and puddling at his feet. His breath came in ragged gasps. "Why—in hell—didn't you run? Climb a tree? Do something?"

"I—I was too terrified to move," Desirée answered, still trembling from her fright.

Jason, too, had been terrified when he saw the alligator stalking Desirée. To him, it has seemed an eternity before he had reached her. Slipping his knife into the scabbard at his waist, he sank to the ground beside her, his weakness partly in relief that she was safe and partly in weariness from fighting the huge creature.

He jerked off one boot, then the other, pouring the water from them. As he sat them aside, his eyes fell on the knot in the rope. He knew it had been disturbed, and he knew who had tampered with it.

Desirée saw Jason eyeing the knot, and as he turned his head to face her, a guilty flush rose on her face.

Jason slammed to his feet, his eyes flashing angrily. "So, you're still bent on escape? Still trying to get back to New Orleans and spread the alarm. You crazy little fool! You wouldn't have gotten a mile before you would have been hopelessly lost. And then you would have slowly starved to death—if an alligator or some wild animal didn't get you first!'"

Desirée knew everything he was saying was true. Escape would have been foolish. She'd never be able to survive in this swamp without him. But she had been so desperate to get away from him that she hadn't even stopped to think. Well, she wouldn't tell him the real reason she had tried to escape. If he thought it was to warn New Orleans, then let him. She'd never let him know how much she feared his power over her. She stared at him mutely.

"I gave you credit for having better sense than to try something as foolish as that, Desirée, but I won't make the same mistake twice. I'm warning you for the last time. Don't try to escape again."

Desirée shuddered at the hard look on Jason's face. At that moment, he looked very dangerous.

"Now, come on," Jason said, taking her arm firmly and pulling her to her feet. "Let's get breakfast over so we can be on our way."

Later, Desirée grimaced as Jason wolfed down his eggs, wondering how he could eat after his close brush with death. Her stomach was still tied in knots. Yet, Jason sat there calmly eating, acting as though nothing unusual had even happened, as if wrestling and killing an alligator were an everyday occurence for him. *Mon Dieu*, does he have nerves made of steel?

Jason glanced up and saw Desirée pushing her food absently around her plate. "Why aren't you eating?"

Desirée looked down at the wild duck eggs. They looked like two yellow eyes staring up at her, and their odor, much stronger than chicken eggs, seemed overpowering. A wave of nausea washed over her. Setting her plate aside, she muttered, "I'm not hungry."

"Well, at least try to eat some of your cereal. Without syrup and milk, it might not be very appetizing, but at least it's filling. It will be a long time until lunch."

Desirée didn't think the Cajun cornmeal mush looked any more appealing than the eggs. She took a hesitant bite and forced it down, then set aside the cup.

Jason frowned, wondering if Desirée's lack of appetite stemmed from being upset over what had happened the night before, or the incident that morning. For a moment, he considered asking her outright, then decided against it. If she was regretting their lovemaking the night before, he didn't want to force the issue. Dammit, all he needed was time to win her over, time to convince her they were destined for each other.

That morning, as they poled down the bayou, Desirée was oblivious to the ducks and long-necked anhingas—called water turkeys—that floated on the water. She didn't notice the otters that cavorted on the bank, the squirrels scampering from tree to tree, or the swamp deer, with its unusually large hooves, bounding through the brush. Nor was she aware of the mocking birds and wrens singing their hearts out, and the blue jays scolding in return. Her thoughts were occupied with her problem, and that problem was Jason.

Escape was out of the question. She'd never find her way out of this land that was part swamp and part bayou, nor could she survive in this strange liquid land. Its beauty and peacefulness were deceptive. Danger lurked everywhere. Yet, she couldn't let herself fall under that strange spell Jason cast over her every time he touched her. Not again. *Non*, there would be no repetitions of what had happened last night. By making no romantic overtures since her capture, Jason had lured her into a false sense of security, and then, when her defenses were down, he had taken quick advantage, his sensual assault quickly reducing her to a mindless, spineless creature. Well, it wouldn't happen again! He had disgraced her once, but never again. She'd watch him like a hawk, never lower her defenses. And if he tried to touch her again, she'd scratch his eyes out!

Feeling reassured by her vow, she shot Jason a defiant look. It was a wasted effort. Jason, standing at the end of the pirogue and facing her, hadn't even noticed the look. His full attention was on the bayou before them.

Desirée glanced around her, wondering where they were. Somewhere between the Mississippi River and Bayou Lafourche, she thought. Probably in that area known as Barataria. Less than a century ago, the pirate, Jean Lafette, had smuggled his goods from Grand Terre to New Orleans through this area, using these same bayous and aided by Cajuns.

The thought of Cajuns brought her attention back to Jason. She watched as he lowered the pole in the water and pushed against the muddy bottom, the powerful muscles in his shoulders and arms bunching. Then he straightened to his full, imposing height. Desirée's breath caught. At that moment, he looked like a pirate captain standing on his quarter deck, a commanding figure, tall and sinewy, darkly handsome and bronzed. All except his eyes. Desirée had always pictured a pirate as having dark, flashing eyes, but Jason's were such a beautiful green, more mysterious than dangerous looking. Except when he was angry. Then Jason appeared very dangerous. No, his eyes didn't look at all like a pirate's eyes, nor did they resemble any Cajun's she'd ever seen.

The longer Desirée looked at Jason's eyes, the more curious she became. Finally, her curiosity got the better of her, and she said, "You told me you were half French. I assume that must be your mother's side, since Steele isn't a French name."

Jason was pleased when Desirée broke the silence between them. She had been quiet and unusually withdrawn all morning. "Yes, my mother was a Cajun, and my father was an American."

So, Desirée thought, Jason's mother had defied convention to marry an American just like her mother, for she knew that the Cajuns were as close knit as the Creoles, rarely marrying outsiders. But how had she met an American way out here in this remote area? Most of the Americans who came to Louisiana stayed close to the cities. They didn't usually wander out into the swamps.

"How did your mother meet your father?"

Jason looked thoughtful for a minute, then said, "I guess that story is best told from my Cajun uncles' viewpoint. One night, they were returning home after taking a load of furs to New Orleans, when they saw two steamboats racing down the Mississippi toward them. They had just pulled their pirogue over to the side to get out of the way, when one of the steamboats exploded, and bodies and pieces of wood and debris flew everywhere. One of the bodies landed in the river near them, and they fished the man out. He wasn't burnt all that bad, but he was unconscious.

"The other steamboat came back for survivors. When my uncles went to transfer the man to the steamboat, the captain told them he didn't have any more room for them to take the man to New Orleans themselves."

"And did they?" Desirée asked.

"No, they decided to take him home with them, since he didn't look that badly injured. It was a week before he regained his memory, and when he did, he had total amnesia. He had no idea who he was or where he had come from. So he just stayed on, thinking it would come back to him. The man was my father. By the time he regained his memory, six months later, he had fallen in love with my mother and they married."

"So he just stayed permanently?"

"Yes. He wanted to go back north to his family in Boston, but my mother didn't want to leave her people. So he stayed, and my uncles taught him everything they knew about fishing and trapping."

"But you did move north eventually," Desirée pointed out. "Did your mother change her mind?"

"No, she never changed her mind about not wanting to leave Louisiana. She died when I was thirteen, and my father and I moved to New Orleans. We lived there a year before going north."

"So that's where you learned to speak English without a Cajun accent. Your father taught you your English."

Jason laughed, saying, "No, actually it was my grandparents who smoothed out my rough edges. They were a genteel people, appalled by my Cajun accent and lack of social graces. They taught me how to behave as a gentleman and saw that my education was brought up to standard."

"Your grandparents?" Desirée asked in surprise.

"Yes, my father died shortly after we moved back north, and my grandparents finished raising me. It wasn't an easy chore for them. I was fourteen at the time. After spending all of my life in these wilds and a year in the Irish Channel in New Orleans, I was half wild and tough as nails."

"I'm surprised they succeeded."

Jason's eyes warmed with remembrance. "They were remarkable people. They had their own brand of toughness. But I don't think they would have succeeded if I hadn't cooperated with them." Jason hesitated, his eyes drifting over Desirée's face, then said, "You see, I had a dream, and I knew I'd never succeed in making it come true without their help."

Desirée was on the verge of asking Jason about his dream, when Jason tensed, saying in an urgent voice, "Desirée, get your hand out of the water."

Desirée jerked her hand from the water, where she had absently been letting it trail, and looked down at the bayou, but all she could see was a frog sitting on a lily pad. And then the water rippled slightly, and the frog took a flying leap. Desirée saw the long shadow in the murky water, a shadow that slowly rose until two beady eyes were staring at her.

She stared down at the long, ugly snout of the alligator and shivered, remembering her close brush with death that morning. She glanced about her nervously, wondering if there were others about, and caught her breath. The whole bank of the bayou was lined with alligators, some as long as sixteen feet. Seeing Jason and Desirée, several of them scampered from the muddy bank and slid into the water to investigate, swimming toward them. Desirée's heart raced in fear.

"There's nothing to be afraid of," Jason said, seeing her pale, frightened face. "They won't bother us here in the pirogue. Just keep your hands in."

Desirée nodded, holding her breath as the alligators circled them. Only when they finally got bored and swam away did she relax, but not for long. Seeing a large log floating in the water in front of them, she tensed, thinking that it was yet another alligator. As they passed and Desirée realized it *was* a log, her fright and revulsion only increased, for lying on it was something just as deadly: a huge cottonmouth sunning itself.

That afternoon was just a long, lazy ride down the winding, sleepy bayou. With the sun warming her, and the soothing, gliding motion of the pirogue, a lassitude crept over Desirée, and despite her worries of how she was going to keep from succumbing to Jason's magnetic male appeal, she lay back, allowing her overtaxed mind to drift aimlessly.

"I wonder where the word bayou came from?" she asked. "It's not a French word."

"No, it isn't," Jason said. "Bayou is derived from *bayuk*, a Choctaw word for creek, which was passed on to the French."

"Indian?" Desirée asked in surprise.

"Yes. Many of the words used here in Louisiana have Indian origins. For example, I'm sure you've heard of the Bayou Teche. It was taken from the Indian word, *tenche*, meaning snake."

Desirée had heard of Bayou Teche. An ancient path of the Mississippi, it was considered the most beautiful bayou in Louisiana, its banks lined with magnificent plantation homes and huge oak trees, some with trunks that were twenty feet in girth. "But why did the Indians name it *tenche*? Because it was so infested with snakes?"

"No, the name came from an Indian legend concerning the bayou. They claim a huge silver snake was terrorizing the area. The Indians killed it with their clubs and arrows, and as it lay dying in agony, its twisting body cut grooves into the earth which later filled with water and became the bayou."

That evening, they again made their camp beside the bayou. All during their meal, Desirée was tense, dreading the night and wondering if she had the inner strength to repel Jason's advances. She sat stiffly, emotionally preparing herself for battle and avoided looking Jason in the eye.

When she saw him preparing their pallet for the night, she jumped to her feet and said in a determined voice, "I'll sleep on the other side of the fire tonight. Alone!"

All day, Jason had been anticipating the night and making love to Desirée. Her words came as a big disappointment to him. So, she *is* regretting, he thought. He fought back the urge to take her in his arms, kiss her until she was breathless, crush her resistance. No, he told himself firmly. Don't push her. She needs time.

"If you like," Jason replied, his facial expression showing none of the disappointment he felt.

As Jason prepared a second pallet on the opposite side of the fire, Desirée watched him warily, hardly believing he would bow to her demand without an argument. Was he trying to trick her, she wondered, as she walked to her pallet, suspiciously watching Jason as he lay down. Well, if he thought he was going to sneak up on her later, he was going to be in for a big surprise, she vowed.

Desirée sat on her pallet and removed her boots. Jason pulled up his blanket and rolled to his side with his back to her. Desirée stared at his broad back through the dancing flames of the fire, every muscle in her body tense.

Minutes passed, the only sound the popping and crackling of the fire. When Desirée realized that

Jason wasn't going to make any move toward her, she felt strangely let down. The unexpected emotion surprised her and filled her with self-disgust. What's wrong with you? He left you alone. He made no advances. Isn't that what you wanted? Well, isn't it?

But Desirée's body knew better. Now that it had experienced Jason's sensuous lovemaking and her passion had been fully awakened, it was making demands of its own. She ached for his touch, his kiss. It was a long, miserable night for Desirée.

Chapter 7

The next morning, they entered another deep cypress swamp. The hair on the nape of Desirée's neck rose as she looked about her nervously, for the fog-shrouded swamp looked eerie with the Spanish moss swaying ghostlike in the gentle breeze. There was a total silence and stillness here. The only hint that anything lived in this swamp was the faint rustle of a fern, a ripple in the water, the quiver of a leaf. And not knowing what had caused that rustle, that ripple, that quiver, only increased Desirée's apprehension.

And then a bloodcurdling scream rent the air, and Desirée almost jumped from the pirogue in fear.

"There's nothing to be afraid of, Desirée," Jason said in a calm voice. "It's only a mink."

"A mink?" Desirée asked in total disbelief. "A mink makes that noise? It sounded human."

"Yes, it does," Jason said. "A lot of the noises they make sound almost human. But they're vicious, bloodthirsty little animals, often killing animals much larger than themselves and eating them, particularly muskrats."

Jason's words, "vicious" and "bloodthirsty," did

nothing to allay the tension Desirée felt. Her nerves were already stretched taut from her long night of twisting and turning, followed by the uncomfortable silence between her and Jason that morning. She knew she had done the right thing by insisting upon sleeping alone. Then why did she feel so miserable?

As they poled out of the eerie swamp and into another bayou, Desirée looked about her in awe. The Spanish moss was so thick on the trees that hardly a speck of green could be seen. Rather than looking eerie, as the swamp had, the bayou had a dismal look about it. It seemed as if the whole world had turned grey, even the water taking on that color as it reflected the moss.

"I've never seen so much *molesse*," Desirée mumbled to herself using the Creole word for the moss.

"You mean *barbe espagnol*?" Jason asked.

"Spanish beard?" Desirée asked in surprise. "Is that what you Cajuns call the moss?"

"Yes. And the Spaniards call it Frenchman's wig and the Indians call it maiden's hair. I guess everyone had their own name for the moss."

Desirée had heard the Spaniard's name for the moss but never the Indian's. "Maiden's hair? Is that what the Indian's call it?"

"Actually I'm not sure what they call it. I was referring to their legend that explains the Spanish moss. They tell of a young maiden who was killed by an enemy tribe during her wedding ceremony. Her mourning family cut off her long black hair and draped it over the limbs of the oak tree she was buried under. The hair flew from tree to tree, and as time passed, turned grey, just as it would have if she'd grown to be an old woman. The legend is supposed to be a tribute to those doomed not to live out their love."

Desirée was touched by the sad tale and decided

136

that of all the things the moss had been likened to, she preferred the Indian's. She knew from then on she would always think of the moss as maiden's hair.

Then her eyes widened in surprise as she saw the first human being she'd seen since the patrol boat had steamed by them two days before. The "moss gatherer" stood in his pirogue and hooked the grey festoons with his long pole, heaping them into the bottom of his canoe. The moss would be used to stuff mattresses, furniture, and horse collars. Braided, it would become bridles; spun into a ropelike material, called tarabi, it would become horse blankets, and mixed with mud, it would be used to make bricks and reinforce chimneys. Some people even used the moss for medicinal purposes, placing it over open wounds.

Desirée stared at the moss gatherer, knowing that he could lead her out of the swamps. Would he help her if she called to him? Surely, he would if she told him Jason was a Yankee spy who had abducted her.

"Don't try it, Desirée," Jason said in a low, warning voice. "He won't believe you."

Desirée realized that Jason had read her thoughts. Her head snapped around to face him; her black eyes blazed. "And why not?"

"Because I'll tell him in Cajun French that I rescued you after you got lost in the swamps, that you haven't been right in the head ever since your harrowing experience, that you're subject to delusions and hysterics. Besides, he'd never believe a Cajun would join the Yankees and spy for them."

Desirée was angry and frustrated at being thwarted. "Don't be too sure of yourself!" she snapped. "He might believe *me*."

Jason shrugged, saying, "That would be a shame if he did. Then I'd have to kill him."

"You'd kill him?" Desirée asked in a shocked

voice.

"If need be, yes. Can you stand that on your conscience, Desirée? Knowing an innocent man died because he tried to help you?"

Desirée couldn't, making her even angrier. "You're nothing but a cold-blooded, murdering Yankee!"

Desirée's words cut Jason to the quick. The way she had said Yankee had made him feel as if he were the scum of the earth. Tight lipped, he looked away, once again concentrating on the bayou.

Other signs of civilization began to appear. they passed several Cajun ribbon farms, narrow strips of land that fronted the bayou. The small, "shotgun" farmhouses were sided with weather-beaten cypress cladding. Most of the houses had small galleries supported with heavy but unadorned cypress columns and had exterior staircases leading to the upper story. But all of the farms had one thing in common: the inevitable cypress piers jutting into the bayou's sluggish waters.

That afternoon, when they approached a small Cajun town, Jason poled the pirogue over to the pier. Tying the canoe to the pier, Jason vaulted to it and then turned to Desirée, saying, "The same holds here as it did for the moss gatherer, Desirée. If you try to get someone to help you, an innocent person will die. And don't try to sneak off and hide, either. I'll be watching you from the window."

Jason turned and walked down the pier. Desirée glared at his back, mute with anger. When he disappeared into a small store at the end of the pier, she turned her attention to the town.

Several Cajuns wandered from store to store. She noticed that they all wore brown clothing. Even the children, playing tag in the nearby woods, wore clothes of the same brown material. She frowned in

138

puzzlement.

Jason returned, carrying a gunnysack and several brown dresses flung over one arm. He tossed the dresses down to Desirée before he jumped into the pirogue.

"What's this?" Desirée snapped.

"I thought you could use a change of clothes," Jason answered, placing the gunnysack at his end of the pirogue.

"I won't wear them!" Desirée spat, tossing the dresses to the bottom of the canoe. "I won't take anything from a Yankee."

Jason jerked the rope holding the canoe to the pier and turned. "Stop being childish, Desirée. Your clothes are torn and, after three days, none too clean."

"I don't care! I won't wear them."

"You'll wear them—if I have to strip you and put them on you myself!"

One look at the determined look on Jason's face and Desirée didn't for one minute doubt his threat. She decided to take a different approach. "I don't like brown."

"I'm sorry about that, but I didn't have a choice of color."

"Why is all of your clothing brown? Do you Cajuns have an aversion to color, or are you like the Puritans, who only wear dark, drab colors?"

"That material is made from the brown cotton we grow. It can be dyed with indigo to make it blue, or ragweed to make it yellowish green, or darkened with onionskins. But it's simpler for everyday clothes just to wear it as it is. And, no, we aren't like the Puritans. If you've ever heard any of our lusty Cajun music, you'd know that."

Desirée glanced down at the dresses lying in a heap at the bottom of the pirogue. She noticed that the material wasn't a dull, flat brown, as she had thought, but had uneven, soft shades of brown mixed in it, giving it an almost iridescent appearance. She finally decided that the unusual color was rather pretty, but she'd be damned if she'd admit it to Jason.

As they floated down the bayou, Desirée kept sneaking glances at the gunnysack, curious to know what it held. And then, as a faint, familiar odor drifted back to her, she frowned. Fish? But why would Jason buy fish, when he could catch them himself?

Desirée didn't get the answer to her question until they had made camp that afternoon. After Jason had started a fire and was still kneeling on the ground, he pulled the gunnysack to him. Desirée, unable to contain her curiosity any longer, craned her neck to look over his shoulder. He pulled out a long loaf of French bread and a package of rice and set them aside. Then he rose and dumped the rest of the sack's contents out onto the grass.

Desirée looked down and, seeing the ingredients of her favorite dish, cried, "Gumbo? We're having gumbo tonight?"

"Yes," Jason answered. "Do you like it?"

"It's all right," Desirée answered with a casual shrug of her shoulders, trying very hard to hide her delight. Already, her mouth was watering at the thought of the spicy dish.

She glanced down at the ingredients lying on the grass and then looked around her, saying, "But—"

"But what?"

"Where are the tomatoes?"

"Tomatoes?" Jason asked in a horrified voice. Then he shook his head, saying sternly, "No, Desirée, the holy trinity of Cajun cooking is onions, celery, and bell peppers. We might add some garlic every now and then, but *never* tomatoes."

"But you can't make gumbo without tomatoes," Desirée objected.

Jason was getting a little irritated. *No one* told a Cajun how to make gumbo. "Desirée, I've been cooking gumbo since I was six years old and went on my first trapping foray with my uncles. Why, I bet you've never cooked a thing in your life. How would you know what goes into gumbo?"

Desirée's dark eyes flashed. "It's true I've never cooked, but I could if I had to. I spent enough time in the kitchens watching, particularly if they were cooking gumbo. And I say you can't cook a decent gumbo without tomatoes!"

"You're wrong," Jason retorted. "You don't use tomatoes in gumbo, not if you're going to prepare it correctly. We Cajuns cook pure French. We haven't adulterated our cooking like you Creoles have."

Desirée was furious. Like Jason, she was proud of her French heritage. She raised her aristocratic nose and said in a haughty voice, "Are you suggesting that you're a purer French than me?"

Jason chuckled to himself. To him, she looked absolutely delightful with her little nose stuck up in the air and her dark eyes flashing. "No, I'm not suggesting any such thing. What I'm saying is Cajun food is very old French cooking. My Arcadian ancestors brought it with them when they left southern France and moved to Nova Scotia in the early sixteen hundreds, and then, after *Le Grand Derangement*, to this country. Since we've always lived in rather isolated communities, our cooking hasn't been influenced by other ethnic groups like you Creoles' cooking has, particularly your black cooks."

"*Eh bien!* I don't care how old your cooking is. I still say gumbo isn't gumbo without tomatoes!"

141

Jason was at the end of his patience. "Well, tonight you're going to eat gumbo without tomatoes whether you like it or not. Besides, I don't see what good we're doing arguing about it, since I don't have any of the damned things!"

Jason turned and placed the pot of water over the fire, then sat down and started peeling the shrimp, ignoring Desirée. For a few minutes, Desirée glared at him and then sank to the grass. As she watched him at his work, she felt useless and bored to tears. She was used to an active life, not sitting around in a canoe and drifting down a bayou all day. Finally, she reached for a knife and started chopping the vegetables. Jason looked at her in surprise.

"What's the matter?" Desirée snapped. "Aren't the pieces small enough to suit you?"

Jason looked down at the small pieces of onion, celery, and bell pepper, then grinned, saying, "No, they look fine to me."

There was something about that engaging grin that disarmed Desirée. From then on they worked in silence, until Jason started browning the flour in oil that made the roux. Jason preferred a lighter roux, Desirée a darker one. They finally compromised.

Soon the spicy gumbo was simmering over the fire and filling the air with its aroma. When Jason prepared the rice that accompanied the dish, he watched Desirée warily from the corner of his eye, expecting another disagreement. When she nodded with approval, he almost sighed in relief. And then he shook his head in self-disgust, wondering what was wrong with him. Why should he care if she approves or not? It's his gumbo. And no one can cook gumbo as well as a Cajun!

Finally they sat down to eat. Jason glanced at Desirée warily as she dug into the gumbo. Her offer to help with the meal had surprised him. Was she calling a truce between them? He had heard of instances in this war between the two sections of the country, where the soldiers fire at one another all day with deadly intent and, then at night, socialized with their enemy, even exchanging coffee and tobacco, only to be back at the grim business of war with the light of day. Those men had declared an unspoken truce from dusk to daylight. But if Desirée was declaring a truce, Jason wasn't sure what the rules were. With her, the bullets might start flying at any moment.

When Desirée had finished eating, she sat her dish aside, just a little shocked at how much she had eaten. As much as she loved gumbo, she had never eaten three helpings of it. She looked up to see Jason watching her. Without even thinking, she said, "That was delicious." Then, seeing the smug look on his face, she added, "But it would have been much better with tomatoes."

Jason fought down a sigh of exasperation. Picking up their dirty dishes, he headed for the bayou to wash them. Stubborn little mule, he thought as he walked. She'd die before she admitted she was wrong about anything. Yes, with her, he certainly had his work cut out for him.

That night, as Jason started preparing their separate pallets, Desirée felt that same feeling of disappointment creeping over her. She felt so torn, a part of her desperately wanting Jason to make love to her, another part fighting for reason. She felt as if a battle had taken place in her, her emotions tangled in one big lump in the center of her chest.

She rose and wandered down to the bayou, weaving her way through the willow trees. When she reached the stream, a full moon was just rising, bathing everything in a soft white light and making the bayou look like a glittering silver ribbon as the water reflected the moonlight. The long willow branches around her waved gently in the whisper-soft breeze, the air heavy with the smell of honeysuckle. A hushed silence lay over the bayou, and Desirée stood, taking in the breathtaking sight and letting the beauty soothe her tangled emotions, emotions that had taken a battering ever since she had met Jason.

Desirée heard Jason's soft footsteps behind her. She closed her eyes, seeing him in her mind as he walked up to her with his graceful, catlike stride and the breeze ruffling his dark hair. A warm feeling curled deep inside her.

Jason stood behind her and gazed at the bayou, saying in a soft voice, "It's beautiful, isn't it?"

His deep voice was a sensual caress to Desirée's ears. She could feel his heat surrounding her like a warm cocoon, then smelled his scent, a scent that sent her senses reeling. She clenched her fists, fighting the heady feeling that was invading her.

Then, when Jason made no move toward her, her nerves began to crawl. Breathlessly, she waited, a strange tension filling her, feeling as if she would explode if he didn't take her in his arms and kiss her. Unaware of her movement, she leaned back, the act a silent plea that came from her subconscious mind.

Jason's warm hand brushed her throat as he lifted her hair and softly kissed the nape of her neck. Desirée trembled with need, her hand clutching his arm as he slid it around her waist and drew her back to him. Meeting no resistance, Jason's lips slipped to her throat, and Desirée arched her neck to him, hungry for the feel of his mouth there. When he slipped his other arm around her, his hand cupping, then stroking one breast, her bones melted.

Totally forgetting her vow to never let him touch her

again, Desirée turned in the circle of his arms and looked up to see his eyes were smoldering, a look that made her heart race even faster. Sliding her hands over his broad shoulders, she lifted her head, her lips aching for the feel of his. Jason's warm mouth covered hers, his tongue playing teasingly at the corners before it slipped inside to gently ravish the heady sweetness there. Sensation erupted in Desirée. A moan of desire rose from deep inside her as she pressed her body even closer to that flame which threatened to consume her, wanting this kiss to last forever.

With soft exploring kisses and tantalizing caresses, Jason undressed her, stopping to dally at her breasts, his tongue laving, his lips nibbling, and then lingering again at her navel. By the time the last garment dropped to the ground, Desirée was a quivering mass of jelly.

Jason stepped back, his eyes hungrily sweeping over her rosy, naked flesh. God, she's beautiful, he thought. Every curve and hollow a perfection, a virtual goddess of desire.

Desirée flushed under that warm ardent gaze. And then suddenly, she wanted to see him: all of him. She stepped up to him, blushing at her own audacity, and with trembling fingers unbuttoned his shirt, pushing it back off his shoulders and down his arms, thrilling to the feel of those powerful muscles under her fingertips. As she reached for his belt, Jason stood perfectly still, excited by her surprisingly bold action, yet hesitant to move for fear she would turn shy on him.

Desirée struggled with the awkward belt buckle, acutely aware of the huge bulge straining at Jason's pants just below her fingers. Finally slipping the belt loose, she unbuttoned one button, then another, and another, her heart racing at the feel of his throbbing

145

heat as her fingers brushed against his skin.

At the feel of Desirée's fingers brushing his aroused sex, Jason's mouth turned dry. And then, feeling her fingers sliding down his thighs as she pushed the pants down, he sucked in his breath. As if in a daze, he lifted one foot, then the other as Desirée slipped the pants off and tossed them to the side.

Desirée sat back on her heels and looked up. Her breath caught at the impact of seeing Jason totally naked. With his powerful, muscle-ridged body bathed in moonlight, he looked like a magnificent silver god, tall and proud and fierce.

"You're beautiful," Desirée whispered in awe.

A brief flicker of amusement passed over Jason's lip at Desirée's compliment, but still he stood perfectly motionless, actutely aware of his state of arousal and afraid Desirée would be frightened or repulsed by his blatant maleness.

But Desirée wasn't in the least frightened or repulsed. If anything, she was fascinated with his male beauty. Her eyes drifted over his broad shoulders, then down the wide expanse of his chest and taut abdomen to lock on the proof of his masculinity, his manhood jutting from the dark curls that surrounded it, standing long and full and proud before her eyes. Her mouth turned dry.

Jason stroked her shoulders and arm, saying in a ragged voice, "You're so beautiful, Desirée. So incredibly beautiful."

Jason was a dark silhouette against the full moon as he drew her down on the soft moss on the bayou's bank and embraced her. Desirée gasped as his heated skin touched hers, acutely conscious of the dark hairs on his chest rubbing against her aching nipples, his hair-roughened thigh between her soft ones, and his manhood, rigid and throbbing, pressing against her

146

loins. Her heart quickened, every nerve tingling as her skin hungrily absorbed the feeling of his.

She trailed her fingertips down the crisp hairs on his chest, marveling at the powerful muscles quivering in response to her touch. Continuing her exploration, she traced his ribs, one by one, then the taut muscles on his abdomen, lower and lower. Then, realizing the direction her hands were taking her, she hesitated.

Jason's heart was racing madly as Desirée explored him, each touch leaving a burning flame on his skin. When she hesitated, he took her hand and guided it to him, whispering, "Touch me, Desirée. Hold me."

Desirée's breath caught at the feel of Jason's hot flesh in her hand. It feels like velvet over steel, she thought. *Mon Dieu*, no wonder she had felt as if he was ripping her apart the other night. A quiver of fear ran through her. Then, as she felt him growing even larger and harder, her eyes widened. Instinctively, she moved her hands, and Jason groaned in pleasure. Encouraged by his response, she stroked him sensuously, feeling an incredible excitement filling her, her pleasure almost matching his.

Jason clenched his teeth and hands as Desirée explored and fondled him, feeling as if he would explode at any minute. A fine sheen of perspiration broke out on his forehead. And then, as Desirée's hands slipped lower, cupping the twin sacs heavy with need, he groaned and reached for her hands, stilling them and whispering hoarsely, "No more, or it will all be over."

Desirée was lost in sheer sensation as Jason's mouth lowered on hers in a deep, fierce kiss that robbed Desirée of her breath and all reason as his hands caressed and stroked, teased and tantalized. When Jason's warm hand slid between her thighs, she opened her legs willingly, her body arching to gain

147

release from the throbbing there. As Jason's slender fingers stroked and tantalized, her blood coursed hotly through her veins, her senses whirling. And then, as those rapturous waves of delight began, she moaned, every muscle in her body quivering.

Jason entered her while those spasms of delight were still rocking her body. His breath caught at the feel of her muscles clutching him greedily, her warmth surrounding him. For a minute he tensed, trembling as he struggled for control, then slid deeper. He lay, just savoring the feel of his rigid length being inside her tight, silken sheath, feeling a wonderful contentment stealing over him, as if he had come home.

"See how perfectly we fit together," he whispered, nuzzling Desirée's ear. "Like two halves of a coin, we're not whole unless we're together. Don't you see? We were meant for each other."

But Desirée was lost in pure tactile sensation. She didn't even hear his words. The feel of him deep inside her, filling her completely, his throbbing flesh pressed against hers and lighting fires in nerve endings she had never dreamed existed, occupied all of her awareness. And then, as he started his slow, sensual movements, his mouth capturing hers in a searing, searching kiss, she felt as if electric shock waves were traveling up her spine.

With bold, masterful, exquisitely sensuous strokes, Jason swept her up that lofty, spiraling path and Desirée clung to him, straining once again, driven by an urgency she didn't understand. Higher and higher she went, her senses expanding. And then the world seemed to turn on its axis. Time stood still for a long minute as she hovered on that apex, and then she hurtled over in a soul-shattering explosion, spinning through space in a bursting firestorm.

As Desirée drifted back down, her body still trembling, she opened her eyes and saw Jason gazing down at her and smiling. *"Mon Dieu!"* she muttered weakly in an awed voice. "I—I never knew. I never knew it was so—so—"

Jason's smile widened, a smile that played havoc on Desirée's already shaken emotions. "So beautiful?" he whispered.

"Oui." And then suddenly Desirée began to cry from the wonder of it, from the beauty of it, from sheer reaction to the shattering experience. Jason held her in his arms, tenderly brushing the tears away, caressing her with gentle, soothing hands, feeling the sting of tears in his own eyes.

And when her tears were spent, he scooped her up in his powerful arms and carried her back to his pallet by the fire, the moon dappling their naked bodies with soft light as he walked beneath the willow trees, the branches whispering softly in the breeze.

Placing her gently on the pallet, Jason lay down beside her, pulling the blanket up over them. But before he could take her in his arms, Desirée snuggled up to him, subconsciously knowing that's where she belonged. She lay her head on his shoulder, nuzzling his warm neck, her fingers tangled in the damp curls on his chest, her thigh nuzzled between his hair-roughened ones. And then in exhaustion and utter contentment, her eyelids fluttered down.

Jason held her as she slept, staring up at the full moon and once again thinking. He had known sharing ecstasy with Desirée would be wonderful, but he had never dreamed just how beautiful it could be. Now, he knew the difference between making love and loving someone with your body. There was no comparison. Making love lacked heart and soul.

And Desirée? Had the love she made just been a physical expression or had she given him a part of her

149

heart and soul? Jason couldn't be sure which was the case, but he did know he was closer to making her truly his than he had been before.

Satisfied that he was at least making headway in his quest to fulfill his dream and their destiny, he closed his eyes and slept.

The next day all traces of civilization disappeared as Jason took them deeper and deeper into the swamps. Desirée looked around at the forbidding landscape, then at the huge, darkly brooding cypresses. A strange apprehension filled her.

"Where are we going?" she asked. "To your Cajun relatives?"

"No, I'm afraid not, Desirée," Jason answered. "In the first place, I haven't seen them for fourteen years. They may have moved, for all I know. Besides, they're probably just as fiercely loyal to the southern cause as you. When they've found out what I am, what I've done, they'd be torn between their loyalties to family and the South, having to choose between helping me or turning me in. I won't put them in that position. No, I'm taking you to some friends of mine. You'll be safe with them while I'm gone."

"Gone?" Desirée asked in a shocked voice. "Where are you going?"

"Back to New Orleans."

"But I thought you said you were going to lay low until after the battle."

"No, I said for awhile, until Farragut had time to make his move. How am I going to know way out here in these swamps what's going on in New Orleans? It takes months for any news to reach this isolated back country. No, the only way I'll know what is going on is to go back to the city and see for myself."

"You're going to leave me out here with total strangers?" Desirée asked in an apprehensive voice.

"You'll be safe with my friends," Jason assured her. "I wouldn't leave you with them if I wasn't sure of that."

"Who are these people, these friends?"

"Some slaves I helped escape many years ago. I found them in the swamps, frantically trying to get away from the bounty hunters who were pursuing them."

"You helped runaway slaves?" Desirée asked in a half-shocked, half-angry voice.

"Yes, I did," Jason replied calmly. "The girl was exhausted and terrified, not so much of the hounds and men who were chasing them, but of going back, of the punishment that might be awaiting them. The young man was trying to help her through the swamps, half dragging and half carrying her, determined not to leave her behind, although she was slowing him down. And then, when they saw me they froze. I guess they expected me to call to the bounty hunters and give away their position. Even though I was only eleven at the time, I knew that I should do just that; that aiding runaway slaves was against the law. But I couldn't do it. There was a cornered-animal look in their eyes that touched something deep in me. Compassion, I guess. Instead, I helped them into my pirogue and took them deep into the swamps, so deep that even those vicious hounds couldn't follow, someplace where they'd never been found. And I've never regretted it. That's why I know they'll help me, that they won't turn me in. Unlike my Cajun relatives, they have no loyalty to the South. No, the only thing they feel honor-bound to is the debt they feel they owe me."

Desirée knew that there were escaped slaves hiding

out in these swamps. It was even rumored that there were whole communities of them in places. Ordinarily, Desirée wasn't afraid of blacks. She had grown up among them, had an almost family fondness for those house slaves. And Mammy Lou was like a mother to her. She never had been afraid of her father's field slaves, for although she had hardly known them, she had known they were no threat to her. But runaway slaves were different. Desirée had heard that they were dangerous, some of them having even murdered before they ran.

"How do you know they won't hurt me?" she asked in a fearful voice. "They're runaways. They probably hate all whites."

"No, Desirée. Not all whites. As I said, these people are my friends. I helped them build their home and got to know them. I even visited with them several times after that. They won't hurt you."

But Desirée didn't feel at all reassured by Jason's words. And when they floated up to a small pier jutting out into the murky water late that afternoon and she looked at the small cabin sitting in the thick copse of cypress trees at the other end of it, her apprehension only grew.

Jason helped Desirée out of the pirogue, and they walked up the pier, Desirée's legs trembling badly. They stopped before the cabin, and Jason scanned the area, saying, "I guess they didn't recognize me when they saw us coming. They're probably out in the swamp hiding. Wait here while I find them."

To Desirée, it seemed an eternity before Jason returned. And then she saw him walking back through the clearing from the swamps. Her eyes darted to the black couple walking beside him. The man was huge, dwarfing the woman beside him. But it wasn't the man's size that made Desirée's eyes

152

widen. It was the sight of the horrible scars that crisscrossed his broad chest and back, scars that seemed to leap out at her before he bent down and picked up his shirt lying on a nearby woodpile.

Mon Dieu! Desirée thought, sickened by what she'd seen. That man had been whipped horribly, cruelly, and undoubtedly the one who had done it had been white. He had to hate whites, Desirée thought, her fear rising. After suffering through that agony, how could he not? Her heart raced with terror; her legs turned weak beneath her.

When Jason stepped up to her, he said, "Desirée, these are my friends, Raul and Benitta. They've agreed to your staying with them until I can return for you."

Desirée smiled weakly at the two blacks. The only acknowledgement of the introduction was a nod from the woman and a deep grunt from the huge man.

Desirée stepped closer to Jason, seeking the protection of his big body. She ignored the woman and looked up, way up, into the black man's eyes, expecting to see hatred glittering there. Instead, his eyes were totally devoid of any emotion. She felt even more terrified.

Without a word, the man and woman turned and walked into the small cabin behind them. Desirée whirled and faced Jason, saying in a frantic voice, "Don't leave me here, Jason. They're dangerous, particularly the man. He's been whipped, Jason. He has to hate whites. He'll kill me once you're gone."

"Desirée, they won't hurt you," Jason said in a firm voice. "Yes, Raul has been whipped horribly. That's why he ran. But he doesn't blame all whites. He knows that we're all not cruel, like his former master was."

"No! Please don't leave me here with them,"

Desirée pleaded. "Take me to New Orleans with you. You can lock me up, tie me, gag me, anything! Only don't leave me here with them."

Jason knew Desirée was truly frightened of his friends. But he also knew they wouldn't harm a hair on her head, and not just because they felt they owed him a debt but because they were both good, gentle people. But he knew he was never going to convince Desirée of that. For a minute, he considered taking her back with him, but then he remembered that New Orleans was about to be attacked. He had no idea how fierce the fighting might be. Desirée might be in far more danger there than she would ever be here. No, he decided, she would be safer here in the swamp with his friends, even if she was terrified of them. She'd just have to learn for herself that they weren't dangerous.

"No, Desirée," Jason said in a firm voice. "That's impossible. You'll be safe here with Raul and Benitta. Believe me, they won't harm you, they don't hate you."

"No, Jason. They don't like me, I can tell. They didn't say a word to me."

"It's just their way. They've been out here in the swamp so long by themselves that they don't need words to communicate with each other. They've forgotten how to communicate with others."

Desirée couldn't believe her ears. Jason knew she was terrified. She had begged him to take her with him, and still he had refused. After his fervent love-making, she had thought he cared for her, might even have loved her. But he couldn't leave her like this, not if he cared anything about her.

Blind anger at Jason replaced Desirée's fear. "Then go!" she shrieked. "Go back to New Orleans and see if I care! Go on! Get out of here!"

"Desirée," Jason said in a pleading voice, "listen to me." He reached for her, hoping he could reason with her, explain why he couldn't take her with him.

Desirée backed away from him, her eyes flashing dangerously. "Don't touch me," she hissed. "Go back to New Orleans and leave me alone! Go, damn you!"

Then she whirled and ran from the pier, not stopping until she reached a huge willow across the clearing. There, she stood, panting from her wild run, glaring at him.

Jason felt as if his heart would break, knowing that once again the war and his duty had put a breach between them. He had hoped that after what they had shared the past few days, she would trust him more, would realize he loved her. And now, he would have to start all over. He fought the urge to go to her, take her in his arms, kiss her until she was breathless, tell her of his love. But he knew it wouldn't do any good. He still had to leave her. And she would be just as angry then as she was now.

Sighing in resignation at what he had to do, he turned, walked to the end of the pier, and jumped into the pirogue. He picked up the small bundle of her clothing and placed it on the pier. Then he picked up the pole and pushed off.

Not once did he look back, knowing if he did, he wouldn't be able to leave her behind. And no matter how much he wanted to close that gap between them, how much he wanted her love, he couldn't take the chance of endangering her life.

Desirée watched in disbelief as Jason poled away from her, feeling as if her life were slowly seeping from her body. She still hadn't believed he would truly leave her. That he did it without so much as a backward glance hurt deeply, drowning out even her anger. And then, when he had disappeared from view, she threw herself on the ground and wept long and bitterly.

Through a small window in the cabin, the black couple watched as Desirée cried. Had Desirée seen the look on their faces, she wouldn't have been nearly as frightened, for their dark eyes were filled with compassion.

Chapter 8

Jason paced the small dingy hotel room restlessly, then walked to the window and peered out over the tin-roofed shanties and grog shops to the harbor below him. Still nothing, he thought irritably. Where in the hell was General Butler and his troops?

When he had returned to New Orleans, he had been stunned to learn that nothing had happened yet. Feeling the attack was imminent, he had holed up in this hotel overlooking the harbor, not wanting to take any unnecessary chances of being seen by the Confederate officers he had worked with, officers who might question why he was still in New Orleans, when they thought he had gone back to South Carolina.

And then, as the days had passed and nothing had happened, he had begun to worry. Had the courier been apprehended by the enemy? Was Farragut still waiting for his dispatch?

Then, on Good Friday, April 18, he had been awakened by the sound of excited cries in the streets below him. With their masts disguised with bushes and their hulls covered with reeds and willows, a Union fleet had sneaked up the Mississippi, around the sharp bend at Plaquemine Bend and attacked Fort St. Phillips and Fort Jackson.

With the forts sitting ninety miles below New Orleans, Jason had no way of knowing how the battle was going. Like the people of the city, he had waited anxiously for news. For two days the Union bombardment had continued, and then word had arrived that the Yankees had tried to blow up the chains in the river and had been unsuccessful.

The news had been greeted with cheers from the people of New Orleans. For Jason, it had been a stunning blow. What if the fleet couldn't make it past those chains? Then, Butler would have to march overland, and that might take months. He couldn't leave Desirée out in the swamps for that long. And yet, he didn't dare bring her back to New Orleans, either.

And so he had waited and paced.

And then, on April 24, word had arrived that the Federal gunboats had broken the chains across the river, virtually destroyed the Confederate fleet stationed there, passed the forts with a furious barrage, and were now sailing up the Mississippi to New Orleans. Jason had stood and watched from his hotel window as the city had gone wild, burning anything they thought might be of value to the enemy, setting fire to warehouses, the wharves, and all the ships in the harbor, including their beloved ironclad, the *Mississippi*. When the Union fleet had come into sight the next day, the whole city had been covered with a pall of thick black smoke, the stench of burnt cotton and sugar filling the air, the boats lining the levees still blazing.

When Farragut had sent a detachment of sailors and marines ashore, their faces grim, their bayonets fixed, Jason had left his hotel room and followed them, curious to see if the proud city would surrender without a fight. With the bells of Christ Church ringing in his ears and sounding like a death toll, he had stood at the back of the angry, hissing crowd that had followed the Yankees and watched as the Union naval officer had faced the Creole mayor and demanded the city's surrender. Despite himself, Jason felt a twinge of pride as the fierce, little Frenchman had crossed his arms over his chest and raised his chin, stubbornly refusing. And then, as the Yankees had pulled down the state flag, Jason had felt a twinge of sadness as he had watched the proud pelican flag fluttering down.

The next day, the Stars and Stripes had been pulled down by the angry burghers of New Orleans, and Farragut, furious at their refusal to surrender, had threatened to fire on the city. Jason had held his breath, terrified that the Union naval captain would follow through and destroy the beautiful city he loved as his second home. And then, as the days passed and nothing happened, he sighed in relief and, like the city itself, waited to see what would happen next.

When the people of New Orleans had received word that the forts had surrendered a few days later, the fight had gone out of them. Shocked and dazed, they had watched as the Confederate Army pulled out, taking everything and anything they could with them, railroad cars, river vessels that had not been burnt, horses, wagons, carriages, food supplies, ammunition, medicines. They had even managed to completely dismantle their armaments factory and take it with them.

And so completely abandoned by their army and left totally defenseless, the proud city had surrendered. On April 29, Farragut had sent another detachment of marines into the city, two hundred and fifty strong and accompanied by a howitzer battery. Once again, the Stars and Stripes had been raised, and this time it had not been challenged.

And now, as Jason paced restlessly, he again wondered where General Butler and his army were. The city had surrendered, but it was yet to be occupied by Union forces. And Jason was getting anxious to get back to Desirée, determined he would fill in the breach that had once come between them. How much longer would he have to wait? Days? Weeks?

To hell with Butler! There wasn't going to be any battle, and it was safe to bring Desirée back to the city now. He'd report in after they got back to New Orleans. If the general didn't like it, that was just too bad!

Picking up his saddlebags, he flew from the room, taking the steps two at a time, his heart already racing in anticipation.

Desirée sat at the end of the pier, totally unaware of the beauty around her, lost in deep thought.

Where was he? It had been over two weeks since Jason had left her here. Was the battle in New Orleans still raging? Or had it already been won? And if so, by which side? If the South had won, had Jason completely deserted her? Was he already on his way back north, fleeing for his life? Was she doomed to spend the rest of her life out here in the swamp, believed dead by her family and abandoned by Jason?

On the other hand, maybe the North had won. Then why hadn't he come back for her as he had promised? Desirée could only think of one reason for that: He had been killed in the battle. An empty feeling filled her as fresh tears shimmered in her eyes.

There must be a good reason why he hasn't returned. It hadn't been all that long. But to Desirée it had seemed an eternity. She had cried until there were no more tears left that afternoon after Jason had left. And then, as if in a daze, she had followed Benitta back into the cabin for the evening meal. Then, lying in the little room off the main cabin, she had stared at the door most of the night, trembling with fear, still afraid that the blacks would rush through the door and hack her to death as she slept. When she was awakened the next morning to the sound of the birds singing and the warm April sun coming in the small window, she had been amazed to find herself still alive.

Since then, she had found that she had nothing to fear from Raul and Benitta. They had been kind to her in their own strange way, for although the cold look had left their eyes, they rarely spoke. As Jason had said, they seemed to communicate silently, leaving her feeling left out and even more alone.

The screech of an angry egret tore Desirée from her musing. She looked up at the next in the cypress tree towering over her and saw that, once again, a stray egret had invaded the air territory of the nesting egrets and was being attacked by the male. The fight going on was mostly wing flapping. And then, as the invader flew away, she smiled.

The nesting egrets had helped Desirée pass her time, and she had been amazed at how hard the parent birds had to work to satisfy their chicks' almost insatiable appetites, coming and going all day long, back and forth, their monotonous *cuk-cuk* filling the air as they braked for a landing. Once, one of the parent birds had almost been pushed from the nest by an overzealous chick anxious to get the food from its parent's beak, and Desirée had laughed out loud at the horrified look in the adult's eyes as it had flapped its wings frantically to maintain its balance.

Seeing that the egrets were settling down for a brief

161

rest, Desirée looked back down at the murky waters before her. Then her eyes widened. Even from this distance, she recognized that tall, bronzed figure slowly poling his way toward her. Jason! He was back!

Her heart raced with joy, and Desirée told herself she wasn't happy to see him, that she was just glad to be getting out of here. She watched anxiously as he tied the pirogue to the pier and then stepped from it. Be careful, she warned herself. Remember his powerful, male magnetism. For you, he's dangerous.

Jason eyed Desirée warily, not really knowing what to expect. Was she still angry with him for leaving her? There had been a sparkle in her eyes when he glided up to the pier. For a minute, he had thought she was glad to see him. But now, it was gone, and she was watching him just as warily as he was her.

"It's over, Desirée," Jason said softly. "I can take you back to New Orleans, now."

Desirée frowned, having completely forgotten about the battle. And if Jason was going to take her back to the city, that had to mean the North had won. "Was the fighting bad? Was much of the city destroyed?" she asked.

"There wasn't any battle at New Orleans, Desirée. All of the fighting took place at the forts below the city, except for a few shots exchanged between the Union fleet and the Chalmette and McGehee batteries as the ships passed. New Orleans surrendered without a single shot being fired."

Desirée couldn't believe her ears. The city had surrendered with no resistance at all? If they had fought bravely and lost honorably, it wouldn't have been so bad. But to surrender without evening firing a shot was humiliating.

"But the army stationed in New Orleans? Didn't

they fight?" Desirée asked, still disbelieving.

"No. Apparently they had orders to withdraw, and that's what they did."

"But why?" Desirée asked in an anguished voice. "Why didn't they stay and fight?"

Jason knew what Desirée was feeling. He ached for her disappointment in her army. "I don't really know the answer to that, Desirée. I'm sure they must have had good reasons. Perhaps they knew they weren't strong enough to defend the city, and rather than see it destroyed needlessly, they retreated."

Jason's words made Desirée feel a little better. Thinking it was their reluctance to destroy the beautiful city and not cowardice soothed her. And then the full impact of his news hit her. The Union fleet had taken the city, not the army. Somehow those ships had gotten past the chains in the river, and Desirée remembered only too well how they had known about those chains. Jason had sent then that information. Because of him, her beloved New Orleans was now in enemy hands.

Her eyes narrowed as she spat, "You did it! You told them about those chains! Are you satisfied now? Are you happy?"

Desirée's word were like a knife in Jason's heart. He could feel the gap between them widening. "Desirée, I had a job to do, and I did it. What kind of a man would I be if I betrayed my own beliefs, ignored my commitments, shirked my duty?"

But Desirée was still too shocked and hurt by the news of the surrender and too angry at Jason for his part in it to listen to reason. She glared at him.

"Desirée," Jason said, stepping closer. "Please listen to me."

More than anger, the fear of Jason's strong magnetic attraction made Desirée react violently. "*Non!*

Don't touch me. Do you think I'd ever let you touch me again after what you've done? *Non*, you're my enemy. I hate you! Do you hear? I hate you!''

Jason watched as Desirée ran from him and down the pier, feeling an emptiness filling him. Had he lost her for good? Would she ever be able to forgive him?

Desirée refused to come out of her small room that night for the evening meal. She lay on the lumpy mattress stuffed with Spanish moss and stared at the cypress beam above her, her emotions reeling in confusion. A part of her hated him, and yet, another part of her didn't hate him. And even now, her body was aching for him.

Mon Dieu, Desirée thought. It's bad enough that just knowing he is near can make this body of mine betray me, but what am I going to do about this rebellious heart?

The next morning, Desirée was awakened by a knock on the door and Jason's voice calling, "Wake up, Desirée. It's time to leave."

After they had eaten breakfast and said good-bye to Raul and Benitta, Jason pushed the pirogue back out into the swamp. Desirée was determined not to look at him or speak to him. It shouldn't be such a hard thing to do, she told herself. After all, she'd managed to survive without looking at him for over two weeks, and she'd lived in virtual silence all that time.

But as the day wore on, it turned out not to be such an easy thing to do after all. Despite her vow she kept stealing glances at his tall, sinewy body and those mysterious misty-green eyes with their dark thick eyelashes. The glances only made her more miserable as the aching returned.

Several times, Jason tried to start a conversation

164

with her. Each time, Desirée's heart leaped with joy, and it was all she could do to remember her vow and give him an icy glare before turning her head away.

Jason was just as miserable. He had paced half the night trying to find a solution, fighting his body's demands that he go to her and force her into submission. If only she would listen to reason, he thought, let him convince her that it was wrong to let this war stand between them, to let hate destroy love.

That night, when Desirée made her pallet on the opposite side of the fire from him, Jason didn't object. A hopelessness had invaded him. Loving her would prove nothing if she wouldn't listen to reason. When it was over, they'd be right back where they had started.

Desirée was hurt by his seeming indifference. Didn't he even find her desirable anymore? Wasn't he even going to attempt to make love to her?

Desirée wondered what was wrong as she lay down, furious with herself. Would she let her body rule her mind? Desire destroy her honor? But despite all, she lay staring up at the stars, her body throbbing, her heart aching strangely.

The next day was even worse. A tension lay in the air all around them, so thick it was almost palpable. Both felt their nerves crawling, both struggled to control their emotions.

That night, they lay on their separate pallets, each acutely aware of the other, each burning for the other. Desirée tossed and turned restlessly. Jason muttered oaths and squirmed uncomfortably, feeling his heat rise and his manhood hardening.

Dammit! I ought to go right over there and take her. I know she wants me as much as I want her. I can feel it. Stubborn little mule!

The next morning, when they glided up to the trapper's shack where Jason had taken Desirée the night she had discovered his true identity, Desirée looked at it with surprise. How had they managed to get here so soon? Why, it had taken them twice as long when Jason had taken her to Raul and Benitta's cabin. And then she realized that Jason had deliberately wandered around in the swamps. Had he done it because he had wanted to be alone with her longer? Or had he only done it to confuse her? Desirée found herself hoping that it had been the first.

When Desirée realized Jason had only brought his horse, she was unnerved. She couldn't ride with him. Not the way her body was already aching. Why, being that close to him, touching him would be sheer agony. She whirled, saying, "Why didn't you bring me a horse?"

Jason fought to control his patience. His nerves weren't in any better condition than they had been the night before; if anything they were worse. "Desirée, when the Confederate Army pulled out of New Orleans they took everything with four legs with them. I wouldn't even have my horse if I hadn't hidden him in the woods outside New Orleans before I entered the city."

"Then I'll just walk!" Desirée said stubbornly.

Jason was at the end of his patience. All he wanted to do was get Desirée back to New Orleans, and the sooner the better. He knew he'd never make one more night suffering the agonies he'd gone through last night. No, one more night alone with Desirée and he'd lose all control.

"Like hell you will!" he thundered.

Then, before Desirée could even react, he lifted her and tossed her into the saddle. In a flash he was behind her, and they were off. Desirée was reminded of the first night when he had done the same thing. She should have known it was fruitless to object. She was helpless against his superior strength.

As they rode, Desirée fought a constant battle against himself. Her body was hungry for Jason. Almost as if it had a will of its own, she would find herself pressing against him, savoring the feel of his warm, masculine body against hers. And then, shocked by what she was doing and furious with herself, she would jerk away and sit up in the saddle, every muscle rigid with concentration.

Jason was bewildered by Desirée's behavior. One minute she was snuggling up to him as if begging him to love her, the next minute she was sitting up as if daring him to touch her. What kind of crazy game was she playing? Was she deliberately trying to drive him mad?

As they rode closer to New Orleans, Desirée was shocked by what she saw. The road was crowded with people fleeing the city, not only whites but slaves, who had run away from their masters, thinking they were free now that the North had taken over the city. Desirée noticed that most of the people were on foot, carrying what possessions they could with them. Apparently, what Jason had said was true. The fleeing Confederate Army had taken everything they could find. And more than once she noticed Jason's horse being eyed with envy. Would they try to overpower them and take Jason's horse away from them? Why, Jason didn't even carry a weapon except for his knife.

Trying to go upstream against a steady flow of people proved to be slow and tedious. Several times, they were forced off the road by sheer numbers. By afternoon, under the hot sun and goaded by not being able to make better time, many of the people grew short tempered. Curses filled the air; shoving matches began; there were even a few fights.

167

Not liking the ugly mood of the crowd and only too aware of the looks being given his horse, Jason decided to take to the country. He realized they weren't going to be able to reach New Orleans before nightfall, and he had no intention of being caught anywhere around this surly crowd in the middle of the night.

Desirée didn't object. She was just as anxious to get away. The crowd had frightened her and shocked her. How could ordinary people, courteous to each other under normal circumstances, become so rude, so mean?

Jason took them deep into the woods. He didn't stop until he was positive they were in a safe place.

That night, as Jason watched Desirée walk to her pallet, he decided to make one more effort to reason with her. This was their last night together. Tomorrow, they would separate, and he might never get another opportunity to be alone with her. It was now or never.

He rose, saying in a firm voice, "No, Desirée, don't go to bed yet. We need to talk."

"Talk?" Desirée asked in a surprised voice. Then remembering he was her enemy, she said, "*Non!* There's nothing to talk about." She turned her back on him and started to sit down on her blanket.

Jason caught her arm, whirling her about, saying, "Oh, but there is. We're going to get the air cleared between us once and for all. Desirée, this war has nothing to do with us."

When Jason caught Desirée's arms, she had felt an electric shock go through her. Frightened by her reaction to his touch, she jerked her arm away, saying in a frantic voice, "Us? There isn't any us! Have you forgotten I'm betrothed to another man?"

"You don't love him, Desirée. You couldn't. A

woman like you could never give herself to another man the way you did me, not if you really loved him."

Jason had hit a vulnerable spot in Desirée. She wasn't sure how she felt about Beau anymore. But to admit, even to herself, that she didn't love him would be leaving herself wide open to the feelings Jason had been stirring in her, feelings that frightened her with their intensity, and she was determined to destroy them.

Jason shook her so hard her teeth rattled, and he said, "Admit it, Desirée! Say you don't love him!"

Again Desirée jerked away. "*Non!* I do love Beau. I love him and—" Her eyes flashed with determination. "And I'm going to marry him."

Jason saw red. After knowing the sweetness of Desirée's body, the beauty of loving her, the thought of any other man making love to her made his blood boil. No, she was his, now, and for always. A sudden, overpowering need to possess her rose in him.

He caught her in a bone-crushing embrace as his mouth came crashing down on hers, kissing her almost savagely, his tongue plundering, demanding a response. Frightened by the suddenness and intensity of Jason's kiss, Desirée struggled, her heart pounding frantically as she fought for breath.

Jason forced her to the pallet on the ground, throwing himself half over her, pinning her down as he continued to kiss her fiercely, his tongue hot and ravishing, his hands roaming urgently, possessively over her body. And then, as Desirée felt his hand close over her breast, the fingers teasing the bud to a hard, throbbing peak, all resistance fled. She moaned deep in her throat as her body went weak with longing.

Sensing her surrender, Jason's hands gentled, his mouth softened. The abrupt change from fierce, hot kisses to achingly tender ones was disastrous for

Desirée. His tender, butterfly kisses, his gentle, yet tantalizing caresses, and then, the sensuous strokes of his tongue against hers played havoc on her love-starved body. Within minutes, every nerve in her body was tingling, her blood surging hotly through her veins from Jason's sensuous lovemaking.

She was so lost in sensation she never even knew when Jason undressed her and stripped himself of his clothes. Only when she felt the feverish heat of his skin against hers and his rigid, pulsating hardness against her thigh did she realize how far their love-making had gone. By then, she couldn't have objected, even if she had wanted to. Her need for him was too great, too overpowering. She pressed herself even closer, her arms enfolding him in a fierce embrace, wishing there was some way she could take him completely into herself, hold him there forever.

Each kiss was an ecstasy, each touch a fire that heightened her desire as Jason continued his sensual, ardent assault on Desirée's senses. She moaned as his lips nibbled and his tongue laved her breast and then gasped as his teeth gently raked one throbbing nipple before rolling it around his tongue. Her hands caught in the soft curls at the nape of his neck, and she arched her back to get even closer to that mouth that was making her feel so wonderful.

And then as Jason's lips left her breast, she uttered a small protest and then sighed in bliss as his mouth closed over the other nipple, his tongue swirling and sending ripples of pleasure through her.

When Jason's dark head descended to explore her ribs and abdomen, Desirée didn't object. The feel of his thick sideburns against her feverish skin as he lowered his head was almost as exciting as his lips and tongue. And then, when he stopped at her navel, his tongue lazily circling, then flicking, Desirée felt as if

170

she would burst from need.

"Please, Jason, now," she pleaded with a weak voice.

But Jason ignored her plea as he continued his explorations. The feel of his lips on the insides of her thighs was almost more than Desirée could endure. Her whole body felt as if it were a flaming torch. She whimpered.

When she felt Jason's hands sliding under her hips and lifting her, she arched her back in anticipation of his lunge, knowing that she would soon find release from this torment. And then, when she realized that it was his tongue and not his manhood that was parting her, pressing against her there, her eyes flew open in shock.

"Non!" she cried, catching his head with her hands, trying to pull it up and away from her.

But Jason was determined he wouldn't be cheated of the taste of Desirée's sweetness. He held her hips firmly, ignoring her frantic pleas to stop, his tongue laving her moist lips, the taste of her nectar and the scent of her womanliness exciting him wildly.

Desirée's eyes widened in wonder. *Mon Dieu!* she thought as she felt Jason's warm tongue circling, stroking sensuously, flicking like a fiery dart. And then, as the sweet ripples began, she parted her legs, thinking she would die if he didn't stop and yet not wanting him to stop. And then, when his tongue darted inside and the ripples turned into exquisite spasms, rocking her body, Desirée did think she was dying from sheer rapture.

And when Jason drove into her in one powerful thrust, she felt as if a bolt of lightning had entered her, sending shock waves racing up her spine and exploding in a blinding flash in her brain as her whole body convulsed.

She opened her eyes, dazed, and saw Jason smiling down at her. Then aware that he was still inside her, rigid and throbbing, she wondered vaguely what had happened.

But Jason didn't give her time to wonder for long. His mouth closed over hers in a deep, searing kiss, and Desirée tasted herself on his tongue. And then he was moving, slow, sensuous strokes that slowly stoked her fires. Each thrust was an ecstasy, each retreat an agony. Over and over he brought her to the shuddering brink, and Desirée thought she would go mad if he didn't end this exquisite torture. She writhed beneath him, moaning, begging for release. And then, as his tempo increased, wave after wave of ecstasy washed over her, until she finally found release in a shattering explosion that left her weak and trembling as she slowly floated back down to reality.

And when she finally opened her eyes, Jason was again smiling down at her. "Did you like that, Desirée?" he asked softly.

There was a taunting quality in Jason's voice that told her he wasn't talking about what she had just experienced. She knew he was referring to the way he had made love to her with his mouth.

"*Non!*" she lied. "It was indecent!"

Jason laughed softly and bent his head, nibbling at her throat. "You're lying, Desirée," he whispered in her ear. "You loved it and you know it. And before this night is over, you'll do the same for me."

Desirée really was shocked. Make love to him with her mouth? There? "*Non!*"

"Oh, yes, my sweet. And not because I ask you to. No, you'll do it because you'll want to."

Suddenly, Desirée was afraid of him. His power over her terrified her. She pushed at him, trying to get away.

172

But Jason held her in a firm grip, saying, "No, my sweet. I'm not through with you yet. If this is to be our last night together, I intend to make it a memorable one. I'm going to love you in every possible way a man can love a woman."

"*Non!*" Let me go!"

Jason's eyes glittered with determination. "You may marry another man, carry his name, even bear his children, but I'm going to place my brand on you, Desirée. Even though your husband will make love to you, even though you may take other lovers, they'll never be able to satisfy you. It will only leave you aching for me. Yes, Desirée, you may be able to lock me out of your life, but you'll never be able to get me out of your blood. You'll never be able to forget me."

For the second time that night, Desirée realized he was still inside her. She could feel him growing and hardening. And then as he started to move, she sobbed, *"Non!"*

"Oh, yes," Jason said in a husky voice before his mouth closed over hers.

And Jason did everything he had promised.

Chapter 9

Jason guided his horse through the cobblestone streets of New Orleans the next morning, feeling a remorse like he had never known. He was ashamed of himself for what he had done to Desirée the night before, not for loving her but for how he had done it. He had used his body to subjugate her. And it had proven nothing. Obviously, it hadn't changed her mind about loving Beau. If anything, he had only alienated her more.

He didn't know what had possessed him; only the thought of another man's loving her was more than he could endure. And in his pain, his frustration, he had taken it out on her, as if by forcing her to admit her passion for him, he could make her deny her love for Beau. Before, she had hated him for being the enemy, for his part in the fall of New Orleans. But now, he had given her more personal reasons for hating him. Undoubtedly, she'd never forgive him.

Jason would have been surprised to know that what Desirée was feeling wasn't hate but fear, and not of Jason himself but of his power over her. She was firmly convinced that if she stayed in his company any longer, she would lose not only her heart but her soul, too. And *that* terrified her.

Desirée knew that he had put his brand on her for life, just as he had said he would do. *Mon Dieu*, she thought, blushing in remembrance, the things he had done to her and the things he had made her do to him. *Non*, Desirée admitted, he hadn't made her do those things. She had done them willingly, even eagerly. And she had loved every minute of their long night of continuous lovemaking. Of course, she would never admit that to anyone else, and certainly not to Jason. She would die before she let him know the power he held over her body. Yes, she had to get away from him, put a safe distance between them, before she lost control of her rebellious heart, too. For then, she would be lost.

"Where do you live?" Jason asked when they got farther into the city.

"On the corner of St. Phillips and Daulphine Streets."

Jason was surprised to learn Desirée lived in the heart of Vieux Carre, the French Quarter. With her American father, he would have expected her to live in the Garden District where the Americans had built their large, elaborate houses, sitting them in the middle of spacious lawns with plantings of shrubs, flowers, and hedges and wide flagstone walks. And if not there, then on Esplanade Avenue where the wealthy, fashionable Creoles had built their new homes. Apparently Desirée's Creole mother had wanted to stay in her family's old French home, and Jason was pleased. He preferred the old homes in Vieux Carre. They had a charm, a warmth that the newer homes lacked, no matter how elaborate they were.

They rode down Bourbon Street and passed the Absinthe House, and then a few blocks down, the French Opera House, or the *Theatre d' Orleans*, as the Creoles called it. Desirée looked fondly at the opera house, remembering all the times she had walked up its red-carpeted entrance and stood below its huge crystal chandeliers before walking up the stairs to the boxes that formed a huge horseshoe around the stage. She smiled, thinking how seriously the Creoles took their opera. More than one duel had been fought between men who had disagreed on who was the best soprano. But personally, Desirée thought Adelina Patti had the most beautiful voice she had ever heard.

Desirée looked around her as they rode, thinking how much she loved this old section. To her, Vieux Carre was New Orleans. She took a deep breath, relishing the smell of fresh baked bread and spicy Creole cooking mixed with the sweet odor of jasmines, magnolias, and gardenias. Her eyes drank in the beauty of the houses they passed with their pale blue, pink, and yellow stucco and their tall galleries with their lacy ironwork posts and scrolled panels of fili-gree, their french doors with their fanlights over them. Oleanders bloomed in a profusion of pinks, reds, and white, while roses of every shade and hue, some trailing up the iron posts and cascading down over the galleries in a riot of color, added their sweet scent to the air. And as if this wasn't enough color, there were pots of geraniums, ferns, and begonias sitting on the galleries, and the streets were littered with the laven-der petals of wisteria, looking like the confetti the merrymakers threw at each other at Mardi Gras. *Oui*, she loved this city. There was only one place she loved more: Whispering Oaks.

When they reached St. Phillips Street and turned left, Desirée could see her home at the next corner. Her heart raced with excitement. She was home! Soon she would see Papa and Mammy Lou. She'd take a bath in hot water and sleep in a real bed. Oh, how wonderful it would be!

After, Jason had lifted her from his horse, Desirée's feet had barely touched the *banquette* before she was off. Jason ran a few steps and caught her arm, saying, "Wait a minute, Desirée. I'm coming in with you."

Desirée whirled. "Coming in with me? But why?"

"Desirée, you've been missing for three weeks now. I'm sure your father has gone through sheer hell in that time. I feel the least I can do is explain."

"Explain?" Desirée said in disbelief. "Why, he'll shoot you when he finds out what you've done!"

"Shoot me?" Jason asked in surprise. Then his eyes narrowed. "Why? Because of what happened between us? Because I compromised you?"

Desirée had no intention of telling anyone what had happened between them, least of all her hot-tempered father. He might get the crazy idea of challenging Jason to a duel. And her father would be no match for Jason. "*Non*, not for that," Desirée muttered, flushing with embarrassment. "Maybe I shouldn't have said he'd shoot you. It's just that my father is so hotheaded." Her eyes flashed with remembered anger. "But he will have you arrested for abducting me!"

"Arrested for abducting you?" Jason asked in an incredulous voice.

"*Oui!* You took me away against my will!"

"Desirée," Jason said in a patient voice, "New Orleans is under martial law now. Do you honestly believe the provost marshal is going to arrest me for doing my duty? That he's going to arrest me for keeping you from warning New Orleans about the attack?"

Desirée was stunned. New Orleans was under martial law? There weren't any civil authorities they could complain to? But Jason should be punished for what he'd done. Not bad, but—well, just a little. After all, look at all the worry he had caused her father.

"Desirée, I hope you can convince your father not to do anything rash."

"Then you're not coming in after all?"

Jason frowned. "No, not if your father is as hot-headed as you say he is. He might react before he thinks. Start yelling, maybe take a swing at me. Then, the next thing we'd know, the house servants will have the whole story spread all over New Orleans, and we'd have a scandal on our hands for sure."

"Scandal? What are you talking about?"

Jason shook his head, saying in an exasperated voice, "Desirée, up to now the only two people who know where you've been for the past two weeks is you and I. Now you know as well as I do how these Creoles are. Nobody loves a scandal like they do. And if word ever leaks out where you've been for the past three weeks, your reputation will be torn to shreds."

Mon Dieu! He's right, Desirée thought. Why even if nothing had happened between them, she'd still be condemned. Respectable young ladies, Creole or not, simply didn't spend a night alone with a man, regardless of the circumstances. Her face blanched of all color.

"I see you understand," Jason said in a grim voice. "And for that reason I hope you can convince your father to move cautiously."

Jason knew it was time to say good-bye, but he didn't want to, not now or ever. He waited, hoping that Desirée might give him some sign his company might be welcomed. But she just stood, staring off into space, as if she had completely forgotten he was there.

Finally, Jason said, "Good-bye, Desirée." He turned, walked back to his horse, mounted, and rode off, refusing to give in to his urge to look back.

At first Desirée had been stunned by the predicament she had found herself in. And then, her mind had been occupied with trying to think of some plausible explanation for her sudden disappearance one that wouldn't put her reputation in jeopardy. When she finally looked up, Jason was halfway down the street.

She started to call to him, and then furiously reminded herself that she wanted him to leave, that putting a distance between them was the only way she could save herself. But still, a part of her rebelled.

Then, remembering that she was home, she turned and ran to the small wrought-iron gate that opened onto the *banquette* at one side of the house. To her surprise, she found the gate locked. What was going on? She never remembered this gate being locked before, not even when her family was out of town, for there were always servants in residence.

She peered into the dim walkway that lined the side of the house, trying to see into the courtyard. Then she rattled the gate, calling, "Hello in there! Open the gate! It's me, Desirée!"

She waited and nothing happened. Again, she rattled the gate, the iron bars clattering loudly, and called, "What's going on in there? Open this gate!"

Desirée waited impatiently, and then she saw Moses, her father's old black coachman and groom, slowly shuffling down the pathway. Desirée smiled in recognition and then said in a stern voice, "Moses, what's this gate doing locked? You know we never lock our gates."

The old man came to an abrupt halt, and even in the dim walkway, Desirée could see his dark face blanch. Even his grey woolly hair seemed to turn whiter. And then he backed away, the whites of his

179

eyes looking huge on his black face as his eyes widened in terror.

"*Mon Dieu*, Moses! What's wrong with you? Open this gate!"

Slowly Moses backed away, his big body trembling with fright, saying, "No, sir, I ain't opening that gate. I ain't opening that gate for *no* ghost!"

"Ghost?" Desirée asked in an incredulous voice, then said impatiently, "What in the devil is wrong with you, Moses? I'm not a ghost. It's me—Desirée!"

"I know who you are. But you're dead, Miss Desirée. You got lost in those swamps and died."

Desirée finally realized why the old man was so frightened. "*Non*, Moses. I didn't get lost in the swamps. I'm not dead."

But to her horror, Moses kept backing slowly down the dark walkway. "Moses, listen to me!" Desirée called. "A man took me off into the swamps. He just brought me back to New Orleans this morning."

Moses peered around the corner of the house. "What man? What are you talking about?"

"I was riding that night, Moses. Down by the bayou. I saw this man talking to another man, and I got curious. He was a Yankee spy, Moses. He caught me before I could get away and took me off into the swamps so I couldn't warn anyone about the Yankees coming to attack New Orleans."

"Then you're not dead, Miss Desirée?" Moses asked, still half disbelieving.

"*Non*, I'm not dead. Now please open this gate."

Moses shuffled up the dim walkway and opened the gate. Pushing it forward, he said, "I'm sorry, Miss Desirée. But I thought you were a ghost. Lawsy, you sure scared the devil out of this old man."

"That's all right, Moses. I understand now. I'm

sorry I frightened you," Desirée said, stepping back as the gate swung open.

And then Desirée realized that a crowd of curious onlookers had gathered around her, obviously drawn by her rattling the gate and calling to Moses. She turned and found herself surrounded by a group of blacks, darkies she recognized as the house servants of the Creoles who lived all around her. Most of the servants were looking at her curiously, eyeing her ragged riding outfit. And then she noticed several of them grinning broadly.

Desirée's heart sank to her feet. She knew how fast the black grapevine moved. The slaves always knew what was going on in New Orleans long before the whites. And she had just blurted out the whole story. Within hours, every Creole in New Orleans would know she'd been alone in the swamps with a man. And to make matters worse, they would think she'd been out there alone with him for three weeks, and since the man was a Yankee and the women of New Orleans considered all Yankees rapists, they would assume she had been defiled. She would be considered a ruined woman. No respectable woman would ever talk to her. And it wouldn't do any good to deny it. They'd never believe her. After all, what woman would admit to something like that?

For a minute, Desirée considered pleading with the servants to keep their mouths shut. But then, seeing Madame Gayarre standing at the back of the crowd, she felt actually ill. The Creole woman lived just down the street from her and was known as one of the biggest gossips in New Orleans. Already her eyes were glittering with anticipation of spreading the newest scandal.

"Lawsy, Miss Desirée, you're pale as a sheet. Did you get swamp fever while you were out there?" Moses

181

asked.

Sudden, overwhelming tears flooded Desirée's eyes. She whirled, tearing past Moses, flying down the dim walkway and then through the sun-dabbled courtyard. She stumbled up the stairs and ran into the foyer, where she collided with the big body of Mammy Lou.

Not even giving the astonished old woman a chance to recover from the shock of seeing her beloved baby alive, Desirée threw herself in Mammy's arms, sobbing out everything, except the intimacies she had shared with Jason, and ending with, "Oh, Mammy, Jason warned me. It's my own fault. Because of my own stupidity, I'm ruined!"

Mammy Lou had been reeling under a maelstrom of emotions ever since Desirée had rushed in and thrown herself in her arms; first shock, followed by an overwhelming relief and happiness, then, as Desirée told her story, anger at the man who had carried her off. When Desirée said she was ruined, the old woman's blood boiled at the injustice of a woman's being blamed for the rape, as if she had committed the crime and not the man.

"Now, you stop that silly talk right now," Mammy Lou said in a firm voice. "I don't care what those uppidy white folks say. You're not ruined. You're the same sweet li'l gal I raised from a baby."

But Desirée knew she wasn't the same. She was a woman now. And if Mammy meant she was innocent by calling her sweet, she couldn't lay claim to that, certainly not after last night. Her face turned beet red in remembrance at what she had done.

Seeing Desirée's flushed face, Mammy Lou's anger turned to cold fear. Had her baby been raped by that man? Was that flush on her face caused by shame and humiliation at being degraded? Fighting down her fear, she said in as calm a voice as she could muster, "Did that man do something to you out there in those swamps? Did he hurt you, honey lamb?"

Desirée knew what was going on in her mammy's mind. Mammy had seen her flushed face and thought she was ashamed because she'd been raped. For a minute, she considered lying to her and telling her yes. But she couldn't do that to Jason, pin the horrible label of rapist on him. Besides, for some reason, she didn't want Mammy Lou to think badly of him.

"You don't have to be ashamed to tell me," Mammy Lou said. "I know it wasn't your fault. And you know I'd never tell anyone. I love you. Now, you tell your old mammy the truth. Did that man hurt you? Force himself on you?"

Desirée didn't want Mammy Lou to think badly of her either. And she knew the old woman would be shocked if she knew how freely she'd given herself to Jason, and disappointed in her, too, particularly after all of Mammy's hard work to make a lady out of her. And *Mon Dieu*, what she had done last night certainly hadn't been ladylike.

"Don't you start lying to me now," Mammy Lou said in a stern voice when Desirée hesitated. "You've never lied to your old mammy."

"No, he didn't force me, Mammy," Desirée admitted reluctantly. Then her chin rose stubbornly. "But he did seduce me!"

Mammy rolled her eyes in exasperation. She'd never been able to understand these white folks' way of thinking. First, that business about being ruined, and now, this foolishness about being seduced. As far as Mammy was concerned, there was no such thing as seduction. The woman was either willing, or she wasn't. There was no in between. And if her baby hadn't been forced, then she must have been willing. But rather than being shocked, Mammy was more surprised. She knew her baby wasn't one of those bad girls. Had something else happened out there in those swamps? Had her baby fallen in love with that man? And what about the man? Had he just been using her or did he love her, too? Then Mammy Lou remembered Desirée's telling her about Jason's warning to keep quiet about her whereabouts. If the man had been concerned about her reputation, then he must have cared something about her. Her dark eyes narrowed thoughtfully.

"Oh, Mammy!" Desirée wailed. "I really and truly am ruined. Now Beau will never marry me. No man will."

Mammy Lou didn't think Beau was any great loss. But she knew her baby would fall in love someday and want to marry. "Don't you worry your pretty head about that. This here talk will die down. It always does. And if it doesn't, we'll just move someplace else after this war is over. Then you can find yourself a nice husband and have lots more babies for old Mammy to love."

"But my husband will know the first time he—" Desirée paused and blushed, then continued, "he makes love to me that I'm not a virgin."

"No, sir, he won't! He won't know nothing, unless you tell him. There's ways of fooling those men."

"But that would be dishonest," Desirée said in a shocked voice.

"Humph! You think those men come to the marriage bed pure as the day they're born? No, sir, they don't! What they don't know won't hurt them."

Mammy Lou had never talked so frankly to Desirée. She knew men weren't expected to stay pure, but for the first time in her life, she questioned why they

184

were allowed to live by one set of rules, while the women had to live by another. Why, it wasn't fair, she thought. And she had a sneaky suspicion it had been the men who had initiated those rules.

Curious, she asked, "How do you fool them, Mammy?"

Mammy tossed her head, saying, "Never mind about that! When the day comes, your old Mammy will take care of it. Now," Mammy said, leading her to the stairs, "let's get you out of those dirty rags and into a tub of hot water."

Desirée pulled back, saying, "But I want to see Papa first." She turned and started walking back toward the back of the house to her father's library, where he usually spent his Sundays in quiet solitude.

Mammy Lou turned ashen, then said, "He ain't there, child."

Desirée turned, saying, "Not here? Why, he's always here on Sundays."

"Not this Sunday, he ain't. He's away—on business."

"Oh," Desirée said in a disappointed voice. "Well, I guess I might as well bathe first."

Mammy Lou followed Desirée up the stairs, a grim look on her face, racking her brain on how she was going to tell her baby the bad news. Even while she was helping Desirée bathe, she was still trying to decide the right words to use.

As Desirée was slipping on her wrapper, she said, "Mammy Lou, you won't tell Papa about me being seduced, will you? I don't think I could bear for him to know that."

"No. I won't tell him."

There was a strange choking sound in Mammy Lou's voice that made Desirée turn and look at the old woman. Seeing the tears streaming down the black woman's face, Desirée said in an alarmed voice, "What's wrong, Mammy Lou? You're crying."

"Come here, child," Mammy Lou said, leading Desirée to the big four-poster. Sitting down on the side of it and pulling Desirée down beside her, she said in an ominous voice, "I've got something to tell you."

Desirée had a strong feeling of foreboding. "It's about Papa, isn't it?"

"Yes, honey lamb, it sure is. Your papa's dead."

"Dead?" Desirée asked in a shocked voice. "But how?"

"When your papa heard about the Yankees coming up the river, he said no damned Yankee was going to get his cotton. So he went to the river and burned all of it."

"Papa set fire to his warehouses?" Desirée asked in disbelief.

"Yes. And so did all those other white folks. It was terrible. Black smoke everywhere, the air stinking of burning sugar and cotton. Why, I could see the flames leaping up in the sky clear from here."

"Then he got killed in the fire?"

"No, honey lamb. When all the white folks started burning their warehouses, the river riffraff went down there with wheelbarrows, trying to pick up all the corn and rice that had spilled out on the wharfs and carrying off everything they could get their hands on. Then they started breaking into the stores. Your papa saw one of them doing that and tried to stop him. Then the man just hit him right over the head with a big stick. Mr. Broussard, down the street, saw it happen. He's the one that brought your papa home that night."

Mon Dieu, Her father had been murdered! Desirée felt sick.

186

"I sent word to your uncle, and he and your cousin came to New Orleans and took your papa up to Whispering Oaks. They buried him right next to your mama."

Yes, Desirée thought, that's where her father had wanted to be for a long time, with her mother.

"Lawsy, that poor man," Mammy Lou said half to herself. "What he didn't go through. First you disappearing. He was just like a wild man. And then that terrible news about your brother coming—" Realizing what she'd just said, Mammy Lou's eyes widened in horror.

Desirée head snapped up. "What news about Thad?"

Fresh tears filled Mammy Lou's eyes. "Oh, honey lamb, I didn't mean to let that slip. I wasn't gonna tell you that just yet. It's too much for a li'l gal to take all at once."

That same horrible feeling of foreboding filled Desirée. "What? What weren't you going to tell me?"

Mammy Lou just sat, her black eyes glittering with huge tears, and shook her head.

Desirée caught her big shoulders and shook her, saying, "Mammy! Tell me!"

To Desirée, it seemed a lifetime before Mammy finally spoke. She stared off into space, saying in a flat voice, "There was this battle, in some place called Shiloh." Then Mammy Lou broke down completely, tears streaming down her face, sobs racking her big body. "He's dead!" she cried in an anguished voice. "Those devil Yankees killed my baby boy!"

"*Non! Non*, not Thad!" Desirée cried in anguish. "*Non*, Mammy, please don't tell me that!"

"It's true. Oh, lawsy, lawsy, I wish to God it weren't true, but it is. My poor baby. My poor baby boy."

Desirée threw herself in her mammy's arms, and

the big woman rocked her as they both cried out their grief and anguish. Mammy was the first to recover, for during the past few weeks she had already spent most of her grief for the young man she had loved as much as any mother.

Then she sat holding Desirée in her big arms, rocking and crooning, just as she had done when Desirée was a child, saying over and over, "Cry it out, child. Cry it out. Get it all out of there."

And when there were no more tears left for Desirée, Mammy Lou dressed her in her nightgown and slipped her beneath the covers of the big four-poster, just as she had done when she was a child. Tucking the sheet around her, she said, "Now, I'll get you a nice bowl of hot soup."

"No, Mammy, I'm not hungry," Desirée said in a lifeless voice. "I don't think I could eat if I had to."

"Now, don't you go arguing with your old mammy. I know what's best for you."

When Mammy returned to the room with a tray, Desirée was lying and staring up at the ceiling, feeling empty and totally washed out, wishing that she could wake up and find the whole thing was just a bad nightmare. Mammy's heart bled for her. It was a wound to the soul that only time could heal.

When Desirée had finished drinking her soup, Mammy Lou handed her a cup, saying, "Now, you drink this nice tisane I made for you. It'll help you sleep."

Desirée felt too numb to argue. She lifted the cup and took a swallow, then gagged. She looked up at Mammy saying, "Why is it so bitter?"

"It's just because you've been crying, honey lamb. Your mouth is dried out. Now, you go ahead and drink it."

Desirée forced the bitter liquid down and handed

188

the cup back to Mammy. Mammy placed the cup back on the tray, tucked Desirée's covers around her, and then sat in the rocking chair by her bed, saying, "Now, you go to sleep, child. I'll be right here if you need me."

"No, Mammy," Desirée said. "You're exhausted yourself. Please don't sit up with me tonight. Go on to bed. I'll be all right."

"No!" Mammy said in a firm voice. "I'm gonna stay right here, just like I've always done when my baby's feeling poorly."

Mammy crossed her arms over her big bosom and started rocking, a determined look on her face. Desirée knew it was hopeless to argue. Once Mammy had her mind made up to something, no amount of arguing, reasoning, pleading—nothing could change it. It would be easier to move a mountain.

Desirée lay back down and, within minutes, was asleep. Mammy Lou sat and rocked, her black eyes filled with compassion and love as she watched Desirée sleeping, the rocking chair squeaking under her heavy weight.

My poor baby, Mammy thought as she rocked. She'd lost so much. Her mama, her papa, her brother. But she still has her old mammy. And thank the Lord, she drank that tisane I gave her. The last thing my baby needs now is a baby of her own.

Desirée smiled weakly as Mammy Lou brought her breakfast tray in the morning. "Good morning, Mammy."

Mammy Lou stood at the foot of the bed and looked down at Desirée, saying, "How are you feeling, honey lamb?"

"I'm feeling better," Desirée said, sitting up in bed

189

and leaning against the headboard. "It still hurts, but a good night's sleep helped." Desirée looked down at the sheet covering her lap and fingered it absently for a minute, then looked up at Mammy, saying, "I know it doesn't sound right, but it's Thad that I feel so bad about. Papa hasn't been the same since Mama died. I don't think he'd really been happy since then. But Thad was so full of life, so eager for all it had to offer." Fresh tears glittered in her eyes. "He was too young to die. It seems like such a waste."

Mammy nodded in silent agreement.

"Well, at least it gave me a new perspective of things," Desirée said in a firmer voice. "Yesterday I was feeling sorry for myself because I'd lost my reputation. Now I'm ashamed of myself. Compared to Thad, I'm lucky. Look what he lost. I still might be able to regain my good name, but Thad will never be able to regain his life."

Mammy Lou smiled. Her baby was beginning to grow up.

Mammy Lou placed the tray over Desirée's lap. Desirée looked down at the bowl of oatmeal and frowned.

"I'm sorry, child, but that's all the food we've got left. When those no'count niggers ran away, they took all of the food they could carry with them."

Desirée's eyes shot up from the tray. "Are you telling me the other darkies ran away?"

Mammy Lou's dark eyes flashed angrily. "They sure did! Talking about how they're free now and the Yankees gonna take care of them. How they're gonna wear silk and satins and never have to work another day in their lives. Humph! They're crazy!"

Desirée was stunned. "And you and Moses were the only ones who stayed?"

"No, there's Benjie and that li'l gal, Tassy. They

190

stayed."

Desirée wasn't surprised that Benjie and Tassy had stayed. Benjie was only nine years old, and Tassy wasn't quite right. She never knew what was going on around her. But it hurt Desirée that the other darkies had fled. She had been fond of them and had thought they would be more loyal.

She glanced down at the oatmeal, saying, "Mammy, you know where Papa keeps his cash box. Why didn't you take some money out of it and buy some food?"

"I did. But those people, down at the marketplace, said it ain't good no more. They said that Confederate money is worthless, now that the Yankees have come."

As Mammy Lou's words sunk in, Desirée paled, remembering that her father had converted everything to Confederate script after the beginning of the war. Not only was all of his ready cash worthless, but everything he had in the bank, too. And to make matters worse, he'd burned his cotton and warehouses.

"What's the matter, baby?" Mammy asked, seeing Desirée's pale face. "Are you feeling poorly?"

"Yes, I am," Desirée said, feeling her stomach ball up in a tight knot. "I just realized we're paupers. Everything Papa has is in Confederate script."

"You mean, we ain't got no money at all?"

"Not unless we find some money lying around in the drawers," Desirée said, flipping back the sheet. "Come on, let's look."

Mammy Lou and Desirée searched the entire house. They went through drawers, all of Desirée's old reticules, her father's and brother's old pants' pockets. When they had finished, Desirée looked down at the money in her hand saying, "This won't even feed us for a month."

"What are you gonna do, baby?" Mammy asked in a worried voice.

Desirée was proud. She hated to ask for favors, even from relatives, but she knew she would simply have to bury her pride and ask for help. She had four people besides herself to feed. "We'll just have to go to Terre Doux and ask *Oncle* Paul for help. Surely he'll let us stay there. Besides, I'd just as soon get out of New Orleans with all these Yankees around," Desirée answered, thinking that would put an even greater distance between Jason and her.

"How're we gonna do that? We don't even have horses and a carriage no more. Those soldiers took them when they pulled out."

Ever since Jason had taken Desirée, she had been forced to face one ugly reality after the other. The latest bit of news hit her like a physical blow. She collapsed on the chair behind her, fighting back tears. She had to get to Terre Doux, to the safety and security of her uncle, and she had to have some means of transportation to get there. She and Benjie and Tassy might be able to walk that distance, but there was no way Mammy Lou and Moses could. They were both too old. Then she remembered something.

Handing Mammy Lou some money she said, "You go on to the market and buy us some food. On your way out, tell Moses I want to see him."

When Moses shuffled into the room a few minutes later, Desirée said, "Moses, did the soldiers take that old wagon we had in the carriage house? You know, the one that was half buried under junk in one corner?"

"No, Miss Desirée, they didn't take it. They didn't even want it. That wagon ain't no good. The wheels are warped."

"But it still rolls?"

"Yes'm, it rolls—just barely."

"Moses, I want you to look around New Orleans for a horse. I can't spend a lot of money, though."

Moses frowned, his wrinkles making even deeper creases across his black face. "I don't think there's any horses left in New Orleans, except for the Yankees' horses, but I'll look anyway, Miss Desirée."

Moses combed New Orleans for a week before he finally found a horse, a miserable, half-starved creature that looked like it was going to keel over any minute, and it took almost every cent Desirée had to buy him. Early the next morning, the five of them piled into the wagon, taking only a basket lunch and one small trunk that held a change of clothes for each of them.

The trip was miserable. With the warped wheels, they were jolted about so badly Desirée feared for their bones. Even over the comparatively smooth cobblestone streets of the city, they felt as if they were riding over railroad ties.

They were stopped at the outskirts of the city by Union soldiers looking for contraband. Desirée and Mammy Lou stood on the side of the road glaring at them as they searched their trunk and lunch basket, remembering that Thad had been killed by men like these men—Yankees.

Once in the countryside, they were forced to move at a snail's pace, not only because of the warped wheels and the condition of the horse but also because of the road. Rutted under normal conditions, the holes had been cut even deeper by the retreating Confederate Army dragging their heavy howitzers behind them.

It was afternoon before they finally lumbered into the shell driveway of Terre Doux and drove beneath the shade of a towering magnolia near the front steps of the plantation house. Desirée was never so happy to see her uncle's plantation. The trip that usually took only a few hours had taken most of the day, and they had arrived hot and thirsty, weary and bruised.

Desirée had barely stepped down from the wagon when Jeanne Marie rushed down the front stairs of the plantation house and caught her in a fierce hug, crying, "Oh, Desirée, it's true! You *really* are alive!" Then, holding her back and searching her face anxiously, she said in a deeply concerned voice, "That horrible Yankee didn't hurt you, did he?"

Desirée felt sick, knowing that the story of her abduction and her shame had preceeded her to Terre Doux. "Then, you know?"

Jeanne Marie looked away, suddenly unable to look her cousin in the eye. "*Oui*, we heard. Madame Breaux, from down the road, stopped by yesterday and said she had heard the news in New Orleans." Then Jeanne Marie whispered so Desirée's servants couldn't hear, "Desirée, he didn't do *that* to you, did he?"

Desirée knew what *that* was. Rape. "*Non*, he didn't do that. He didn't hurt me in any way," she answered in all honesty. She wondered briefly if she should tell Jeanne Marie it was Jason who abducted her and then decided against it. For some strange reason, she didn't want her cousin to think badly of him.

"Oh, I'm so glad," Jeanne Marie cried in relief. Then, remembering what had happened to Desirée's father and brother, tears came into her eyes as she said softly, "Oh, Desirée, I'm so sorry about your papa and Thad."

This time it was Desirée who couldn't look her cousin in the eye. Seeing Jeanne Marie's tears brought on a fresh wave of grief, an emotion she couldn't

194

afford to succumb to just yet. First, she had to talk to her uncle and see if he would allow them to stay at Terre Doux. She wasn't just seeking refuge for herself but for her slaves, too; darkies who, because of their age and mental disability, might be considered an added burden.

It might be all her uncle could do to feed his own slaves right now. Why, he might even suggest she sell them, since she was destitute and needed money. But she would never do that. They were her black family.

"Thank you," Desirée muttered in response to Jeanne Marie's sympathy. Then she said in a firmer voice, "Jeanne Marie, where is *Oncle* Paul? I need to talk to him."

"He's not here, Desirée. When he heard about the Yankees coming, he joined Armond's regiment. They're both gone. They left when the army pulled out."

"*Oncle* Paul?" Desirée asked in a shocked voice.

"*Oui*, many of the older planters joined up at the last minute."

"But who will run Terre Doux while he's gone?"

"*Maman*, with the help of an overseer Papa hired before he left. Besides he said they wouldn't be gone long, that the South would recapture New Orleans as soon as they could regroup, that the South would never allow the Yankees to keep their queen city. He expects to be back before the cane is cut."

Desirée didn't feel so confident. She had heard that Butler had eighteen thousand men in his Army of the Gulf. And General Grant's army in Tennessee, just north of them, was even larger. But then, maybe her uncle was right, and New Orleans would soon be back in the hands of the South. She had no idea how many men the South had in the area, and certainly her uncle knew more about it than she did. War was men's business, not women's.

"Since *Oncle* Paul is gone, I'll have to speak to *Tante* Josephine," Desirée said, thinking outloud.

"*Non!* You can save your breath," a biting voice said from behind them.

Desirée whirled and saw her aunt standing on the steps of the plantation house, a cold, hard look on her face, her dark eyes glittering.

"I know why you're here," Josephine said in an ugly, clipped voice. "To seek refuge with us. The answer is *non*. You're not welcome here anymore."

Desirée couldn't believe her ears. She stared dumbly at her aunt.

"*Maman!*" Jeanne Marie cried in a shocked voice. "You can't mean that! Desirée is family. You wouldn't turn her away."

"I certainly will!" Josephine replied hotly, her dark eyes flashing with anger. "She has disgraced us all. I won't have her in my home."

"But she couldn't help what happened to her," Jeanne Marie objected. "She was abducted!"

"*Oui*, and Desirée brought it all on herself. I told you she was wild. Riding alone in the middle of the night. What were you doing out there, anyway?"

"Just—just riding," Desirée stammered, still stunned by her aunt's refusal to let her stay.

"That's not what the people of New Orleans are saying. They say you were meeting a lover. *Mon Dieu!* The humiliation of it! A niece of mine, betrothed to one man, sneaking out at night to meet another."

"That's not true!" Jeanne Marie said with surprising vigor. "Desirée would never do that!"

Josephine whirled on her daughter, spitting out, "And that's precisely why she's not staying. She's a bad influence on you. Why, you've never talked to me

196

like that. I'm your mother and I won't tolerate it!"

Desirée expected Jeanne Marie to burst into tears and go running into the house. But the dainty, shy girl surprised her. Instead she faced her mother, her own dark eyes flashing, and said, "You can't do this. I won't let you. It's inhuman. Turning out your own family. Papa will be furious!"

Josephine paled, her eyes widened in disbelief at her meek daughter's sudden, fierce resistance. But Desirée had already made up her mind. She knew now that her aunt hated her, that she was only using her disgrace to lash out at her. And Desirée had her pride.

"*Non*, Jeanne Marie," Desirée said in a firm voice. "Don't argue with her. I wouldn't stay now, even if she begged me."

Jeanne Marie turned, saying, "But, Desirée, you can't stay in New Orleans all by yourself, particularly with the Yankees there."

"I'm not by myself," Desirée replied in a stubborn voice. "I have my darkies. We'll do just fine." Her dark eyes flashed. "And I'm *not* afraid of the Yankees."

Josephine turned and walked stiffly back into the house. Jeanne Marie watched her and then turned back to Desirée, saying, "She'll change her mind, Desirée. She's just upset now. But she'll come to her senses, and when she does, we'll send for you. In the meanwhile, maybe one of your father's friends will take you in."

"Yes, perhaps," Desirée said, anxious to be away from Terre Doux and her aunt's hatred. But she knew she would never ask for help from her father's friends, even if they would accept her despite her disgrace. In the week that she had been in New Orleans, she had learned that almost everyone was in the same financial position as she. They, too, had converted their money to Confederate dollars. The pawn shops were full of the once wealthy selling their personal possessions to buy food for their families and darkies. She wouldn't ask any of them to take on five extra mouths to feed. No, she'd do just like the rest of the people in New Orleans. Sell her jewels and her household furnishings to survive and hope the South would retake the city soon.

As Desirée started to climb back into the wagon, Jeanne Marie's eyes widened, for the first time noticing the miserable wagon. *"Mon Dieu!* What are you doing riding around in that?"

"The army took all of the horses and carriages when they pulled out of New Orleans. I'm lucky to have this."

"We have an extra carriage you can have, and horses, too." Jeanne Marie turned to Moses, saying, "Moses, go down to the stable and tell—"

"Non, Jeanne Marie," Desirée interjected, determined she would take nothing from Terre Doux. "The Yankees would only take them away from us." She motioned to the broken-down wagon, saying, "At least no one wants this, and it does give us some means of transportation."

"Why, you can't get back to New Orleans in that by nightfall. At least stay the night."

"I'm not going back to New Orleans tonight. I'll go to Whispering Oaks. We'll spend the night there and leave in the morning. Besides, I want to visit Papa's grave."

"Will you be all right? Do you have enough money to get by until you can find someone to stay with?"

Desirée frowned. Had Jeanne Marie guessed she was destitute? "What do you mean?"

"Well, doesn't it take awhile for wills to be straightened out, or whatever they do?"

No, Desirée thought, Jeanne Marie had no earthly idea of her financial position. Hadn't her uncle converted to Confederate script too, or had he kept the bad news from his family, not wanting to worry them? Whichever, Desirée would never let Jeanne Marie know of her distress. She couldn't help her. *Tante* Josephine controlled the money during her husband's absence. And knowing Desirée's financial predicament would only upset Jeanne Marie more.

"*Non*, that's already been taken care of," Desirée lied smoothly. "I've already seen Papa's lawyers. Money is no problem. Why, I'm a wealthy woman now."

The two cousins hugged each other, and as Desirée climbed into the wagon, Jeanne Marie said, "You'll be sure and let me know where you're staying?"

"Yes, I'll let you know," Desirée answered, settling herself between Moses and Mammy Lou on the wagon seat, both of the old blacks looking at her with compassion in their eyes.

As they drove off, Jeanne Marie called, "Be careful!"

"We will!" Desirée called back.

As they drove by the plantation house before turning back down the shell driveway, Mammy Lou glared fiercely at the house, saying angrily, "That old devil woman! She's the meanest woman I've ever seen."

Moses grunted in agreement.

Desirée sighed, saying, "She hates me, Mammy Lou. I don't know why, but she does."

A puzzled look came over Mammy's face. "Yes, sir, it sure looks like she does. I don't understand it."

"Neither do I, but I'm not going to waste my energy worrying about it."

As they turned down the road leading to Whispering Oaks, Mammy Lou asked, "What are we gonna do when we get back to New Orleans?"

Desirée looked at the worried faces of Mammy Lou and Moses. She turned and looked at Benjie, his eyes wide with apprehension, and then at Tassy, staring off into space as if she didn't even know where she was.

She squared her shoulders and turned back, saying in a determined voice, "Why, we'll just do like everyone else in New Orleans, Mammy. We're going to survive."

Oui, Desirée thought fiercely, raising her head proudly. We're going to survive. We're going to survive, despite *Tante* Josephine and despite the damned Yankees!

Chapter 10

By the middle of May, 1862, the Union controlled New Orleans, Baton Rouge, and Natchez on the Mississippi. Everything in between was still in Confederate hands. As the war raged in the swamps and bayous all around them, the isolated people of New Orleans fought their own battle, that of surviving under Union occupation.

Surviving wasn't easy, as Desirée discovered over the next few weeks. With everyone selling their valuables and overloading the market with jewels, silver, china, priceless paintings, and furniture, the prices for these items plummeted. Desirée cried bitter tears when she was forced to sell her grandmother's silver candlesticks for a mere pittance.

While the prices for luxury items plunged, the cost for necessities skyrocketed, since the Union blockade was still in effect. Desirée decided she could save money by planting a garden and then discovered, to her horror, that she wasn't the only one who had thought of that, for even the price of seed had spiraled.

She stood and watched as Moses and Benjie dug up the plants on the sunniest side of the courtyard, feeling sick at heart as she saw her favorite rose bushes and the azaleas that her mother had planted wrenched from the soil. And then when the ground was dug up, she knelt beside the two darkies and placed the seeds in the fertile ground, praying the sun wouldn't scorch the tender seedlings this late in the season.

Since all of the household slaves had left, she and Mammy Lou took over their chores. Desirée discovered she liked cooking, but loathed doing housework and laundry. After standing out in the hot sun and stirring the pot of boiling water, sweat dripping off of her forehead as she wrung out the heavy clothes by hand and rinsed them, she was exhausted, both from the heat and the strenuous work. And since Mammy, due to her size and age, couldn't get down on her hands and knees, it was Desirée who had to scrub the floors. By the end of the month, Desirée's hands were chapped, and the long nails she had been so proud of were ragged and broken.

Tassy wasn't any help, although the girl was only two years younger than Desirée. It wasn't that she wasn't willing or sullen in any way. She simply wasn't capable. Desirée would put her to work dusting tables and come back an hour later to find her still dusting the same spot, that vacant stare in her eyes. Then Desirée would lead her to another table, and Tassy would say, "Yes'm," moving the dusting rag over and over the same spot. It finally became easier for Desirée to do it herself. And she didn't dare trust Tassy in the kitchen for fear she would cut or burn herself.

Sometimes Desirée would watch the girl, wondering what, if anything, went on in her head. She was a pretty girl, slender, yet shapely, with eyes as soft as a doe's. Her comeliness was the reason Desirée's father had kept her as a house servant, where she could be watched over, fearing that she would be taken advantage of by the male field slaves. And Desirée had a soft spot in her heart for her. When she heard people refer to Tassy as a half-wit or idiot, it infuriated her. To Desirée, she just wasn't quite right.

The blacks didn't fare any better in New Orleans that summer. The slaves who had stayed with their owners shared their miseries. The slaves who had run away, thinking the Yankees had freed them, found themselves declared contraband of war. General Butler put them to work cleaning out the canals and ditches and building roads, and the bewildered slaves found themselves working as hard, if not harder, than they ever had.

But the biggest scourge in New Orleans that summer was General Butler himself, who marched his troops into New Orleans on May 1, to the tune of "Yankee Doodle Dandy." Union flags went up everywhere, all along the streets and over the *banquettes* as the Yankees flaunted their victory. But Butler soon learned that the city of New Orleans may have surrendered, but the people had not stopped resisting. They refused to walk under the flags and took to the streets to avoid passing his soldiers. Incensed by the people's refusal to bow to the victors, Butler issued a series of punitive enactments. All citizens over eighteen had to register and swear allegiance to the United States, and if they refused, their homes were confiscated and they were told to leave town or imprisoned. Union soldiers ferreted out Confederate sympathizers, and if so much as a Confederate flag, button, or newspaper was found, the home was confiscated and the owner expelled. Slaves were encouraged to inform on their owners with the promise of freedom if they did so. Families were removed from their homes that General Butler's staff wanted to occupy. When Butler was refused a choice suite in the St. Charles Hotel, he took over the entire hotel.

And still, the people resisted. Ministers were sent to prison for refusing to pray for the president of the United States. St. Louis Cathedral was barred and locked. An editor was fined and imprisoned for printing the names of Confederate soldiers who had died or been wounded.

Like everyone else in the city, Desirée hated "Beast Butler" with a passion. She refused to sign the loyalty oath and throw away her Confederate buttons and flags. And she, like the rest of the city, prayed a yellow fever outbreak would come and wipe out the hated Yankees.

And then came Butler's crowning blow, his infamous Women's Order. Desirée stared down at the newspaper in utter disbelief as she read it.

General Orders No. 28
As the officers and soldiers of the United States have been subject to the repeated insults from the women, calling themselves ladies, of New Orleans, in return for the most scrupulous noninterference and courtesy on our part, it is ordered hereafter when any female shall by word, gesture or movement, insult or show contempt for any officer or soldier of the United States, she shall be regarded and held liable to be treated as a woman of the town plying her avocation.
By command of Major-General Butler

"*Mon Dieu!*" Desirée cried angrily. "I can't believe it! That animal!"

"What's the matter?" Mammy asked, her eyes

wide with alarm.

"Look at what 'the beast' has done now!" Desirée said, handing the newspaper to Mammy Lou.

Mammy Lou stared down at the newspaper dumbly. Then, realizing what she'd done, Desirée took it from her, saying, "I'm sorry, Mammy. I was so upset, I forgot you can't read. Here, I'll read it to you."

Mammy Lou listened as Desirée read the new order to her, but with all of the unfamiliar words in it, she didn't know any more about what it said than she had when she had looked at the newspaper. When Desirée was finished, she asked, "What does 'plying their vocation' mean?"

"It means if any soldier feels he's been insulted or offended by any one of the ladies of New Orleans, he can treat her like a prostitute. *Mon Dieu*, Butler's giving his army license to rape at will!"

"Why, that's terrible!" Mammy Lou spat, her black eyes flashing angrily. Why, those no'count Yankees ain't nothing but a bunch of pigs. Ain't a gentleman in the whole lot of them."

A pair of misty-green eyes flashed through Desirée's brain. "Well, maybe one or two of them are decent," she muttered.

Desirée walked to the window and stared out at the courtyard. She hadn't been able to forget him, just as he had promised her that last night. Visions of his eyes and sensuous smile would flash through her mind at the oddest times. Putting a distance between them hadn't helped at all. At night, she would lie in bed, tormented by memories of his lovemaking.

Where was he? Had he left New Orleans and gone back north, or was he still here with General Butler's army? And if he was still here in New Orleans, why hadn't he made any attempt to see her? Had he completely forgotten about her? A small tear trickled down her cheek.

But Jason hadn't forgotten about Desirée, and he had come to see her.

After reporting to General Butler, Jason had been promoted to major at Captain Farragut's recommendation for his part in the taking of New Orleans. Had Jason been promoted for distinguishing himself in the field, he would have been proud, but to be promoted for spying didn't sit too easily with him. It left him with a strange feeling of accepting blood money, a feeling he knew came from his torn loyalties.

And then he had learned that, because he spoke French and understood the customs of the predominately French population in New Orleans, he had been assigned as one of the liaison officers between the Union Army and the Creoles of the city. Jason had been disappointed. He had hoped for a field command like the one he had had before his last assignment. He was used to being outdoors in the fresh air and sunshine, not locked away in some dark, musty office. Besides that, he hadn't felt he was up to the job. He was Cajun, not Creole.

Jason had objected, pointing out to his commanding officer that he was Cajun and spoke a patois French, not a pure French like the Creoles in New Orleans did. He had explained that his French was a shortened standard of French grammar, an old country French, mixed with scraps of English, Spanish, Italian, Portugese, Indian, and a few black gumbo words, and that he doubted that the Creoles would even understand him.

But his commanding officer had been deaf to Jason's explanation, replying that if the Creoles and Cajuns could make themselves understood at the state legislature, where French was spoken exclusively, then

Jason could make the New Orleans Creoles understand him.

Besides, the colonel had pointed out, Jason was still half French and understood the French people better than any other officer in Butler's army, and since Lincoln was anxious for New Orleans to begin reconstruction, needing the people's cooperation to do so, Jason was still the best man for the job.

So Jason had gone to his new assignment the next morning, wearing a new gold-embroidered leaf on his shoulder strap and dreading the thought of sitting in a stuffy office all day. And just as he feared, the first time he opened his mouth and rattled off his Cajun French, the Creole he was interviewing had been horrified at his outrageous French. As the day wore on, irritation was added to Jason's frustration, for he began to suspect many of the Creoles spoke just as good English as he and were only pretending to speak French exclusively to thwart the Yankees.

That night and every other free minute he had, Jason labored over French grammar books, but the more he studied, the more confused he became, having particular trouble with the feminine adjective forms, since his Cajun French used only the masculine forms. By the end of the week, he realized he was learning more of the Creole French by just listening to them talk than from all of the books he had studied. The grammar books were tossed into the trash can.

And so, because Jason had been busy taking a self-imposed crash course in French and because he had wanted to give Desirée's hot-tempered father time to simmer down, Jason didn't attempt to visit Desirée that first week. And the night he did go to her house was the night Desirée was gone, spending the night at Whispering Oaks after being turned away by her aunt.

Finding Desirée's house dark and locked up tight, Jason had been left to assume her father had taken her to Terre Doux where it would be safer. He had mixed emotions. A part of him was glad she was in a safe place, yet another part of him was keenly disappointed. He had left feeling depressed, not knowing if it would be months or years before he saw her again.

After that, Jason had thrown himself into his work, and although his French steadily improved, his frustrations only increased. It was his job to get the Creoles to cooperate with the reconstruction efforts, but Butler and his punitive enactments were seriously encumbering him. As the army confiscated more homes and personal property and more people were sent to prison, Jason's office was flooded with irate Creoles. And while Jason tried to soothe and explain, he found himself feeling like a hypocrite, silently cursing Butler for his stupid insensitivity.

As a liaison officer, Jason tried to reason with the general, pointing out that the Creoles were a proud people, that the more he tried to force them into submission, the more they would resist; that this was an instance where diplomacy would accomplish more than brute force. But all of Jason's reasoning and pleas of leniency were to no avail. Butler only continued with his vigorous repressive orders, and the people continued to resist.

And of all the resistors, the ones who aggravated Butler the most were the women. It infuriated him that the ladies of New Orleans refused to welcome his officers into their dining rooms, that they showed contempt for his men by pulling their skirts away when they passed or holding their noses, that they taunted his soldiers by wearing Confederate flags and buttons and singing snatches of "The Bonnie Blue Flag" within their hearing. When Butler learned that the women of the city called him "the beast," he retaliated by calling them "the she-adders of New Orleans."

But the women's resistance wasn't just limited to the respectable ladies of the town. Jason had been present when Butler heard that some of the ladies had pasted his picture to the bottom of their chamber pots. The general had been absolutely livid, his puffy face turning purple, the veins on his short neck standing out as if they would burst, his slightly crossed eye—earning him the name of "Old Crossed Eyes" by some of the people of New Orleans—looking as if it were going to pop right out of his head.

The day Butler issued his Women's Order, Jason's office had been overflowing with shocked, furious Creoles. And Jason had been just as shocked and just as furious. He had rushed to Butler's office to complain in the name of the Creoles of New Orleans, only to be told by the other officers waiting there that he could save his breath. Decent, God-fearing men, they had been just as shocked, both personally and as officers of the Union Army. They had feared that they would no longer be able to control the unsavory among their men, men who felt that rape and plunder was their due as victors. One officer had told Jason that there had already been reports of women being accosted and rumors of rape. Another officer had said that he was ashamed to be in General Butler's army, that he felt a black mark was being put on them all, that history would remember them for this and not for the good things they had tried to accomplish. When Jason had left, he was cursing Butler and thinking that "beast" was too good a name for him.

Several days after Butler's Women's Order was

issued, Desirée and Mammy Lou went to the French Market. They walked down Daulphine Street to St. Anne's Street and then turned toward the market, giving Gallatin Street, which sat to the other side of the market, a wide berth. Neither wanted to go anywhere near that notorious street where crime and wickedness flourished.

There sat a reeking collection of saloons, gambling joints, nickel and dime hotels, fence's shops, and bordellos, headquarters of thieves and murderers, with its saloons and whores who danced in the streets naked. On that narrow street and in its dark, dank alleys, there were nightly killings, stabbing, and riots. Even a policeman didn't venture down there without a partner, and then reluctantly.

As they passed Jackson Square, Desirée admired the crepe myrtle blooming in profusion and filling the park with splashes of reds, whites, lavenders, and pinks. And then she came to a halt, seeing Beau's mother standing and talking to several other women near the statue of Jackson.

Why, she had completely forgotten about Beau, Desirée thought. He'd been with Thad, and he, too must have been in the battle at Shiloh. Had he survived it? Or had he been wounded or killed like Thad? Desirée felt a sense of sadness at the thought that Beau might be dead but the feeling was not as intense as she expected. Why didn't the thought bother her more? Didn't she still love him? Was it because she knew he would never marry her now that she was disgraced? Whichever, she had known Beau all her life. She had to at least know how he'd fared in the battle.

"There's Beau's mother over there, Mammy," Desirée said. "I'm going over to ask her about Beau. For all I know, he might have been killed or wounded at

Shiloh."

Mammy frowned as Desirée walked away and then followed her in resignation.

Desirée walked up behind the group of Creole women and then, when there was a break in the conversation, said, "Madame Fortier, may I speak with you?"

The three women turned and then, seeing it was Desirée, their eyes widened with surprise. Then two of the women gave Desirée an icy glare, turned, and walked off haughtily. Desirée wasn't particularly bothered by their behavior. She'd become resigned to being snubbed by the women. But she hadn't expected to see the anger on Madame Fortier's face. Why, the woman was absolutely livid, her normally pale skin mottled with rage.

"How dare you!" Madame Fortier hissed, her short, dumpy body trembling with anger. "How dare you speak to me in public, after the way you disgraced yourself and humiliated my son."

"I only wanted to ask about Beau. Is he all right? He wasn't—"

"My son is none of your concern anymore!" Madame Fortier snapped, interrupting Desirée. Then her dark eyes narrowed as she said, "I hope to God you don't think he will marry you after what you've done. Why, no Creole would marry a woman with even the slightest hint of scandal about her."

"I know that," Desirée answered, wondering why not marrying Beau didn't bother her either. "I just wanted to—"

"It's disgraceful," Mrs. Fortier said in a disgusted voice, rudely interrupting Desirée for the second time. "What were you doing riding out there in the middle of the night?"

Suddenly, Desirée's own anger rose. Beau's mother

211

knew nothing of what had happened between her and Jason. No, she was condemning her for something she wasn't even sure had happened. Why, she could be as pure as the day she was born, and she'd still be guilty in this woman's eyes. It wasn't fair, and she had no intention of putting up with any more of this woman's rudeness. Who did she think she was?

Desirée's eyes flashed hotly as she raised her head proudly and said, "Since I'm no longer your son's betrothed, *that* is none of your damned business!"

With the sound of Madame Fortier's shocked gasp in her ears, Desirée whirled and walked proudly away. Mammy gave the Creole woman a murderous look, then turned and followed Desirée away, grinning and thinking that she'd never been so proud of her baby.

But, when Mammy Lou caught up with her and saw the tears glittering in Desirée's eyes, her grin turned to a frown. Did her baby still love that Beau? Was that why she was crying? Or had that mean old woman made her feel guilty for betraying him, for giving her virginity to another man?

Humph! Mammy thought. What right did Beau have to demand purity from her baby? Why, she knew for a fact that he had one of those *femmes de couleur*, one of those uppidy niggers who thought they were better than other black folks because they had white blood in their veins. He'd kept his mistress on Rampart Street the whole time he and Desirée had been betrothed, and she had been terrified that the news would get back to Desirée and hurt her baby. He had betrayed her long before her baby had been seduced. Men! They're disgusting! It was all right for them to slip off the straight and narrow path, but not a woman. And using the excuse that they couldn't help themselves because they had a more passionate nature. Humph! Women were just as passionate as men, except they weren't supposed to show it.

"Now, don't you go letting that hateful old woman upset you, baby," Mammy said in a soothing voice. "There ain't no reason for you to—"

Desirée whirled, her black eyes flashing. "I'm not upset, Mammy. I'm just plain mad!" Desirée said angrily, stamping her small foot to emphasize her words. "What right do these people have condemning me? I may have to answer to God for what I've done, but I don't have to answer to them!"

"That's right!" Mammy said, nodding her head so vigorously her turban almost fell off. "It's none of their business!"

As they walked into the marketplace, the aroma of freshly baked French pastries and hot coffee filled the air. Desirée's mouth watered and her stomach grumbled. To save money, they had existed on the plainest and cheapest food, and coffee and sugar weren't cheap. It seemed ages since she'd had some sinfully rich or spicy Creole food. Her rebellious spirit already aroused by her confrontation with Beau's mother, she decided to splurge, regardless of the consequences.

"Mammy, tonight we're going to eat a decent meal for a change," Desirée said in a determined voice. And then her eyes sparkled as she said in an excited voice, "We're going to have gumbo!"

A dreamy look came over Mammy's face. "You mean, with shrimp and oysters and crawfish?"

"Yes, I do." Desirée's mind flashed back to the last time she had eaten gumbo. Her eyes glittered with determination. "And tomatoes, Mammy. Lot and lots of tomatoes!"

"Of course, we're gonna have tomatoes. Why, I've never heard of gumbo without tomatoes."

"That's right, Mammy. That's just exactly what I said. Gumbo isn't gumbo without tomatoes."

Mammy looked at Desirée, wondering why she was acting so strangely.

Desirée and Mammy spent a long while wandering about the market, determined they would have the freshest and best of everything. One by one the pink shrimp, the oysters, still in their greyish shells, and the crayfish that looked and tasted like miniature lobster went into the shopping basket. And then the vegetables were added; onion, bell pepper, celery; velvety green okra pods, garlic, and, at the very end, so that they wouldn't be crushed, six huge red tomatoes. Then, deciding that the gumbo wouldn't be complete without it, Desirée bought a huge loaf of French bread, almost three feet long.

Handing the loaf of bread to Mammy, since Desirée was carrying the shopping basket, Desirée said in an excited voice, "Let's hurry home, Mammy. I can hardly wait to get this on the stove."

They wove their way through the stalls and crowd of shoppers, stepping to the side to avoid bumping into the street vendors who carried their trays of pralines, honey, and rice cakes, and pots of coffee and hot chocolate. As one vendor passed, Desirée looked longingly down at the pastries filled with dark, rich chocolate topped with whipped cream and pecans. Only with supreme effort was she able to fight down the urge to buy some of the delicacies.

As they walked down the *banquette*, Desirée kept urging Mammy to hurry. After a few blocks, the old woman was panting to keep up with her, her black skin glistening with perspiration under the hot afternoon sun.

"You go on ahead, baby. We're almost home, and I'm too old to be running like this," Mammy Lou finally said, knowing full well it was her weight, and not her age, that prevented her from keeping up with

214

Desirée. "I'll be right behind you."

"All right," Desirée said. "I'll get everything started."

As Desirée rushed away, Mammy Lou called, "Now you leave those smelly shrimp for me to peel. It ain't right for you to be smelling like some fishwife."

Desirée laughed, thinking how ridiculous it was for Mammy to be worrying about her ladylike behavior at this point. During the past month, she had been doing many things that no lady would be caught doing: scrubbing floors, beating rugs, boiling laundry, even emptying chamber pots.

At Dauphine Street, she turned and almost collided with three Union soldiers. The men leered at her. Without even thinking, Desirée raised her head proudly, pulled her skirt to the side, and stepped off into the street.

"You see that?" one of the soldiers asked the other two. "Why, she's snubbing us."

"Yeah," another said, spitting a wad of tobacco juice to the *banquette*. "Don't know about you fellas, but I'm insulted."

"That's right," the third said, his eyes glittering with lust, his eyes raking Desirée's body. "And you know what General Butler said. We don't have to put up with these whores insulting us no more. I say we put this slut in her place."

As the three men moved toward her menacingly, fanning out to prevent her escape, Desirée froze in terror, saying in a frantic voice, "Stay away from me."

"Why, you little slut," one of the soldiers said, grabbing Desirée's arm and yanking her back up on the *banquette*. Desirée tripped, and the shopping basket went flying. And then, before she could think or scream, she was thrown against the wall of a building with such force that it knocked the breath

215

from her.

"What's going on here?" a stern, authoritative voice said.

Desirée looked up, but, with the three men crowded around her, she couldn't see who the man was.

One of the soldiers whirled angrily and then froze, seeing the officer towering over him and glaring at him. Then, remembering the general's order, his courage returned, and he said, "This here woman insulted us, major. We were going to teach the little slut a lesson on how to respect us Yankees."

Jason struggled for control, fighting down the urge to smash his fist in the man's face. The behavior of these soldiers sickened and angered him. But what infuriated him even more was that he couldn't do a damned thing to the men, not even reprimand them. They knew what Butler had said, and the officers were helpless, unless the officer was willing to get personally involved.

"I'll take care of this," Jason said in a clipped voice.

"Now, wait a minute, major," the man said in a surly voice. "There are three of us here. She insulted us all. You gonna tell us we can't teach her a lesson?"

"I said, I'll take care of this," Jason answered in carefully measured words.

There was a warning tone in Jason's voice that made the men reconsider. They eyed him warily, noting his wide shoulders, his clenched fists, the determined set of his jaw. And then, seeing the steely glint in his eyes, a shiver of fear ran up their spines. This man is dangerous, they all thought. Regardless of the odds, he would tear them all apart.

"All right, major, if you say so," one of the more prudent soldiers said, his demeanor suddenly respectful. He turned and walked away. Soon he was joined

216

by the other two, casting resentful looks over their shoulders.

Jason turned from watching the men walk away and, seeing Desirée, said in a shocked voice, "Desirée!"

Jason was stunned. He hadn't recognized her from the back. Realizing what could have happened to her terrified him, leaving him weak with fear. And then, remembering the way she had shunned the men, giving them the excuse they were looking for, his anger at her putting herself in such a dangerous position surged to the surface.

Desirée hadn't been able to see past the three men until they walked away. When she saw it was Jason, she had been filled with sheer happiness. She drank in the sight of him, thinking that he looked even more handsome in the blue uniform than he had in the grey, for the color brought out the green flecks in his eyes, making them more startling against his bronzed skin. She was so overjoyed to see him, she wanted to throw herself into his arms.

Catching her by the arm, he shook her, saying angrily, "You crazy little fool! Haven't you heard about the Women's Order? Don't you realize you could have been raped?"

Hurt that Jason hadn't acted glad to see her, Desirée's own anger rose. "Take your hands off me!" she demanded.

Jason's eyes narrowed, seeing the edge of the Confederate flag that Desirée had tucked in her bodice. Holding her firmly against him with his hand, he slipped his slender fingers inside Desirée's bodice and pulled out the flag. Desirée gasped, feeling an electric shock go up her spine at the feel of Jason's fingers on her breast.

"My God, Desirée, it's bad enough that you

217

snubbed those men and risked being raped, but are you trying to get yourself thrown in prison, too?" Jason asked in exasperation.

"Since when is loyalty to your country and hating your enemy a crime?" Desirée spat, jerking her arm from Jason's hand, then added in a venomous voice, "*Major* Steele. I suppose you got *that* as a reward for your spying."

Jason winced, both at Desirée's referral to his promotion and her reminder that he was her enemy.

For a minute, they stared at each other, Desirée glaring her defiance and Jason fighting his frustration at not being able to reason with her. Then Desirée turned, picked up her shopping basket, and started putting her precious groceries back in it. Jason bent to help her.

"I don't need your help!" she snapped.

"For God's sake, Desirée. Stop being so damned mule-headed!" Jason retorted, picking up one of the bell peppers and tossing it into the basket.

And then they both reached for the same tomato. Their hands brushed, and they both felt the electric shock caused by the brief contact. Their eyes rose and locked, both remembering that day—and that night. For a long minute, they stared at each other.

Then Desirée remembered that Jason had been in New Orleans all this time and had made no effort to see her. And here she was, gazing into his eyes like some moonstruck idiot and making a damned fool of herself. She jerked her eyes away and looked down at the tomato in Jason's hand. Seeing that it was half crushed, sudden tears came to her eyes, tears that had nothing to do with the tomato.

She snatched the tomato from Jason's hand, saying, "Now look what you damned Yankees have done. You've ruined my gumbo!" She whirled and ran down the street, choking back sobs.

Jason watched as Desirée fled, fighting the urge to go after her and throttle her. He knew that she had remembered, knew that she had wanted him just as much as he had wanted her, despite what he had done that last night they were together. And why in hell had she gotten so upset over one damned tomato?

He turned and then came to an abrupt halt, seeing the most ferocious-looking black woman he'd ever seen standing before him. It wasn't the woman's size that made her look so formidable, for although she was big in girth, her head hardly came to the middle of his chest. No, it was the flashing black eyes and the angry expression on her face that made her look so fierce.

Then, noticing the long loaf of bread she held up in the air with one hand, Jason's lips twitched with amusement. He looked her directly in the eye and said, "Are you going to hit me with that?"

When Mammy Lou had seen the three men surrounding Desirée, she had rushed to her defense as rapidly as her squatty legs would carry her, which wasn't very fast. She didn't arrive on the scene until Jason had turned and recognized Desirée. Mammy had known instantly who he was, for there was only one Union officer who could possibly know her baby's name. She knew this was the man who had abducted Desirée, and she glared at him angrily, not because he had made love to her, but because of the position he had put Desirée in. Because of this man, her baby had been turned away by her family and snubbed by the other women, forced to struggle just to survive. But Mammy had completely forgotten about the loaf of bread, and now, realizing it was a weak weapon, she felt ridiculous.

Sheepishly lowering the loaf, Mammy said, "No,

sir, I ain't gonna hit you." Then, remembering what had almost happened to Desirée, her black eyes flashed again. "But I'd sure thrash those other devils if they'd hurt my baby."

Jason's dark eyebrows rose. Her baby? Yes, that explained why the woman had looked like a lioness guarding her cub. This must be Desirée's mammy.

"Are you Desirée's mammy?"

"Yes, sir, I sure am. I'm Mammy Lou." Her dark eyes narrowed. "And I know who you are, too. You're that Yankee who took her off into those swamps."

Was that why she was so angry with him? Had Desirée told her mammy what had happened between them? Did the old woman think he had taken advantage of Desirée? He expected to see the loaf of bread come flying at him any minute. But Jason wasn't concerned about what Mammy Lou thought of him. His concern was Desirée's safety.

"Then maybe you can reason with her, Mammy Lou," Jason said. "You saw what almost happened here. After what that damn fool Butler pulled, it isn't safe for women to be on the streets."

Much of Mammy's anger fled at Jason's words. She realized he was truly concerned about Desirée. Besides, any Yankee that called Butler a damned fool couldn't be all bad.

"I'll try to, but that li'l gal has got a stubborn streak in her a mile wide."

Jason knew how stubborn Desirée was. Her obstinacy infuriated him at times, and yet it was a part of her, and for that reason, he even loved that quality. He smiled, a warm look coming in his eyes, and Mammy's sharp eyes didn't miss it either.

"Then ask her father to talk to her," Jason said. "Surely after he hears what almost happened here, he'll lay down the law to her."

"Her papa's dead," Mammy Lou said in a bitter voice. "He was killed in those riots when he was burning his warehouses."

"Dead?" Jason asked in a shocked voice. He glanced back in the direction Desirée had fled, then said in a quiet voice, "Is she taking her father's death hard?"

"Not as hard as her brother's," Mammy Lou answered, fresh tears stinging her eyes. "He's dead, too. Was killed at Shiloh."

"Oh, my God, no," Jason groaned. My poor Desirée, he thought. And undoubtedly, she hated the Yankees even more now—all Yankees. Once again, he felt that gulf widening between them. And then a sudden thought came to him. "Then what's she doing here in New Orleans? Why didn't she go to her uncle's plantation?"

"She did!" Mammy spat, her black eyes flashing angrily with remembrance. "But that hateful aunt of hers wouldn't let her stay. She said it's because my baby disgraced herself, but that ain't true. She hates my baby. I don't know why, but she does."

Jason knew instantly what disgrace Mammy was talking about. "How did that news leak out?" Jason asked angrily.

Mammy wasn't about to tell Jason Desirée had blurted the news herself. "I don't know, but it did."

"Then Desirée is staying here in New Orleans all alone with no one to protect her?" Jason asked, his fear for her even stronger.

"She's *not* alone," Mammy said indignantly. "She's got me and Moses. We protect her."

"Is this Moses a big man? Big enough to protect her from trash like that?" Jason asked, nodding his head in the direction of the soldiers had taken.

Moses was a big man, but he was old and had lost

most of his muscle. But Mammy knew that he'd fight to the death to protect Desirée. "Yes, sir."

"And he's loyal to Desirée?"

"Yes, sir, he sure is!"

"All right, Mammy. See if you can't get her to stay in the house, and if not, don't let her go anywhere without you or Moses going along."

Mammy Lou was pleased that Jason had included her. There weren't very many men who would give a woman, especially an old, black woman, credit for being able to protect anyone. A seedling of respect for this man crept into Mammy.

Jason hesitated, then said, "Is she doing all right Mammy? Does she need anything? Money?"

Mammy knew that Desirée was too proud to accept financial help from anyone. "No, sir. We've got plenty of money."

Jason was vastly relieved. He knew the financial position of many of the Creoles. Thank God, Desirée's father had been wise enough not to convert everything to Confederate currency.

"If there is anything I can do to help, anything you need, you let me know. You can find me at the customs house. Just ask for Major Steele."

"Yes, sir, I will," Mammy promised.

Jason wheeled, took a step, then turned back to Mammy, saying, "I didn't want to put her in that position, Mammy. I never wanted to hurt her."

Mammy Lou looked deep into Jason's eyes and saw the pain and regret there. She nodded wordlessly.

As Jason walked away, Mammy Lou watched him until he was out of sight, a thoughtful look on her face. Then she nodded her head, muttering, "Yes, sir, that Yankee's in love with my baby."

* * *

A few days later, Desirée was in the salon when she heard Mammy Lou screaming at the top of her lungs, "You get out of here. You can't come in this house!"

Desirée ran into the foyer just in time to see a Union officer shoving Mammy Lou aside, saying, "Get out of my way, you damned nigger. Who do you think you're talking to?"

Mammy Lou's big body went rigid. She called other blacks nigger when she was angry with them or wanted to insult them, but she had never been called one, at least not to her face.

"What's going on here?" Desirée demanded, furious at the way the officer had treated Mammy Lou.

The officer turned, then said, "Who are you?"

"I'm Desirée McAllister and this is my house you're trespassing in."

"Your home?" The officer scoffed, saying, "You mean your father's or husband's."

"No, *my* home. My father is dead and I'm not married."

"Then why haven't you registered or signed the loyalty oath? This house isn't registered to anyone."

Desirée's blood ran cold. She realized that she was in danger of having her home confiscated. She cursed herself for her stubborness. She didn't want to lose her home. It was all she had left. "I didn't realize I was supposed to," she lied. "We just returned to New Orleans a few days ago, and we've been busy setting up housekeeping. I'll see to it today."

The officer shot her a suspicious look, then turned and walked into the salon.

"What do you think you're doing?" Desirée asked indignantly, following him.

The man walked around the room, eyeing it critically. Then he turned, saying, "I'm looking, Miss McAllister. If this house suits me, I intend to move into it. It's much more convenient to headquarters than my present quarters."

"But you can't do that!" Desirée blurted.

"Can't I?"

Desirée paled under the man's cold blue eyes. He could, she realized, and there was no one to stop him.

The colonel smiled, a smile that never reached his eyes. Then he turned and continued his browsing. When he picked up a picture of Thad, sitting on a small table, and looked at it, Desirée ran to him and snatched it out of his hands, saying, "Take your hands off that, you pig!"

The colonel smiled smugly, then he said, "Did you hear that, men? The lady called me a pig!"

Desirée whirled, for the first time seeing the three enlisted men who had followed their superior officer into the house, and then into the salon. Seeing them leering and grinning at her, Desirée's heart raced with fear.

"Yep, Colonel Anders, we heard what the *lady* said," one of the soldiers answered, sneering at Desirée.

"Search the house!" Colonel Anders barked.

After the enlisted men had left, Desirée paced the floor nervously. Mammy Lou stood in one corner of the room, wringing her hands and wishing Moses hadn't left the grounds. Colonel Anders sat in an overstuffed chair, his legs casually crossed, and he peered over his steepled hands, a smug smile on his face.

Desirée studied him from the corner of her eye. He was of medium height and middle aged, his sandy hair receding at the temples, the paunch on his stomach straining at his unform coat. But it was his eyes that disturbed Desirée. They were cold and hard and—evil, Desirée thought. That's why he frightens me so badly. He's evil!

A few minutes later, the soldier returned, grinning even wider.

"Look what we found, colonel," one of the soldiers said, handing the officer a handful of Confederate buttons.

Colonel Anders rose, saying to the soldiers, "Wait for me outside."

The men scowled in disappointment. Desirée realized that they had hoped to participate in the rape the colonel was planning—if that was what he was planning. Her heart raced in fear.

"Get out, I said!" Colonel Anders thundered.

"Yes, sir!" the men said in unison, rushing from the room.

Colonel Anders turned to Mammy, saying, "You, too!"

Mammy crossed her arms over her big bosom, saying, "No, sir! I ain't going nowhere. I'm gonna stay right here with my baby."

Desirée saw the murderous look in the colonel's eyes. "No, Mammy. You wait outside. If I need you, I'll call."

Mammy Lou refused to budge. "Please, Mammy," Desirée pleaded.

Shooting Colonel Anders a hot, angry look, Mammy Lou left the room, closing the door behind her softly. Desirée noticed that the door didn't click and knew that Mammy was probably watching through the crack.

Colonel Anders turned, smiling that same cold smile, saying, "Now, Desirée, you and I are going to have a little talk."

"Talk? About what?"

"About how you're going to be my mistress. My *willing* mistress."

Desirée couldn't believe her ears. "You're insane!"

"No, my dear, I'm not insane. I could rape you right now and no one would say a word. You insulted me. Even my men heard you. But you're a beautiful woman, and I know my lust would only be temporarily sated."

His cold eyes raked her, and Desirée shivered, feeling as if a snake had crawled over her.

"No," Colonel Anders continued, "I've decided to make you my mistress, and you'll cooperate. Because if you don't, I'll have you thrown into prison."

"Prison?" Desirée asked in a shocked voice. "But you can't do that."

"Yes, I can," Colonel Anders answered with supreme confidence. "You're a Confederate sympathizer. I have the evidence right here in my hand. And there's another piece of evidence," he said, pointing to Thad's picture. "He's wearing a Confederate uniform."

"But you can't send me to prison for that," Desirée objected. "You can only confiscate my home."

"No, my dear, you're wrong. What happens to the sympathizer is very much left up to the arresting officer. And I happen to feel very strongly about traitors, just as my friend, General Butler, does. Besides, I strongly suspect you deliberately haven't registered and signed the loyalty oath, and *that* is punishable by imprisonment."

Desirée sank to the chair, muttering, "*Mon Dieu.*"

"It really won't be too bad, my dear," Colonel Anders said in a voice that made Desirée's skin crawl. "You'll be able to stay in your own home, and I can be generous, providing you're willing to perform to my satisfaction."

"*Non!*" Desirée screamed, slamming to her feet. "I won't do it!"

The colonel's cold blue eyes glittered dangerously. "Don't make any rash decisions," he warned. "You haven't seen our prisons. They're infested with rats and lice and fever. People die in them all the time. Certainly, your virtue isn't worth your life." He smiled coldly, saying, "I'll even be generous enough to give you a few days to consider."

Desirée bit her lips to keep from screaming. But she needed that time, she reminded herself. Then maybe, she could escape, leave the city.

As if reading her mind, Colonel Anders said, "And don't try to sneak out of the city. "I'll have the sentires watching the roads on the lookout for you. And don't be so foolish as to ask your friends here in the city to hide you. You wouldn't want your friends going to prison for harboring a fugitive, would you?"

Desirée felt sick. The room spun crazily. Once again, she sank weakly to the chair.

The colonel smiled arrogantly, then strutted to the door. Opening it, he looked back at Desirée, saying, "I'll be back in two days for your decision."

After Desirée heard the front door slam, she looked up and saw Mammy Lou watching her, a worried look on her face. "You heard?" Desirée asked.

"I heard," Mammy replied in a grim voice.

Desirée rose and paced the room, thinking. She wouldn't let that man touch her. She couldn't stand it. It was bad enough that he lusted after her body, but there was something else about him, something that terrified her.

Despite what he said, she could still try and sneak out of the city. She knew back roads the Yankees didn't even know existed. But where would she go? She couldn't go to Terre Doux. The swamps perhaps? But she knew nothing of surviving in the swamps, and neither did Mammy or Moses. Besides, at their age, they'd probably die during the first cold, damp winter.

Then she'd just go to prison, she decided. But what would happen to her black family if she did that? They'd be declared contraband of war, and Moses would be put to work cleaning out the filthy canals. Why, he'd never survive that work at his age. As it was, he could hardly walk because of his arthritis. And Mammy Lou? What did they do with the old women? And Tassy? She shuddered, fearing she knew just how they'd use her. No, she wouldn't go to prison. Her black family needed her.

Then maybe she would have to be his mistress. At least, that way she could stay in her own house and keep her darkies. He had said he would be generous if she could satisfy him. Desirée shivered, refusing to contemplate what that might entail.

"But I can't do it!" Desirée cried silently. "I can't! I'd die if that reptile touched me!"

She turned, saying to Mammy in an anguished voice, "*Mon Dieu*, Mammy Lou! What am I going to do?"

Chapter 11

While Desirée didn't know what she was going to do about Colonel Anders, Mammy Lou knew exactly what *she* was going to do. To her way of thinking, the only one who could protect Desirée from a Union officer was another Union officer, and she knew just who that particular Yankee was.

But Mammy Lou couldn't leave the house without arousing Desirée's suspicions, so she convinced the girl she needed a nap and then she would be able to think much clearer, once she was rested. When Desirée protested, saying she couldn't possibly sleep, Mammy Lou suggested one of her tisanes.

After Mammy Lou had tucked Desirée in for her nap, she went downstairs and pulled Benjie to the side.

The boy stood wide-eyed while Mammy Lou said, "Moses and I are gonna be gone for awhile. Miss Desirée is upstairs, asleep. Now, you stay here and watch over her. After Moses and I leave, you lock that gate, and you don't let nobody in. You hear? Nobody!"

"I hear," the boy answered solemnly.

Then Mammy Lou walked to the carriage house. Seeing Moses sitting in front of it and whittling on a stick, she said, "Moses, you hitch up that old horse to that wagon. We've got important business to attend to."

Moses frowned, saying, "Business? What are you talking about, old woman?"

"I'll tell you about it on the way."

As Moses drove the rickety old wagon down the street, Mammy Lou told him what had happened. Moses was furious, but he didn't think the solution to the problem was another Yankee.

"What makes you think that Yankee is gonna help Miss Desirée?" Moses asked. "From what I've seen, they're all a bunch of white trash."

"Not Major Steele. He's different."

Moses grunted, then grumbled all the way to the customs house.

When the horses pulled up in front of the Union headquarters, they stopped, and Mammy asked Moses, "You coming in with me?"

"No, sir, I ain't. I'm gonna sit right here and see none of these no'count Yankees steals my horse," Moses said, suspiciously watching the Yankees walking all around them.

Mammy Lou climbed from the wagon. With her size, her exit was not the most graceful in the world, and several of the passing Yankees guffawed. Mammy Lou glared at them and then, with all the dignity she could muster, walked into the building.

After asking for directions several times, Mammy Lou finally found Jason's office. Squaring her chunky shoulders, she opened the door and stepped in. The waiting room was crowded with Creoles sitting on long wooden benches against the walls, the Frenchmen looking at her with surprised faces. Ignoring their looks, she waddled up to the desk and said to the lieutenant sitting behind it, "I've got important

230

business."

The lieutenant glanced up, then scowled, saying, "Look, if you're one of those runaways looking for a handout, you've got the wrong office. Now, you go down to—"

"I ain't one of those no'count runaways," Mammy interjected in an indignant voice. "I'm here to see Major Steele."

"Major Steele?" the lieutenant asked in a surprised voice. "What do you want to see him about?"

"That ain't none of your business!"

A snicker came from behind the big black woman, and hearing it, the lieutenant's face turned red with anger.

"Well, you can't see him today," the lieutenant said in a brisk voice. "He's busy. He's still got to see all of these people. Come back tomorrow."

"No, sir, I ain't coming back tomorrow. I'll just wait."

Mammy Lou turned, walked to one of the benches, and sat down, wedging her big body between two of the Creoles.

"Now see here," the lieutenant said in a stern voice. "You can't wait in here. Niggers—" The officer came to an abrupt halt, seeing Mammy Lou's black eyes flashing angrily. Dammit, he thought, what had Major Steele told him to call these people? Darkies or black folks? Hell, how was he supposed to know? He'd never even seen one until he came to New Orleans. "Black folks aren't allowed in here. You go stand out in the hall."

"I ain't going nowhere. I'm gonna sit right here," Mammy Lou said stubbornly, folding her arms over her bosom and lifting her head with determination.

For a minute, the lieutenant considered forcing the woman out of the room but, realizing that Mammy

Lou outweighed him by at least a hundred pounds, decided against it. Frustrated, he glared at her and then, worried that the Creoles might be offended by her sitting with them, he glanced around. But instead of looking shocked, the Creoles' eyes were twinkling with amusement. The lieutenant knew they were enjoying seeing the woman thwart him, but what he couldn't figure out was how they understood what was going on if they didn't speak English, as they claimed. He had the uncomfortable feeling that he was being made a fool of by both the Creoles and the big black woman. His anger rose.

He slammed to his feet, saying, "Now you get out of here! Major Steele is too busy to fool with the likes of you."

"I told you, I ain't going nowhere!" Mammy retorted, eyes flashing.

"I'll have you thrown out!"

Mammy Lou's eyes narrowed. "I wouldn't do that if I were you," she warned. "Major Steele is gonna be mighty mad if you don't let me talk to him. I told you. My business is important."

The lieutenant glared at Mammy Lou. Mammy Lou glared back. "Oh, all right!" the lieutenant said in an exasperated voice, throwing his pencil on the desk. "Who shall I say wants to see him?"

"Mammy Lou."

"Mammy Lou who?"

"Just Mammy Lou! He knows who I am."

The lieutenant walked angrily to the inner door, rapped on it a few times, and opened it.

Jason, sitting behind his desk, looked up, then said in an irritated voice, "Yes, Lieutenant Benton?"

"Excuse me, Major Steele, but there's a woman out here who insists upon seeing you."

Jason frowned. "A woman?"

232

"Yes, sir. She says her name is Mammy Lou and she has important business."

Jason shot to his feet so fast, Lieutenant Benton almost jumped out of his skin. "Did you say Mammy Lou?"

"Yes, sir."

"Show her in."

"Now?" Lieutenant Benton asked in disbelief.

"Yes, now!" Jason barked.

"But—but what about him?" Lieutenant Benton asked, nodding to the Creole sitting in front of Jason's desk and watching curiously.

Jason picked up his pen, bent, and quickly scrawled his name at the bottom of a piece of paper on his desk. Then he walked around the desk, shoved the paper into the dapper Frenchman's hands, and practically lifted him from the chair.

"*Merci, merci,*" the surprised Creole said as he beat a hasty retreat from the room.

Jason turned to the lieutenant saying, "Now. Show her in."

Jason waited impatiently for Mammy Lou, a worried frown crossing his wide brow. Had something happened to Desirée? Mammy Lou had said it was important. When Mammy Lou walked into his office and Jason saw the troubled look on her face, his apprehension only grew.

The door had barely closed behind Lieutenant Benton when Jason asked, "Did something happen to Desirée?"

"Yes, sir, something happened, Major Steele. Something bad. My baby's got big troubles."

Then Mammy told Jason everything that had transpired. As she talked, Jason got angrier and angrier. When she finally finished, Mammy Lou shivered at the murderous look in his eyes.

"Do you know the name of this man?" Jason asked.

"Yes, sir. He said his name is Colonel Anders." Mammy watched as Jason's face paled. "What's the matter, Major Steele? Do you know that man?"

"Yes, I know him," Jason said in an ominous voice. "Or rather, I know of him. I've heard some things about him. Ugly things."

"What things?"

"That he's a sadist."

Mammy frowned, then asked, "What does that mean?"

"It means he's not like normal men. He can't gain satisfaction without inflicting pain on others, particularly women." Jason gave Mammy a penetrating look, saying, "Do you understand what I'm saying, Mammy Lou?"

Mammy Lou's face had turned ashen. "I understand. I knew that man was bad. I saw the devil in his soul."

Jason's anger had turned to stark fear. The thought of Desirée in the hands of a man like Colonel Anders made his blood run cold. He walked to the window and stared out of it thoughtfully, then turned to Mammy Lou, saying, "There's a problem here, Mammy Lou. I can't just walk in and demand the colonel leave Desirée alone. The man outranks me and he's a personal friend of General Butler. Even if I put her under my protection, make her my mistress, I wouldn't be able to stop him from sending her to prison, not if she deliberately refused to sign the loyalty oath."

Mammy Lou was terrified. "You mean, you can't help my baby?"

"There's only one way I can protect Desirée, Mammy Lou. But I'm not too sure she'll agree."

"What's that?"

"Marry her."

Jason watched as the words sank in, then continued: "If Desirée married me, she could claim she didn't think the loyalty oath applied to her, since she knew she was going to marry a Union officer soon. She might receive a reprimand, but I don't think Butler would send her to prison, not the wife of a Union officer and particularly not now, when many of the officers are already up in arms over his Women's Order. No, I don't think even Butler would be that stupid. And as for their confiscating her home, once we're married all of Desirée's property will be in my name."

Mammy Lou was shocked when Jason had talked of marriage. She had expected him to simply step in and tell Colonel Anders to leave Desirée alone. She had never realized how complex the problem was.

As Jason talked, Mammy Lou studied him thoughtfully. She knew he loved her baby. She also suspected Desirée had some tender feelings for him. But to Mammy Lou, that wasn't enough. Marriage was a serious step, a step that would affect Desirée's entire future. She knew nothing of this man, only that he was a Yankee officer and a gentleman. That Desirée might care for him didn't mean much to Mammy Lou either. She didn't trust Desirée's judgement of men, not after Beau. No, she wanted to decide on Jason's character for herself.

She looked Jason over, seeing a handsome, splendid physical specimen of manhood. But Mammy Lou wasn't interested in the surface features. She wanted to see the inner man, the real man. By this time, Jason had stopped talking. Mammy looked deep into his eyes, eyes that met hers levelly, and searched his soul. What she saw was a man of strength, a powerful spirit that would never falter, never waver. But Mammy Lou saw something else, something that impressed her even more. Here was a man of sensitivity, a man of rare insight.

Jason was aware he was being judged and, for the first time in his life, he was afraid he wouldn't pass the test. He knew if Mammy decided she disapproved of him and sided against him, he'd never be able to convince Desirée to marry him. And knowing what would happen then, he felt weak with fear for her.

Pleased with what she saw, Mammy Lou grinned and said, "I reckon that's what you're gonna have to do, major. Marry my baby."

Jason let out a silent sigh of relief, then said, "I'm afraid it's not going to be that simple, Mammy. Desirée has reasons to hate me. First, I'm a Yankee, her enemy. Second, I've hurt her by disgracing her in her people's eyes and robbing her of a marriage to the man she loves. And marrying me will only hurt her more. Then she won't only be disgraced but hated by her people for marrying a Yankee, for betraying her country. She isn't going to like being forced into marriage, particularly to me, the very man who's responsible for the position she's in. You know how proud she is and how stubborn. She may very well refuse, regardless of the consequences."

"But my baby's *got* to marry you!" Mammy Lou cried. "If she don't, she'll go to prison. Or that devil man will get her."

"I know, Mammy. Just pray that, for once, she'll listen to reason."

Desirée never missed Mammy Lou and Moses that afternoon. After her nap, she stayed in her room and paced for hours, trying to find a solution to her predicament. She still had not found one that evening, and she was still pacing, this time in the salon.

Hearing a knock on the front door, she froze, fearing it might be Colonel Anders returning to tell her he had changed his mind and wanted an immediate decision.

"I'll get it," Mammy Lou called from the hallway.

When Desirée saw the hated blue uniform, she went weak with fear. And then, realizing it was Jason and not Colonel Anders, she asked in a surprised voice, "Jason? What are you doing here?"

"We're going to have a talk, Desirée," Jason replied in a firm voice. "I know about Colonel Anders."

"But how?" Desirée asked in bewilderment.

"I told him," Mammy Lou said, stepping into the room.

Desirée had no idea Mammy Lou knew Jason, but she realized that she should have suspected something when Mammy let him in the house without any resistance. And Mammy Lou had gone to him and told him the whole humiliating story? She glared at Mammy resentfully.

"I'm sorry, honey lamb, but I couldn't let you go to prison. And I couldn't let that devil man get hold of you, either. So I did the only thing I could think of. I went to Major Steele for help."

Desirée could accept Mammy Lou's interference. She knew she loved her and had only done it out of concern. But Jason? He didn't care anything about her. She didn't want his help. She didn't want anything from him.

"That's all right, Mammy. I understand," Desirée said. Then she turned to Jason, saying in an icy voice, "Thank you, Major Steele, but I don't need your help."

"Yes, you do, Desirée. Whether you want to admit

237

it or not, you do."

Desirée dark eyes flashed. "I said, I don't want your help! Now get out!"

"No, Desirée, I'm not leaving," Jason said in a firm voice. "For once, you're going to listen to reason."

Desirée saw the steely look in Jason's eyes, the rigid set of his jaw. She glanced at Mammy Lou and saw the same determined look. "Oh, all right! Say what you've got to say—then get out!"

Jason turned to Mammy, saying, "Would you like to stay?"

Mammy Lou grinned, then said, "No, sir. I think you can handle it."

Jason watched as Mammy Lou walked from the room, wishing that he felt as confident as she did of the outcome. He turned to Desirée, then said, "I'll come right to the point, Desirée. I want you to marry me."

Desirée was shocked speechless.

"It's the only way I can protect you from Colonel Anders. He wouldn't dare accuse the wife of a Union officer of southern sympathies."

Desirée had recovered from her shock. No mention of love, she thought bitterly. All he was offering was his protection. Did he feel he owed it to her for putting her in this position? No, she couldn't accept that. It would be humiliating to have a man marry her just to pay off a debt of honor.

"No, Jason. I won't marry you. I've decided to accept Colonel Anders's proposition."

"Desirée, you don't know what you're saying! Colonel Anders is a cruel man, a sadist."

Desirée stood mute, glaring at him defiantly.

"I'm not making this up, Desirée. Anders's perversions aren't common knowledge, but I have a friend

238

in the provost marshal's office who confided to me that they've had complaints from some of the madams about Anders abusing their girls. He'll do things to you, Desirée," Jason said in an ominous voice. "He'll hurt you so bad, you'll wish you were dead."

Desirée had sensed all along that Anders would sexually abuse her, but her pride ruled her reason. "I don't care! I still won't marry you."

Fear for Desirée made Jason lose control. He crossed the distance between them in two swift strides, caught her by her shoulders, and jerked her to him roughly. "Dammit, you're going to listen to me!"

"Take your hands off me!" Desirée spat, struggling to get away from him.

"No, I won't!" Jason snapped, holding her firmly. "I'll shake some sense into you if I have to!" Then his eyes narrowed as a sudden thought occurred to him. "Do you think Colonel Anders is going to let you keep Mammy Lou and Moses? He won't, you know. He hates darkies. He can't stand to be near them. He'll get rid of them the first thing."

"You mean he'd sell them?" Desirée asked in a shocked voice.

"No, he can't sell them, only confiscate them. He'll turn them over to the army as contraband."

Suddenly, Desirée knew she was trapped. The only reason she had ever considered Colonel Anders's proposition was to protect her black family. There wasn't any way out, except the one Jason was offering her. If he only cared for her, at least a little. She had to know.

"Why are you doing this Jason? Do you feel you owe me something?"

Jason knew Desirée was on the verge of agreeing to marry him. And he knew why. To keep Mammy Lou

239

and her other darkies from being turned over to the army. While he admired her loyalty, it was a bitter pill to swallow. Marrying Desirée had always been his dream, but he hadn't wanted her to come to him like this, forced by circumstances and a sense of duty to her people. He had wanted her to come to him of her own free will, because she loved him as much as he loved her.

Jason was a proud man, himself. Knowing that she would have chosen any man over him, even a total stranger, if he would have allowed her to keep her darkies, hurt and hurt deeply. He would never admit that he loved her now. He couldn't. It would make him look like a fool.

But Jason knew Desirée was proud, too. If he told her he was only offering marriage because he felt it was the honorable thing to do, she might still refuse. And he couldn't let her place herself in that danger.

He chose his words very carefully. "I'll admit that's part of it, Desirée. I'm partly responsible for what's happened to you. What kind of a man would I be if I turned my back on you now? But that's not the only reason I'm asking you to marry me. You're a beautiful woman. I've always wanted you. From the minute I saw you, I wanted you. And if you'll be honest with yourself, you'll admit that you aren't averse to my lovemaking. I think the physical attraction was mutual between us from the very beginning."

Desirée flushed, knowing what he said was true. Even now, her body was making its own selfish demands. But Jason *had* admitted to some feelings for her. She supposed that should be some consolation. But that wasn't what she had wanted to hear. Even though she was still clinging desperately to her own heart, she had hoped he might feel more for her than physical attraction. Well, she decided, if he could offer marriage without love, then she could accept on the same terms. She could at least salvage a part of her pride.

"All right, Jason, I'll marry you," Desirée said in a brittle voice. She raised her chin, her dark eyes glittering with determination. "But I'll *never* love you."

Why? Jason asked himself. Because she hated him that much? Or because she still loved Beau and always would? Was he doomed to spend the rest of his life with the woman he loved and never be loved in return? It would be sheer hell, and yet, what choice did he have?

Jason released her and stepped back. He took a deep breath and said, "I understand, Desirée."

Was he glad that she'd said she'd never love him? Desirée wondered, feeling even more hurt. Did he want it that way? No emotional entanglements? Well, he didn't have to worry about her. She'd keep a firm grip on her rebellious heart. She'd never let herself fall in love with him. Never!

Fifteen minutes later Jason was riding through the moon-dappled streets of New Orleans, deeply troubled and brooding.

Well, it seemed that he had been right about his and Desirée's destinies being linked. She would be his wife. But how the gods of fate must be laughing at him now. Yes, they had promised that she would be his to love and cherish, but they had never promised she would love him in return.

He had to hand it to them, Jason thought bitterly. Those gods had arranged all the circumstances very neatly—but not resisted the urge to play with them before they finally linked them: throwing them in each other's paths, then separating them by putting obstacles between them, then throwing them together again, moving them around like pawns on a chessboard for their own amusement.

And was their perverse game finished now? Or did those damned gods of fate still intend to interfere in their lives?

Chapter 12

Jason and Desirée were married in a quiet ceremony the following afternoon. The ceremony took place in the rectory of St. Louis Cathedral, since the church was still barred. The witnesses were the rectory housekeeper and gardener. Throughout the entire ceremony, Desirée was aware of their disapproving scowls. She wondered whether they disapproved because she was marrying a Yankee or because she was still in mourning, or both. The ceremony was in French, and Desirée was surprised when Jason spoke his vows and she could actually understand him, his Cajun accent not nearly as pronounced as it had been that day by the bayou long ago.

They walked home from the ceremony, just as they had walked to the church, since carriages were still scarce in New Orleans. Desirée would have enjoyed the walk if it had not been for the looks her Creole neighbors gave her when they saw her with Jason. She had become accustomed to being snubbed, but these were fierce glares. Desirée wondered just how much more hateful those looks would become when they realized she had actually married this Yankee.

Eh Bien! To hell with them! Desirée thought angrily. I don't care what they think. They turned their backs on me when I needed them. I could have starved to death, been raped, or sent to prison, and none of them would have helped me. At least Jason didn't throw me to the wolves. Well, I'll be damned if I'll let them intimidate me or look down on Jason, either.

Desirée raised her head proudly, her eyes flashing their defiance as she tightened her hold on Jason's arm and moved closer to him. Jason glanced down at her in surprise, for he, too, had been aware of the glares and had expected Desirée to be ashamed to be seen in his company. Pleased by her unexpected action, he smiled down at her, thinking that there might be some hope for their marriage, after all.

When they reached the courtyard of Desirée's house, Jason said, "I'm sorry, Desirée. I know it looks insensitive to me to leave my new bride, but I really do need to get back to headquarters."

Desirée knew he was lying. She knew where he was going. To confront Colonel Anders with the news of their marriage. "I know where you're going, Jason. To talk to Colonel Anders."

Jason frowned, then said, "I didn't mean to lie to you. I just didn't want you to worry. I thought I would go and see him right away. Under no circumstances do I want Colonel Anders coming back here and upsetting you."

Desirée didn't want the colonel coming back either, and she hoped to God she'd never have to lay eyes on him again. "You'll be back as soon as it's over?"

Jason heard the apprehension in her voice. "Yes, I'll come right back," he assured her. He bent and kissed her cheek. His fingers cupped her chin as he looked down at her and smiled. "Now don't worry."

"I won't," Desirée replied. She watched as he strode to his horse and mounted. How could she help but worry? She wasn't nearly as confident as Jason that the colonel was going to let her off that easily.

244

And knowing that Colonel Anders was a good friend of General Butler didn't help her apprehension.

Desirée had paced the floor half the night, worrying about this meeting between Jason and Colonel Anders. She had also done some serious soul searching. She had finally admitted to herself that it was she who had placed herself in the predicament she was in, and not Jason, although he blamed himself for a part of it. But Jason's part had been circumstances beyond his control. No, *she* was the one who had stupidly blurted out the story of her abduction that placed her in disgrace, and it was *she* who had refused to register and sign the loyalty oath, her stubborness endangering not only her, but her darkies, too. She had even realized that she couldn't blame Jason for not loving her. Love was an emotion that couldn't be given on demand, or forced either.

And marriage without love wasn't all that bad, Desirée had decided. Her Creole ancestors had always arranged marriages, alliances, not unions based on love. Even her own mother would have had such a marriage, if she had not rebelled and married Desirée's American father instead. At least she and Jason were physically attracted to each other. Oh, it would mean the end of her dream, the dream for the perfect marriage with the man she loved and the man who loved her in return. But she had learned in the last few months that dreams and realities were a world apart.

In the end, Desirée had decided that she was grateful to Jason for coming to her aid and putting her under his protection. She knew that she would always hate the Yankees and remain true to her southern heritage, but she had decided to stop fighting this particular Yankee. And while she was determined she would *never* allow herself to fall in love with him, for her pride would never allow that, she would try to be a good wife.

* * *

Two hours later, Jason was riding back to Desirée's house, a deep scowl on his face. The meeting with Colonel Anders had not gone well. When Jason told the man that he had married Desirée, Anders had been furious. The colonel had threatened to follow through with the charges, vowing that he'd do everything in his power to see Desirée imprisoned. It had been all Jason could do to hold down his anger and keep from killing the man with his bare hands, before he retaliated with his own threats. Colonel Anders had been shocked to learn that anyone in the Union Army knew of his well-guarded perversities and had quickly backed down—after Jason had threatened to expose him.

Jason had left the confrontation with a bad taste in his mouth, for blackmail didn't sit easily with him, that and the knowledge that he had made an enemy for life.

Desirée was waiting in the courtyard when he returned. He knew by her pale face and anxious expression that she had been worrying. "It's over, Desirée. The colonel won't be making any charges," he assured her softly.

"There were no problems?"

"No," Jason lied smoothly. He didn't see any reason for Desirée to know the truth. If she did, she might ask more questions, and Jason didn't want her to know the ugly details.

"Oh, Jason," Desirée cried softly, impulsively throwing herself in his arms and hugging him. "I'm so relieved."

For the second time that day, Jason was surprised by Desirée's action. A little glimmer of hope was born

246

deep inside him.

Desirée raised her head saying, "Thank you, Jason. Thank you for helping me."

Gratitude? Jason thought, as the glimmer died a quick death. But he didn't want that. He wanted Desirée's love. "You're welcome," he answered in a carefully controlled voice, hoping desperately that he hadn't let his disappointment show.

"Are you going anyplace else?" Desirée asked. "Do you have to go back to headquarters?"

"No. I'm free for the rest of the day."

"Then bring your horse in. I'll show you to the carriage house."

As Jason led his horse down the path at the side of the courtyard to the carriage house, he noticed a young black girl wandering aimlessly around the courtyard, a vacant look on her face.

"That's Tassy," Desirée informed him. "I'd introduce you, but I don't think she'd understand. You see, she's—she isn't quite right."

Desirée was relieved to see the compassion in Jason's eyes. Then, as they passed Tassy and Jason made a point of smiling at her, Desirée appreciated his effort but feared it was lost on Tassy.

When they entered the stable that occupied one side of the carriage house, Moses and Benjie walked up to them from the shadows of the building. "Jason," Desirée said, "this is Moses, my father's coachman and groom. And this is Benjie, his *negrillon*. He rode at the back of the carriage and opened and closed the door for my father."

Jason gave Benjie a friendly smile. The boy hung back behind Desirée, eyeing Jason's uniform fearfully. Jason felt a surge of anger, not at the boy, but at war itself, a human weakness that taught children fear and hatred before they were even old enough to

247

understand what they feared and what they hated.

He turned his attention to Moses, shocked by what he saw. This was the man that Mammy had said could protect Desirée? Why, he was an old man, even older than Mammy.

"This is Major Steele, my new husband," Desirée said.

Moses grunted in acknowledgement, his gaze sweeping over Jason distrustfully. And then, as his eyes rose to meet Jason's, Jason saw something else: a warning look that told Jason if he hurt Desirée in any way, Jason would have to answer to him. Yes, Jason thought, Mammy Lou was right. The man was totally loyal to Desirée. He may be old and frail, but he'd fight to the death to protect her.

"Moses will rub down your horse and see that he's stabled, Jason," Desirée said.

Jason handed the reins to Moses, looked him directly in the eye, and said, "Would you mind? I'd appreciate it."

Moses couldn't believe his ears. Sometimes, Miss Desirée would ask him to do things that weren't his usual duties, particularly since the other darkies had run away. But he had never been *asked* by a white man to do something—just told to do it. And to be told that it would be appreciated was a totally new concept to Moses. Was the man funning him? Moses wondered suspiciously.

Once again, he looked Jason in the eye, but he couldn't see any sign of ridicule or amusement there. Moses felt the stirring of something, something that he didn't recognize as self-esteem, and with it was born a seedling of respect for this man. But that didn't mean the old man was ready to let down his guard—yet.

"Yes, sir," he replied in a noncommittal tone of

voice. "I'll do it for you."

Mammy cooked and served dinner that night. When she had gone back into the kitchen, Jason asked Desirée, "Mammy does the cooking now?"

"No, we share it. I usually cook the evening meal, but Mammy insisted she do it tonight, since this is my wedding day."

"You?"

"Yes, me," Desirée answered, enjoying the look of astonishment on his face.

Jason frowned, then said, "I can pick up some kitchen help for you tomorrow."

From where, Desirée wondered. Would he bring home one of the confiscated or runaway slaves that the Union Army considered contraband of war? As far as Desirée was concerned they were stolen property. And even if they weren't, she wanted nothing from the Yankees. "No, I'd rather you didn't. I've discovered that I enjoy cooking."

Jason wondered. His own mother had loved to cook, but she had never had any servants, much less been raised with them to do everything for her. "You're sure?" he asked in a doubtful voice.

"I'm sure," Desirée said firmly.

After dinner, they walked to the salon. Jason glanced around him, noticing the absence of the usual knicknacks on the tables and on the mantle above the fireplace. He looked closer, seeing the discolored areas on the walls where paintings had once hung, and the bare spots in the corners where furniture had once sat, the carpeting still dented. He knew, then, that Mammy Lou had lied to him about Desirée's financial position, and he knew why. To protect Desirée's fierce pride.

He was amazed that Desirée had managed to care for not just herself but four other people over the past

249

months with no ready cash. And now he knew why she had even considered being Colonel Anders's mistress and had not elected to go to prison instead. She hadn't done it to simply protect an investment but to protect the slaves themselves. His admiration for her grew.

A picture sitting on one of the tables caught his eye. He walked over to it and picked it up.

"I won't put it away," Desirée said in a determined voice. "I'll sign the loyalty oath, but that's the only picture of Thad I have. I don't care if he *does* have on a Confederate uniform."

"I wouldn't ask you to," Jason replied in a tight voice.

Desirée heard the hurt in Jason's voice and realized that she had been overly defensive. "I'm sorry, Jason. It's just that—"

"Desirée," Jason interjected, "I'm glad you're willing to sign the oath. I'm afraid I would have insisted on that for your own protection. But I don't intend to tell you how to feel or what to think, just because I'm your husband. I know how you feel about the South."

"Thank you, Jason. And I'll try—try to accept your feelings, too."

Jason laughed softly, saying, "Well, I'm glad that's settled. I'd hate to come home and fight the war every night."

Desirée smiled, then frowned as she noticed that Jason was running his finger under his tight coat collar. "I'm sorry, Jason. You must be burning up in that hot coat. Why don't you take it off?"

Desirée watched as Jason untied the buff sash and unbuttoned the double-breasted uniform jacket. Laying them over a chair, he said, "That's better, but I think it would be even cooler in the courtyard."

"Yes, it is hot in here," Desirée said.

They walked out on the galley and down the stairs to the courtyard. Jason cocked his head, listening. "Is that a fountain I hear?"

"Yes, it's over here," Desirée answered, leading the way to the back of the courtyard.

Jason sat on the brick bench that surrounded the fountain and leaned back, looking up at the branches of the oak tree above them. "This tree must be over a hundred years old."

Desirée, sitting beside him and trailing her fingers in the cool water in the fountain, looked up, then cried softly, "Look! Lightning! That's why it's been so hot and sultry. There's a storm coming."

She looked back down and saw Jason watching her. The warm look in his eyes told her, even before he moved toward her, that he was going to kiss her. And Desirée was anxious for it. It seemed a lifetime since that night outside of New Orleans when he had last made love to her.

His lips were soft and warm as his tongue traced the outlines of her mouth before flicking at the corners and sending shivers of delight through Desirée. She moaned, catching his broad shoulders with her hands. Jason slipped his arms around her, pulling her half over his lap as his tongue slipped inside her mouth, stroking sensuously, then swirling as he deepened the kiss, a soul-searing kiss that seemed to last a lifetime.

Jason's heart pounded in his ears as his mouth moved from Desirée's and brushed across the long, slender column of her throat. Sliding the gown from her shoulder, he teased her collarbone with his tongue, then left a trail of soft kisses down to the warm valley between her breasts. There, he dallied, nuzzling the soft mounds, drinking in her essence, his head spinning from the intoxicating scent and taste of her.

251

He raised his head, his eyes dark with passion, saying in a roughened voice, "Where? Where's your room?"

"The second floor—to the left," Desirée muttered, her senses reeling dizzily.

Jason lifted her in his arms and rose, carrying her across the courtyard in swift, impatient steps. Above them, the moon played hide and seek behind the dark clouds that the approaching storm was scuttling across the sky.

He walked up one flight, then down the gallery and through the open French doors. Desirée lay with her arms around his broad shoulders, her head buried in the warm crook of his neck, her mouth against the thudding pulse beat there.

Jason stopped and looked about the candlelit room, seeing the turned down sheet on the bed. Then, spying the lacy nightgown lying across the end of it, he smiled, thinking there would be none of that foolishness tonight. Then, as Desirée nibbled on his ear and her small tongue darted inside, he sucked in his breath and tightened his grip on her.

He walked to the bed and sat her on her feet beside it, his fingers trembling with excitement as he undressed her. And then he stood back, drinking in her beauty with his eyes, muttering, "God, you're even more beautiful than I remembered."

Desirée stood proudly before him, reveling in Jason's warm admiration and then thrilling when she saw his look turn to hot, naked desire. But as he lifted his hand to touch her breast, she stepped back, saying, "No! Not until you're undressed, too."

Jason stripped impatiently, tossing his shirt to the side, throwing one boot one way, the other, in another direction. As he slipped off his pants and then stood, Desirée's breath caught at the sight of him, tall, bronzed, magnificently male and totally aroused.

Her legs turned to rubber. She swayed, whispering urgently, "Jason."

Jason caught her in his powerful arms as they tumbled to the bed, both gasping at the feel of their naked, heated skin coming together. Their kisses were deep and drugging one minute, fierce and feverish the next, while their hands hungrily explored, rediscovering each other's secrets. Desirée's hand circled his rigid heat, and Jason groaned at the feel of her fingers stroking sensuously, igniting the fire that had smoldered in him to a flaming torch. He dropped his head, his tongue swirling about the soft, silken flesh of her breasts before his teeth gently raked the throbbing peak. Desirée moaned, arching her back to him, and then gasped as he took the nipple in his mouth, his tongue dancing and flicking, sending sparks racing to her loins.

"Now, Jason," Desirée pleaded in a ragged voice. "Come to me now."

But Jason ignored her plea as he slid down her body. He wanted to taste more of her before he buried himself in that warm, silken sheath his body hungered for.

Desirée quivered with anticipation of his mouth there, and then, as his lips supped at her sweet moisture and his tongue worked its magic, stroking, swirling, then flicking like a fiery dart, Desirée felt as if every nerve was shattering as her body convulsed with pleasure.

Jason rose and slipped into her velvety warmth, filling her slowly, deeply, completely. Desirée's eyes flew open, and their eyes locked. For a long minute, they stared deeply into each other's eyes as they savored the exquisite feel of their bodies joined, seemingly throbbing in unison, as if their heartbeat were one. Then, unable to bear the tension any longer, they moved simultaneously, the electric feel of that movement taking their breaths away. Jason's mouth closed over hers, their tongues dancing as they moved in that erotic dance as old as time itself. Together, they strove, bodies straining, fevered skin against fevered skin, heart pounding against heart. Steadily, they climbed up those thundering heights before the universe shattered around them, her cry of ecstasy blending with his groan of pleasure as he gave himself up to her, his seed a searing jet deep inside her.

When it was over, Jason held her, tenderly kissing her temple, her brow. He ached with a need more powerful than the one he had just assuaged, a need that threatened to burst from the depths of his soul—the need to tell her how much he loved her. He buried his mouth in the soft crook of her throat, fighting it down, struggling to suppress it.

Desirée fingered his soft hair, then said softly, "Look, Jason. It's raining."

Jason lifted his head and looked over at the open French doors. The rain was blowing in, and in a flash of lightning, he saw a puddle of water had already formed on the floor. He rolled from Desirée and off the bed, saying, "I'll close the doors."

"No!" Desirée cried softly, restraining him with a hand on his arm. "Don't close them. I love to watch storms."

She climbed from the bed and walked to the open doors, looking out over the galley. Jason came to stand behind her, slipping his arms around her waist. For a long time, they stood in the open doorway, watching the wind lashing the trees and the flashes of lightning against the dark, rolling clouds. Around them, the wind billowed the curtains on the doors and blew the rain over their sweat-slick bodies.

Finally, Jason bent and kissed her shoulder softly, saying in a husky voice, "You're shivering. Come back to bed and let me warm you."

Desirée could feel his rigid heat pressing and pulsating against her back. A tremor of excitement ran through her. She turned in the circle of his arms, and Jason swept her up and carried her back to bed.

Jason fulfilled his promise in a long, achingly sweet, exquisitely tender loving that brought tears to Desirée's eyes and a lump in her throat. When it was over, Desirée knew the true meaning of being cherished.

Desirée wrinkled her nose and sleepily swiped at the annoying wisp of hair that was tickling it. The tickling continued, and she heard a deep male voice saying, "Wake up, sleepy head."

She opened her eyes to see Jason gazing down at her, a long lock of her chestnut hair dangling from his hand. Desirée looked up into those mysterious, misty-green eyes, with their shamefully thick dark lashes, and her heart did crazy flip-flops in her chest and a warm curl formed deep in her belly.

"Good morning, *cherie*," Jason said softly, kissing her brow.

What a wonderful way to wake up, Desirée thought dreamily. She reached up and pushed a dark lock of hair from his brow, muttering, "Good morning."

She glanced over and saw the sun shining in through the open French doors. The smell of freshly washed earth filled the room as a soft breeze fluttered the curtains. "What time do you have to leave for headquarters?" she asked.

Jason bent and softly kissed her nose, then her mouth before answering, "Not for another hour or two."

There was a husky timbre in Jason's voice that sent Desirée's heart racing.

Jason gazed down at Desirée, thinking she looked absolutely delightful with her lips swollen from his passionate kisses the night before and her long hair spread out around her and across one breast. He stared at the rosy nipple peaking through her hair and watched with fascination as it grew and hardened under his gaze, seemingly beckoning to him. Unable to refuse such a sensuous invitation, he bent his head and kissed it before rolling it around his tongue.

"Jason," Desirée gasped, "do we have time—" She gasped again as Jason's warm tongue swirled and his lips gently nipped. "Have time for—"

Jason raised his head and smiled at her, a smile that promised heaven. "We do, *cherie*," he answered in a roughened voice.

Later, Desirée lay in bed, still basking in that warm afterglow and watching Jason as he shaved, then dressed. She was a little shocked at his total lack of embarrassment as he paraded around before her, stark naked—and delighted—for it gave her the opportunity to feast her eyes on his magnificent male physique. She marveled that every muscle, every tendon seemed to be perfection itself, his bronzed skin a smooth, sleek covering that rippled across his broad back as he slid his razor down his jaw, then up his throat. Her eyes drifted down his slim waist and past his lean, taut buttocks to those long muscular legs, with their sprinkling of dark hair. And then, as he turned, wiping the soap from his face with a towel, she lowered her eyes, peeking through her lashes, admiring him as he walked across the room with that feline grace that was so much a part of him. And to think that this perfection of manhood was her husband, every wonderful inch of him. A thrill of pride ran through her.

As Jason dressed, he said, "I've been meaning to ask you something, Desirée. I was wondering if you'd mind if I brought my aide-de-camp to live here with us. It's customary for the men to live with the officers they serve and, if the officer is married, in their homes. He could live at the barracks, but that would be a bit awkward, since he's responsible for caring for my uniforms and personal belongings. But, if you prefer, that can be arranged."

Desirée didn't like the idea of a stranger in the house, particularly a Yankee. But she could hardly refuse, knowing that if hadn't been for Jason, she could well be in the streets, herself, or worse, in prison. "No, I don't mind," she lied gracefully. "Since the other darkies ran, we have plenty of room here."

"He won't be in the way," Jason assured her. "He'll leave with me in the mornings and return in the evenings, and I give him Sundays off to do with as he wishes. You'll hardly know he's around."

Jason walked to the bed and sat down on the edge of it. Leaning over, he softly kissed Desirée on the mouth, saying, "Why don't you go back to sleep for a few hours?" He grinned. "You didn't get much sleep last night."

"Maybe I will," Desirée mumbled, lost in the magic of those misty-green eyes glittering with amusement and that engaging grin that left her feeling weak.

Jason kissed her again, this time more warmly, then rose and walked from the room. *Mon Dieu*, Desirée thought, her senses swimming, if this is what marriage is going to be like, I'm going to love it.

But, as she walked from her bedroom an hour later,

she was forced to face reality again, and that ugly reality was her financial situation. She wished that she hadn't splurged on their dinner last night, particularly the French pastries, but she had felt that their wedding dinner should be something special. Now, she doubted that she had enough money left to buy something for tonight. She should have asked Jason for money before he left, but she had hated to do that, particularly so soon after they'd been married. She'd die of embarrassment if he knew how destitute she was.

Desirée walked into the library, opened the desk drawer, and picked up the money box. Then she walked into the kitchen, saying, "Good morning, Mammy."

Mammy turned, saying, "Morning, honey lamb."

Desirée sat down at the table and opened the money box. Her eyes widened in surprise. "Where did these come from?" she asked, pulling out the neatly folded bills lying in it.

"I reckon Massa Steele put it in there. He asked me this morning where you keep the money for the household expenses."

Desirée noticed that Mammy had called Jason "massa," instead of major, but she was too surprised at what the old woman had told her to comment on it. She unfolded the bills and counted them, then said in a shocked voice, *Sacre Dieu!* There's over a thousand dollars here!"

Mammy's eyes widened. She didn't know just how much a thousand was, but she knew it was much more than a hundred. "Lawsy, that should keep us eating for a long time."

"Yes, it certainly will," Desirée answered absently, preoccupied with her thoughts. Had Jason guessed that she was penniless? And had he known that she

258

hated to ask him for money? Was this his way of saving her from being embarrassed? She knew the answers. Tears of gratitude stung her eyes.

Desirée was in the salon late that afternoon when she heard the front door opening. Knowing it was Jason, she walked to the doorway and looked out, seeing him standing there with an enlisted man at his side. That must be his aide, Desirée thought, quickly scrutinizing the man. Shorter than Jason, he was a big, beefy man, his face ruddy colored, his nose sitting more to one side of his face than the other, as if it had been broken at one time. Thick reddish-blond eyebrows almost covered his blue eyes, eyes that were glancing around suspiciously.

Seeing Desirée, Jason smiled, saying, "Desirée, I'd like to introduce my aide, Sergeant Brian O'Malley."

Desirée smiled politely, saying, "How do you do, sergeant."

The sergeant swept his blue forage cap from his head, revealing a thick head of curly hair the same color as his eyebrows. "Pleased to meet you, ma'am," he said in a tight voice with a thick Irish brogue. Then he stood stiffly, not a hint of a smile on his face, staring straight ahead.

Desirée turned to Jason, saying, "Dinner isn't ready yet. Why don't you take Sergeant O'Malley up to the third floor and let him choose which room he'd prefer?"

"All right," Jason replied, then said to the sergeant, "This way, O'Malley."

Sergeant O'Malley picked up the footlocker lying to one side and, as he passed Desirée, nodded curtly to her and said in a clipped voice, "Ma'am."

Desirée watched as Jason and O'Malley walked up the stairs, the sergeant's back ramrod straight. She wondered whether the man resented Jason's bringing him to live with the enemy, or if the man had taken an instant dislike to her personally.

259

Later, when Jason walked into the dining room, Desirée asked, "Isn't Sergeant O'Malley coming, too?"

"No, he said he'd have his meals in his room."

"Have I done something to offend him?" Desirée asked.

Jason chuckled, then said, "No, *cherie*. That's just his way. At least it has been for as long as I've known him."

"And how long has that been?"

"Just since we've been in New Orleans."

"And he's always like that, so stiff, so unfriendly?"

"Well, I'll admit he has loosened up a bit lately. Maybe he's finally getting over his resentment at being assigned to me. I'm sure he was disappointed when he wasn't assigned to a field commander, where he could get into the fighting and see some action."

"You're not a field commander?" Desirée asked in surprise.

"No. Because I speak French and know the customs of the people here in New Orleans, I've been assigned as a liaison officer, working between the army and the Creoles. My job is to listen to the Creoles' complaints about the military government, solve them if I can, soothe their ruffled feathers if I can't, by explaining why the army is doing what they do, in hopes of gaining the Creoles' cooperation with the reconstruction efforts."

"It doesn't sound like an easy job," Desirée said.

"It wouldn't be easy under any circumstances, but with Butler's high-handed tactics, it's been an almost impossible job."

"Then you don't approve of Butler's proclamations?" Desirée asked in astonishment.

"No, personally, I don't. Some of the other officers agree with me. Like me, they have trouble thinking of women, children, and old men as being the enemy.

However, just as many of Butler's officers agree with him. They feel the South should be punished, and New Orleans should serve as an example. But it doesn't matter what any of our personal opinions are, we're in the army, and we're expected to obey."

Jason pulled Desirée's chair back from the table, and she sat down. While Jason was seating himself, she looked down at her plate thoughtfully. She had never considered how soldiers felt about what they were ordered to do, that they might have doubts or reservations. Apparently, waging war wasn't all black and white but had a lot of grey areas in it.

The sound of Jason's chuckling broke her musing. "What's so humorous?" she asked.

"Talking about obeying reminded me of Sergeant O'Malley. That may have been part of the reason he acted so brisk this afternoon. You see, he wasn't too happy when I told him we were moving our lodgings."

"Why? Does he object to living with the enemy?"

"No, I don't think it was that as much as it was my announcement that we'd be riding to headquarters from now on instead of walking. He told me that he and horses didn't get along, that everytime he had mounted a horse, the damned thing had thrown him. He suggested that I ride and he walk. I told him that it would look ridiculous for me to ride, with my aide walking beside me. Besides, it would defeat my purpose for riding: to save time. I ordered him to get over to the quartermaster and have him issue him a horse. He obeyed, but he wasn't happy about it."

"And did the horse throw him?" Desirée asked curiously.

"No. Army mounts are well trained. But the horse knew that O'Malley didn't know how to handle him and took advantage of it. Everytime I turned around, O'Malley's horse was taking off in the wrong direction. And then, I'd have to wait while the sergeant and the horse went round and round in the street, until O'Malley finally got him headed in the right direction. By the time we got here, O'Malley's temper was more than a little frayed at the edges."

Desirée laughed.

As they walked into the salon after eating, Desirée remarked, "I wondered why your Cajun accent wasn't as noticeable during the wedding ceremony. I guess your talking to the Creoles every day must be responsible for that."

"Then I have improved?" Jason asked in a pleased voice.

"Oh, yes," Desirée answered, then laughed. "I could actually understand you."

That night, as they were undressing for bed, Jason said, "I was wondering if maybe you could help me with my French? Give me a few lessons, so to speak. Point out my mistakes."

"*Oui*, if you like."

A glimmer came to Jason's eyes. "I have an idea. Why don't we limit our conversation to French in the bedroom?"

Desirée nodded in agreement.

When Jason began his lovemaking, he muttered French endearments and love words between his kisses. Then he bent and whispered something in her ear.

Desirée's eyes flew open in shock. "*Mon Dieu*, Jason! That's indecent!" she objected, a thrill of excitement running through her nonetheless.

"*Non, cherie. Francais*," Jason reminded her.

Then he began to whisper in French just what he was going to do to her, his words sometimes very romantic and sometimes shockingly explicit. Desirée found the words tantalizing, especially since Jason

262

was sensuously performing the acts as he whispered descriptions of them, stoking her fires until they were a blazing inferno.

When the torrid, soul-shattering lovemaking was over, Desirée was still dazed from Jason's erotic, exciting attack on her senses when she became vaguely aware of him asking her a question. Had his accent improved? She finally realized what he had asked. *Sacre Dieu!* How would she know, with all that other going on?

"I think we'd better limit our French to the dining room," she answered in breathless English.

Jason chuckled softly against her throat. Desirée had the strangest feeling that *he* had been the one giving the lesson tonight, and he had done it deliberately. He had just taught her that words could sometimes be as sexually stimulating as actions.

True to Jason's prediction, Desirée didn't even know Sergeant O'Malley was in the house, since he continued to take his meals in his room. Desirée never knew whether his self-imposed isolation was due to resentment or his way of showing respect for her privacy.

However, while Sergeant O'Malley didn't make his presence known in the house, he certainly did so in the carriage house, where his and Jason's horses were stabled. Moses resented both the Irishman's intrusion into what the old man considered his domain, and the fact that Jason hadn't let him take over the care of his horses, something that Moses had been trained for his entire life. To make matters even worse, as the days passed, it became obvious to Moses that the Irishman didn't know any more about caring for horses than he did riding one. So Moses was forced to sit back and watch O'Malley mishandle the only decent horseflesh he'd seen since the Confederates had pulled out of New Orleans. To add insult to injury, the Yankee sergeant totally ignored Moses, acting as if he didn't even know the old man existed.

Finally, goaded by his resentment and pity for the horses under O'Malley's care, Moses couldn't take it any longer. One day, when he was watching O'Malley currying one of the horses, he walked up to the Yankee, saying in a hard voice, "Is that the way you comb your hair? Backwards?"

O'Malley whirled to face the old man, snapping, "What in the hell are you talking about?"

"I'm talking about the way you're brushing that horse, mister Yankee man. You ain't doing it right. Here, give me that brush," Moses said, grabbing the brush. "I'll show you."

O'Malley couldn't believe the old man's audacity, to talk to him, a white man, like that. He stared at him in disbelief and then said in an angry voice, "Who do you think you are?" And he snatched the brush back.

"I'll tell you who I am. I'm the groom around here, that's who I am! I know horses, and you don't know nothing about them. Feeding and watering them while they're hot," he said in a disgusted voice. "Humph! It's a wonder they ain't dead."

O'Malley was furious. "These horses ain't any of your business. One is army issue and the other belongs to the major, and I take care of them, myself. Now, get out of my way, you damned nigger," he said angrily, pushing Moses back.

Moses felt the insult like a slap in the face. His glare turned so fierce that O'Malley wondered for a minute if the old man was going to take a swing at him.

When he was finished, O'Malley went to Jason and complained that Moses was interfering with his duties and told Jason what had happened. Jason felt the same as Moses, and yet, he knew he couldn't ask his aide to step aside and let the old groom take over his job. Caring for his personal equipment, including his horse, was his aide's job, and he knew O'Malley would resent the inference that he wasn't capable of the job—even if he wasn't. Jason agreed to have a talk with Moses.

Unfortunately, the talk only served to make Moses more resentful, although Jason admitted to the old man that he knew Moses was much more capable than O'Malley, then carefully explained that, despite that, it was still the sergeant's job. Jason left the stable knowing that he had alienated the old groom, something that he had vowed he wouldn't do. If at all possible, Jason wanted to get along with Desirée's darkies, especially since he knew how fond she was of them. What disgusted him even more was he hated to see his horse going steadily downhill because of O'Malley. But he knew if he suggested to the Irishman that he let the old man teach him how to properly care for horses, the sergeant would only get his hackles up again. How in the hell did he get himself into this mess?

Jason didn't find the solution to his problem until two days later. That afternoon, he returned from headquarters driving an old carriage pulled by a pair of matched greys.

Desirée looked at the horses and carriage in disbelief, saying, "Where did you find them?"

"One of the Creoles I was talking to today told me he had managed to hide them from the Confederate Army," Jason answered. "He wanted to sell them, since food was more important to him than transportation at the present time. He asked me if I knew someone who would give him a good price for them."

Since her struggle to survive, Desirée had become very conscious of financial matters herself. "But Jason, we don't need them," she objected. "Every place I go is within walking distance, and you have your horses to take you back and forth to headquarters."

"Desirée, I have no intention of your going back and forth to church or the market in the cold and rain this winter. Nor do I relish the idea of going to headquarters in it." Jason turned to Moses, who had been standing off to one side. "Moses, these horses and this carriage belong to the family, and therefore, they will be your responsibility. The carriage is old and in poor condition. It will need some patching, a paint job, and the springs are bad, but I'm sure you can handle all that."

Moses had been eyeing the horses and carriage like a child eyes candy. He knew prime horseflesh when he saw it, even if the animals were a little skinny and their coats dull from lack of proper diet. He couldn't hide his excitement as he said, "Yes, sir, I sure can. You give this old man a few days, and I'll have that carriage looking brand spanking new. And those horses, too."

Moses kept his word. Within a few days, he had the carriage repainted, the broken springs replaced with new ones, and the patches in the roof repaired. Even the tears in the upholstery were neatly mended. And the change in the horses was even more remarkable, so much so, that even O'Malley, who had no eye for horseflesh, noticed. The sergeant began to compare his horses to the old groom's and had to admit that his animals looked sad. O'Malley was also aware of the praise Jason had been giving the old man for the good job he was doing. Not wanting to be outdone by a slave that he considered much beneath him, O'Malley

266

started observing everything Moses did and copied him. Within two weeks, his horses were as sleek skinned and healthy looking as the old man's.

Then O'Malley's horse developed a sore on its haunch that refused to heal, no matter what he did to it. Stubbornly refusing to ask the old man how to treat it, O'Malley made a special trip to the army stables and asked the grooms there how they would treat it. But still, the sore refused to heal.

One day, O'Malley stood in the stable and stared in frustration at the red, angry area on the horse's haunch, an area that ruined the animal's otherwise healthy appearance. Aware of Moses, who stood behind him, shaking his head in disgust, he whirled and spat, "All right! I give up! How do you cure the damned thing, I'm asking you."

Moses grinned smugly, then turned and walked to the cabinet where he kept his medicines for the horses. Taking out a jar of ointment, he handed it to O'Malley, saying, "Put this on it in the morning and at night."

O'Malley looked down at the jar suspiciously, saying, "What is it?"

"Never mind what's in it," Moses replied gruffly. "That's my secret medicine, and I ain't telling nobody what's in it. Now, do you want it or not?"

O'Malley fought a hard battle with himself, then finally snapped, "I'll take it." And then, in a effort to regain part of his pride, said, "The least I can do is try it. Couldn't make it any worse than it is."

Within a week, the sore was healed, without a hint of a scar, much to O'Malley's amazement.

From then on, a truce existed in the carriage house between the two men. They were a far cry from being friends, for hardly a word passed between the two as they performed their duties. But much of the resentment had been buried.

The rest of the summer passed uneventfully. Desirée found marriage to Jason much to her liking. She loved the long nights in his arms as he made passionate love to her—the french doors flung open and the moonlight flooding in—and the lazy Sunday afternoons, with the doors closed and the sunlight filtering in through the wooden slats. In the daytime, she found herself missing his company and laughter and waited impatiently for his return each evening. She wondered that the house she had always loved could seem so empty, so lonely without the man who had come into her life so suddenly and unexpectedly.

And Desirée wasn't the only person in the household who came under the spell of Jason's magnetic personality. Catching Benjie in the courtyard one afternoon, Jason had offered to give the boy a few pointers on how to shoot his slingshot. Half fearfully and half distrustfully, the boy handed over his most prized possession to the hated Yankee. By the time the lesson was over, Benjie had buried his fear and mistrust. The next afternoon, he met Jason at the courtyard gate and begged him to let him lead Jason's horse to the carriage house. Much to Benjie's surprise and delight, Jason suggested he ride it instead. From then on, Benjie idolized Jason, following him around like a worshipping puppy.

Even Tassy received her share of Jason's attention. He made a point of stopping and talking to her every afternoon in the courtyard, smiling and pointing out something to her, a pretty flower, a bird's nest, a spiderweb. And though Tassy's only response was a lifeless, "yes, sir," something deep inside her stirred.

But it was the relationship that developed between Jason and Mammy that was the most remarkable. At first, the old woman had looked upon Jason as a knight in shining armor, the man who had rescued her baby from disaster. But as time passed, she found herself liking Jason, not only for the way he treated Desirée but for the way he treated her, too. She enjoyed his teasing even more, as she was able to tease him back, something that she would have never dreamed of doing with another white man. But what impressed her the most was the way he sought her counsel on things concerning Desirée.

The only thing Jason and Mammy disagreed upon was her calling him "massa." Jason insisted that he wasn't her master, that he didn't own her, that he preferred to be called Jason.

Mammy responded by saying, "No, sir, I can't call you by your first name. That ain't proper."

"Then call me Major Steele."

"No, sir, I won't," Mammy replied firmly. "You're taking care of us now. That means you're our massa."

Then Mammy Lou turned and waddled from the room, and Jason knew that the matter had been settled once and for all. No matter how he felt about it, he was stuck with "massa." Mammy had spoken.

When Jason noticed that Desirée never wore any jewelry, he searched out her jewelry box. He wasn't surprised when he found it empty, knowing that was probably the first thing she sold to feed herself and her black family. He went to Mammy and asked her if she knew whether Desirée had sold her jewelry or pawned it.

"Yes, sir, I sure do know," Mammy answered. "She took them to that pawn shop down on Canal Street."

"Can you give a description of the different pieces?"

Mammy knew what Jason was going to do. Tears of gratitude glittered in her dark eyes. "Yes, massa, I sure can. And I thank you from the bottom of my heart. Most of those pieces were family jewels, come from Desirée's mama and grandma. It broke her heart to have to give them up."

"Don't thank me yet, Mammy. I don't know if I'll be able to get them all back," Jason warned. "They may have been sold already."

"If you can get just one piece back, it'll make my baby happy."

"I'll see what I can do," Jason answered. For a minute, he stood, a thoughtful expression on his face, then said, "But please don't say anything to Desirée. I don't think now would be a good time to give them back to her. You know how proud she is. How hard she tried to hide the state of her finances from me."

"Yes, massa. I understand."

Jason found all but one of the jewels Mammy had listed for him and bought them back. He hid them away, concerned not so much in hurting Desirée's pride but fearing that she would accept them with gratitude or, worse yet, think that he was trying to buy her love, and in so doing, scorn him.

He decided to wait for the right opportunity to give them to her. Someday, when she would be able to accept them as the gift they were meant to be—a token of his love—he'd present them to her.

But Jason wondered bleakly if that day would ever come, the day when he wouldn't feel exposed and vulnerable by placing his heart at Desirée's feet; the day when he would no longer fear her throwing back his love in his face.

Chapter 13

Desirée dipped the brush into the soapy water in the pail beside her and bent, furiously scrubbing the foyer floor and muttering very unladylike curses under her breath. *Dieu*! How she hated housework, particularly this back-breaking chore, as she inched her way across the floor on her hands and knees and swirled the brush over the wood planking.

The door at her back opened, flooding the hallway in bright sunlight, but before she could turn and see who had the audacity to walk over her freshly scrubbed floor, Jason roared, "What in the hell do you think you're doing?"

Desirée sat back on her heels, her dark eyes spitting sparks. "What does it look like I'm doing?" she flared back. "I'm scrubbing this damned floor!" She angrily tossed the brush into the bucket, sending suds flying everywhere. Placing her hands on her hips, she glared at the booted feet standing just inside the doorway. "And look at you! You're standing on my clean floor and it isn't even dry yet. Now, you get out of here and come in the back door."

Jason ignored her demand and walked across the foyer in swift, angry strides. He bent and pulled her to her feet, saying, "Now, tell me why you're scrubbing

271

this floor. Where's Tassy?"

Desirée knew that Jason had no idea she had been doing the housework, that he assumed Tassy did it. And Desirée had purposely not corrected that assumption. She hadn't wanted Jason to know the truth. Why, of all days, did he have to come home early and catch her at it?

"Desirée," Jason said in a threatening voice. "Answer me."

"Oh, Jason," Desirée said with an exasperated sigh. "Tassy can't—" She stopped in mid-sentence, for the first time realizing that Sergeant O'Malley had been standing behind Jason.

Desirée flushed. It was bad enough that Jason had caught her in such an undignified position, but for the Irishman to have seen her on her hands and knees, with her rump stuck up in the air, was downright embarrassing. And then, to have him witnessing the shouting match between Jason and herself was even more humiliating.

The little spat between the major and his beautiful wife had surprised Sergeant O'Malley, but what had shocked him was the way Desirée had snapped back at Jason. He had always thought that southern women were meek, mild-mannered women who never raised their voices, and certainly never used the word, damned. And there for a minute, Desirée had looked like she was about to tear her husband to shreds. But now, realizing that she was embarrassed by his hearing her outburst, O'Malley, too, flushed a deep red.

"Good afternoon, ma'am," O'Malley muttered, snatching his forage cap off his head and twisting it in his big hands. Then, nodding curtly, he said, "Excuse me," before backing out the door, and beating a hasty retreat.

Jason frowned as he watched O'Malley disappear

272

down the stairs. He turned to Desirée, saying, "I'm sorry, Desirée. I didn't mean to yell at you. But, why are *you* scrubbing this floor? Is Tassy ill or something?"

"No, Tassy isn't ill," Desirée admitted. "But she can't do housework."

"And why not?"

"Oh, Jason, you don't understand. She's willing enough, but—well, she just can't. I'll put her to work and come back hours later to find her still scrubbing the same spot or dusting the same table. She just doesn't understand when the job is done. It's easier and faster for me to do it myself."

"Are you telling me you've been doing all the housework?" Jason asked.

"No, Mammy helps. But she can't do any of the heavier work. And she certainly can't get down on her hands and knees. Not at her age."

"Why didn't you tell me this when I asked you about getting kitchen help?"

Was he going to offer to bring home some of the confiscated slaves for house servants again? Well, she wanted no part of them! "Because I don't need any help. I'm perfectly capable of performing a few little household chores. There's nothing wrong with my back."

She bent to pick up the bucket, but Jason beat her to it. He glared down at her, saying in a firm voice, "You may be capable, but you're not going to do it anymore. I won't have my wife doing housecleaning or laundry. There's no need for it. Not with servants so easy to come by."

"I told you, I don't want any servants!"

"Why not?" Jason demanded. "Are you going to stand there and tell me you enjoy this work?" He scoffed. "Well, I won't believe it."

For the life of her, Desirée couldn't think of a good excuse for not wanting house servants. She glared at him in angry frustration.

Jason put the bucket down and framed Desirée's face with his hands. His eyes dared her to lie to him. "Now, tell me why you're so determined not to have any new servants."

Desirée tried to jerk her head away, but Jason held it in a firm grip, a determined look on his face. She chewed her lower lip, then spat, "Because I won't have stolen property in my house!"

"Stolen property? What are you talking about?"

"I'm talking about the slaves the army confiscated. They're stolen property!"

Jason chuckled, then said, "I don't have any intention of getting one of them."

"Then where do you plan on getting a servant?" Desirée asked in surprise.

"Buy one," Jason replied calmly. "The Creoles I talk to are always complaining about not being able to feed the slaves they have, with things as they are now. I'm sure I could buy one at a very reasonable price."

Desirée frowned, saying, "I still don't think I want a new servant. She may not fit in. My darkies have been with me for as long as I can remember. They're like family. And bringing a complete stranger—"

"Desirée," Jasons interjected, "I have no intention of you doing this housework. I'm going to either buy a slave from one of the Creoles or hire some domestic help. Now, which is it going to be?"

Hire help? Desirée thought. No, that wouldn't work. Undoubtedly, she'd look down on her darkies because they were slaves, perhaps even try to boss them around. And she knew that Mammy and Moses would never tolerate that. No, another slave would fit in better.

"Well?" Jason asked in a demanding voice.

"Buy one then," Desirée said, still reluctant.

Jason nodded, then picked up the bucket and carried it to the open door. Removing the brush, he tossed the dirty water over the galley and sat the bucket down beside the door. He turned, saying, "Now, don't let me catch you doing anything like that again."

"But I didn't even finish scrubbing the floor," Desirée objected.

"The dirt will still be there tomorrow when the new help comes," Jason replied, closing the door firmly behind him. Then, seeing Desirée's frown, he said, "Stop worrying, Desirée. I'm sure she'll fit in fine."

The next morning, when Jason left for headquarters, he took the matched greys and carriage with him, and when he returned that afternoon, the new slave was sitting by his side. Desirée watched as the big woman climbed down from the carriage, thinking that she certainly looked strong enough. But she still worried that the stranger might not fit in with her close-knit household.

In the days that followed, Desirée learned that her fears had been for nothing. Mattie, the new slave, not only performed her duties with an ease and speed that absolutely amazed Desirée, but she got along well with everyone. She seemed to understand and accept without questioning that Mammy and Moses held a place of respect in the household. But it was her treatment of Tassy that pleased Desirée. Seeing Mattie's patience with the girl, Desirée sighed in relief and relaxed, thoroughly enjoying her free time.

About two weeks after Mattie had arrived, Jason again approached Desirée about getting a cook. They were standing in the kitchen at the time, Jason watching Desirée as she kneaded the bread on the table before her.

She glanced up at his question, a surprised expression on her face. Then she frowned, saying, "No, Jason, I really don't want a cook. I'll admit that I hated cleaning, but I *do* enjoy cooking and my garden. And it's not likely I really have to do a lot of work. Mattie does all the cleaning up in here, and Moses and Benjie help me in the garden. Besides," she said, returning to her kneading, "it gives me something to do with my time."

This time it was Jason's turn to frown. He imagined that she did have a lot of time on her hands now that the people of New Orleans had totally shunned her because she had married a hated Yankee. Cut off from the social life that she had enjoyed before the fall of New Orleans, she had to be floundering for things to do to keep her occupied. He wished that she would have let him introduce her to some of the other officers' wives, as he had offered to do. That way, she might have some female company her own age. But Desirée had firmly refused to have anything to do with "the enemy." But then, he wasn't too sure the northern women would be willing to accept Desirée, a southerner, any more than she would them. He hadn't missed the look of shock and disapproval on many of his fellow officers' faces when they had learned that he had married a southerner. He imagined their wives would be just as disapproving, perhaps even more so. It seemed, to some degree, that he and Desirée were both outcasts. For Jason, it didn't matter, but he hated to see Desirée cooped up in this house with no friends or social life to speak of.

Seeing Jason frowning and having no idea what he was thinking, Desirée assumed he was displeased because she had refused a cook. "Don't you like my cooking?" she asked, a hint of hurt in her voice.

276

Jason smiled, saying with all sincerity, "I love your cooking, Desirée. I think it's amazing that you learned how by just watching your former cooks."

Suspiciously, Desirée searched his face but could see no sign of deception there. She turned her attention back to her bread, placing the long loafs on the pan she had sprinkled with cornmeal.

Jason grinned. His eyes twinkled mischievously. "I've even gotten used to eating cooked tomatoes."

Desirée was taken aback by Jason's words. She realized that she had never once considered his tastes in her cooking. She wondered how she could be so inconsiderate when he had been so kind to both her and her darkies. She frowned with self-disgust.

Seeing her frown, Jason chuckled, saying, "I'm just teasing, sweet." Then he stepped up behind her and kissed her throat softly, saying, "If you change your mind about the cook, just let me know." He turned and strode from the room.

Desirée clutched the pans tightly, feeling that same weak feeling that Jason's touch always aroused. *Mon Dieu*, she thought, would she ever get used to him? Even the most casual show of affection left her senses reeling. And everytime he smiled, or she looked into his misty-green eyes, a strange knot twisted deep inside her.

A sizzling noise drew Desirée's attention to the stove. Seeing her soup boiling over, she rushed to it and, grabbing a dishtowel, yanked it off the fire. Looking down at the crusty mess on the stove, she thought, *oui*, when he's around, you can't even think straight. Why, it's disastrous to even have him in your kitchen.

The next day, Jason was again in Desirée's thoughts as she prepared the evening meal. She was ashamed of herself for not considering Jason's tastes and was determined to make it up to him. But strangely, it wasn't gratitude or guilt that motivated her. She simply wanted to please him. She firmly refused to delve into why she had this urge.

Mammy waddled into the kitchen, drawn by the delicious aroma. "If I ain't mistaken, that's gumbo I smell," she said, her black eyes sparkling with delight.

Desirée looked up from the oven where she was taking out the peach cobbler. Carrying it to the table and sitting it down to cool, she smiled at Mammy, saying, "Yes, it is."

Mammy looked down at the cobbler, the juices still bubbling over the flaky crust, and smacked her lips. "Lawsy, child, if you don't stop feeding us so good, I'm gonna be as big as this house."

Mammy walked over to the stove and picked up the lid of the pot sitting on it. Bending, she sniffed at the steam rising from the simmering gumbo. Then she frowned. Picking up the spoon on the stove, she stirred the gumbo, peering down at it. Frowning even deeper, she asked, "Where's the tomatoes, child? Did you forget them?"

Desirée shot Mammy a defiant look, saying, "No, Mammy, I didn't forget them. We're not having tomatoes in our gumbo anymore."

Mammy looked at Desirée as if she had lost her mind. "What are you talking about? Ain't gonna have tomatoes in our gumbo no more? Lawsy, you can't have gumbo without tomatoes. What's wrong with you? You crazy or something?"

"No, I'm not crazy," Desirée replied in a firm voice. "And you *can* make gumbo without tomatoes. The Cajuns do it all the time."

Mammy looked at her suspiciously, asking, "You spoofing this old woman?"

"No, I'm serious."

"Humph! Who cares how those Cajuns cook their gumbo! That ain't got nothing to do with us."

"Yes, it does. Jason is half Cajun, and he doesn't like tomatoes."

"He don't like tomatoes?" Mammy asked in disbelief, her eyes widening.

"Not in his gumbo, he doesn't. And from now on, I'm fixing it the way he likes it." Seeing Mammy's horrified look, Desirée continued saying, "After all, Mammy, if it wasn't for Jason, we wouldn't even be eating gumbo. You know how things were before I married him. The least I can do is cook it the way he likes it."

Mammy stared at Desirée for a minute, then placed the lid back on the pot. Walking across the kitchen, she said, "That's right!" He's the massa now, and if he don't like tomatoes in his gumbo, then the rest of us are just gonna have to get used to eating it that way."

Desirée shook her head in exasperation at Mammy's words. As far as the old woman was concerned, Jason's word was law, and not just because he was the new "massah." No, Mammy thought Jason hung the moon and stars and was just about as perfect as any man could be. She wondered who idolized him the most, Mammy, Benjie, or Tassy? Even Mattie hung on every word he said. Why, it was downright disgusting!

And what of herself? She wasn't immune to his charms, either. Cooking gumbo without tomatoes just to please him. Mammy's right. She must be crazy.

When Desirée served the gumbo to Jason that night, her doubts had only increased. She found herself hoping that he wouldn't notice the absence of the tomatoes. She didn't want him to know she was trying to please him. It left her feeling too vulnerable.

Why, he even might get the crazy idea she was falling in love with him. And she'd never want him to think that, particularly after he'd made it clear he didn't want any emotional entanglements.

But Jason did notice. Almost as soon as he had sat down, Jason asked, "Where are the tomatoes?"

Desirée cringed. And then, to her horror, she felt a slow flush creeping up her face. Avoiding his eyes, she said, "They didn't have any at the market today."

Jason looked at Desirée, who was suddenly very engrossed with the food on her plate. He distinctly remembered seeing several large ripe tomatoes in the garden that morning and knew that she was lying. And he knew why she had omitted them from the gumbo. To please him. Once more, he sensed she hadn't been motivated by just gratitude. His heart beat wildly against his chest as he replied in as calm a voice as he could manage, "Oh? That's a shame."

"Well, you know fresh produce isn't so easy to find," Desirée said in a defensive voice, still staring down at her plate and nervously moving the food around on it. "That's one reason I like having my own garden."

"Yes, of course," Jason said, then ducked his head, not wanting Desirée to see the amused look in his eyes.

They ate in total silence. When Jason asked for his third helping, Desirée was irritated at the surge of happiness she felt. She was getting more pleasure out of pleasing him than he was. And that was utterly ridiculous. If she didn't watch herself, she'd end up making a complete fool of herself over him.

Later, as they walked from the dining room, Jason put his arm around Desirée's waist and pulled her close to him, saying, "That was absolutely delicious— but I'm afraid I'm still hungry."

Desirée stopped dead in her tracks. She couldn't believe he was still hungry. "There's more gumbo in the kitchen if you want another helping."

Jason turned Desirée toward him and slipped his other arm around her waist. "No, *cherie*, I'm hungry for you. Suppose we skip our little stroll in the courtyard tonight and go straight to bed?"

So early? Everyone would guess where they had gone and what they were doing. She flushed and looked up at Jason, fully intending to object. But one look at those smoldering green eyes and that seductive smile of his, and the words died before they even reached her lips. Then, as Jason pulled her to him. and his mouth closed over hers, his tongue parting her lips to taste the ambrosia within, Desirée's resistance fled.

She hardly noticed as he scooped her up in his powerful arms and carried her to their bedroom, their mouths still locked in that sensuous, devastating kiss. By the time they reached their bedroom and Jason had nudged the door shut with his shoulder, Desirée couldn't even remember what it was she had intended to object to.

Desirée and Jason took to taking long walks through the French Quarter in the evenings, enjoying the sights and smells of the city they loved so much. One evening, they strolled through Jackson Square.

They stepped aside to allow two nuns to pass, the huge white headdresses on their heads bobbing like ships at sea, their beads swaying against their dark blue skirts.

Desirée turned and looked up at the statue of Jackson, a statue that depicted the famous general sitting on a rearing horse. She looked down at the base and scowled. "*Mon Dieu*! It's true! Look what 'the beast' has done now!" she cried in a furious voice, pointing to the inscription that had been etched there. She glared at the words, saying, "I overheard everyone talking about it at the market this morning, but I couldn't believe Butler would do it. What kind of man is he to deface the statues of our heroes?"

Jason looked at the words inscribed on the statue: "The Union must and shall be preserved." He frowned, saying, "Those are Jackson's words, himself, not Butler's. They're what Jackson said to the nullifiers during the War of 1812, when they threatened to secede from the Union. General Butler is trying to make a point, but, as usual, he's being totally tactless."

Desirée was at a loss for words. What could she say? Jackson had left no doubt how he felt about the Union.

Jason gazed at the words thoughtfully. They expressed his sentiments to the letter. He wondered how Jackson would feel if he were living today. Would he still feel as strongly about the Union's being preserved? Would he, like himself, side with the North for that reason? Or would he fight for his native South? And if he decided to fight for the North, how would his fiercely southern wife, Rachel, feel about it? Would she have given him her total support?

Ever since that day on the bayou, when Desirée had accused him of being a traitor to the South, Jason had felt bad. He wanted her to understand why he had taken this position. He decided to explain right now.

Turning to her, he said, "Jackson's words express my sentiments exactly. When the war broke out, I had a hard time deciding which side to fight for. I still loved the South. I always will. But, on the other hand, like Jackson, I knew that the Union must be preserved. I struggled with myself for months before I finally decided. In the end, I had to go with the Union."

Desirée glared at him, saying, "How can you claim to love the South when you fight against her?

"Desirée, this country can't be split in two," Jason replied in an emphatic voice. "Together, we form one strong nation. But divided, we're both too weak to fight off a foreign aggressor. And don't think for one minute that the powers in Europe aren't just waiting for that opportunity." Jason gazed back up at Jackson's statue, saying in a thoughtful voice, "It's the South that concerns me the most. The way they woo the European countries, particularly France."

"We have to!" Desirée argued. "We're not an industrial country, like the North is. What's wrong with asking for their support? And France is our staunchest friend."

Jason sighed in exasperation, saying, "Desirée, Napoleon isn't going to help anyone, not without an ulterior motive. He's only for himself. For years, he's been wanting to get a foothold in the Americas, and now, he's finally gotten one in Mexico. If he takes over that country, he'll be on our border, with just a river between him and Texas. Once he has Mexico in his pocket, what's to keep him from crossing that river and invading the South? Do you really believe that power-hungry egomaniac will settle for just Mexico when he could have the South and all its riches, too?"

Desirée was just a little stunned by Jason's words. If Napoleon were successful in taking Mexico, would he attack the South? Did he have designs on them?

"Then again, maybe he wouldn't even have to attack," Jason said, thinking out loud. "Maybe Napoleon could woo the South into joining him. With Louisiana's majority-French population, this state might even encourage the rest of the South to do just that."

"That's ridiculous!" Desirée cried indignantly. "Just because our ancestors were French doesn't mean we'd be willing to place ourselves back under French rule. Why, we're Americans, just as much as anyone else in the South. And the South is its own nation now. If Napoleon, or anyone else, tried to invade us, we'd fight, just as we're fighting the North."

"But that's just the point, Desirée. Would the South be able to fight off one of the powerful European nations by herself?"

"But we couldn't stay with the North any longer," Desirée objected. "They were stifling us, trying to destroy our whole way of living. They were . . ."

Jason only listened with half an ear as Desirée launched into the southern arguments for seceding from the Union. He didn't have to listen. He had heard them all before. Nor did he bother to argue with her.

As they walked from the square, Jason glanced once more at the statue and thought that he had been foolish to compare him and Desirée to Jackson and his wife. Rachel loved her husband, and undoubtedly, she would have supported his views regardless of her own personal opinions. But then, Jason admitted to himself that he wouldn't want Desirée to agree with him simply because she loved him. He admired her for sticking to her beliefs. He only wished she had shown some understanding in how he felt.

But, unknown to Jason, Desirée did admire him for sticking to his convictions. While she had never really understood his reasons for fighting the North—for she had failed to notice that he had always stressed Union and not North—she admitted to herself that it took a rare courage to fight for his beliefs when he was as torn in his loyalties as Jason obviously was. She glanced up at him as he walked beside her, thinking that the more he revealed of himself to her, the more she liked him as a person.

Because Desirée's summer garden was so successful and the cost of food was still so high, she decided to plant a fall garden. One afternoon, when her dinner was simmering over the fire, she ambled out into the courtyard to do a little weeding.

She passed Tassy, sitting on one of the stone benches and staring at a spiderweb Jason had pointed out to her one day. Desirée wondered if the girl even saw the web, much less the tiny spider that was weaving it, for the same blank look that was always there was in her eyes.

Desirée knelt beside the garden and started pulling the weeds away from the small vegetable plants that had just barely sprouted from the ground. She heard a rustling noise behind her and looked up, seeing Tassy walk over and bend to help her.

"*Non*, Tassy!" Desirée said in a sharp voice, catching Tassy's hand and pulling it back. Rising, she led the girl back to the bench and sat her down on it, saying in a stern voice, "You mustn't touch my garden."

Desirée looked up and saw Jason standing across the courtyard, a frown on his face. She hurried over to him, saying, "I didn't hear you come in."

"I was in the carriage house with Moses," Jason answered, his eyes still on Tassy. "Why didn't you let her help you weed?"

"Tassy? *Mon Dieu*, Jason. She can't tell a weed from a vegetable plant. Why, even I have trouble telling them apart when they're that small. She'll pull up everything."

Jason turned to Desirée, asking, "Have you ever seen Tassy show an interest in anything? Volunteer to do anything?"

"*Non*, I never have," Desirée admitted.

"Then, don't you think it's rather remarkable that she offered to help? I think you should have let her."

"But, Jason, she doesn't know anything about gardening. If she didn't pull everything up, she'd trample it."

Jason turned and scanned the garden. "Why don't you let her have that small section over by the other wall for her very own? Give her the chance and see if she can take care of it?"

Desirée looked over at the section Jason was referring to and frowned.

"Desirée, give her the chance. Even if she ruins it, it's not that big a loss. It's not like we can't afford to buy vegetables or that our lives depend on it."

"Oh, all right," Desirée said reluctantly.

She walked over to Tassy and took her hand, leading the girl to the small section of the garden sitting against one wall. Pointing to it, Desirée said, "Tassy, this will be your garden from now on. It will be your responsibility to take care of it. But you're not to touch the rest of the garden."

Desirée looked at Tassy and knew she wasn't getting through to her. She chewed her bottom lip in frustration, wondering how she could make Tassy understand. Then she remembered how Jason talked to Tassy, using the simplest terms, as if he were talking to a small child.

Again, Desirée pointed to the small garden, saying, "Tassy's garden." Then she motioned to the rest of the garden saying, "Desirée's garden. Don't touch. She repeated, "Tassy's garden. Desirée's garden.

"Yes'm," Tassy replied, staring off into space. Then she turned and ambled back into the house.

Desirée watched Tassy as she walked away, then said to Jason as he strode up to her, "I don't think she understood."

"Don't be too sure," he replied. "I think she understands more than we give her credit for."

The next morning, Desirée rushed out of the house to look at her garden, half expecting to see a plot of totally bare ground. She sighed with relief when she discovered it was still there, plants—and weeds.

She turned and looked at Tassy's garden, her eyes widening with surprise. The little plot had been completely weeded, the vegetable plants standing in neat rows. The darkened circle on the ground around each plant told her that Tassy had already watered them.

In the weeks that followed, Desirée stood by and watched in total amazement as Tassy religiously tended her garden, and it grew by leaps and bounds, far surpassing Desirée's garden. One afternoon, she was observing Tassy as she watered her garden, when Jason strolled into the courtyard.

She turned to him, saying, "Look at Tassy's garden, Jason. Have you ever seen anything like it? I can't believe it."

Jason's eyes swept over the garden appreciatively. "Yes, apparently Tassy has a green thumb."

"Well, it's either that or that singing she does."

"Singing?" Jason asked in surprise.

If it had been anyone but Jason, Desirée would have been reluctant to tell them that Tassy sang to her plants, for fear they would laugh at the girl. But she knew that Jason would never do that. "Yes, she sings to her plants," Desirée explained. "At least I think

287

that's what she's doing. I don't recognize the tune or understand any of the words, but it sounds like that." She turned and gazed thoughtfully at Tassy, saying, "You were right when you said to give her the chance. I'm glad I listened to you."

"Yes, she had a natural knack for gardening, and somehow, she sensed that was her nitch in life. Have you praised her? Told her how well she's doing?"

Desirée frowned, then admitted, *"Non."*

"Why not?"

"I—I didn't think she'd understand."

"Desirée, everyone understands praise," Jason said in a patient voice. "Even animals."

"That's true." Desirée said thoughtfully. Suddenly she felt ashamed of herself. She walked up to Tassy and said, "Tassy, your garden is absolutely beautiful. You've done a wonderful job."

Tassy stared at her blankly.

"Your garden is pretty, Tassy." Desirée pointed to the garden, saying, "Pretty garden."

There are some incidents in everyone's life that touch them so deeply that they remain imprinted on their minds till their death. What happened next was one of those times for Desirée. As long as she lived, she would remember the transformation on Tassy's face. She watched in disbelief as the eyes that had always been dull and lifeless suddenly gleamed, as if a light had been lit in them. A broad smile spread across Tassy's face, a smile that changed her comely features to absolute radiant beauty. And then, Tassy spoke the first words that Desirée had ever heard her say, other than the monotonous "yes'm." Tassy smiled down at her garden and said, "Pretty garden."

Sudden tears sprang into Desirée's eyes. A lump formed in throat. She hugged Tassy fiercely, saying in an emotion-choked voice, "Oh, Tassy. I'm so proud of you."

That day, Desirée turned the entire garden over to Tassy. Following Jason's lead, she made a point of taking time everyday to talk to the girl and praise her. She and Jason were rewarded for their efforts when Tassy started talking in simple sentences.

Chapter 14

Desirée wandered through the French Market, threading her way through the stalls, a smug smile on her face. She had managed to elude Mammy and Moses and sneak off to the market by herself. She had hated to lie to them, telling them that she planned on taking a long nap that afternoon, but she was sick and tired of their following her around the market like watchdogs. Oh, she knew why they did it: because Jason insisted that one or the other always accompany her when she went out of the house if he wasn't around. But he needn't worry. She wasn't going to get into any trouble with any of the Yankee soldiers. Oh, she wasn't about to smile at them or act friendly in any way. But she'd be very careful not to aggravate them. No, she had learned her lesson—the hard way.

Besides, Jason had been at her for weeks to buy something for herself and she didn't want to be rushed, as she would be if Mammy or Moses were tagging along. Since she wasn't sure just what she wanted to buy, she wanted time to browse. But one thing she did know for sure: She wasn't going to buy the new dress Jason had suggested she buy that morning. No, she was in mourning, and just like all the other women in mourning in New Orleans, she would continue to wear black for an entire year.

Seeing a figure through a break in the crowd, Desirée came to an abrupt halt, a surprised look on her face. Jeanne Marie? What was she doing here? And of all things, buying food supplies. But why? The plantation was totally self-supporting. They even raised their own meat.

Desirée rushed through the crowd and up to her cousin. Jeanne Marie, occupied with watching the barrels that were being loaded on the wagon, didn't notice her approach. Desirée stood behind her cousin, her eyes widening as she saw the word stamped on one barrel: Sugar. Why was Jeanne Marie buying sugar? There was a whole row of storehouses on Terre Doux crammed full of sugar that her uncle Paul hadn't been able to sell because of the Union blockade.

"Jeanne Marie, what in the world are you doing?" Desirée asked.

Jeanne Marie whirled about, then cried, "Oh, Desirée! Thank God, you're all right! Why didn't you let me know where you were staying?"

Desirée flinched at Jeanne Marie's question. She hadn't sent her cousin the letter letting Jeanne Marie know where she had gone because she had never left her home. Had her cousin been worrying about her all this time? She felt a twinge of guilt. But Desirée's curiosity overrode her guilt. Brushing it and Jeanne Marie's question aside, she answered, "I'm fine, Jeanne Marie. But what are you doing here buying food supplies? And sugar?" She glanced around the market. "And where is *Tante* Josephine?"

A look of pain crossed Jeanne Marie's delicate features; her beautiful, doelike eyes filled with tears. And then, to Desirée's horror, the tears spilled over as her cousin's small shoulders began to shake with sobs.

Alarmed, Desirée put her arms around Jeanne

Marie, pulling her cousin to her. "*Mon Dieu!* What's wrong? What happened?"

Jeanne Marie struggled to control herself, acutely conscious of the stares from the other shoppers. She pulled back from Desirée, the tears glistening on her cheeks, and said, "So much has happened, I don't know where to begin."

Desirée was also aware of being watched. Spying a small bench behind one of the stalls, she said, "Come over here, Jeanne Marie, and sit down. Then you can tell me everything."

She led Jeanne Marie to the bench and when they were both seated, she said, "Now, tell me what happened."

Jeanne Marie fished in her reticule and pulled out a handkerchief. Dabbing her eyes, she said, "The Yankees came to Terre Doux and burned everything but the plantation house. Oh, Desirée it was awful! They took all of the barrels of sugar out of the storehouses and loaded them on their wagons. They said they were confiscating them, but that wasn't true. They were just stealing them! And then, they set the storehouses, the factory, the slaves' quarters, the stables—everything on fire. They even burnt the sugarcane in the fields and our vegetable garden."

Desirée's face turned ashen at Jeanne Marie's story. She knew General Butler and his army were raiding the plantations all around New Orleans, greedy for the sugar and cotton stored on them. More than once, Jason had complained that the general seemed more interested in confiscating the valuable products and lining his own pockets than fighting the war. But ostracized by the people of New Orleans, she had only caught snatches of conversation in the market and had no idea that the destruction to the plantations had been so rampant and vindictive.

Jeanne Marie continued in a bitter voice, her face filled with hatred. "They took everything: the sugar, the darkies who didn't manage to escape into the swamps, every chicken, cow, and pig we had. They call themselves soldiers. *Mon Dieu!* They're nothing but thieves! I hate them!"

Desirée glanced around nervously, seeing several Union soldiers strolling through the market. Remembering only too well Butler's Women's Order and her own near disaster, she whispered, "Sssh, Jeanne Marie. Not so loud."

"I don't care if they do hear me!" Jeanne Marie spat, her eyes glittering with anger.

"*Oui*, you do," Desirée said in a firm voice. "Believe me, there's nothing to be gained by aggravating them."

Fresh tears glittered in Jeanne Marie's eyes. "I'm glad Papa will never know. It would have broke his heart to see Terre Doux like it is now, everything burnt and blackened, even the fields." Her voice quivered. "You know how proud he was of it."

Fear rose in Desirée's throat. She forced the words from her lips. "Why—why won't he know?"

"He's dead, Desirée. He died of a heart attack when the army was retreating after the fall of New Orleans. Armond wrote and told us about it. He said it happened during a forced march through the swamps, when they were trying to escape the Yankees. Papa kept insisting he could keep up with the younger men. He was even goading them on. And then, all of a sudden, he clutched his chest and staggered. He was dead before he hit the ground."

Desirée was stunned speechless. Her Uncle Paul was dead? Yet another casualty of this terrible war, for the war had killed him just as surely as a bullet had struck him. *Sacre Dieu*, was there no end to the death and destruction? Three out of the four men in their family had been killed. Now, only Armond remained. Stark terror seized her.

"Armond?" she choked out. "Is he all right?"

"As far as I know, he is," Jeanne Marie answered in a lifeless voice.

The two young woman's eyes met and locked for a long minute, each silently communicating their pain and fear. Then Desirée opened her arms, and Jeanne Marie collapsed into them.

They cried quietly, sharing their grief for a few minutes, before Desirée glanced about, saying, "Where's your mother?"

"Back at the plantation."

"She let you come to New Orleans alone?" Desirée asked in a shocked voice.

"I didn't come alone. I brought one of my darkies with me. And I doubt if *Maman* even realizes that I left the plantation. Ever since we heard about Papa, she's been in a state of shock. She doesn't even know what's going on around her. Even when the Yankees came and burned everything, she just stood there and stared out into space."

"Then why didn't you send the overseer your father hired before he left to buy the supplies for you?"

"Because he's gone," Jeanne Marie said in a bitter voice. "He left the day the Yankees came. He said with the sugar fields burned and no slaves to tend them, there was no use for him to stay. Besides, since the Yankees had stolen the stored sugar, he knew we had no way of paying him."

"You have no money?"

"No, Papa converted everything to Confederate script after the war broke out. I didn't even know we were destitute until the overseer told me before he left that day. He said Papa had been staking everything on the cane that was in the ground and would be able to eventually sell the stored sugar. I wouldn't have even been able to buy these supplies today if I hadn't had the grand piano to sell."

"The grand piano?" Desirée asked in surprise. "You sold the grand piano?"

"Yes, that was about the only thing of value the Yankees didn't steal."

"You mean they raided the house, too?" Desirée asked in shock.

"Yes, they took anything they could possibly carry that had any value at all. The silver, the paintings, the china and crystal, the rugs, our jewelry, the smaller pieces of furniture. They even took down the chandeliers. With their wagons so loaded, they didn't have room for the grand piano. And if one of the darkies hadn't hidden that horse and wagon in the swamps, I wouldn't even have had a way of getting it into New Orleans."

Jeanne Marie was right, Desirée thought angrily. The Yankees weren't anything but thieves.

"Oh, Desirée, what am I going to do?" Jeanne Marie asked in despair. "These supplies I'm buying today will never feed us and our darkies until next spring, when we can plant another garden. And it's too late to plant now."

"Then you do have some darkies left?"

"Yes, some of them who ran off to the swamps and hid came back. The others didn't. I don't know whether they were afraid to come back or just took the opportunity to run. I guess I should be glad that more of them didn't return. I can't even feed the ones I have."

"Why didn't you come to me for help?"

"I would have, but I didn't know who you were staying with. You never did write me like you promised."

"Then you didn't go by my house?"

"Why, no." Then Jeanne Marie's eyes widened as she said, "Desirée, you're not still living in your house, with only Moses and Mammy to protect you?"

"Yes, I'm still in my house," Desirée admitted.

"But you can't do that! It's too dangerous with all these Yankee soldiers around." A determined look came into Jeanne Marie's eyes. "You'll just *have* to come back to the plantation and stay with us now."

Desirée knew she was going to have to explain to Jeanne Marie about Jason, but she didn't know how to begin.

"If it's my mother you're thinking about, don't worry," Jeanne Marie said. "She won't even know you're there. She doesn't even know *I'm* there."

"That's not it," Desirée answered. "I can't come because I'm married now."

"Married?" Jeanne Marie gasped. Her eyes filled with disbelief. "But how did that happen?"

Desirée rose and paced for a few minutes. Then she turned to Jeanne Marie and, with a deep sigh, said, "It's a long story."

Desirée told Jeanne Marie everything that had happened to her, beginning with the night she had discovered Jason's true identity and ending with their marriage, omitting only the intimacies she had shared with Jason while they were in the swamps.

Jeanne Marie was stunned by the story. When Desirée had finished, she asked in a somewhat angry voice. "Why didn't you tell me the truth that day you came to the plantation? Why did you lead me to believe you were a wealthy woman?"

"Because I knew that you would insist that I stay, and I couldn't do that. Now knowing how your mother felt. My pride wouldn't let me."

296

"*Mon Dieu!* And now you're married to him—*that Yankee?*" Jeanne Marie asked in a horrified voice.

Desirée winced at Jeanne Marie's last hateful words, feeling them as if she, personally, had been insulted. "It's not so bad," she answered in a defensive voice. "Besides, what choice did I have? It was either that or go to prison. I certainly couldn't agree to become Colonel Anders's mistress." Desirée shivered in revulsion at the thought.

"But what about Beau? Don't you still love him?"

Desirée gazed out over the crowd in the market, her look pensive. "No, I don't," she answered, finally admitting the truth to herself. She turned back to Jeanne Marie, saying, "I don't think I ever really did, although I didn't realize it until just now. Oh, I cared for him, had some affection for him. After all, we grew up together. Then, when he and everyone seemed to expect us to marry, I think I convinced myself that I loved him. But now, I realized that what I felt for him was more friendship than love."

"Then—you're in love with Jason?" Jeanne Marie asked in an utterly shocked voice.

Desirée refused to even consider the question. It disturbed her too deeply. "*Non,*" she denied quickly. "I'm just grateful to him for coming to my rescue. After all, he didn't *have* to marry me. I was the one who blabbed the whole story and put myself into that position. And I was the one who refused to sign the loyalty oath."

"But he's a Yankee!" Jeanne Marie persisted.

Again, Desirée felt defensive. "Yes, he is!" she snapped. "And for that reason, he was the only one who could help me. Besides, he's not like the Yankees who raided your plantation. He's a good man. He's been very kind and generous to both me and my darkies."

Jeanne Marie gave her a doubtful look and then said, "But to be married to a man you don't love. That must be terrible."

It's worse being married to a man who doesn't love you, who will never love you, Desirée thought bitterly. But her pride would never let her admit that to her cousin. "*Non*, it's not so bad," she answered. "After all, we Creoles have always arranged marriages. Why, even your own parents' marriage was arranged."

"*Oui*, I know," Jeanne Marie admitted. "But I've always hoped to marry for love."

So did I, Desirée thought with a heavy heart.

A glum look came over Jeanne Marie's face. "It's just as well I didn't come to you. You can't help me. You don't have any money either."

"*Oui*, I do. I told you, I'm married to Jason now. He gives me money."

"But he won't let you help us. He's a Yankee and we're the enemy."

Desirée was sick and tired of Jeanne Marie's calling Jason a Yankee, as if he were the scum of the earth. She knew her cousin had very good reasons for hating the Yankees, but Jason wasn't like the rest of them.

"Of course, he'll let me help you!" Desirée snapped, exasperated and angry. "I told you, he's not like the rest of the Yankees. He's a good, decent man. And you're not his enemy. You're family."

Jeanne Marie was a little stunned at Desirée's strong defense of Jason. But despite her cousin's assurances, she didn't like the idea of a Yankee in the family one bit. Nor did she like the idea of accepting help from one. In fact, if it weren't for her mother and darkies, she wouldn't even consider accepting his aid.

Desirée continued, saying, "I'm sure when he hears what happened to you, Jason will insist that you and your mother come and live with us."

Live with a Yankee? Jeanne Marie thought of it in absolute horror. *Mon Dieu!* Never! Desirée might. But she had to. She was married to Jason now. But Jeanne Marie wouldn't. Why, she wouldn't even enter their house. Jason might not think of her as his enemy, and he might be a decent man, as Desirée insisted, but he was still a Yankee, and he was still *her* enemy.

"*Non*. Desirée," Jeanne Marie said in an adamant voice. "We won't come to live with you. Armond is counting on me to hold Terre Doux for him until he returns. Besides, it's my home and I won't leave it."

Desirée was surprised at the determined look on Jeanne Marie's face. She gazed at her cousin thoughtfully, amazed at the transformation in her. The meek, shy girl was gone. In her place was a strong-willed, determined woman. She had always loved Jeanne Marie, but she found that she liked this new woman she had become even more.

"All right, Jeanne Marie, it's your decision. But you will let *me* help you, won't you?"

She knew that if she refused Desirée's help, it would hurt her cousin deeply. Desirée would feel it like a slap in the face. And while Jeanne Marie didn't approve of Jason, she could never hurt Desirée, particularly since she had been forced into marrying the Yankee by circumstances beyond her control.

"*Oui*, I'll let you help me," Jeanne Marie answered.

"Good," Desirée said, coming to her feet. She reached into her reticule and brought out a handful of bills. Handing them to Jeanne Marie, she said, "Will this be enough to pay for the supplies you bought today?"

"I can pay for what I bought today," Jeanne Marie objected.

"*Non*, you keep that money in case you need it for

an emergency." Seeing Jeanne Marie's hesitation, she said, "You promised you'd let me help."

"Oh, all right," Jeanne Marie said reluctantly, accepting the money and rising to her feet. "But when the war is over with and things get back to normal, I'll pay it back."

Desirée knew Jeanne Marie's pride was hurting, that she hated taking money from anyone. The fact that the money came from a Yankee only made it harder for her. "Of course. Just consider it a loan," Desirée answered.

As they walked back to the wagon, Jeanne Marie chewed her bottom lip nervously. Then suddenly, she stopped and turned to Desirée, saying, "You've been completely honest with me. I feel it's only fair to let you know that if the soldiers come to Terre Doux again and ask for food, I'll give it to them."

"What soldiers?" Desirée asked in surprise.

"The Confederate soldiers who are hiding out in the swamps around Terre Doux. Oh, Desirée," Jeanne Marie cried in an anguished voice. "you should see them. They're so pitiful looking. They've been out there for months now, eating alligators and snakes and anything they can get their hands on. And still, they're half starved. I was giving them everything I could spare, until the Yankees burned everything." She raised her small chin defiantly, saying in a determined voice, "And if they come back, I'll give it to them again, even if it means me and my darkies go without."

Desirée knew that the Confederate Army was hiding out in the swamps all over Louisiana. Jason had told her that Butler had explained his failure to take the state for the Union by claiming he couldn't fight an enemy he couldn't find, an army that hit and ran, then hid. But Desirée had been so caught up in her own survival that she had never stopped to consider how those men were struggling to live. She claimed to love the South as fiercely as any southerner, and yet, she had done nothing to help it, as Jeanne Marie had. That old guilt for not having escaped Jason and warned New Orleans of the impending attack rose up in her and, with it, her shame and self-disgust. Well, maybe it still wasn't too late to help, she thought.

"What do the soldiers need?" Desirée asked.

Jeanne Marie looked at her curiously, then answered, "Mostly staples. Things like flour, sugar, lard, and salt. And with the winter coming on, blankets."

Desirée looked at Jeanne Marie directly in the eye, saying, "If I buy those things, will you see that they get delivered to the soldiers?"

Jeanne Marie's mouth flew open in shock. Then she recovered, saying, "You can't be serious. Jason may let you help us, but he'd never let you buy supplies for the Confederate Army."

Desirée knew what Jeanne Marie said was true. Jason would help Jeanne Marie because she was a civilian and her family, but he'd never help the enemy army. He was just as fiercely dedicated to the northern cause as she was to the southern. "Then I won't tell him," she said in a determined voice.

"But how will you keep him from knowing? Won't he ask why you need so much money?"

"If he asks, I'll tell him I'm using the extra money to help you. But I don't think he'll even notice. He never pays any attention to how much money I spend. And I never have to ask him for it, either. He just puts it in the money box each week. As I said, he's very generous."

Jeanne Marie laughed, saying, "Oh, how wonderful—and how fitting. First, the Yankees steal from us,

301

and now, we steal from them. Do you honestly think you can get away with it?''

Desirée winced at Jeanne Marie's words. She had never thought of it as stealing. And she wouldn't be stealing from the Yankees, as Jeanne Marie had said. She'd be stealing from Jason. And she really didn't like the idea of deceiving Jason either, particularly after he'd been so kind to her. Doubts assailed her.

"Oh, Desirée, the soldiers will be so grateful," Jeanne Marie said, not noticing the look on Desirée's face. "Why, it might even save their lives."

A vision of the men in the swamps filled Desirée's mind. Among their faces were familiar ones: friends of her brother's and father's and old personal acquaintances. They seemed to be staring at her, their eyes sucken and accusing, their faces pale and gaunt. She couldn't refuse them, even if it did mean deceiving Jason. If those men died of starvation, she'd never be able to live with herself. No, she had to do it.

"When do you think we can begin?" Jeanne Marie asked, excited as much at the idea of getting revenge on the Yankees as helping her beloved South.

"How about next week?" Desirée answered, turning and walking once again to the wagon. "You can come by the house and pick me up, and then, we can come over here and buy the supplies you think they'll need. Do you think if we send them something every week, it will be enough?"

"Oh, I'm sure it will be," Jeanne Marie replied in a confident voice. "But I don't think I should stop by your house. If Jason knew you were buying supplies that often, he might get suspicious. Why don't we meet here at the market?"

Desirée realized what Jeanne Marie said was true. Jason might not suspect anything if Jeanne Marie came into town for supplies once a month, but

302

weekly? No, he probably would get suspicious.

"All right," Desirée answered. "I'll meet you here every Wednesday."

They had almost reached the wagon when a sudden thought occurred to Desirée. She was risking Jason's wrath if he discovered what she was doing, but Jeanne Marie was risking much more. She stopped dead in her tracks, her face ashen.

"What's wrong?" Jeanne Marie asked.

"Maybe we'd better not do it, Jeanne Marie. If you got caught sneaking supplies to the Confederates, you'd be thrown into prison."

A determined gleam came into Jeanne Marie's eyes. "I'm *not* going to get caught. I'll take the old bayou road. Why, hardly anyone here in New Orleans even knows about it, much less the Yankees. How do you think I planned on getting the supplies I bought today back to Terre Doux? I'll be damned if I'm going to let those Yankee bastards steal them, too."

Mon Dieu, her cousin had changed, Desirée thought, surprised by Jeanne Marie's clear thinking and just a little shocked by her language. But the old bayou road was dangerous, a mere pathway through thick canebrakes and marshland. Why, Jeanne Marie might be attacked by a wild animal or, worse yet, by one of the runaway slaves or army deserters who hid out in the swamps.

"Who did you bring with you?" Desirée asked, knowing Jeanne Marie would need protection.

"Him," Jeanne Marie answered, nodding to the slave who was climbing into her wagon.

Desirée gasped. She had never seen such a huge man in her entire life. He was at least seven feet tall, with shoulders almost as broad as the seat he sat on and arms that looked like tree trunks. *"Sacre Dieu,"* Desirée whispered in an awed voice. "Who's he?"

"One of my father's field hands. The only one who came back after the Yankees left. The rest were all house servants. *Mon Dieu*, I don't know what I would have done without Sam these past weeks. He was the one who took the horse and wagon into the swamp and hid them. And we would have never got that piano into the wagon without his help."

Desirée wasn't worried about her cousin driving down the old bayou road anymore. With Sam sitting beside her, a man would have to be a fool to attack her. No, now, she was concerned for another reason. "But can you trust him to help you carry supplies to the soldiers?" Desirée whispered. "Remember, the Yankees encourage the darkies to divulge information about their masters. He might inform on you."

"He won't do that," Jeanne Marie replied in a confident voice. "Sam's as loyal to me as Moses and Mammy are to you. And don't let all that brawn fool you. He's intelligent, too. He knows the Yankees didn't come down here to rescue the darkies. And after what they did to Terre Doux, he hates them as much as I do."

Jeanne Marie turned and, with Sam's help, climbed into the wagon. Once she was seated beside him, looking like a doll up against his massive size, she asked, "What time should I meet you next week?"

"Would you be able to make it by one o'clock?"

"We'll be there," Jeanne Marie answered.

Desirée watched as they drove off. Then she turned and walked out of the market, deep in thought, not even aware of the hawkers calling their wares or the crowds jostling her.

Now, she was doubly glad that she had managed to slip away from Mammy and Moses today. She feared that neither of them would approve of what she was

304

going to do, not because she would be helping the Confederates but because she would be deceiving Jason, a man they had come to respect and admire. She wished that she didn't have to do it, that she could tell Jason the truth. But she knew that he would feel honor-bound to stop her. She frowned, realizing that she would have to deceive Mammy and Moses, too, by finding some way to slip out of the house every week to meet Jeanne Marie.

Deeply troubled, she wandered through the old French Quarter instead of going straight home. For over an hour, she walked aimlessly through the streets, not even aware of her surroundings, until she found herself standing in Beauregard Square. She looked about the park. Here, the slaves came in the dark of the night and danced their ancient dances, the air filled with their eerie chants and the throbbing beat of their African drums. It was rumored that even some voodoo was practiced on those dark, moonless nights; dancing with snakes that symbolized their deities wrapped around their bodies, animal sacrifices to their gods, the selling of charms, love potions, and gris-gris. Despite the heat of the day, Desirée shivered.

She turned and walked in hurried steps from the park, still torn between her desire to help her beloved South and her loyalty to her husband. She had promised herself that she would try to be a good wife to Jason, and here she was, planning to deliberately deceive him. But everytime she remembered what the Yankees had done to Terre Doux, her blood boiled, and everytime she thought of the starving men in the swamps, her heart filled with compassion.

And then, she remembered that Jason, too, had been torn by his loyalties. Yet, he had still decided to fight for the North. If he could support his side, and still claim that he and she weren't enemies, then why couldn't she support her side? After all, what was fair for the goose was fair for the gander. Her decision finally made, she hurried home, her small chin set with firm resolve.

Desirée waited until she and Jason were strolling in the courtyard that night to tell him about what had happened at Terre Doux and her promise to help Jeanne Marie financially, hoping that if her eyes and facial expression gave her away, he wouldn't notice in the dark.

Jason stood and scowled as he listened to Desirée describe the destruction at Terre Doux, feeling an anger filling him. He knew the army condoned the raids on the plantation, arguing that they were necessary since that was where the Confederates were getting their food supply. He also knew the army condoned the confiscation of the slaves and the stored sugar and cotton. As for the looting and burning, that had been an ugly reality of war since the beginning of time. And yet, it angered and sickened him to know that his army was doing those things and that he was a part of it. He had chosen to fight for the Union for what he considered honorable reasons, and yet, there was nothing honorable about burning and looting and stealing. He wondered bitterly why righteous causes had to be fought by such unrighteous means.

Desirée's hand trembled as she traced the lip of the stone jar sitting beside her, a jar filled with alum and charcoal to purify the river water for drinking. "So you see," she finished, "Jeanne Marie is destitute now. She doesn't even have enough money to buy food. I promised to help her out financially. I hope you don't mind."

Jason heard the nervous quiver in Desirée's voice. My God, he thought, does she expect me to refuse?

What kind of monster does she think I am? Just because the Yankees who burned Terre Doux rode off and left them; does she actually believe I'd stand by and let two helpless women and a handful of slaves starve to death?

"Of course, I don't mind," Jason answered, hurt that she would think him so heartless.

Desirée sighed in relief and said, "Thank you."

She turned and walked toward the old, weathered fountain. Jason strolled beside her, the heels of his boots clicking rhythmically on the cobblestones. Then he turned to her and said, "In fact, I'll drive the supplies to Terre Doux, myself. That way, Jeanne Marie won't have to worry about a Union patrol confiscating them."

Panic rose in Desirée. "No, that won't be necessary, Jason. Jeanne Marie plans on taking one of the old bayou roads, one of the back roads the Yankees don't know about. Besides, Jeanne Marie might be willing to bury her pride and accept help from me, but it would embarrass her to have you bring her the supplies."

"Of course, I should have thought of that. But don't you think mortified would be the more correct term? After all, I'm a Yankee, one of the hated enemy."

Desirée heard the hurt in Jason's voice, and it tore at her heart. What made it worse was that she knew that it was true. Despite all of her assurances that Jason was a decent man, she knew that Jeanne Marie still considered him the enemy. In a way, her cousin's attitude angered her, and yet, she had felt the same way until she had gotten to know Jason.

"Oh, Jason try to understand. Jeanne Marie has been through so much. After what happened to Terre Doux, it's only natural that she should hate the

307

Yankees even more than ever."

"I do understand, Desirée. It's just that I was hoping she wouldn't think of me as a Yankee, but as one of the family."

"She will eventually. But, Jason, you've got to give her time to let the wounds heal."

"I know," Jason replied, then wondered bleakly if the wounds being inflicted in this war of countryman against countryman would ever heal, if the bitterness and hatred would ever be forgotten. If Desirée still had her doubts about him, then how long would it take for the two sections to forget and forgive?"

A month later, Jason returned home from headquarters early. He headed straight for the library and pulled out the money box, intending to put the weekly household allowance into it. But when he opened the lid and found the box almost empty, he frowned. Had he forgotten to put the money in last week? No, he distinctly remembered doing it. He knew Desirée was helping Jeanne Marie out. He'd even increased the allowance to allow for that. But why would it take so much to buy supplies for Terre Doux if Jeanne Marie only had a few slaves left to clothe and feed? But then, maybe that wasn't where the money had gone. Perhaps, Desirée had bought some new furniture and he hadn't even noticed.

He wandered through the house but could see nothing new, nor was there any sign of Desirée. He walked into the kitchen and found Mammy Lou sitting there and paring potatoes.

"Good afternoon, Mammy."

Mammy looked up in surprise. "Oh, Massa Steele. I didn't even hear you come in. You're home early today."

"Yes, I am," Jason answered absently. He looked around him, saying, "Where's Desirée? Is this the week she's meeting Jeanne Marie at the market?"

"No, sir. That was last week. She's up in your bedroom, taking a nap."

Jason frowned. He knew Desirée wasn't in their bedroom. He'd already looked in there.

"What's the matter?" Mammy asked, seeing Jason's expression.

"Nothing, Mammy, nothing," Jason answered in a distracted voice. He turned and walked from the kitchen, a strong suspicioun in his mind.

Fifteen minutes later, Jason stood in the French Market, looking about him. Then his eyes narrowed, and he stepped behind a stall. There, he watched as barrels and barrels of flour, lard, cornmeal, salt and sugar were loaded onto the wagon Desirée and Jeanne Marie stood beside. Behind the barrels came armload after armload of blankets. His suspicion had proven true. Desirée wasn't just helping Jeanne Marie. The two young women were slipping supplies to the Confederates.

He wondered what he should do. Aiding the enemy was a crime punishable by prison. As a Union officer, he was honor-bound to turn them in. But he couldn't do that. Desirée was his wife, the woman he loved, and Jeanne Marie was her cousin, a relative by marriage. He knew that he could put an end to it by simply walking over and telling them he knew what they were doing. But he wasn't too sure he wanted to do that either. He knew that they were motivated by something more than just the desire to help the South. Both were driven by deeper emotions, needs that would only grow with time unless they were assuaged. By slipping supplies to the Confederates, Desirée was easing the guilt that ate at her, and Jeanne Marie was getting revenge on the Union Army for burning her home.

Would it really be so terrible to let them continue? Oh, he knew starving the enemy out was an age-old military tactic, but it had never sat well with him. To him, it seemed cowardly and underhanded, a less than honorable way of forcing the enemy to surrender. Besides, what the girls were slipping through was a mere drop in the bucket, not enough to begin to feed the thousands of men hiding out in the swamps, and certainly not enough to seriously hamper the Union war effort.

But what about the danger to Jeanne Marie? Then he remembered that Desirée had told him she was using an old bayou road to slip the supplies to the plantation. If it was the same road he thought it was, there wasn't much danger of her being caught by a Union patrol. And even if she was stopped, the patrol would only confiscate the wagon and horse, since they had no way of knowing that the supplies weren't going to the slaves at Terre Doux.

He finally decided to let them continue, but he'd keep an eye on them from now on. He couldn't let them try anything foolish, like trying to slip guns or ammunition out of the city. That would be too risky for them. Nor could he stand by and watch guns being infiltrated to the enemy. There was a big difference between arms and food. No, if they tried something like that, he'd have to step in and stop them, both for their protection and his honor.

Jason turned and walked out of the French Market, making a mental note to add more money to the cash box. He grinned, thinking that it was a good thing that he had another income besides his officer's pay. Otherwise, he might not be able to afford Desirée and Jeanne Marie's little project.

Chapter 15

In October, word of Lincoln's Emancipation Proclamation arrived in New Orleans. Jason and his fellow officers learned of it almost the same time the news hit the streets. That afternoon, Jason dreaded going home and facing Desirée. He knew that she wasn't going to like it.

He walked into the kitchen and found her, as usual, in the midst of cooking the evening meal. She stood by the stove, stirring something in a pot. She looked up when Jason walked in and glared at him.

Seeing that heated look, Jason said, "I assume you've heard about Lincoln's Emancipation Proclamation."

"I've heard," Desirée replied in a tight voice.

"What are you going to do about your darkies?"

Sparks flew from Desirée's black eyes. "Do?" she snapped. She slammed the lid back on the pot, saying, "I'll tell you what I'm going to do! The same thing everyone else in the South is going to do. Absolutely nothing!"

"Desirée, New Orleans isn't in the same position as the rest of the South. Undoubtedly, most of the slave owners in the South will ignore Lincoln's proclamation. But New Orleans is an occupied city. The Union

Army has been ordered to protect the slaves' freedom, an order that came directly from the president himself."

"Whose president?" Desirée asked, venom dripping from her voice. "Not mine. My president is Jefferson Davis. Lincoln can't tell me what to do. He has no authority over me."

"Desirée, don't try anything foolish. General Butler said—"

"You don't have to tell me what General Butler said," Desirée interjected angrily. "I can just imagine. Now, 'the beast' has something else to shove down our throats. And I'm sure he'll enjoy it immensely, particularly since he's an Abolitionist." Her eyes bored into Jason. "You know, I've always wondered how he could claim to hate slavery so much when it was his idea to declare the slaves within the Union lines contraband of war. What difference does it make to a darkie if he's a slave to the army or to an individual? Either way, he's still a slave; he's still not free."

"At least the army pays the confiscated slaves," Jason pointed out.

Desirée laughed harshly, saying, "Pays them? Why, it's such a small amount it isn't even a token payment. If anything, it's an insult. No, the slaves were better off with their former masters, and they know it. At least he took care of them. Why, no slave owner in Louisiana would have ever put his slaves to work building railroads and dredging out those filthy canals. It's too dangerous!'"

Jason knew that what Desirée said was true. When the railroad and canals were built to Lake Ponchartrain, cheap white labor was used, mostly Irish. The men dropped like flies from malaria, yellow fever, and cholera. No, slaves weren't used for fear of killing them. They were much too valuable. "That's irrelevant, Desirée. The fact remains that the slaves have been freed, and the army has been ordered to protect that freedom. Now, what are you going to do about your darkies?"

"Why are you rushing me?" Desirée said in a resentful voice. "Lincoln said if the southern states rejoined the Union by the first of the year, we could keep out slaves."

"Desirée, we both know that Louisiana isn't going to rejoin the Union," Jason said in a patient voice. "Lincoln may not know it yet, but *we* do. Why put it off till the last minute?"

Desirée glared at Jason. He met her look levelly, hating being put in this position. She *had* to free her slaves. To refuse would be too dangerous for her. And yet, he didn't want to force her. He know how stubborn she was. If he insisted, she'd be all the more determined not to. No, he wanted her to do it on her own.

He also realized that *he* could free them. As her husband, they were legally his property. But Jason had never considered them as such. Besides, if he overrode Desirée on this, it would infuriate her. So far, their marriage had gone rather smoothly, surprisingly so. He didn't want to put any new barriers between them. Damn this war!

Finally, Desirée threw her hands up in exasperation, saying, "Oh, Jason, it's not that I mind freeing them. To be honest, I never really considered them slaves. If any one of them had ever asked to be freed, I would have gladly given them their manumission papers. It's just that it infuriates me for some damned Yankee to tell me what to do with my property—and then *force* me to do it! It makes me so mad I could—I could spit!"

At that minute, Desirée did look fighting mad and,

with her dark eyes flashing, very beautiful and very desirable. Jason fought back the urge to sweep her up in his arms, carry her to their bedroom, and make passionate love to her. Instead, he asked, "Then you will free them?"

"Yes, I'll free them," Desirée said with a defeated sigh. "And I suppose you're right. Why put it off to the last minute?" A worried look came over her face; she chewed her bottom lip. Then she said, "Jason, would you mind breaking the news to them?"

"Me?" Jason asked in surprise. "Why me?"

"Because I'm afraid if I tell them, they'll think I'm throwing them out."

"They know better than that."

"Yes, I suppose they do," Desirée admitted. "But still, you're so much better at explaining things."

Jason was secretly pleased that Desirée was asking for his help. "All right, I'll tell them," Jason said. "But I want you there when I do. I don't want any of them to think I'm forcing you to do this."

That evening, Jason and Desirée invited all the slaves into the dining room and asked them to sit down. There was a palpable tension in the air and a frightened look in the black peoples' eyes as they seated themselves at the table. Even Tassy was apprehensive, sensing the disturbed emotions of the others.

Jason began by saying, "I'm sure you've all heard about Lincoln's Emancipation Proclamation."

"Then it's true?" Moses asked in an ominous voice. "We're gonna be freed?"

"Yes, it's true," Jason answerd. "The president said we didn't have to do it until the first of the year, but Desirée and I have decided to do it now. You're all free. If you want, you can leave. We won't try to stop you. No one will."

"But where will we go?" Mammy cried, a terrified

314

look in her eyes. "Who's gonna take care of us? I'm too old to get a job."

"You don't have to leave," Jason replied in a soothing voice. "I'm only saying you can if you want to. Personally, Desirée and I would prefer you to stay, but as our servants, not as our slaves. If this is what you decide to do, we'll take care of you, just like we've done in the past. The only difference is we'll pay you a small salary, not as much as we would if you weren't still living with us since we'll still be feeding and clothing you."

"Salary? What's that?" Moses asked.

"That means we'll pay you money for working for us," Jason replied. He scanned the black faces, then said, "Now, I'd like to know from each of you what your decision is." He turned to Mattie, saying, "What about you Mattie? Are you going or staying?"

"I'm staying. I like it here."

Desirée sighed in relief. Mattie was really the only one she had any doubts about staying. She had dreaded the thought of having to resume doing the household chores, even for the brief time it would take to find a new servant.

Hearing Desirée's sigh, Jason smiled, "We're both glad and happy to have you, Mattie." He turned to Mammy, saying, "What about you, Mammy?"

Everyone knew it was a perfunctory question. Just as expected, Mammy answered, "I'm staying." She lifted her chin and looked Jason directly in the eye, saying, "But I ain't gonna take no money."

"But that's the agreement, Mammy," Jason objected. "If you stay, I'll pay you."

"No sir! I don't want no money. If you're gonna take care of me, I don't need it."

"I'm staying, but I ain't gonna take no money, either," Moses chimed in, his look just as determined as Mammy's.

"But you can buy things with it," Jason pointed out. "Surely, there must be something you want. Something personal."

"Like what?" Mammy asked. "One of those fancy silk dresses and silly hats with feathers that those uppidy free niggers wear? Humph! Now, wouldn't this old woman look like something in that?"

In spite of themselves, every adult at the table, except Tassy, laughed. Benjie started to giggle and Mammy shot him a hot look, then crossed her arms over her bosom in her typical stubborn stance, and said, "No sir! I ain't taking no money."

Jason frowned, then said, "I'm afraid that's going to create a problem for Desirée and me. You see, if we don't pay you, everyone will think we haven't freed you, that you're still our slaves." Jason waited for this to sink in before he said, "You wouldn't want us to get into trouble, would you?"

The two old darkies looked aghast at Jason's words. "No, sir," Moses said with a worried look on his face. "We sure don't want you getting into trouble because of us."

"Then please take the money," Jason replied.

Mammy and Moses looked at each other, both scowling deeply. Then Mammy turned to Jason, saying, "We ain't trying to be stubborn. It's just that Moses and I are old. Nobody's gonna hire us. Nobody wants us. And you don't really need us old folks. It's not right for us to take your money."

For the first time, Desirée spoke up. "That's not true, Mammy. I do need you. Why, you're like family to me. No amount of money can buy that."

"I love you, too, honey lamb," Mammy answered, tears shimmering in her dark eyes. "But you don't have to pay money for that kind of needing."

316

"I'm afraid I'm going to have to disagree with both you and Moses, Mammy," Jason said in a firm voice. "We do need you." He looked her directly in the eye and said, "You may be old, but you still perform a lot of services around here, like taking care of Desirée and helping with odd chores. If we didn't have you, Desirée would need a personal maid, and I might even have to hire another servant to help Mattie out."

"That's right," Mattie said, giving Jason her support. "I do the heavy work, but Mammy does a lot of the light work, things I don't have time for."

Seeing Mammy's thoughtful look, Jason knew that they had convinced her of her worth. He turned his attention to Moses, saying, "And Moses, I can't believe you really think you're not needed. Why, you're probably the best groom in Louisiana. No one knows horses like you do. And a man's not born with that kind of knowledge. It's something that's learned over the years. How many good *young* grooms have you ever seen? Not many, I'd wager."

Moses looked deep into Jason's eyes. The old darkie knew he meant every word he said. A flush of both pride and embarrassment crept up his dusky face.

"Now, I don't want to hear any more foolish talk about not being needed," Jason said in a firm voice. "And I want you to take the money. If nothing else, you can buy gifts with it."

Mammy and Moses exchanged quick glances. Then they both grinned, knowing just who those gifts would be for.

"All right, Massa Steele," Mammy said. "I'll take the money." Moses nodded his grey woolly head in agreement.

"I'm afraid that's something you're going to *have* to stop now, Mammy," Jason said. "You can't call me massa. There aren't any slaves and masters anymore."

"But you said I'm free," Mammy objected.

"That's right. You are free."

Mammy lifted her head, saying stubbornly, "Then I can call you anything I want to, and I'm gonna call you massa."

"But—" Jason began.

"No, sir!" Mammy said in a determined voice. "No damned Yankee up in Washington is gonna tell me what to say. Even if he is the president. I'm free now. I can call you anything I like."

Jason looked at Mammy in total exasperation. Then he shook his head, saying, "All right, Mammy. I know when I'm licked."

Mammy grinned. "Yes, sir, I reckon you do."

Desirée, Moses, and Mattie laughed. Jason, chuckling himself, turned his attention to Benjie.

He looked thoughtfully at the wide-eyed boy, wondering if he should offer him the same choice. What if the boy elected to leave? Jason couldn't let him do that, knowing that Benjie had no way to fend for himself. Then Jason saw the naked fear in the boy's eyes and realized that the boy was afraid he was going to say he didn't need him and ask him to leave. Compassion filled Jason as he said, "You'll stay, too, won't you Benjie?"

A look of vast relief came into Benjie's eyes. A broad grin spread across his face. "I'll stay."

"I have a different proposition to offer you in the way of payment," Jason said. "I was thinking I wouldn't pay you as much—"

"I understand. I'm just a boy. I don't do that much work."

"No, Benjie, that's not what I mean. I was thinking that I'd put the better part of your money away for you. That way, when you're a grown man, you'd have

318

a tidy sum to buy something really substantial, like a piece of land."

"What do I want land for?" Benjie asked. "I'm gonna be a groom, like Moses."

"A house then," Jason replied. "Remember, you're free now. There aren't any masters to take care of you. When you've grown, you may not be provided living quarters as part of your job. You'll need your own home then."

Jason glanced at the adult darkies, silently seeking their support. "He's right," Moses said in a firm voice to the boy. "You listen to the major."

"I think you should put aside all his money," Mammy Lou said. "Benjie's just a boy. He'll just waste all that money, spend it on a heap of foolishness he don't even need."

"No, Mammy," Jason replied. "He'll be receiving wages the rest of his life. He needs to know how to manage his money. This will be training for him."

He turned to Tassy. The girl's doelike eyes darted apprehensively to the others sitting around her. Jason knew that she didn't know what was going on. He patted her hand reassuringly, saying, "There's nothing to be afraid of, Tassy. You'll stay with Desirée, just like you always have. We'll take care of you."

Jason's touch and tone of voice soothed Tassy's apprehension more than his words. She smiled in mute acceptance, knowing that this man would never do anything to hurt her.

Jason turned to the others, saying, "I'll put Tassy's money aside also. If she ever shows any sign that there's something special that she wants, I'll give the money to you and you can buy it for her. Otherwise, the money will be there, just in case something should happen that Desirée and I wouldn't be able to take care of her. It will be in our wills. I want you all to remember that, so no one can cheat her out of it."

The other blacks nodded their heads in understanding, the adults thinking what a remarkably kind and compassionate man Jason was.

Jason watched the darkies thoughtfully as they walked out of the room. Undoubtedly, the Abolitionists were lauding Lincoln's proclamation, but he wondered how many of them had really thought the problem through. Oh yes, freeing the slaves sounded good enough in principle, but how many of those who advocated it had stopped to consider what would happen to the very young, the old, and the handicapped. Or any of them, for that matter. There were a few slave who had trades that could support them, trained by their former masters as masons, carpenters, blacksmiths, seamstresses, cooks, or grooms. But the majority of the slaves were common laborers. They would go out into the world to compete for jobs with the unskilled, uneducated whites. But the blacks would be handicapped. Unlike the whites who had been taught the art of survival from birth, the slaves had been cared for all of their lives. In many ways, they were like children, having no idea of how to handle money or fend for themselves.

"I don't think Lincoln did the slaves a favor," Jason remarked in a quiet voice.

"He didn't do it for the benefit of the slaves," Desirée replied bitterly. "He didn't free those slaves in the North or the border states. No, it was a threat to the southern states. Either rejoin the Union or lose your slaves."

"I know, but I still think freeing the slaves was inevitable. Sometime, in the near future, they'll all be freed. Unfortunately, I fear it will be just like this when it happens, catching the slaves totally unprepared in fending for themselves. It's a shame it couldn't be a gradual process, where the slaves could be trained in trades or skills before they're thrown out into the world.''

He really cares, Desirée thought. Not just about the slaves but all people. She remembered how angry Jason had been at one of his fellow officers for sending his troops on a practice forced march with full packs in the heat of the summer. The men had dropped like flies from heat exhaustion.

And she, like everyone else around him, had felt the results of his caring and concern. She only wished he could feel more for her.

Tassy's garden turned out to be so productive that Desirée had a hard time keeping up with canning the vegetables. At the height of its yield, everyone in the household, except Jason and Sergeant O'Malley was put to work. While Tassy and Moses picked the produce, the women pared and sliced the vegetables, then canned them.

Within a few days, the entire pantry was filled with jars of green beans, beets, carrots, corn, peas, tomatoes, lima beans, and black-eyed peas. And still, the garden produced, until every table, every shelf, every nook and cranny in the kitchen was filled.

One afternoon, Desirée sat at the kitchen table, wearily resting her head on her hand. Her feet ached; her hands were numb from wielding the paring knife, and her clothes were soaked with perspiration from the steam.

Jason walked in, chuckling softly. Desirée raised her head and asked, "What's so funny?"

"I probably shouldn't be laughing about it," he answered. "It's something you southerners would be expected to appreciate, but not a Union officer. And yet, I can't help but see the humor of it. Do you know Father James Mullon, down at St. Patricks?"

"Not personally, but I've heard of him. Isn't he the Irish priest who refused to let General Butler confiscate the church bells for the Union war effort?"

"That's right. And now he and Butler have locked horns again. It seems Father Mullon refused to bury a Union soldier and the general severely rebuked him for it."

"That doesn't sound so funny to me."

"No, it was the priest's answer that tickled my fancy. I can almost see the fiery southerner saying it."

"Saying what?" Desirée asked impatiently.

"Father Mullon snapped back, 'Sir, I stand ready to bury the entire Union Army.' "

"And what did Butler have to say to that?"

"Nothing. I understand he turned three shades of purple."

Desirée smiled wanly. Jason frowned, for the first time noticing how tired she looked. "What's wrong, sweet?" he asked. "You look exhausted." A suspicious gleam came into his eyes. "You haven't been scrubbing the floors again, have you?"

"*Non*. It's just all this canning that's getting me down." She motioned to the jars sitting all around her. "*Mon Dieu*, look at it! Who would have dreamed that such a small garden would produce so much? I've sent cases and cases to Jeanne Marie and we still have enough here to last us for two years."

"Then why are you killing yourself canning?"

"Oh, Jason, I can't just let it rot. With so many people starving in the South nowadays, that would be a crime."

"Why don't you just give it to the neighbors?"

"I would, but you know how they feel about me. They'd starve to death before they'd accept anything from me."

"What about letting Tassy give it away? Maybe they'd take it from her, particularly if she told them she grew it."

"I doubt it," Desirée replied with a sigh.

"It won't hurt to try."

The next morning, Desirée sent Tassy and Benjie around with two baskets crammed full of fresh vegetables to give to the neighbors, telling them to explain to the Creoles that the food came from Tassy's garden, not hers. Much to Desirée's surprise, the vegetables were accepted. It seemed the Frenchmen had learned that while pride fed the ego, it did nothing for an empty stomach.

For the next week, the baskets of vegetables went out daily. Then Desirée watched in amazement as the Creoles began sneaking into her courtyard to ask Tassy's advice on growing vegetables. Desirée always hovered in the background, out of sight, afraid that the haughty Creole might laugh at Tassy's simple speech or ridicule her in some way. But with the evidence of her expertise growing profusely all around them, none of the neighbors dared to doubt Tassy's word or her skill. As the Creoles listened intently to every word she said, Tassy beamed. Desirée could almost see her self-confidence and self-esteem growing. She blinked back tears of happiness for Tassy and blessed Jason for his wisdom.

Chapter 16

It was a week later that Desirée awakened and lay in her bed, fighting back the waves of nausea that swept over her. She clenched her teeth and squeezed her eyes shut, forcing herself to remain absolutely still.

Mon Dieu! What in the world was wrong with her? For almost two months, she had been bothered with this strange nausea and tired feeling. At first, she had thought that she had one of the fevers that plagued this swampy country. And then, she had blamed her symptoms on the canning: the exhaustion from the hard work and the nausea from the mixed odors of the steaming vegetables.

Careful not to move too suddenly, she rolled to her side and winced as her tender breast pressed against the mattress. Her eyes flew open as the answer to her strange malady came to her. *Sacre Dieu!* She was *enceinte!*

Mammy Lou opened the door and waddled into the room. "Lands sake, child, are you still in bed? You sure have gotten to be a lazy bones now that you're married. Why, Massa Steele had been up, eaten breakfast, and left the house hours ago."

Desirée ignored Mammy as she walked to the

windows and opened them. The waves of nausea were washing over her again, each one worse than the one before. Every bit of her concentration was being spent to fight them back.

Mammy turned and said, "Now, what would you like for breakfast this morning? How about some nice crisp bacon? And some fried eggs, just like you like them, sunny-side up. And some of my biscuits, just dripping with butter and molasses?"

At Mammy's words, the bile rose, and this time, she couldn't force it back down. Desirée bolted up in bed.

"Lawsy, child! What's wrong with you? Why, you're plumb green."

Desirée threw the sheet back and flew from the bed, making a beeline for the chamber pot. When it was over, Mammy led her back to the bed, patting her face with a wet cloth.

Desirée sat on the edge of the bed, feeling weak and drained. She looked up at Mammy and said in a small voice, "I'm going to have a baby."

Mammy grinned, a grin that stretched from one side of her broad face to the other. "I know, honey lamb. The only thing that can make a woman look that green is a baby. Her dark eyes sparkled as she hugged herself. "Oh, lawsy. I'm so happy. Now, I'm gonna have me a new baby to cuddle and love."

Desirée frowned. Mammy might be happy with the news, but she wasn't so sure she was. In fact, she wasn't sure how she felt about the baby. Did she want it? In a way she didn't want anything else binding her to Jason, since he didn't love her and she couldn't love him back. And how would he feel about the baby? Maybe he wouldn't want it either, since he had made it clear he didn't want any emotional entanglements. Would he consider a baby an emotional entanglement?

She realized that she couldn't think straight right now. She was still in a state of shock. She needed time to sort out her feelings. But until she did, she didn't want Jason to know. "Mammy, please don't say anything to Jason just yet," Desirée said, her eyes pleading silently.

"I understand. You want to pick a special time to tell him."

"Yes, that's it," Desirée answered, jumping at the excuse Mammy gave her.

"How far along are you?"

"I don't know," Desirée admitted.

"When's the last time you had your monthly?"

Desirée's brow furrowed as she thought back. "About two weeks before I married Jason."

"Then you must have gotten this baby right after you married. Maybe even on your wedding night." Mammy grinned, a devilish twinkle coming into her eyes. "Lawsy, that Massa Steele is sure potent."

Desirée flushed and looked away from Mammy's knowing eyes. "Virile is the word, Mammy."

Mammy Lou laughed, her whole big body shaking. "It don't matter what you call it, honey lamb. That Massa Steele is a lot of a man."

In the weeks that followed, Desirée sorted out her feelings about the baby. She decided that she wanted it. She regretted that it couldn't have been conceived in love, but vowed that, even if Jason didn't want it, she would love it. It would be *her* baby. As the days passed, she became fiercely possessive of it, her love for it already growing. She had already decided that it would be a boy and look exactly like Jason.

One afternoon, Jason rode home from headquarters

later than usual, a worried look on his face and he wondered how he was going to break the news to Desirée.

That afternoon, he had been called into General Butler's office and told by the general that there was going to be a dance that night for the Union officers, and that Jason and his wife were expected to attend. When Jason tried to excuse himself, the general had been furious. For over fifteen minutes, Butler had paced the office and raved about how displeased he was with Jason, how he felt Jason was showing too many southern sympathies because of the way he had sided with the Creoles in many of his proclamations. The general had ended the tirade by telling Jason he wanted him to show more loyalty to the North, in fact, demanded it of him. Then Butler had ordered Jason to attend the dance, or else.

As Jason dismounted in the courtyard and untied the box attached to his saddle, he considered telling Desirée that he had been ordered to attend the dance. Then he decided against it, not wanting her to know Butler was displeased with him, for fear it would worry her.

When he walked into their bedroom, Desirée was sitting at the vanity and brushing her hair. Jason placed the box on a chair and walked up to her.

Seeing his reflection in the mirror, Desirée turned, saying, "You're home late. Is anything wrong?"

"Not exactly. I just got detoured this afternoon and had to stay over to finish up."

"We went ahead and ate. I didn't know what time you'd be in." She rose, saying, "I'll heat it up for you."

"Don't bother," Jason replied, stripping off his sash and tossing it on the bed. Unbuttoning his coat, he said, "I don't think I'll have time to eat."

"Why? Do you have to go back to headquarters?"

"No. I have to bathe and get dressed for the dance."

"What dance?"

Jason tossed his coat aside. He turned and faced her. "The dance General Butler is having for his officers tonight. We've all been ordered to attend." A determined gleam came into his eyes. "We're going, Desirée."

Jason couldn't have shocked Desirée more if he had thrown a bombshell into the room. She stared at him in horrified disbelief, then said, *"Non!* I won't go any place where 'the beast' is, much less a social event."

"I'm not asking you, Desirée. I'm telling you. We're going. I've been ordered to attend."

"You can't possibly expect me to go to a Yankee dance, to mingle with my enemies."

"Yes, I do," Jason said in a firm voice.

Desirée's dark eyes flashed. "Well, I *won't* go. Go by yourself!"

"No, we're *both* going," Jason answered in an adamant voice. "I've been ordered to attend, *and* brim my wife."

Desirée couldn't believe Jason's obstinacy. She decided to try a different approach. "I can't go to any dance. Have you forgotten? I'm in mourning."

Jason sat down on a chair and jerked off his boots, saying, "It's been six months since Thad and your father died. That's long enough for mourning."

"Not in the South it isn't! Maybe you cold-blooded Yankees don't mourn for a full year, but *we* do!'"

"Desirée, this isn't just a social occasion," Jason said in a hard, clipped voice. "It's a duty I must perform. They'll be other Union wifes there in mourning for lost loved ones. They'll be there for the same reason I'm asking you to attend. Because their hus-

328

bands have been ordered to do so. We're going."

A sudden gleam came into Desirée's eyes. "I can't go," she said smugly. "I don't have anything suitable to wear. I don't have a black ballgown."

Jason picked up the box on the chair where he had left it earlier and walked to the bed. Placing it on the bed, he opened it and pulled out a dark blue ballgown. Holding the gown in his hand, he turned, saying, "Yes, you do. You'll wear this."

"I can't! It's not black. I told you, I'm in mourning!"

Jason's patience was almost at an end. "Desirée, it's ridiculous for a woman to wear black for a full year. Mourning isn't something you have to prove to the world. It comes from the heart. Besides, I'm sick and tired of seeing you in nothing but black."

Desirée's persistence in wearing black disturbed Jason deeply. Everytime he looked at the color of her clothes, he felt a twinge of guilt, knowing that her brother had been killed by Union forces and that her father's death had inadvertently been caused by Yankees. The black seemed to reach out and slap him, reminding him not only of her loss but of their separate stands, of the war that stood between them like a wall.

"I don't care what you think!" Desirée retorted hotly. "I won't wear that dress!"

Jason caught Desirée's arm and jerked her forward. His grip wasn't painful, but it was like a band of steel around her arm. He towered over her, his green eyes glittering like shards of splintered ice. A twinge of fear ran through Desirée.

Jason looked down at her, saying in a low, carefully measured voice, "Oh, yes, you will wear this dress. Either you'll dress yourself, or I'll strip you and do it for you. I've asked very little of you in this manner, but this is important to me. Now, dammit, we're going to that dance, and you're wearing this dress!"

Desirée couldn't believe that he could be so insensitive, so cruel as to force her to mingle with her enemies. What had happened to the kind considerate man she had come to know over the past few months? Had it all been an act? Was this cold-blooded brute the real Jason? Her anger rose. She glared at him.

There eyes locked in a silent struggle for a long minute, each pitting their will against the other. But Desirée knew that she couldn't win any match against *this* Jason. There was a hard, unbending quality about him now. The knowledge made her angrier.

"All right! I'll go!" she shrieked.

Jason released her arm and stepped back. Desirée raised her chin, her black eyes glittering with rage. "But you'll be sorry," she threatened.

They dressed in total silence. When Jason tried to help her into the carriage, Desirée jerked her arm back and climbed in by herself. She perched in the opposite corner from Jason, refusing to talk or even look at him.

Jason sat in his corner of the carriage, watching her sit stiffly and stare out the window. His frustration grew. Dammit, he hadn't wanted to force her. He knew that it wouldn't be easy for her, but Butler hadn't given him any choice. Why couldn't she understand the position *he* was in? He had told her that he had been ordered to do it, that it was important to him. Couldn't she give him her support just this one time, for just this one night? By the time they reached the St. Charles Hotel, where the dance was being held, Jason was angry himself.

As Desirée stepped down from the carriage in front of the hotel, she glanced up at the hotel's white dome, seeming to glow with a life of its own in the moonlight. The sight brought back memories of the times she and Thad had stood on the open turret above that dome and drank in the breathtaking view of the city far below them.

Jason's hand on her elbow brought her back to the present. She looked around her, seeing the Yankee officers and their wives milling around them, laughing and talking. A fresh anger filled her: at the officers and at the man who was forcing her to mingle with her enemy—the same enemy that had killed her brother. She jerked her arm away from Jason and walked stiffly away from him, her mouth tight set, her eyes flashing angrily.

Jason flushed, aware that some of the couples had witnessed Desirée's silent show of temper. He caught up with her in two swift strides and took her arm again, holding it tightly against him. When she tried to pull it away, he hissed from the side of his mouth, "Cut it out, Desirée! I know you're angry at me for making you come, but I'd appreciate it if you'd save our personal quarrels for the privacy of our own home."

Desirée glanced about her, seeing the smug smiles that were sent their way. Did they know who she was—a southerner? Did they know Jason had forced her to come? Were they enjoying her humiliation? As much as she longed to spit in their faces, claw their eyes out, she'd be damned if she'd make a spectacle of herself in front of some damned Yankees. No, she wouldn't give them satisfaction. She'd show those uncouth animals the real meaning of good breeding.

She raised her head proudly and walked regally across the huge lobby and up the stairs, a dazzling smile pasted on her face. Only Jason, walking beside her and feeling the stiffness of her body, knew she was seething. To those descending the stairs, she was a vision of breathtaking beauty and grace, and many of the men cast admiring glances over their shoulders as she passed, a few even turning and gawking openly, much to the embarrassment of their wives.

The swelling music reached their ears long before Jason and Desirée reached the huge oval ballroom that stretched seventy feet across and twenty feet high. And when they stepped into the room, Desirée couldn't help but gasp. She had never seen it so crowded, not even at Mardi Gras. And the whole room was filled with the hated blue uniforms. To have the St. Charles Hotel, the pride and joy of New Orleans, filled to the brim with the enemy, seemed yet another desecration to Desirée. Bitter tears stung at her eyes.

Jason took her into his arms and swung her on the dance floor. Desirée danced stiffly, staring at his broad shoulders. Jason looked down at her, feeling a twinge of pity for her.

For several dances, they were left to themselves, but at the end of the fourth dance, a pleasant-looking, sandy-haired officer tapped Jason on the shoulder.

Jason turned, then said, "Hello, Bob."

The major smiled, saying, "I see you and your beautiful wife made it to the dance, after all. I looked for you earlier but couldn't find you."

Jason knew there was no way out. Whether Desirée liked it or not, he was going to have to introduce her to his friend. He turned to her, saying, "Desirée, this is a good friend of mine from the provost marshal's office, Bob Gregg."

Bob smiled, saying, "I'm pleased to meet you, Mrs. Steele."

Desirée stood woodenly, aware of Jason's penetrating gaze on her. After what seemed an eternity to Jason, she replied, "My pleasure, Major Gregg."

"May I have the next dance?" Bob asked, then turned to Jason, saying, "That is if you can bear to give her up for a few minutes."

Again, Jason knew there was no graceful way out. He shot Desirée a warning look and said, "I imagine I can tolerate it," adding for Desirée's benefit, "since we're such good friends."

Desirée shot Jason a murderous look and, as the music began, she turned to the major in furious resignation. I hate him, she thought, as the major swung her on the dance floor. I'll never forgive him for subjecting me to this.

As they whirled around the ballroom, Bob said, "You have a beautiful city here, Mrs. Steele. My wife has fallen in love with it. I'm beginning to wonder if I'll ever get her back to Michigan."

"Thank you, Major Gregg," Desirée answered stiffly.

As they danced, Bob continued to make pleasant conversation, and by the time the dance was finished, Desirée had discovered something that utterly shocked her. Despite the blue uniform, she liked him.

As the evening wore on and Desirée was claimed for more dances by the officers, she found herself torn. She had come to the dance determined not to enjoy it, to hate every minute of it, and yet none of the officers were the animals she had imagined them to be. All were just as polite and charming as any southern gentlemen. The revelation was disturbing. She was finding it increasingly difficult to hate them.

At the end of one dance, Desirée looked about her. Surely, they could leave now, she thought. But to her dismay, she couldn't see Jason anywhere in the crowded ballroom.

"May I have this dance, Mrs. Steele?" a voice asked from behind her.

Desirée turned and then gasped, seeing Colonel Anders standing in front of her, a mocking smile on his face and that same cold glitter in his eyes.

Fear and revulsion rose up in her. She fought the urge to turn and run. She stepped back, saying stiffly, "No, I don't—"

Before she could finish, Colonel Anders stepped forward and took her in his arms, whirling her off into the dance floor.

The feel of his cold hand on hers made goose bumps rise on Desirée's skin. As he ran his other hand over her back, Desirée felt the bile rising in her throat. Frantically, she looked around her for Jason.

"Looking for your husband?" Colonel Anders asked in a low, tight voice. His eyes flared briefly before he quickly hid his anger. "Well, he won't always be around to protect you."

Desirée's head snapped up at the implied threat. Anders smiled down at her blandly, but she could feel the hatred radiating from him in powerful waves.

"Oh, you think you pulled a fast one on me, don't you?" Anders hissed. "Well, I'll get my hands on you one day, and when I do, you'll be sorry. Some day I'll have you where I want you, and when I do . . . "

His voice deliberately lowered so others couldn't hear, Colonel Anders described in lurid detail the horrible, sadistic things he would do to Desirée, all the time smiling down at her and looking as if he were behaving like a perfect gentleman. Desirée couldn't believe her ears as she danced woodenly, shocked speechless as he spewed out his obscene filth. Not until he started calling her vile and vulgar names did she finally recover. Suddenly, her anger rose and erupted.

She jerked away from him and spat, "You filthy pig!" Her hand flew out and slapped him—hard, the noise sounding like the crack of a pistol shot over the music.

Desirée looked up at the vivid red mark on the colonel's face, stunned by what she had done. She glanced around her apprehensively, seeing that the couples who had been dancing around them had stopped and were staring at them with shocked expressions on their faces. Suddenly, the music stopped, and everyone in the ballroom turned to see what had happened.

Desirée was acutely conscious of everyone staring at her and of Colonel Anders glaring down at her, his arms held stiffly at his side, his fingers twitching with the urge to hit her back. And then, a short man, with a pot belly and a bushy black mustache on his face, pushed his way through the crowd.

When he stood before them, the officer demanded angrily, "What's going on here, Colonel Anders?"

"I'm afraid I don't know, General Butler," Anders lied adroitly. "All I did was simply ask the lady to dance, and then suddenly, for some unknown reason, she seemed to take affront. The next thing I knew, she was calling me a pig and slapping my face."

General Butler? Desirée was shocked. This pudgy, baldheaded man was "the beast" himself?

"Of course, I suppose it was a foolish thing to do, asking her to dance," Anders continued.

"Why do you say that?" Butler asked.

"Why I should have known she'd pull something like that," Anders answered smoothly. "Jump at the first chance to insult a Yankee, just like all the rest of her kind."

Butler blinked his eyes, a confused look on his face.

"You do know who she is, don't you, Ben?" the colonel asked. "She's Major Steele's wife, one of those Creoles he's always coddling."

General Butler's eyes widened with surprise. Then he glared at Desirée. How dare this haughty rebel come to this dance and insult one of his officers!

Desirée watched in horror as the general's look turned livid, his double chins shaking with his fury, his face turning red clear up to the top of his shiny baldhead, his crossed eye twitching furiously. Why, he believes him, she thought. He actually believes Colonel Anders's claim to innocence and that she had attacked him with no provocation at all. She glanced around her, hoping that someone had heard what the colonel had said to her and would come to her defense. But everyone around her was glaring at her angrily.

Jason shouldered his way through the crowd and stepped forward. "What is the meaning of this, Major Steele?" General Butler demanded, shaking with fury.

Jason had seen Desirée slapping Colonel Anders from across the ballroom. Other than that, he had no idea what had happened. All he could remember was her threat to make him sorry that he'd forced her to come to this dance. He was both angry at her for putting them both in this position and afraid for her, fearing he wouldn't be able to protect her from Butler's wrath, particularly since the general was already displeased with him.

Jason shot Desirée a hard look and then said in a tight voice, "I'll be happy to explain, general." He looked around at the crowd surrounding them. "But I don't think this is the time or the place. I'll see you in your office the first thing in the morning. I'll answer any questions you have then."

Before Butler could object, he took Desirée's arm in a tight grip and rushed her through the crowd, his stride quick and angry.

One of the Union wives standing at the back of the crowd watched as Jason led Desirée away, furious herself. But it wasn't Desirée she was angry with. It was Colonel Anders. She had danced past Desirée and the colonel and had heard him calling her vile names. His behavior had shocked and disgusted her. Even more infuriating was the way he had deliberately lied to cover up for himself.

Desirée had a hard time keeping up with Jason as he rushed her from the ballroom. She looked up at his angry face, saying, "Surely, you don't believe Colonel Anders."

"You said you'd make me sorry for forcing you to come to the dance, but I never dreamed you'd go that far," Jason said in a tight voice, staring straight ahead as he threaded their way through the crowd. "Well, dammit, I hope you're satisfied!"

"But I don't mean that," Desirée objected. "I was angry at the time."

"Yes, and you were still angry when we got here, too," Jason snapped back. "I saw the way you were behaving."

"But, Jason, you don't know what happened. Colonel Anders—"

"Asked you to dance," Jason interjected, as he pulled her out the front door of the hotel. He turned to her, a furious look on his face. "Dammit, I know you don't like the man, but you could have at least danced with him for appearance's sake. After all, what could have happened to you on the dance floor with everyone there? But no, you just had to make a scene, humiliate me."

"No, it wasn't like that. He—"

"I don't want to hear any more about it!" Jason thundered.

Desirée watched as he turned and signaled for their

337

carriage, feeling stunned. She regretted her rash threat, but she couldn't believe that Jason would side against her, particularly when he knew what Anders had tried to do to her. A deep hurt filled her.

The return trip to their home was spent in total silence, Jason glaring angrily out the window, Desirée nursing her hurt. As soon as they had reached the house, Jason took her upstairs, then left her in their bedroom without another word. Desirée threw herself across the bed and cried for hours, both hurt and angry. Finally, she rose, undressed, and fell back into the bed, quickly falling asleep in total exhaustion.

But Jason didn't sleep that night. He spent it pacing the library floor, worrying, his fear for Desirée finally overriding his anger at her. He had to protect, he thought. But how? What excuse could he give Butler for her behavior? The last thing he wanted to do was tell the general about Anders's threat to force Desirée to be his mistress. Then Butler might confront Anders and learn that Desirée had refused to sign the loyalty oath, and as angry as the general was at Desirée right now, he didn't know what Butler might do to her.

The next morning, when Desirée awakened, Jason was standing by the bed, shaved and dressed. Before she hardly got her eyes open, he said, "I'm leaving now."

Still groggy, she asked, "So early?"

"Yes, I promised General Butler I'd be there the first thing this morning." He ran a hand wearily through his thick, dark hair, saying, "I only hope he'll believe my explanation. I plan to tell him you've been upset and not too emotionally stable since the death of your brother and father, that you hadn't wanted to go to the dance but I forced you to, that suddenly you saw the blue uniform and something snapped. The last thing I want to tell him is how we've crossed swords with Anders before. He might start asking too many questions, and I don't want him to know you refused to sign the loyalty oath until we were married."

He walked to door and opened it. Then he turned, saying, "Just hope he accepts the story. Personally, I don't think Anders is any more anxious than we are for Butler to know the truth."

But you don't know the truth either, she thought bitterly as he closed the door behind him. She wondered if it would have done any good to tell General Butler the truth. No, the colonel would have denied it, and there was no doubt in her mind who Butler would have believed. Of course, he'd take the word of one of his officers over hers, particularly if he was a personal friend.

She remembered how drawn and tired Jason had looked, but she had seen no sign of the anger he had shown the night before. She finally realized that he was worried about her, afraid he wouldn't be able to protect her from General Butler's anger. Jason was right, she admitted reluctantly. She shouldn't have lost her temper. She would have been better off if she had endured Anders's threats and insults. There, in the middle of the crowded ballroom, he couldn't have done anything else to her. Now, considering how furious General Butler had been, she might yet go to prison. She had put both herself and Jason in a precarious position, and she couldn't help but wonder if the devious Colonel Anders hadn't planned the whole thing.

For a long time, Desirée lay in bed, worrying. Then she rose and slipped on her wrapper. She was sitting at the vanity and brushing her hair when Jason walked back into the bedroom.

She turned, surprised to see him back so soon. "What happened? Did General Butler believe you?"

"I didn't even have to offer him any explanations. In fact, I didn't even see him. He left word with his adjutant that it wasn't even necessary."

"Not necessary? But, why?"

"According to the adjutant, who overheard everything, one of the officers' wives overheard Colonel Anders calling you vile names. She was infuriated with Anders, both by his behavior and by his lying to General Butler to cover for himself. She gathered a delegation of officers' wives together and they went to General Butler to complain, not only about Colonel Anders but about Butler's Women's Order. They told him that they thought the order was an insult to all respectable women and threatened if he did anything to you, they'd send an official letter of complaint to the War Department."

"Then, that's the end of it?" Desirée asked in disbelief.

"Apparently. I understand Butler was still furious, but this time at the delegation of women. No, I don't think he's going to do anything to you. He knows his hands are tied."

Desirée was a little stunned at being told that a group of Yankee women had come to her defense. A wave of gratefulness washed over her. "Do you know who the woman was who gathered the delegation?"

"Yes, I do. Do you remember Bob, the officer I introduced you to last night? It was his wife, Dorothy."

She remembered. She promised herself she would visit the woman and thank her personally. But not today. She was much too tired from all the worry and excitement.

Jason frowned at Desirée, saying, "Why didn't you

tell me Anders had insulted you?"

Desirée's dark eyes flashed with remembered anger. "I tried to, but you wouldn't listen."

Jason winced at her words, knowing that they were true. He had gotten just as caught up in his anger as she had. "I'm sorry I lost my temper, Desirée. I thought you were trying to get even with me for forcing you to go to the dance. Just what *did* Anders say?"

Desirée told Jason everything, shivering with fear and revulsion as she related the horrible things Colonel Anders had threatened to do to her. As she talked, Jason's anger slowly rose. When she finished telling him the filthy names Colonel Anders had called her, Jason exploded. "That son of a bitch! I'll kill him!"

He turned and stormed from the room, a murderous look on his face. For a minute, Desirée sat, stunned by his anger. Then, she rose and ran after him, calling, "No, Jason!"

But Jason was already stalking angrily through the courtyard, ignoring her calls. Desirée ran after him and, realizing that she was only wearing her wrapper, she turned and hurried back into the house.

When she entered the foyer, Mammy Lou was standing there. "What's going on? What's the massa so mad about? Who's he gonna kill?" she asked, her eyes wide with alarm, her face a pasty-grey color.

"I can't explain now, Mammy. I've got to catch him before he does something rash." Desirée hurried down the hall, calling over her shoulder, "Tell Moses to bring the carriage around while I get dressed."

Thirty minutes later, Desirée and Moses drove up in front of headquarters. Desirée rushed to Jason's office, only to discover that he hadn't checked in that morning. As they drove back home, Desirée chewed her lip anxiously. She had no idea of where to look for him.

As she walked back through the courtyard, Desirée saw Sergeant O'Malley leading his horse from the carriage house. Seeing her, he dropped the reins and walked up to her, saying, "Good morning, Mrs. Steele."

"Good morning, sergeant."

"Do you know where the major went?" O'Malley asked in a bewildered voice. "I saw him rushing off about an hour ago and thought he'd be back. Did he go on to headquarters? Was there some kind of emergency I didn't know about?"

Desirée could understand the Irishman's bewilderment. He and Jason always rode together to headquarters. "No, I don't know where he is, except he's not at headquarters. I just came from there. I've been looking for him myself."

O'Malley scratched in head in puzzlement.

"There is an emergency that has come up. I really need to talk to him. Do you think you could find him for me?" Desirée asked, holding her breath for fear O'Malley would ask what the emergency was.

But O'Malley had been a soldier too long to ask any questions. "Well, now, ma'am. I can try."

Desirée paced the floor while O'Malley was gone. By the time he returned, three hours later, her nerves were crawling.

He limped into the room, looking hot and weary, saying, "I'm sorry, ma'am, but I can't find him anywhere."

"Is something wrong with your leg, sergeant? You're limping."

"No, ma'am. It's just that I'm not used to riding that damn— His normally ruddy face flushed three shades of deeper red. "Excuse my language, ma'am. I mean danged horse."

342

"Then you have no idea of where he could be?" Desirée asked.

"Well, it's possible he went off with one of the other officers. There's some places that we enlisted men ain't allowed to go, you know."

Desirée remembered Dorothy Gregg. Maybe her husband could find Jason. "Do you by any chance know Major Gregg's address?"

"Why, yes, ma'am, I do. It just so happens the major had me drop some books off at his house a few months ago. Do you want me to look there?"

"No, if you'll just tell me the address, I'll have Moses drive me over. I've been planning on visiting Mrs. Gregg anyway."

Fifteen minutes later, Desirée knocked on the Greggs's door. When a tall, slim, dark-haired woman opened the door, Desirée vaguely recognized her from the dance the night before. "Mrs. Gregg? I'm Desirée Steele, Jason's wife. I'd like to thank you—"

"Oh, thank God, you're here," Dorothy interjected, taking her arm and pulling Desirée into the house. "I've been wondering how I could get in touch with you. I didn't dare ask Jason your address for fear he'd get suspicious."

"What are you talking about?" Desirée asked.

"Jason is threatening to challenge Colonel Anders to a duel. Oh, Desirée, you've got to stop him," Dorothy said in an urgent voice. "Dueling is against army regulations. At the very least, he could be court-martialed. And if he killed Colonel Anders, he'd be tried for murder."

For the first time in her life, Desirée felt faint. Seeing her deathly pale face, Dorothy said, "Oh, my God. I shouldn't have broken it to you so suddenly. Come in here and sit down."

Dorothy led her into the drawing room, supporting

343

Desirée as she walked on wobbly legs. Once she was seated, Dorothy asked, "Should I get some smelling salts?"

"No, I'm fine now. I was just momentarily stunned." She looked up to see Dorothy watching her, her grey eyes full of concern. "When he rushed off angry this morning, I was afraid he'd do something rash. I've been looking all over for him."

"Well, you don't have to look any further. He's here."

"Here?" Desirée asked in surprise.

"Yes. When Jason couldn't find Colonel Anders this morning, Bob talked him into coming over here. They're in the library. Bob's still trying to reason with him, but I don't think he's making much headway. Jason's determined to challenge Anders to a duel. I've never seen him so angry."

Neither have I, Desirée thought. "May I see him?"

"Of course. That's why I wanted to get in touch with you. I was hoping you could reason with him. But do you feel up to it right now?"

"I'm fine now," Desirée assured her, rising to her feet.

As they walked down the hallway to the library, Desirée could hear the raised voices of the two men arguing. Dorothy knocked on the door, but because of the noise, the two men didn't hear. The second time, she pounded on it.

The door was flung open, and Bob looked out, an angry look on his face. Then, seeing Desirée, his look was replaced with one of immense relief. "Thank God, you're here, Mrs. Steele," he said. He shot Jason a hot look, saying, "Maybe you can talk some sense into this mule-headed husband of yours."

Desirée glanced at Jason. He had that same hard look that she had seen the night before. She knew that she had a formidable task on her hands. "I intend to try," she replied.

After she had walked into the room, Bob excused himself and left, closing the door behind him.

For a long minute, Jason and Desirée stared at each other across the room. Jason broke the silence, saying, "You can save your breath, Desirée. You're not going to talk me out of it. I've made up my mind. I'm challenging Anders to a duel. I intend to kill that bastard."

"Why?"

"Why?" Jason asked, as if she had just asked a stupid question. "Because he threatened and insulted you, that's why."

"But he threatened and insulted *me*, not you. I've had my revenge. I obtained that when I insulted him right back and slapped his face. Now, I just want to forget it."

"My God! What kind of a man would I be if I stood by and let a man treat my wife that way and did nothing about it?"

"A sensible man."

"Sensible?"

"Yes, sensible. I can't believe you'd do something as foolish and stupid as challenge a man to a duel. Besides that, it's selfish, too. I thought better of you."

"Selfish?" Jason asked in disbelief.

"Yes, selfish! I told you, I've had my revenge. I'm satisfied. No, it's your stupid male honor, not mine, you're defending, your face you're trying to save, with no regard for my feelings at all."

"No," Jason objected. "I'm doing it for you."

"No, you aren't. If you cared anything about me, you'd realize that fighting this duel would only leave me unprotected. Dorothy told me about the army's regulations regarding duels. What good would you be

345

to me if you went to prison or were hung for murder?"

Jason frowned.

"If you don't care anything about me, then at least consider your baby. He'll need your protection and support."

Jason's dark head snapped up. "Baby? What baby?"

"The baby I'm going to have next spring."

Jason's eyes flew to her stomach and then back to her face. "Why didn't you tell me?"

Desirée didn't want to tell him because she feared he didn't want the baby. "Because—because I didn't know for sure until just recently, and I was waiting for a special time to tell you. I certainly hadn't expected to tell you like this."

A perplexed look came over Jason's face.

Desirée took quick advantage of his indecision. "Oh, Jason, don't you see?" she implored. "There's no way the baby and I can gain from you fighting this duel. Either way, we lose."

"He deserves killing," Jason argued. "He's a monster."

"I agree. But let someone else do it. Besides, no real harm was done, not enough for you to risk our entire future over."

Jason didn't want to endanger their future, the future he had such great hopes for. And he certainly didn't want to leave Desirée and his child unprotected. And they would be if something happened to him, particularly since Desirée had no family to turn to for help, other than Jeanne Marie, another defenseless woman. His love and sense of responsibility finally overrode his anger.

Desirée could tell by the expression on Jason's face that she had won. She sighed in relief, saying, "Let's go home, Jason. I'm tired."

Silently, they walked from the room and down the hall. When they reached the parlor door, Bob stepped out and looked at them. One glance at Jason's face told him all he needed to know. Desirée had succeeded where he had failed.

He smiled sheepishly at Jason, saying, "Will you forgive me for calling you all those awful names?"

Jason grinned. "You mean mule-headed fool, obstinate son of a bitch, and stupid bastard?"

"My God," Dorothy said with a small laugh. "Is that what he called you?"

"Yes, and everyone of them was true," Jason replied good-naturedly. He turned to Bob, saying, "Thank you for everything. If you hadn't delayed me, I'd already done something I'd live to regret."

"Won't you stay for dinner?" Dorothy asked.

Jason seriously doubted that Desirée would be willing to dine with his Yankee friends. "No, I don't think so. We've both been through a lot in the past twenty-four hours. We're both tired."

"Would you come for tea tomorrow?" Desirée asked Dorothy.

Jason looked at her with surprise.

Jason wasn't the only one surprised by Desirée's invitation. She had surprised herself. The words had just seemed to slip out, with no forethought. But now, she found that she couldn't regret them. She owed much to this northern woman. Strangely, Dorothy didn't seem like the enemy any longer. But then, maybe Dorothy didn't want to socialize with her. Dorothy's coming to her defense might have been motivated by the desire to simply see justice done, and her invitation to dinner, only good manners.

"I'd love to," Dorothy answered with a warm smile, surprising Desirée for the second time.

That night, as they were undressing for bed, Desi-

347

rée looked at Jason from the corner of her eye. He'd been very quiet and thoughtful ever since they had left the Greggs's home. Was he displeased about the baby? She had to know.

"Jason, how do you feel about the baby?"

Jason turned, his eyes once again flicking from her stomach to her face. "I'll admit I was stunned at first. I hadn't expected a child this soon." He grinned. "But then, I don't know why. As often as we've made love, it was inevitable."

Desirée flushed. Yes, she thought, that was one appetite that they fed frequently and lavishly, and yet, it never seemed to be satisfied. But he still hadn't told her how he felt. "Then you're not particularly pleased?"

Jason walked to her and took her in his arms. Nuzzling her hair with his chin, he said, "No, to the contrary. I'm very pleased."

Was he only saying it or did he mean it? Desirée wondered. And then she was distracted from the thought as Jason lifted her chin and kissed her.

Soon, she was lost in Jason's warm, heady kiss and the feel of his hands caressing her as he deftly stripped her of her petticoat and chemise. When he lifted and carried her to the bed, she snuggled dreamily against his broad chest, loving the feel of his strong arms around her and her bare breasts pressed against his naked skin, the crisp hairs there tickling her nipples.

He laid her gently on the bed and, stripping off his pants, he joined her. Lying on his side and propped up on one elbow, his eyes leisurely drifted over her. *Mon Dieu*, Desirée thought, just his looking at her could make her melt and tingle all over.

Jason's hand caressed her stomach. "You don't look any different. Are you sure?"

"I'm sure."

Jason gazed at Desirée's stomach. It was hard to believe that their child was actually living, already growing within her. His love surged through him. He bent and kissed her stomach, an act of love for both the baby and its mother.

Desirée was stunned by his tender act. Was he kissing the baby or just her? And then again, her thought was swept away by the feel on Jason's warm hand on her breast.

"Yes, they are fuller," Jason said as his slender fingers gently stroked one mound. "I'm surprised I hadn't noticed. But then, you always had such beautiful, full breasts."

Desirée flushed. His complimenting her so intimately both embarrassed and thrilled her. As he bent and kissed her breast, her heartbeat quickened in anticipation of their lovemaking.

Jason lifted his head and kissed her lips tenderly, then flipped the covers up over them. He lay back down, placing her head on his shoulder. Desirée waited for something else to happen, but Jason made no more advances. Desirée felt a deep disappointment filling her—and something more.

He wasn't going to kiss her like that, caress her like that, start those fires to smoldering, and then leave her dangling, was he? Why, she wouldn't sleep a minute all night. What was wrong with him? Didn't he desire her anymore? Did the thought of making love to a pregnant woman repulse him? Was she doomed to lie by his side, night after night, tormented by memories of his beautiful, exciting lovemaking for the duration of her pregnancy. *Mon Dieu!* That would be sheer torture!

She summoned up her courage and asked, "Is something wrong? I thought you were going to—" She flushed, very aware of those misty-green eyes on

349

her.

"To make love to you," Jason finished for her. "I was, but you look so exhausted, I decided it would be selfish of me."

"I'm not tired," Desirée objected.

Jason rose over her, saying, "You're sure?"

Suddenly, Desirée felt embarrassed. *Mon Dieu!* She was practically begging him. "Yes, but if you don't want to . . ." Her voice trailed off.

Jason ducked his head and nibbled her earlobe, whispering, "*Ma cherie*, I'd have to be dead and in my grave before I'd stop wanting to make love to you." He chuckled. "Even when we're old and grey, I'll be hobbling around the room, chasing you."

Old and grey? Of course, they were married for life. Strangely, the thought didn't disturb her but pleased her immensely. And I'll let you catch me, too, she thought, a smile on her lips.

Jason made slow, tender love to Desirée, his kisses achingly sweet, his caresses deliberately gentle. Even when he entered her, he was very careful, his thrusts slow and well controlled, holding his passion in rein for fear of inadvertently hurting her.

Desirée floated back to earth and lay, long after Jason had fallen asleep, staring at the canopy above her. While he had satisfied her with his tender, sweet lovemaking, and while she appreciated his concern for her condition, she didn't particularly like being treated like a piece of fragile crystal. Oh, it was all right for a change of pace, but she hoped Jason wasn't going to deny her of his fiery, passionate lovemaking just because she was going to have a baby. *Ma foi!* She wasn't sick or crippled. A little exercise wasn't going to hurt her.

The next morning, Desirée lay in bed enjoying her daily treat: watching Jason shave and dress. When he had finished, he walked to the bed and kissed her good-bye.

Rising, he looked down at her and said, "Why don't you stay in bed today and rest?"

Desirée frowned.

Ignoring her look, Jason said in a firm voice, "And another thing. I'm going to hire a cook. That job is entirely too much for you now that you're going to have a baby."

Desirée shot from the bed. She stood before him, stark naked, her hands on her hips, her dark eyes flashing. "*Sacre Dieu!* If you think I'm going to lie around and get fat and lazy just because I'm going to have a baby, you're crazy! I refused to be coddled. There's nothing wrong with me. I'm not sick or suddenly fragile. I'm just *enceinte*! And I intend to keep up with everything I've been doing—including my cooking!"

"All right, Desirée," Jason conceded, seeing the determined look on her face and just a little stunned by her fierce outburst. "Just promise me you won't overtire yourself."

"I won't. *Mon Dieu!* I'm not stupid either!"

Jason turned and walked from the room, a wide grin on his face. He should have known Desirée wouldn't let her pregnancy slow her down or use it as an excuse to be pampered. And God, she had looked magnificent standing there naked, with her hair flying wildly about her face and shoulders and her eyes flashing. Jason's body responded to the memory. He stopped, seriously considering going right back and making torrid, passionate love to her. Then, remembering he was already late, he forced himself to walk down the hall and out of the house.

That afternoon, Dorothy Gregg came to tea. Desirée had expected their meeting to be a little stilted and tense, however, much to both women's pleasure, they found they had much in common: their tastes in music, books, theatre, even fashions.

By silent, mutual consent, they avoided mentioning the war or anything vaguely political. As the afternoon wore on, Desirée realized she had sorely missed the company of another woman her age. She wondered if that was why she was enjoying herself so much. And then, she realized with surprise, that was not the case at all. She liked this slender, plain-faced woman, with her wide smile and sparkling grey eyes. Her conversation was stimulating and not at all silly or dull as it had been with some of her southern friends.

"I've fallen in love with your city," Dorothy confessed. "It's like visiting another country, with its Spanish and French architecture and its continental air." She looked about her, saying, "This is the first time I've actually been in one of these Creole homes. It's just as beautiful and charming as I imagined it would be." She laughed. "I used to make Bob drive me through the Vieux Carre, so I could admire the homes, wishing I could see the inside, too."

"Would you like to see the rest of the house?"

"I'd love to," Dorothy answered, her grey eyes sparkling.

When they had finished their tour, Dorothy said, "Oh, there's so many places in New Orleans I've heard about and would just love to see, but Bob and I don't know our way around all that well and he's so busy. I've been tempted to just take off on my own, but I know I'd get lost."

"Perhaps, I could take you."

"Would you?"

Desirée was proud of her city. She could think of nothing more enjoyable than showing it to someone who would appreciate its old world charm and beauty. "I'd love to."

As Dorothy rose to leave, Desirée said, "You know, Dorothy, I'll have to admit that you surprised me."

"In what way?"

Desirée hesitated, flushing, then said, "Well, I always thought northern women were cold and haughty."

Dorothy laughed, then confessed, "And I always thought southern women were weak, spoiled, and insipid. It seems we were both wrong."

From then on, Dorothy and Desirée spent much of their free time together. Desirée gave Dorothy a tour of the city that only a native of New Orleans could give, showing her not only its famous landmarks but little out-of-the-way places that reeked of history and old-country charm. Within a week, their friendship was firmly cemented, and Desirée extended an invitation to dinner to both of the Greggs.

After they had finished eating, Dorothy sighed contentedly, saying, "I love these Creole dishes. I've been after Bob to find me a Creole cook, but apparently, they're not easy to come by. But then, I can't blame anyone for not wanting to give them up."

"That's right," Bob agreed. "We've been eating at one of the restaurants when our hunger for Creole food gets the best of us, but I'm afraid not as often as we'd like. They're terribly expensive."

"I suppose your cook had been with you a long time," Dorothy remarked, a hint of envy in her voice.

Jason's lips twitched. Desirée grinned, saying, "Yes, all my life."

"That's what I thought," Dorothy said in a despairing voice.

"Desirée cooked this meal," Jason said, smiling proudly.

"You cooked this?" Dorothy asked in astonishment.

"Yes. Why do you act so surprised?"

Dorothy blushed, making her freckles stand out even more. "Well—I—I just thought all southern women had cooks."

"I did have until—" Desirée flushed. She had almost blurted until the Yankees came." Until New Orleans fell and the majority of my slaves ran away, including my cook. I did it out of necessity and discovered that I enjoyed cooking. Jason's been after me to hire a cook, but I don't want to give it up. I guess it's my French blood coming out in me. You see, most French like to dabble with cooking, even the men. Why, Jason can cook a gumbo as good, or better, than mine."

Jason's dark eyebrows shot up at Desirée's words. Desirée ignored his look of surprise at her oblique compliment and continued, saying, "In fact, there was even a French nobleman who lived in Louisiana who insisted upon doing all of his own cooking."

"Really?" Dorothy asked in surprise. "Who?"

"He was a duke," Desirée answered, "the crown prince of Naples and Napoleon's nephew." Desirée chewed her bottom lip thoughtfully, then said, "Yes, I remember. His name was Charles Louis Napoleon Achille Murat."

"My God!" Bob gasped. "All those names for just one man?"

Jason chuckled, saying, "Yes, the nobility do have a way of getting carried away with their names and their titles."

"And he actually cooked?" Dorothy asked in amazement.

"Yes," Desirée replied with a grin, "but it was what he cooked that made him so notorious. You see, he didn't cook ordinary food. He had strange tastes. He preferred owls and rattlesnake and alligator, and fed them to his horrified guests. Of course, the guests could hardly refuse to eat them, being as he was nobility and all, but, needless to say, they never accepted another invitation to dine."

Everyone at the table laughed.

"Oh, he was one of the most colorful characters that Louisiana has ever seen, and believe me, we've had more than our share of them," Desirée continued. "He was always experimenting with things he found in the swamps. He got the notion in his head that the bark of the wild cherry tree had values that improved physique and endurance and fed it to his slaves, and then had to nurse them back to health when they almost died from poisoning."

"He was a character," Bob remarked, chuckling.

"But what was he doing here in Louisiana?" Dorothy asked.

"He had a plantation," Desirée answered. "Many of the lesser nobility toyed around with them. But Murat was a complete failure as a planter. I understand he once fell into one of his sugar vats when he got too close. He was furious, not because he might have been burned but because he had to bathe, something he hated to do."

"But I would have thought nobility would have meticulous personal habits," Dorothy commented.

"Not Murat," Desirée said with a laugh. "He wore unpressed clothing, and his hair looked as if it had never been touched with a comb or brush. He even took an old, shaggy dog around with him everywhere he went."

"Well, he couldn't have been too bad, if he was an animal lover," Bob remarked.

"Oh, he didn't care a thing about the dog," Desirée

said. "You see, he chewed tobacco, a habit that was absolutely abhorrent to Louisiana's elite society. The dog had a purpose. If Murat couldn't find a cuspidor, he spat his tobacco juice into the dog's shaggy fur."

"My God, he was eccentric," Bob remarked, shaking his head in disbelief.

The four sat around the dining table, still chuckling over Desirée's tale. Finally, Desirée said, "If you'd like, Dorothy, I'd be happy to teach you Creole cooking."

"Would you? Oh, I'd love to learn, Desirée." She turned to her husband, saying, "Wouldn't that be wonderful, Bob? Then, when we go back home, we can still have our Creole food."

"Then I do have hopes of getting you back to Michigan after all?" Bob asked in a teasing voice.

"Well, maybe. Just maybe," Dorothy teased back.

Desirée felt a twinge of sadness. As anxious as she was for the Yankees to leave New Orleans, she would miss her friend.

One day in December, Jason walked into the house, a big smile on his face.

"Well, you look awfully pleased about something," Desirée remarked.

"Yes, I am, and so will you be when you hear the news. In fact, I'm surprised everyone in New Orleans isn't out in the street celebrating."

"What news?"

"General Butler is being replaced. It seems his Women's Order was his undoing."

"You mean because Jefferson Davis declared him an outlaw, to be hung on sight if caught by southern forces?"

"No, that's not why Lincoln is replacing him.

Davis made that proclamation months ago, and besides, I don't think Lincoln gives a damn what the president of the South had to say on the matter. No, it was foreign disapproval that put the pressure on Lincoln. It seems the House of Parliament condemned Butler for it, and the French government sent Lincoln an official complaint in the name of the Creoles in Louisiana."

When General Butler left the city a few days later, Desirée was as happy as everyone else in Louisiana to see "the beast" leave. She only wished Colonel Anders had gone with the hated general.

Chapter 17

Sergeant O'Malley walked down the dark, deserted street, a scowl on his face and grumbling under his breath. "Dammit, it was bad enough the major married a southern woman, but why did he have to go and marry one of those foreigners, those Creoles? Now, whoever heard of celebrating New Years instead of Christmas. Why, it's the most ridiculous thing I've ever heard. A sacrilege, no less."

Well, he'd be damned if he let Christmas go by without celebrating it, he thought, even if he had to do it all by himself. O'Malley grinned, lovingly patting the bottle of whiskey that strained at his tunic pocket.

He walked through the courtyard to the carriage house. After lighting a lamp, he settled down on a stack of hay and, pulling out the bottle, he uncorked it and lifted it in salute to the horses standing in the stall, saying, "Merry Christmas, you four-legged bastards!"

O'Malley took a long swig and then glared at the horses, wondering why God put such miserable creatures on earth. As far as he was concerned, they were the most stubborn beasts there were. A real pain in the ass. He laughed, thinking, they were that, for sure. Everytime he rode one of the stupid things, his ass hurt.

For a few minutes, he drank silently, thinking that celebrating by himself wasn't much fun. When Moses entered the carriage house, O'Malley glanced up, a thoughtful expression coming over his face. Then O'Malley shook his head, thinking he must be crazy to consider asking a nigger to join him. But then, it was Christmas, wasn't it? A time for brotherly love and all that rot. Well, Moses was better than those horse, he decided. At least he could talk.

"How about having a drink with me?" O'Malley asked Moses.

Moses looked at him suspiciously. The Yankee had never been over friendly.

O'Malley saw Moses's look and said defensively, "Well, it is Christmas, you know. A time for celebrating." He rose and, picking up a cup, he poured a generous amount of whiskey into it. Handing it to Moses, he said, "Merry Christmas."

Moses looked down at the cup doubtfully.

"What's the matter?" O'Malley asked in an irritated voice.

"I ain't never drank whiskey before."

"You a teetotaler? You got something against drinking?"

"Nope. Just never had any."

"Then drink up. A little won't hurt you. It'll put hair on your chest."

Moses watched O'Malley as he settled down in the hay, bewildered by the sergeant's last remark. He already had hair on his chest. Is that why white men drank? To grow more hair? Did they think the more the manlier?

Seeing Moses still hadn't taken a drink, O'Malley glared at him, saying, "What's the matter? You think you're too good to drink with me?"

Moses could see O'Malley was getting agitated. The last thing he wanted was another squabble with the man. Then, he'd go running to the massa and tell him Moses was giving him trouble again. Reluctantly, Moses raised the cup and took a big swallow. His eyes widened as the liquor went down his throat, burning like fire. He choked, his eyes watering.

O'Malley laughed, saying, "Has a kick like a mule, don't it? But you'll get used to it."

Moses found O'Malley's words to be true. After a few swallows, a warm glow suffused him, and he didn't even notice the terrible taste anymore. When O'Malley leaned over and filled his cup the second time, the old man didn't object.

"Ah, Christmas always reminds me of my home," O'Malley said in a longing voice, feeling mellower by the minute.

"Where's that?"

"Ireland. The Emerald Isle, we Irish call it. Ah, it's the most beautiful place in the world, I'm telling you. Ain't been there for a long while, though. Ain't seen my mother for over twenty years now. Not since I come to this country as a wee lad." He looked at Moses, asking, "How long has it been since you've seen your mother?"

"Don't remember my mother. I was sold away when I was a li'l boy."

"You mean you don't even know where she is or if she's still alive?" O'Malley asked in horror.

"Nope. But I reckon she's dead by now. I'm pretty old, myself."

"You ever been married?" O'Malley asked, his curiosity aroused.

"Yep. I jumped the broom once."

"Jumped the broom?"

"Yep. That's how we black folks get married. We

360

jump over a broom handle."

"Then where's your wife?"

A look of pain crossed the old man's eyes. "She's dead. She died having my baby. It died, too."

O'Malley heard the anguish in Moses's voice and saw the pain in his eyes. He's human, he thought with amazement. And he's suffered, too. Hell, he thought he'd had some tough breaks in his life, but they were nothing compared to what this old man had gone through. Shame for how he had treated Moses filled O'Malley.

Moses picked up his banjo and started strumming on it softly. "Can you play 'John Brown's Body'?" O'Malley asked.

Moses scowled. He knew the Union's favorite song, but he'd be damned if he'd play it for this Yankee. He turned to O'Malley, saying "Nope." Then he grinned. "But I know 'Dixie.' "

Moses launched into the old minstrel tune that had become one of the South's favorite songs, second only to 'The Bonnie Blue Flag.' O'Malley glared at him as he played the familiar southern tune, knowing that Moses was deliberately goading him. Black bastard, he thought hotly.

And then, as Moses played and sang an old Negro spiritual, O'Malley stared at him in awe, deeply touched by the hauntingly beautiful music and amazed at Moses's rich baritone voice.

Moses saw the look of admiration in O'Malley's eyes. He hadn't missed the look of compassion in the Irishman's eyes when he told him about his wife and baby either. He regretted goading the sergeant. For that reason, the next song he chose to play was a popular one, a song loved equally well in both the North and the South. He grinned when O'Malley joined in, singing lustily.

When Desirée learned from Benjie that Moses and O'Malley were getting drunk in the carriage house, she marched to the library where Jason was. Flinging open the door, she said in a demanding voice, "Jason, you've got to stop them."

Jason looked up from his papers on the desk in surprise. "Stop who?"

"Sergeant O'Malley and Moses. They're getting drunk in the carriage house. You've got to stop them."

"Why?"

"Moses has never had a drink in his life. He'll get sick."

Jason shrugged. "They'll probably both get sick."

"But, aren't you going to stop them?"

"No, I'm not, Desirée," Jason said in a firm voice. "Moses is a grown man. If he didn't want to drink he could have refused. I'm sure O'Malley isn't forcing it down him."

"Then if you're not going to do anything about it, I am!" Desirée said angrily, turning to walk from the room.

Jason jumped from his seat and quickly moved around the desk, catching her arm. Whirling her around, he said, "Leave them alone, Desirée. This may be just what they need. Sometimes, it's easier for men to settle their differences over a bottle than any other way."

He turned, leading her firmly toward their bedroom, saying, "Now, let's go to bed and leave those two to do their own celebrating."

Later, as Jason lay sleeping soundly, Desirée lay awake and listened to the laughing and singing coming from the carriage house. As the noises got even louder and more boisterous, she thought that it was a good thing her neighbors weren't talking to her. Otherwise, there'd be a steady stream of irate Creoles at her front door tomorrow morning complaining about being kept awake all night by that noise. In spite of her anger at O'Malley and Moses she laughed.

The next morning, the only sounds coming from the carriage house were the moans and groans of Moses and O'Malley, both men having terrible hangovers.

Moses rolled to his side, his color a peculiar dusky-green shade. "I'm sick," he moaned, holding his stomach. "I've never been this sick. I'm gonna die. I know I am."

"Oh, God, my head hurts," O'Malley groaned, holding his pounding head. "Jesus, Mary, and Joseph, it feels like there's somebody up there with a sledgehammer."

"Who's gonna feed the horses?" Moses muttered.

"To hell with the stupid beasts!" O'Malley spat, then winced as his head pounded even harder.

Desirée threw the carriage door wide open and marched in. Both men sat up in surprise. Then their hands flew to their eyes to protect them from the glaring sunlight.

"Shut the door, Miss Desirée. That bright light hurts my eyes."

Desirée ignored Moses's plea. She looked at the two men. They both looked ghastly with their pasty coloring and bloodshot eyes. She glared at them, hands on her hips, saying, "Well, I hope you're satisfied. Was your little celebration worth it?"

"Please, Mrs. Steele, don't yell," O'Malley said. "My head is killing me."

"I'm not yelling!" Desirée shrieked. Both men groaned, holding their heads.

"Look at you!" Desirée continued. "Both of you! Two grown men getting stinking drunk. You'd think

363

you'd have better sense. Well, don't expect any pity from me. I should just leave you here and let you suffer. Then maybe you'd learn your lesson."

O'Malley was wishing that she *would* leave. Then, he could suffer in peace and quiet.

Desirée took a bottle and tablespoon from her apron pocket. She opened the bottle and poured the liquid in the spoon, then said in a firm voice, "Open your mouth, Moses."

"What's that?" Moses asked suspiciously.

"Something to cure your hangover."

"There ain't nothing that can cure a hangover. Only a little peace and quiet," O'Malley said in a disgusted voice, shooting her a meaningful look.

"Mammy says this will," Desirée retorted.

"Mammy?" Moses asked. "Humph! What does that old woman know about hangovers?"

"Enough to know that if you drink too much, that's what you end up with the next morning. Which is more than you apparently know," Desirée said to Moses. "Now, open your mouth."

Reluctantly, Moses opened his mouth, and Desirée shoved the spoon in. As he swallowed, he made a terrible face, then spat, "Lawsy, that stuff tastes worse than that old woman's spring tonic."

Desirée ignored his comment and poured another spoonful, saying, "Open up again."

"Again! Oh, no! I ain't taking no more of that stuff. Please, Miss Desirée. I'd rather die."

"Oh, yes, you are, Moses," Desirée said in a determined voice. "Mammy said two spoonfuls. Now, open your mouth."

Moses wrinkled his nose and obediently opened his mouth, making an even more horrible face as he swallowed the second spoonful of the bitter brew.

Desirée turned to Sergeant O'Malley, saying, "Now

you, sergeant."

"Me?" O'Malley asked, his bushy eyebrows rising in surprise. Then he scowled, saying, "No, ma'am, you won't be shoving that stuff down *my* throat."

"If I have to force you, I will, sergeant. And right now, I don't think you're strong enough to fight me off."

O'Malley realized what she said was true. He felt as weak as a newborn kitten. Why, he doubted if he could fight off a fly, much less this determined woman standing in front of him, even if he did make two of her.

"Now, wait a minute, Mrs. Steele. I'm not a servant, like Moses here. You can't tell me what to do. I'm your husband's aide, and a soldier in the United—"

Desirée shoved the spoon in O'Malley's mouth as he talked, almost laughing outloud at the astonished look on the Irishman's face. He gagged, then swallowed, a horrified look on his face.

"My God! That's the foulest tasting stuff I've ever had in my mouth. What did the old woman put in it, anyway? Rat's nests?"

"I have no idea what's in it, sergeant," Desirée answered calmly. "Perhaps she did."

O'Malley turned pale at the thought. Then, seeing Desirée pouring another spoonful, he said, "No, ma'am!"

"Yes, sergeant," Desirée said sternly.

"That's right," Moses said. "If I've got to take two spoonfuls, then so do you."

O'Malley stubbornly clamped his big jaw shut, glaring up at Desirée. Desirée glared back.

Minutes passed.

Finally, the Irishman spat in disgust, "Give it to me, then! I'll take it myself. I'm no baby to be spoon-fed."

Desirée handed him the spoon. After he had swallowed the brew, he handed the spoon back, his look murderous.

"Now, lay back down, both of you," Desirée said. "You should be feeling better in about thirty minutes."

"She's crazy," O'Malley thought, lying back down. All that nonsense about curing a hangover. There ain't nothing in the world that will cure a hangover.

"What are you doing, Miss Desirée?" Moses asked.

"Feeding the horses," Desirée said from the stall. "No reason for them to suffer because you two haven't got the sense you were born with."

Feeding the horses? O'Malley was surprised. Now, what would a lady like her be knowing about horses? He watched her from the corner of his eye as Desirée fed and watered the animals, crooning to them as she did. She's the damnest woman I've ever seen, O'Malley thought with grudging admiration. Who'd ever think a little thing like her would have the nerve to boss a big brute like me around?

When Desirée was finished, she walked back to the two men lying in the straw. "Are you feeling better?"

"Yes, ma'am," Moses answered. "Maybe I ain't gonna die after all."

Desirée smiled, then turned to O'Malley. "And you, sergeant?"

O'Malley hated to admit it, but he did feel much better. He nodded his shaggy head curtly.

"Good," Desirée said. "Then I'll tell Mammy to start your breakfast." She turned and walked from the carriage house.

O'Malley watched her as she walked out, a thoughtful look on his face. "Is she always like that? So determined?"

"She sure is. When Miss Desirée gets something in her head, there ain't nothing or nobody gonna change it."

O'Malley remembered the way Desirée had flared at her husband the day the major and he had come home early and found her scrubbing the floor. Then and today, she had reminded him of some fiery Irish colleen and not the pampered meek little creature he had always thought southern woman to be. And he hadn't been scolded and fussed over since he was a lad. Why, she had treated him just like she had Moses, as if he were one of the family. A warm feeling filled him as a broad grin spread across his ruddy face.

From then on, O'Malley ate his meals in the kitchen with Moses, and never a cross word was said between them. Desirée was forced to admit that Jason had been right. The drinking bout had apparently settled their differences.

In the week between Christmas and New Years, Desirée went to the French Market for her weekly rendezvous with Jeanne Marie.

She awakened that morning with a sore throat and headache, but despite how she felt she was determined to stick to her end of the bargain. As soon as lunch was finished, she went to her bedroom, giving Mammy her usual excuse that she was going to take a nap. Then picking up her cloak, she slipped out the door, walked down the galley, and then down the stairs to the courtyard.

The day was grey and dreary, the weather foul as a cold drizzle fell. She shivered and pulled her cloak closer, wondering if she should ask Moses to take her in the carriage. Then, she decided against it. She had been very careful not to let him or Mammy learn of her agreement with Jeanne Marie. There was no need to risk their disapproval just because of a little bad weather.

By the time she reached the market, she was chilled to the bone. She looked about the almost deserted place but could see no sign of Jeanne Marie anywhere. She walked to one of the stalls and sat on a barrel sitting outside it, leaning into the wall in an effort to get some protection from the fine rain and cold wind.

There, she waited for hours, shivering and feeling miserable. Not until the stalls began closing did she finally give up her vigil.

Desirée trudged back home, her head pounding, her throat raw, and her chest aching, wondering why Jeanne Marie hadn't come. For weeks, they had been planning this shipment of supplies for the soldiers in the swamps. It was going to be a special shipment for the men's holidays, and she knew that only something drastic would keep Jeanne Marie from delivering it to them.

When she walked into the house, Mammy was waiting for her in the foyer, where she had been pacing for hours with worry. Mammy pounced on her the minute she closed the door. "Where have you been all this time? And look at you. You're sopping wet."

"I—I went to the market. I—I promised Jeanne Marie I'd meet her there today and we'd do some shopping together for New Years."

"They why didn't you take the carriage? Ain't you got any sense at all? Going out in this cold and rain."

"It wasn't raining when I left," Desirée lied. "Oh, Mammy Jeanne Marie didn't come."

"Lawsy, child. She ain't gonna come out in this

weather. Ride all that way in this rain and cold."

"She would too come," Desirée insisted. "She wouldn't let a little rain stop her, particularly since we were going to buy supplies for New Years for—for her darkies. I'm worried about her."

"Worried about her? And what about you and that baby? Humph! Wouldn't surprise me if you didn't get sick."

Desirée didn't dare tell her Mammy that she was already sick, that she had felt ill even before she left for the market. She'd never hear the end of it.

The door opened behind her, and a fresh blast of cold air blew into the hallway as Jason stepped into the foyer. Closing the door, he turned and looked at Desirée and Mammy in surprise. And then, seeing Desirée's wet clothing, his eyes narrowed.

"She walked to the market to meet Miss Jeanne Marie today and got sopping wet," Mammy informed Jason. "Humph! Would have thought I'd taught her better sense than that."

Jason was stunned. He hadn't followed Desirée to the market that day because he'd never dreamed she'd got out in the bad weather. Was she that dedicated to her cause?"

"Look at you, child. You're shivering," Mammy said. "Now, let's get you to your bedroom and out of those wet clothes. What you need is a hot bath."

Jason hung up his slicker and followed Desirée and Mammy. When they walked into the room, Mammy said, "Now, you get out of those clothes, and I'll get the hot water."

Mammy stalked angrily from the room, and Desirée walked behind the screen to undress. Long before Desirée came out from behind the screen, Mammy, Benjie, and Mattie had lugged the buckets of hot water into the room and filled the tub.

Wondering what was taking her so long, Jason stepped behind the screen. Desirée was struggling with her underclothes, her hands shaking so badly with cold that she couldn't manage the small buttons. Jason shoved her hands away and started deftly unbuttoning her chemise.

"I can—can—do it," Desirée objected, her teeth chattering.

"Like hell you can!" Jason ground out, angry at her himself and wishing now that he'd never let her get involved in her little scheme to help the Confederates. He hadn't minded as long as she hadn't endangered herself. But to put her cause before her health was something he wouldn't tolerate.

When she was undressed, Jason slipped her wrapper around her and led her from behind the screen to the big tub.

"I—I really don't have time for a bath. I need to get my dinner started," Desirée said, clenching her teeth to keep them from chattering.

"I'll get dinner after I've helped you with your bath," Mammy said.

"No, I'll help Desirée with her bath," Jason said. "You go ahead and start dinner, Mammy."

As Jason helped her into the tub, Desirée fervently wished she could just go to bed. She felt terrible and very weak. And then, as Jason was soaping her shoulders and back, a wave of dizziness swept over her. "Jason," she muttered, "I don't feel so good."

Jason saw her flushed skin, a flush he knew had nothing to do with the hot water. Alarmed, he quickly rinsed off the soap and helped her from the tub. As he reached for the towel, Desirée's vision blurred. The room spun crazily. And then, total darkness.

Jason caught her as she collapsed and swept her up into his arms. Looking down at her flushed face and feeling the heat radiating from her feverish body, a terror like none he had ever known seized him. Frantic with fear, he called, "Mammy! Get in here!"

An hour later, Jason anxiously paced the floor, casting worried glances over to the bed where Desirée lay as the doctor examined her. When the doctor finally rose from his examination and walked to him, Jason's breath caught at the concerned look on the man's face. He could barely force the words from his mouth: "What's wrong with her, Colonel Davis?"

The colonel took his glasses off and wiped them with his handkerchief before answering, an act that seemed an eternity to Jason. Placing them back on, the doctor said in a solemn voice, "I'm afraid it's influenza, complicated by pneumonia, Major Steele. A very dangerous, life-threatening condition under any circumstances, but even more so for your wife with her pregnancy. At this point, that's just an added burden for her."

"Then you think she'll lose the baby?" Jason asked.

"It's a very distinct possibility. Forgive me if I sound cold-blooded, Major, but I hope she does. It might be her only chance to survive, and then, I can't guarantee it."

Mammy had been standing behind the two men as they talked. Her black eyes glistened with tears as she said in a soft, but firm voice, "I ain't gonna let my baby die, doctor. No, sir! She ain't gonna die."

Jason had been stunned by the doctor's words. Were the perverse gods of fate still playing their games with him and Desirée? Did they think to give him this brief time of happiness and then snatch her away from him! By God, no! He'd fight those damned gods for her!

"She's right," Jason said in a steely voice, a deter-

371

mined look on his face, stupefying the doctor with its intensity. "Desirée *isn't* going to die!"

From then on, Jason and Mammy nursed Desirée as she struggled for her life. Jason refused to leave her side even for a minute. They sponged her when her fever raged, warmed her when the chills shook her body, and forced the medicine and any fluids they could down her throat. They rarely spoke, this fiercely determined man and teary-eyed, stubborn woman, too intent on their battle for her life, each wishing they could take the pain for her.

In the long days, and even longer nights, that passed, the entire household joined in, even Sergeant O'Malley, who insisted upon carrying the heavy buckets of hot water used for Desirée's croup tent. New Years passed, the joyous ringing of the city's bells sounding like a death knell to those fighting for the young woman's life.

Desirée was oblivious to all around her as she thrashed and twisted in delirium. The only thing she knew was her pain and her suffering.

Her chest felt as if an iron bar was lying over it, forcing the air from her lungs. She struggled to breathe. It felt like her lungs were on fire. Was she making that strange gurgling sound? What in the world was wrong with her?

And now her stomach hurt, way down low. *Mon Dieu*, it hurt worse than her chest. Great waves of pain were washing over her, each one worse than the last. It was tearing her in two, ripping her apart. She couldn't bear it. Go away! Please, God, make it go away.

What was that wet, sticky feeling between her legs? No matter. The pain in her stomach was finally gone. What a relief. What a blessed relief. Now she could concentrate on her breathing. But she was tired, so terribly tired. She didn't have the strength to breathe. It hurt too bad. It took too much effort.

Then, she was free of the pain, free even of the bonds of gravity, drifting in a wonderful weightless world. It was so peaceful here, floating in this warm, rosy haze. But what were Mammy and Jason doing there? Why was Mammy crying, and why did Jason look so anguished? And who were they bending over? Her? No, it couldn't be her. She was up here.

Suddenly, it was dark. She was floating down a long, black silent tunnel. She wondered why she wasn't afraid. Then, she saw a light at the end, the most brilliant light she had ever seen. And standing in that beautiful light were Thad and her father—and her mother! Why, she hadn't seen any of them in ages. Her mother was holding something in her arms, and they were all smiling at her, beckoning for her to join them. Yes, she wanted to join them. I'm coming, she called silently, amazed that she no longer had to say the words.

"Desirée! You can't die!"

Jason? But where was he? She couldn't see him. Only her family, beckoning to her.

"Desirée! Come back!"

But she didn't want to go back. Not to the pain and suffering. It was so peaceful here, the most beautiful place she had ever seen.

"Desirée! I need you! Come back to me!"

Jason needed her. Then she must go back. I'm sorry, she said silently to the beckoning specters. I can't come now.

She drifted backward, through the long, dark tunnel, back to the world of pain, back to struggling for each breath.

When Desirée regained consciousness, Jason was dozing, slumped in a chair, his dark head beside her on the bed. She gazed down at him, shocked at how thin and haggard he looked.

Sensing her eyes on him, Jason lifted his head and looked at her, a wave of tremendous relief washing over him. "Thank God, you're finally awake."

"What happened?" Desirée asked.

"You've been ill. Very ill. You had pneumonia. You almost died."

Desirée remembered her strange experience. Had she just dreamed she had floated free of her body, had viewed that beautiful place, had seen her parents and Thad? No, it had been too vivid, too real. It had actually happened. She *had* died, and then, come back! But no one would ever believe her.

She raised her hand to stroke his stubbled jaw, shocked at how weak she was. "You need a shave."

Jason took her hand in his and kissed her palm. "I'll do it later when you've gone back to sleep."

Awareness slowly returned to Desirée. It still hurt to breathe but not nearly as bad as it had. This, she could bear. And that other pain was completely gone. Her eyes widened; her hand flew to her abdomen where her baby was. But it wasn't there.

"My baby?" she asked in a strangled cry.

"You lost the baby, Desirée," Jason said gently.

"No! Oh, no! Not my baby!"

Jason cradled her while she cried, one hand stroking her head, his own eyes glittering with tears. He felt as if his heart would break for her anguish.

Desirée never mentioned the baby after that. Days passed, and Jason and Mammy wondered at it, but were both glad, fearing she would get hysterical and have a relapse.

One day, after Mammy had bathed her and was tidying the room, Desirée asked, "What was it, Mammy? A boy or a girl?"

374

Mammy looked up in surprise, then answered, "A boy."

"I had a feeling it was," Desirée said sadly. She gazed out of the window, then asked, "Where is it buried?"

"At Whispering Oaks, beside your mama and papa. Massa Steele took the baby up there and buried it himself. He thought that's where you'd want it."

Yes, that's where she wanted her baby, at Whispering Oaks, with her parents. Suddenly, she realized that was what her mother had been holding. Her baby son.

"Lawsy, child," Mammy said. "That was the saddest thing I ever saw. The massa took the baby from between your legs, himself, and then he cried. I ain't never seen a strong man like him cry before. It plumb tore me up."

Jason had actually cried when she had lost the baby? He had told her he was pleased about the baby, but she never dreamed he had loved it that much already. She remembered the night he had kissed her abdomen so tenderly. He had loved it even then. She never considered his feelings for it. She selfishly thought of it as *her* baby. Now, it was dead because she had acted so foolishly. She should have never gone out in that bad weather, knowing she was already ill. She had put her commitment to the South before her husband's feelings and the safety of the baby. Guilt overwhelmed her.

"And I've never seen a man take care of someone the way he did you, honey child," Mammy continued. "He stayed right here by your side, not even leaving for meals, helping me all the time. The only time he left was those few hours he went to bury the baby, and that wasn't until you was better. Lawsy, I've never seen a man love a woman as much as he does you."

Desirée thought Jason's concern had been more for the baby than for her. Hadn't Mammy just said he'd cried when she lost it? "No, Mammy, Jason doesn't love me. He only married me to protect me from Colonel Anders and because—" She flushed. "And because he desired me. He admitted it before we were even married."

"Humph! I know better than that! Anyone can tell he loves you by the way he treats you, not just when you're sick but all the time."

"Jason's just a good man," Desirée countered. "He's kind to everyone. You know that. Naturally, he'd be good to me, his own wife."

Mammy knew different. She'd seen the naked look of love in Jason's eyes when he didn't think Desirée was watching, and the fear and anguish in his eyes when he thought he was going to lose Desirée. Mammy wondered if she should tell Desirée that Jason later explained he had cried for several reasons: partly in relief, knowing that Desirée couldn't handle the burden of the baby and still survive; partly in grief for the baby because he knew that Desirée was going to be very disappointed. But the old woman realized that she couldn't tell that to Desirée. It would be betraying his trust. Besides, if Jason had never told Desirée he loved her, there must be a good reason. Perhaps he felt that Desirée had to see it for herself. But how the girl could be so blind was beyond Mammy, and it angered her.

She glared at Desirée, saying, "I'm gonna tell you something. Not only does that man love you, but you love him, too."

"No, I don't!" Desirée said. She turned her head, unable to look the old woman in the eye. "I'm just grateful for everything he's done for me, that's all."

Mammy couldn't understand Desirée. In some

ways she had matured drastically in the past year, yet in other ways, like this business of denying her love for Jason, she was still behaving like a child. Would she ever grow up, become the mature woman she longed for her to be? Until she did, Mammy Lou couldn't feel her job in raising Desirée was completed.

"You're lying! Not only to me, but to yourself, too. Just like some li'l child."

"Little child?" Desirée asked, both surprised and hurt by Mammy's words.

"Yes, li'l child! Until you can admit to yourself, and to that man, that you love him, you aren't grown up."

Desirée watched as Mammy stalked from the room. But, you don't understand, Mammy, she thought. I can't let myself fall in love with Jason. He doesn't want my love.

A few days later, Jeanne Marie came to visit.

Mammy walked into the salon where Desirée was sitting, a broad smile on her black, chubby face, and she said, "Guess who's here?"

Jeanne Marie stepped out from behind Mammy. "Jeanne Marie!" Desirée cried in surprise.

After Mammy Lou had left, Jeanne Marie rushed to Desirée, saying, "Oh, Desirée, I was so worried when you didn't show up at the market the last two weeks. And then, when you didn't come today, I decided to come over here and make sure he hadn't done something to you."

"He?"

"Yes, Jason."

"Jason would never hurt me, Jeanne Marie. Whatever gave you a silly idea like that?"

"Well, I remembered how dangerous looking he'd been at the dance last spring and, after all, he *is* a Yankee. Are you sure he hasn't hurt you? You look awfully pale and thin."

"No, Jason hasn't hurt me. In fact, it's the other way around. I'm the one who's hurt him." Seeing the puzzled look on Jeanne Marie's face she continued: "I went to the market the week before New Years and waited for you in the cold rain. I should have never gone. I was ill in the first place. I got pneumonia and lost the baby. Jason's baby. The baby he wanted so badly." Tears glittered in Desirée's eyes. "Oh, Jeanne Marie, I feel so awful about it. Because I was so determined to help the South, I robbed Jason of his child. It was wrong."

"Mon Dieu," Jeanne Marie said, her own face pale as she sat on the couch beside Desirée. "We tried to come that day, but the wagon broke down. By the time we got it fixed, it was too late to come. I had no idea you'd wait all that time in the rain."

"I know. It wasn't your fault. It was mine. And to make matters worse, Jason has been so good to me, so sweet and considerate. He thinks I'm grieving for the baby, but it's more than that." She chewed her lips to keep the tears back. "I feel so terribly guilty."

Jeanne Marie realized that she had taken advantage of a good man, a man who had given her financial aid with no questions asked, no reservations. Her own guilt rose to the surface.

Desirée looked her cousin in the eye, saying, "I'm sorry, but I won't buy supplies for the soldiers anymore. I'll help you, but I can't help them. I love the South just as much as you do, but I can't deceive Jason any longer. It's wrong. He's my husband, not my enemy."

"I understand, Desirée. If I do anything else, I won't ask you to get involved."

Both girls nearly jumped out of their skins when a deep male voice said from the doorway, "Why, Jeanne

Marie! What a pleasant surprise."

They turned to see Jason walking into the room. Jeanne Marie's breath caught in her throat. *Mon Dieu*, she had forgotten what a handsome man he was, with his dark coloring and those striking green eyes. Struggling to compose herself, she said, "Hello, Major Steele."

He smiled, saying, "Jason, please. After all, I'm part of the family now." He turned and bent, kissing Desirée on the cheek. Rising, he asked, "How are you feeling, *cherie*?"

"Much stronger," Desirée answered. "I walked around the room a bit today with Mammy's help."

Jason nodded, obviously pleased with Desirée's small accomplishment. "Would you like to go down to the courtyard? It's a sunny, rather mild day. You and Jeanne Marie can visit out there. The fresh air will do you good."

"Yes, that sounds lovely," Desirée replied.

Jeanne Marie watched while Jason lifted Desirée in his arms and carried her out of the room, and she followed behind them. When they reached the courtyard, he gently placed Desirée in a metal chaise lounge and then, taking a lap blanket from a nearby table, he tucked it carefully around her legs.

"Would you like me to send Mammy down with some hot chocolate and pastries?" Jason asked.

"Pastries?" Desirée asked in surprise. "Where did they come from?"

"I stopped at the French Market on my way home. I believe you like the ones with the chocolate filling and whipped cream and pecans on top. Am I right?"

Desirée's mouth watered. "Yes, they're my favorites."

Jeanne Marie had watched Jason's tender ministrations to Desirée in amazement. It seemed impossible that such a strongly masculine man could be capable of such gentleness. In fact, she had never seen any man act so caring. Jason certainly didn't seem dangerous now. Oh, she suspected he could be very dangerous for his enemies but never for Desirée.

As Jason turned and walked toward the stairs, Desirée called, "Are you coming back?"

"No," Jason called over his broad shoulder. "I'll leave you and Jeanne Marie to your visit."

Jeanne Marie hurried after him, calling, "Jason?"

He turned and waited until she caught up with him.

"I wanted to thank you for the supplies you sent to Terre Doux," Jeanne Marie said.

"I was happy to be able to do it," Jason replied warmly.

He really means it, Jeanne Marie thought, her guilt for having used him rising to the surface once more.

Jason gazed over Jeanne Marie's head at Desirée, sitting in the distance. Jeanne Marie was stunned by the look of deep love in his eyes. His gaze still resting on Desirée, he said in a low voice, "I hope you come often and visit Desirée. She's taking the loss of the baby very hard. She needs some cheering up."

"Yes. I'll come often."

Jason tore his eyes away from Desirée and looked down at Jeanne Marie. "Thanks," he said, then turned, saying, "Call me if she looks like she's getting tired."

Jeanne Marie watched as he walked up the steps. Would a man ever love her so deeply? She felt just a little envious of Desirée.

Jeanne Marie and Desirée visited for hours in the courtyard. Jeanne Marie watched her cousin thoughtfully as they talked, noticing that Desirée's eyes strayed to the house several times. Finally, Jeanne Marie said, "You fallen in love with him, haven't you?"

Desirée jerked her eyes away from the house where they had once again strayed, an almost guilty look on her face. "Jason?"

"Yes, Jason," Jeanne Marie answered, looking her in the eye.

Desirée averted her eyes, saying, "No, I don't love him. I told you. I'm only grateful to him, now more than ever. He saved my life when I had pneumonia. Mammy said—"

Jeanne Marie listened with only half an ear as Desirée related everything Mammy had told her. She knew Desirée was lying, not only to her but to herself.

During the weeks of Desirée's recovery, Jason made a point of coming home early from headquarters to keep her company, hoping to distract her from what he thought was her grief over the baby. One blustery February afternoon, they sat before a cozy fire in the salon as Jason told her the latest news of the war in Louisiana.

"Well, I'll have to say one thing for my new commander, General Banks. At least, he appears to be more interested in fighting the war than General Butler was. With Galveston retaken by the South in January, he feared an attack from Texas and sent General Wertzel up the Bayou Teche to clear out the Confederates. But I'm afraid it will land up just another wild-goose chase."

"Why do you say that?" Desirée asked.

"Because he sent Wertzel after General Mouton and his men. No one has been able to catch that sly fox and his swamp guerrillas. At first, Mouton plagued General Butler all along the Bayou Lafource, so badly Butler couldn't spare the men to attack as he'd been ordered. And now, General Wertzel has been bushwhacking his way up the Bayou Teche, expecting to catch Mouton just around the next bend, only to discover he'd disappeared again. No, Mouton's playing the same cat and mouse game he's played all along. Hell, he's a master at guerrilla warfare. Hit and run. There one minute and gone the next. We'll never catch him."

Desirée looked at Jason curiously, saying, "You almost sound as if you admire this General Mouton."

Jason grinned sheepishly, saying, "I suppose I shouldn't admit it, being a Union officer and all, but to be honest with you, I do admire him. I don't know if it's because he's a military genius or if its just my French blood coming out in me. He's Cajun, you know."

A glimmer of recognition teased in the back of Desirée's mind. "Is he by any chance related to the Mouton that was the first Cajun governor of Louisiana?"

"Yes, his son, Alfred. He's made quite a name for himself here in Louisiana, as much a hero to the Cajuns as Beauregard is to you Creoles. And everytime he wins a victory or eludes us, I can't help but feel a little twinge of pride. I guess my Cajun blood is too strong for me."

Desirée thought it was more than Jason's Cajun blood that made him secretly proud of the man who was a thorn in the Yankees' side. She suspected he was still torn in his loyalties. She could understand. She felt torn between the South and him. She wondered if Mouton could have possibly been the man Jeanne Marie had been slipping the supplies to. In a way, she hoped he was. Knowing that Jason admired him eased her guilt over deceiving him.

From then on, Jason and Desirée followed General Mouton's campaign as closely as the rest of Louisiana.

At the end of February, the doctor pronounced Desirée fully recovered, and Desirée was thrilled, anxious to fulfill the vow she had made. She had promised herself she would have another child to make up for the pain she had caused Jason.

That night, Desirée told Jason what the doctor had said and hinted that it was all right to resume marital relations. When Jason undressed and lay down on the cot beside her bed, where he had been sleeping during her illness and entire convalescence, Desirée stared at him in dismay. Hadn't he understood? *Mon Dieu*, how explicit did she have to be?

But Jason wasn't obtuse. He knew what Desirée was hinting at, but he didn't agree with the doctor. As much as he wanted to make love to her, he thought that she was still too weak, remembering all too well how she had almost died.

In the days that followed, Desirée became increasingly frustrated, not only because Jason was thwarting her plans to have another baby, but because she was hungry for his lovemaking. One night, she lay in her big canopied bed and watched as he undressed and walked to his cot. Her eyes drifted over his broad shoulders and the wide expanse of his bronzed chest with its mat of dark hair. She followed that line of hair as it tapered down his taut abdomen and then flared at his groin. As he lay down and flipped the covers over him, she swallowed hard and jerked her eyes away to stare at the canopy above her. *Mon Dieu*, she thought, how could he be so cruel? To parade around naked like that, and then nothing. It was like dangling food in front of a starving man and then snatching it away.

For a minute, she considered coming right out and asking Jason to make love to her. But then, she remembered the night she had told him she was pregnant and how embarrassed she had been, feeling as if she were begging. She tossed that idea aside. No, there must be a less obvious way to get him into her bed. A sudden gleam came into her eyes. Of course, She'd seduce him!

She rolled to her side and said, "Jason, would you do me a favor?"

Jason rolled and propped himself on one elbow, answering, "Of course, *cherie*. What is it?"

"Would you rub my back for me?"

"Your back?" Jason asked, a worried look coming over his face. "What's wrong with your back?"

"Oh, it's nothing serious," Desirée answered. "Just sore muscles. I've had these little backaches on and off ever since I was a child. Mammy used to rub my back for me and they'd go away. Would you mind?"

"No, of course not," Jason answered, flipping the covers back.

Desirée's breath caught at the sight of his magnificent male nakedness as he walked to the bed, her heart racing in anticipation.

As Jason sat on the edge of the bed, Desirée rolled to her side and, placing her hand in the small of her back, said, "Right here is where it aches."

For a while, Desirée lay still as Jason massaged her back, then said, with a devilish gleam in her eyes. "Wait a minute, Jason. Let me pull up my gown. The material is getting all bunched up."

Desirée twisted and turned, pulling the gown up high on her back, and then she lay back down. Jason stared down at her nakedness and felt his mouth go dry, his heartbeat accelerating. He hesitated, doubting that he could touch that soft, satiny skin and not give in to his passion, a passion that he had been fighting a constant battle against whenever he was around Desirée.

384

Desirée peeked over her shoulder and saw the hungry look in Jason's eyes, elated that her plan was working. "You're not going to stop, are you? It felt so much better when you were rubbing it."

Jason felt like a heel and silently cursed his baser nature. Steeling his resolve to keep himself under control, he bent and began to rub Desirée's back again.

"Oh, Jason, that feels so good, but would you mind rubbing a little lower and down the back of my legs? The ache seems to radiate down them."

Jason groaned, a sound not missed by Desirée's sharp hearing, and began to massage her shapely buttocks. As he rubbed her thighs, he was acutely conscious of that soft woman's place he ached to touch just inches from his fingers. His heat flared. A sheen of perspiration broke out on his forehead.

Desirée squirmed and twisted seductively, muttering, "Oh, yes, that helps." Deliberately, she brushed her hip against his groin.

She didn't even have to look to see what effect that promising little brush had on Jason. She could feel his manhood growing and hardening against her hip. And then, as his hands began to caress instead of rub, and his warm lips placed soft kisses on the small of her back, she knew she had been successful. It was all she could do to keep from crying out loud with joy.

Jason dropped soft, butterfly kisses up Desirée's back. When he reached the bunched material at her shoulders, he frowned at the obstruction. With a small snarl of impatience, he sat Desirée up and quickly stripped off her gown, tossing it aside, and then rolled her once more to her stomach.

Jason's hot breath scalded her skin as he left a trail of fiery kisses from her shoulders to her feet, licking the sensitive instep before he made the return trip.

Pushing her long hair aside, he nibbled at the nape of her neck, softly nipping her shoulders, his hand stroking her thighs. Desirée squirmed impatiently, not liking the position. She wanted to kiss him, touch him, taste him.

"Jason, I want to turn over," she said, trying to roll over.

Jason nipped her earlobe, muttering, "Not yet." His hair-roughened thigh hooked over hers to hold her down.

And then Desirée gasped in pleasure as his hand slipped between her thighs, his fingers seeking her warm moistness, teasing, taunting, then slipping inside as he mouthed the long column of her throat and her shoulders. It was heaven. It was hell. She didn't want him to stop, and yet, she wanted to kiss and touch him.

"Please," she sobbed.

He chuckled, the deep sound a sensual caress to her ears, and rolled her to her back. Desirée's fingers tangled in his dark hair, pulling his head down. She placed hot, greedy kisses over his face, her hands sweeping over his broad shoulders and bronzed back, and she reveled in the feel of the powerful muscles contracting under her fingertips and his chest hair tickling her breasts.

Jason caught her roving mouth with his; their tongues met and danced. The kiss grew wilder as he kissed her hungrily, his tongue an instrument of soft, sweet savagery that sent both of their senses reeling and their blood coursing hotly through their veins.

She reached for him and felt his gasp of pleasure as her hand closed around him. And then, as she stroked that rigid, pulsating man-flesh, she gloried in the shudders that wracked his big body.

Jason tore his mouth from hers and stilled her

hand, saying in a breathless, ragged voice, "Easy, *cherie*. Or else, it will be over right now."

He kissed her throat, slowly descending. As his tongue drew lazy circles around her breast, she sobbed in anguished anticipation, then cried out softly as his mouth closed over the hardened peak, his tongue rolling it, then flicking, sending a bolt of fire to her loins.

She couldn't stand it any longer. She reached for him again, guiding him to her. He drove into her, his thrust true and deep. Desirée's legs trembled; her breath caught at the feel of him, immense and throbbing, inside her. He withdrew, and Desirée sobbed in frustration.

"Please, Jason, no more," she begged as the hot tip of his swollen shaft teased and tormented. "I can't bear any more of this torture."

Chuckling softly, he plunged into her the second time, groaning as he felt her muscles greedily contracting around him. Desirée locked her legs around him tightly, pulling him deeper, determined that this time he wouldn't get away from her.

She looked up into those shimmering green eyes, darkened with passion, feeling as if she were drowning in those emerald depths. And then, as his mouth captured hers in a deep, drugging kiss and he moved inside her, harder, deeper swifter, she soared to the heights of heaven, climaxing in an intense sweet rush of sublime ecstasy as Jason's arms tightened convulsively around her, and he shuddered in his own exquisite throes of release.

They lay for a long time, their sweat-slick limbs still entwined. Finally, Jason rolled from her and lay on his back, staring at the canopy above him.

He knew there was nothing wrong with Desirée's back, or Desirée, either, not after all those gyrations she had gone through. He strongly suspected that the backache had only been an excuse to get him in bed with her. The little minx!

Desirée was thinking her own thoughts, pleased with how well her plan had worked. *Mon Dieu*, she just might have to have a backache every night if it brought those results! But then, why wait until tomorrow night to experience all those exciting, wonderful sensations again? She smiled and, casting Jason a sly look, complained softly, "My back still aches."

Jason grinned, then hovered over her, his misty-green eyes shimmering with a mixture of amusement and anticipation. "Would you like for me to rub it for you?"

"Oh, yes," Desirée breathed.

Chapter 18

Jason rode his horse through the French Quarter a few weeks later, a worried frown on his face. A month before, he had been relieved of his position as liaison officer and assigned a field command. Ordinarily, he would have been pleased, but he had been placed under the command of Colonel Anders, and Jason strongly suspected Anders had something to do with it.

He hadn't told Desirée of his transfer, knowing that she would be upset by the possibility of his having to go to war. He hadn't wanted to take any chances of her having a relapse. But he couldn't put it off any longer. They had just received orders to move out for spring operations the following morning.

On several occasions that evening, Jason started to tell Desirée the news, then backed down, cursing himself as a coward. It wasn't until they were in their bedroom and undressing for bed that he finally told her, knowing that he was running out of time.

"Desirée, there's something I've been meaning to tell you. I requested a field command a few months ago, and the transfer came through last month." Jason frowned. He hated lying to her, but he feared if he'd told her the truth, she ask too many questions, and he didn't want to mention Anders to her.

Desirée was stunned. He had asked for a dangerous field command when he could have a safe office position? "Why did you ask for a transfer?"

"I've always wanted a field command, Desirée. I'm a soldier, not a pencil pusher." He took a deep breath, steeling himself for her reaction, and said, "We're leaving tomorrow to start spring operations."

Desirée was shocked speechless, reeling under an onslaught of sudden emotions: anger at Jason for deliberately putting himself in a dangerous position; fear for his life; and hurt that he had done so right on top of her recent illness and loss of their baby, when she needed him the most. Then, something else occurred to her: With Jason gone, how could she get pregnant? She had to rid herself of this terrible burden of guilt she felt.

She forced the words from her mouth. "How long will you be gone?"

Jason hated leaving Desirée at this particular time. "I don't know. It could be a few months—or years," Jason answered, feeling miserable himself.

Years? *Mon Dieu*, she couldn't wait years to have another baby. "Why didn't you tell me sooner?" she asked angrily.

"We didn't know ourselves until today."

Jason saw the hurt and anger written all over her face. He walked to her and took her shoulders in his hands. Desirée jerked away from him and whirled away, standing rigidly with her back to him.

Jason couldn't stand the thought of leaving her like this. He slipped his arms around her waist and pulled her back to him, saying against her throat in an anguished voice, "Please, *cherie*. This is our last night together. Don't be angry with me."

Desirée wasn't just angry with him. That was only

a part of it. She was worried about him and frustrated, too. *Mon Dieu*, she would miss him. And his last night might be her last chance to conceive for a long time.

She turned in the circle of his arms, her sob smothered by Jason's mouth as he kissed her long, deeply, lovingly. Their lovemaking that night had both a desperate edge and a poignant edge to it: Desirée determined to conceive before Jason left, and Jason fearful that this might be his last time to make love to Desirée.

Their kisses were feverish and greedy; their caresses urgent and demanding. Even after they had reached their peak in a blinding, soul-shattering climax, they clung to each other desperately. Time was their enemy, and each longed to hold back the dawn as they made love over and over, as if they were trying to squeeze months, even years of loving into this one night. Finally, they dozed, not because they had satisfied their desperation but simply because they were exhausted.

Jason held Desirée in his arms as she dozed and watched the silver streak in the sky turn to a rosy glow. He ached to tell her he loved her. The long night of loving seemed meaningless without the words.

"Desirée," Jason whispered, shaking her lightly.

She opened her eyes and looked up at him, saying, "Yes?"

Looking down at her beautiful face, he couldn't say it. If something did happen to him, her knowing that he had loved her would only make it harder. Instead, he said, "It's time for me to leave."

In the weeks that followed after Jason's departure, Desirée was shocked at how much she missed him. She found herself listening for his firm step and deep voice in the hallway, announcing his arrival home from headquarters. She missed looking at him across the dining room table and their nightly walks. But she missed him the most at night. Then, she would lie in their big bed, feeling miserable and lonely, aching for his touch and the sound of his voice. A listlessness invaded her. She felt as if her very life had left her.

Therefore, when Dorothy visited at the end of the week, Desirée was more than happy to see her friend, hoping that she might be able to cheer her up.

As soon as they were seated in the salon, Dorothy said in a concerned voice, "Are you all right, Desirée? You don't look too well."

"I'm not ill, Dorothy. I just miss Jason so terribly much."

Dorothy's eyes flashed angrily. "Yes, everyone thinks it's terrible what Colonel Anders did to Jason. Back-stabbing him that way."

At the mention of the hated Anders, Desirée's heart raced with fear. "What do you mean?"

"Didn't Jason tell you?"

"Tell me what?"

Dorothy hesitated.

"What are you talking about?" Desirée insisted. "What did Colonel Anders do to Jason?"

"Me and my big mouth," Dorothy said with self-disgust. "I guess Jason didn't want you to know, but Colonel Anders told General Banks that General Butler didn't think Jason was a good choice for a liaison officer because he was too sympathetic to the Creoles, since he was half French and married to you. Anders suggested General Banks relieve Jason of his position and give him a field command instead—under him. Of course, General Banks didn't know anything about what happened that night to you at the dance or how angry Jason was about it, so he agreed."

Desirée turned pale. "Are you telling me Colonel Anders is Jason's immediate commanding officer?"

"Yes."

Jason hadn't requested a transfer, Desirée realized. It had been plotted by Anders. And Jason hadn't told her because he didn't want her worrying. She remembered Ander's threats the night of the dance. The colonel had told her he would get his hands on her someday, that Jason wouldn't always be around to protect her. Sheer terror rose in her, not for herself but for Jason.

"Desirée, what's wrong?" Dorothy asked, alarmed by her friend's deathly color and the frightened look on Desirée's face.

Desirée didn't want to tell Dorothy that she feared Anders was seeking revenge on Jason. Dorothy had heard Anders's insults but not his threats. And Desirée didn't want her friend asking questions. Then she'd have to tell her the whole story, and Desirée couldn't bear for Dorothy to know Jason had married her not out of love but only to protect her from Anders.

"You don't think Jason will change his mind and challenge him to a duel, after all, do you?" Desirée asked, hoping to make Dorothy think that was why she was so frightened.

"Oh, no, Desirée," Dorothy assured her. "Jason was just angry that day. And rightly so. No, I'm sure Jason wouldn't do anything to jeopardize himself."

Desirée knew that Jason was more than capable of protecting himself in a dangerous situation. His years in the swamps had honed his instincts until they were razor sharp. And Jason knew Anders hated him. Surely, Jason would be on guard. But then she remembered that Colonel Anders was an evil, cunning man, a treacherous man. A hard knot of fear formed deep in her belly.

During the next few weeks, Desirée awaited news of the war anxiously, still unable to shake the feeling that something terrible was going to happen to Jason. Then, in the last week of May, word arrived that a fierce battle had taken place at Port Hudson on May 23. The North had been firmly repulsed by the South, and the Union casualties were unusually high. Desirée watched as one hospital ship after the other arrived in New Orleans and unloaded the northern wounded, her apprehension growing each day.

One evening, when Desirée was sitting in the salon and trying to force herself to concentrate on the book she was holding, she looked up and saw Sergeant O'Malley walking into the room, followed by Mammy. One look at their anxious faces told Desirée that what she had feared had come to pass.

Her face blanched of all color. She could hardly force the words from her mouth. "Something has happened to Jason, hasn't it?"

O'Malley was alarmed by Desirée's appearance. She looked as if she might faint. "He's not dead, ma'am," he said in a rush of words. "Just wounded."

Desirée sucked in a deep breath of air; she hadn't realized she had been holding her breath. "Oh, thank God," she muttered. Then she asked, "How bad is he wounded?"

"Pretty badly, I'm afraid. It's his leg, and the doctors are thinking they may have to amputate it. The major don't want them to. He sent me to ask you if you would come."

Amputate his leg? Desirée thought in horror. Then she rose, saying, "Of course, I'll go to him. Where is he? At the St. Charles?"

"The St. Charles?" O'Malley asked with a frown. "Do you mean the hotel?"

"Yes. I understood that's were they were taking the wounded now, since all the hospitals are filled."

"No, ma'am. The major's not here the city. He's in a field hospital, outside of Baton Rouge."

Desirée was stunned. "Baton Rouge? But I thought they were bringing all the wounded back to New Orleans."

"They are—as fast as they can. But there were so many wounded, they haven't been able to bring them all back. The major gave up his place on a hospital ship to a man more seriously injured."

Yes, Desirée thought, that sounds like something Jason would do. Then, gathering her wits, she asked, "How soon do you think we'll be able to board a boat for Baton Rouge?"

O'Malley shook his head, saying, "I'm afraid we won't be catching any steamer to Baton Rouge, Mrs. Steele. Port Hudson has been put under siege, and the navy's not allowing any unauthorized boats into the area. We'll have to go overland. That's how I came."

For the first time, Desirée realized the state O'Malley was in. His uniform was filthy, and he looked totally exhausted. He must have ridden straight through, she thought. "You get some sleep, sergeant. We'll leave the first thing in the morning. We'll take the carriage in case we need to bring the major back to New Orleans."

The sun was just rising the next morning when Desirée and O'Malley walked to the carriage house. While O'Malley was placing Desirée's valise and the wicker basket crammed full of food for their long trip into the carriage, Moses said, "I'm coming, too, Miss Desirée. You might need my help."

Desirée had expected this, but she knew the old

man wouldn't be able to keep up with the pace she and O'Malley intended to set. Besides, they were going into a war zone. It was dangerous enough for her to venture into an area where skirmishes between the two opposing armies were everyday occurrences, but she was determined she wouldn't risk Moses's life, too. "No, Moses, I can't leave the women and Benjie here by themselves with no man to protect them and take care of them."

Moses's brow wrinkled while he thought Desirée's words over. "I reckon you're right, Miss Desirée," he finally said reluctantly. Then he beamed, his chest expanding with self-importance. "Don't you worry about nothing here. I'll take care of everything."

When O'Malley turned to help Desirée into the carriage, Desirée said, "No, sergeant. I'll ride on the driver's seat with you. If I sit back there in the carriage all by myself, I'll do nothing but worry all the way there."

O'Malley drove the horses as fast as he could without exhausting them. That afternoon, they were stopped by a Union patrol. When O'Malley explained where they were going, the lieutenant in charge of the patrol ordered them to go back to New Orleans, saying it was too dangerous to take a woman into a war zone. O'Malley stubbornly told the lieutenant that he was following *his* commanding officer's order, *Major* Steele, and would do no such thing.

As they drove off, Desirée looked back over her shoulder and almost laughed at the shocked look on the lieutenant's face.

The second day, they were forced to leave the road and hide in the thick brush to keep from being caught by a Confederate patrol. After the soldiers had passed in a flurry of choking dust, Desirée's heart was racing in fear. As O'Malley drove the carriage back onto the road, she said, "That was too close for comfort. Maybe we should stop in the next town and buy you some civilian clothes, sergeant. If we're stopped by a Confederate patrol, you'll be taken as a prisoner of war."

The Irishman's blue eyes flashed. "No, ma'am. I won't do that," he said in a determined voice. "I'm a Union soldier and proud of it. I wouldn't hide in civilian clothes. Those Johnny Rebs won't catch me."

Twice more that day, they were forced to hide from the Confederates, one patrol so close Desirée thought she could have reached out and touched them. Desirée was weak with fear by the time they had disappeared around the bend in the road.

The last day was the longest and most grueling. That morning, just north of Donaldsonville, they heard gunshots in the distance and knew that a skirmish was taking place. Both were tense, fearing that they would suddenly find themselves caught in the middle of the fight. When the sounds diminished and finally faded away, they both let out long sighs of relief.

In the middle of the afternoon, a violent thunderstorm swept through the area. For over an hour, the rain came in torrents as lightning cracked all around them and the carriage was buffeted by gusts of wind. When it was over, the road was one long mud puddle. Twice, the carriage got bogged down in the deep mud. At these times, Desirée had to get down from the carriage and pull on the horses' reins, urging them forward, while O'Malley pushed the carriage from behind.

By evening, they were both mud-splattered and exhausted.

But as tired as she was, Desirée found she couldn't sleep that night. The next day, they would reach

397

Baton Rouge, and she feared for Jason's condition. She knew that the wound must be very serious if the doctors were considering amputation.

She climbed down from the carriage where she had been sleeping at night. O'Malley sat on the ground, propped against one of the wheels, staring absently up at the glittering stars above them.

"Tell me about the battle," Desirée said.

O'Malley glanced at Desirée, wondering if he should. It was hardly a tale for a lady's ears. But then, Desirée was a very unusual lady, O'Malley silently admitted to himself. Not once on the long trip had she complained, and if she had been afraid, she had never revealed it to him. He admired her guts and determination.

"Ah, ma'am, it was a disaster. We should have never attempted an attack on Port Hudson. Why, that place is as well fortified as Vicksburg."

Desirée knew that was true. Port Hudson was almost as important to the South as Vicksburg. It guarded that part of the Mississippi where the Red River entered it. If Port Hudson fell, the South would be deprived of its important supply line from the west. And with the entire southern coast under Union blockade and the upper and lower Mississippi in northern hands, the Red River was about the only way of getting guns and supplies into the South.

"It was bad, then?" Desirée persisted.

"Yes, that it was. We came up the Bayou Salk in our boats, and as soon as we were landed, the major's battalion was ordered in."

"Jason's battalion?"

"Yes, ma'am." O'Malley stared off into space, a haunted look in his eyes. "They sent us on an impossible task. There was no earthly way we could storm those high bluffs overlooking the river. Why, they went straight up in the air. And with all those heavy gun batteries up there, we were like sitting ducks, we were. Oh, the navy was there. But their guns didn't have a long enough range. They didn't get anywhere near those rebel batteries. It seemed like we were squatting down there for years, instead of hours, before they finally sent in the other battalions, shells exploding all around us, the smoke choking us and so thick we couldn't see our hands before our faces. It's a miracle we weren't totally wiped out.''

O'Malley stopped talking, a thoughtful expression on his face. Then he looked Desirée directly in the eye, saying, "No, I take that back. It wasn't a miracle. It was the major that kept that from happening." O'Malley smiled sheepishly, saying, "I'll be honest with you, ma'am. When I was assigned to your husband, I wasn't too happy about it. I wanted to be in the middle of the fighting, not playing valet to some desk officer. But as I got to know the major, I came to respect him. I'd never known anyone who cared about people the way he did, except maybe a priest or a doctor. It impressed me. But then, when he was assigned a field command, I had my doubts about him. Seemed to me such a good man wouldn't make a good field officer. To my way of thinking, a good field commander had to be a hard, cold-blooded son of a bitch, if you'll forgive my language. Well, I was wrong about the major. He proved to me that he could care about his troops and still be a good commander. Oh, don't get me wrong. He didn't coddle them. He was tough. But he didn't risk them unnecessarily, either. And because the men knew he really cared about them, they never questioned his orders. They never hesitated. If he told them to stay put, they did. If he told them to move, they moved. That's the reason we didn't get wiped out. The major said dig in, and we did."

"But why didn't they send more troops right away?" Desirée asked.

"I don't know," O'Malley said, shaking his head glumly. "But I do know when they did send them in, it didn't make any difference. They couldn't storm it either. And they fared much worse than we did. They didn't dig in. They didn't have any protection, and they were dropping like flies all around us. After what seemed an eternity of hell, they called the order to retreat, and that was even worse. Most of the men panicked—and to be honest with you—a few of the officers, too. But the major wouldn't let us do that. I've never seen anyone as cool under fire as he was. He got us out of there as systematically as if he'd planned the whole thing himself, with hardly any casualties at all, and what wounded we did have, we took with us."

"Then when did he get shot?"

"It was after we were loaded on our boats. You see, all the time we were loading, we could hear this soldier out in the clearing between us and the bluffs. He was badly wounded and his officer had left him behind. He kept crying out for someone to help him, and we could tell by his voice that he was just a lad. And then, when his begging and pleading didn't do any good, he started calling his mother. I'm telling you, ma'am, it tore us all up. But we knew it would be suicide to go back for him. And then, when we were all loaded, the major went after him."

"Jason?" Desirée gasped.

"Yes. And I've never seen anything like it, I'm telling you. It was the bravest thing I've ever seen. The major flung that lad around his shoulders, like he was a sack of potatoes, and came tearing across that clearing through a furious artillery barrage, dodging shells exploding all around him. The men on the boats started hollering and cheering him on. He almost made it, too. But right before he got out of their firing range, a shell caught him. He went flying one way and the lad the other. Threw the boy clean out of the clearing. Several of the men went running to him and carried him back to the boats, the lad sobbing his thanks all the way."

"And Jason. Who went after him?"

A slow flush crept up O'Malley's face.

"You did, didn't you?" Desirée asked, tears of gratitude shimmering in her eyes. "Why, you were as big a hero as he was."

"No, ma'am. It wasn't that dangerous for me. Like I said, he was almost out of their firing range when he got hit. Besides, if I hadn't gone after him, someone else would have. Everyone in our battalion knew they'd be dead if it hadn't been for him. There wasn't a man among us who wouldn't have done the same thing I did. And not just out of gratitude, either. After that day, there wasn't a man who didn't admire and respect him."

O'Malley gazed off, saying in a thoughtful voice, "Yes, I sure misjudged the major." His eyes swiveled back to Desirée. "And you, too, ma'am. I didn't approve of the major marrying you, a southerner, the enemy. And then for a long time after we came to live in your house, I was resentful. I didn't feel like I fit in. I didn't feel like I belonged until—" A broad grin spread across his face. "Until that day you gave me and Moses hell for getting drunk, and then took care of us."

Desirée smiled, remembering that day. It seemed the drinking bout had not only settled the differences between the two men but had wiped out O'Malley's resentment toward her, too.

* * *

The next morning, when Desirée and O'Malley arrived at the field hospital outside of Baton Rouge, the place was in an uproar. Soldiers ran here and there, dodging orderlies carrying the wounded on litters to the waiting wagons.

"What's going on?" O'Malley called down from the carriage to an orderly running by. "What's all the excitement about?"

The orderly turned, saying, "The Confederates have been spotted at Simmesport, just north of here. We're expecting an attack at any minute. We're evacuating our wounded—at least those that can be moved."

O'Malley helped Desirée down and led her into one of the tents. The orderlies were so busy evacuating the tent that no one paid any attention to them. Desirée scanned the long rows of low cots that the wounded were lying on, but could see no sign of Jason.

"He was right here when I left him," O'Malley said, pointing down at an empty cot.

"Maybe he's already been evacuated," Desirée suggested, refusing to even contemplate the other possibility: that he had died.

O'Malley caught the arm of an orderly rushing by, saying, "Where's Major Steele?"

"He's been moved to the surgical tent across the road," the orderly answered before hurrying off.

Desirée's heart rose in her throat. *Mon Dieu*, had they already amputated? She tried to imagine Jason with only one leg but the thought was too disturbing and the vision wouldn't come. She turned and followed Sergeant O'Malley, dreading what she would see—or wouldn't see—when they found him.

When they entered the surgical tent, Desirée feared she might faint. Men with blood-stained bandages thrashed and moaned in pain. The odors were intensified by the June heat, and the tent reeked with the smell of antiseptic mixed with blood, vomit, urine, and death. Bile rose in her throat, and she turned away, fearing she would throw up.

Her eyes settled on the bloody dressing on a stump that had once been some man's leg. Horrified, she looked up at a man's face and almost cried out in relief when she saw it wasn't Jason.

O'Malley walked up to her and took her arm, saying, "This way, Mrs. Steele. They said the major was back here."

Jason lay on a cot in one corner of the tent. Desirée was shocked when she saw him. A week's beard covered his lower face, and there were dark circles under his eyes, eyes dulled with pain. Perspiration dotted his brow, mute testimony to his agony.

Desirée glanced quickly over him, seeing the blood-spattered, torn uniform before her eyes found what they were looking for: his injured leg. But it wasn't the blood-soaked dressing covering his leg from knee to groin that terrified her. It was the putrid odor that rose from it.

She dropped to her knees beside him and took Jason's hand in hers, alarmed at how feverish his skin felt. Despite his pain, Jason managed a weak smile, whispering in a hoarse voice, "You came."

"Yes, I came," Desirée answered, fighting back tears.

An urgent look came into Jason's eyes. "They want to amputate. You won't let them do it, will you?"

"No, I won't let them," Desirée said, smoothing back the damp hair on his forehead.

Jason closed his eyes and clenched his teeth as another excruciating wave of pain washed over him. Seeing him suffer, Desirée was suddenly furious. She rose to her feet, whirling, her dark eyes flashing dangerously. She stopped an orderly passing by, asking in an angry voice, "Why haven't you given him something for pain? Can't you see he's suffering?"

"Because your bull-headed husband has stubbornly refused to take anything!" an equally angry voice said from behind her.

Desirée turned and saw a tall, heavy-set, grey-haired man. His shirt sleeves were rolled up to his elbows, and the blue of his uniform trousers could be seen beneath his blood-splattered apron. "And who are you?" Desirée demanded.

"I'm Colonel Bennett, your husband's doctor." Dark piercing eyes looked down at her. "I assume you *are* Desirée, Major Steele's wife."

"Yes, I am."

"Then maybe you can talk some sense to your husband. As I said, he's refused to take anything for the pain."

"But why?"

"He's been afraid we'd amputate his leg while he was unconscious. Mrs. Steele." The doctor's voice took on an intense timbre. "We *must* amputate. That leg is dangerously infected. He may have already developed gangrene. If we don't take it off, he'll die."

"No!" Jason said in a weak but determined voice from the cot. "I don't want you to. You can't cut off my leg."

"Do you see what I mean?" Colonel Bennett said in exasperation. "He's beyond reasoning."

"Desirée," Jason pleaded from the cot.

Desirée knelt beside him and once again took his hand in hers, saying, "Jason, maybe you should listen to what the doctor says."

"No! I won't have my leg cut off at the hip—or anywhere else. I'd rather be dead than a cripple the rest of my life. Please, don't let him do it."

404

Desirée hesitated. She knew that Jason meant exactly what he had said. He *would* rather be dead than crippled. But maybe it wasn't as bad as the doctor said, Desirée thought. Colonel Bennett had said he *might* have developed gangrene. But if it was just badly infected, she knew that Mammy could cure him. She has all kinds of poultices that drew out infection, poultices that the doctors ridiculed and scoffed—but worked.

"Please," Jason pleaded.

Desirée made her decision. "I won't let them amputate, Jason," she said in a firm voice.

"You promise?" he asked, using the last of his strength to squeeze her hand for emphasis.

"I promise."

A ghost of a smile played across Jason's cracked lips before he closed his eyes. He allowed the blackness to engulf him, finally giving in to the pain he had kept at bay for over a week.

"You shouldn't have made a promise you aren't going to keep," Dr. Bennett said in disapproval.

Desirée rose and turned to face the doctor, a determined gleam in her eyes. "Oh, but I intend to keep that promise, Dr. Bennett. I'm not going to let you amputate. I'm going to take my husband back to New Orleans for my old mammy to nurse."

Dr. Bennett stared at her in shocked disbelief for a minute, then exploded, saying "Are you insane?"

"No," Desirée replied calmly. "Mammy can cure him."

"With what?" the doctor spat. "A bunch of voodoo charms and mumbo jumbo?"

"No, with medicinal herbs and poultices."

Blood rushed to the doctor's face. For a minute, Desirée feared he would have a stroke. "All right, Mrs. Steele," he said in a tight, angry voice, barely able to contain his fury. "I wash my hands of the whole thing. But remember, you were warned. If your husband dies, it will be *your* fault!" He turned and stalked angrily away.

They left the field hospital almost immediately. If the Confederates were anywhere around, Desirée was determined Jason wasn't going to be captured.

All the way on the long trip back to New Orleans, a trip that seemed to last an eternity to her, Desirée anguished over whether she had made the right decision. Jason would regain consciousness for a few minutes, and then fall back into his dark world. His skin was burning with fever, and sometimes, his breathing was so shallow that Desirée feared he had died.

That last night, when O'Malley climbed into the carriage to see if she needed anything else before he retired, Desirée looked down at Jason lying so deathly still, with his head in her lap. She could hardly get the words past the lump of fear in her throat. "Maybe I should have let the doctor amputate."

"No, Mrs. Steele, you're doing what the major wants. No matter how it works out, just remember that."

Desirée was never so happy to see her old mammy as she was the evening they drove into the courtyard. After O'Malley had carried Jason up the stairs to their bedroom, and Mammy and Desirée had stripped and bathed him, Mammy Lou removed the dressing from his leg.

Desirée was totally unprepared for what she saw. Jason's left leg had a gaping hole in it, stretching from his knee almost to his groin, a horrible wound that was oozing blood and pus. She swayed dizzily as bile rose in her throat, her eyes wide with horror. "*Sacre Dieu*," she whispered. "I should have let the doctor amputate. He'll die for sure!"

"He ain't gonna die," Mammy said, staring down at the wound and feeling her own stomach rebel at the horrible sight and odor.

"*Mon Dieu*, Mammy, look at it!" Desirée wailed. "He'll die! And it will be my fault. Mine!"

Mammy turned and shook the hysterical girl so hard Desirée's head bobbed. "You hush up that talk," she said in a furious voice. "I told you, he ain't gonna die. You hear me? He ain't gonna die!"

Desirée looked down at Mammy's face. "Do you really believe that, Mammy?" she asked, tears shimmering in her eyes.

"I *know* it, honey lamb. Didn't I save you and Thad from that old yellow jack? If I can do that, then I can lick this, too. No sir!" Mammy said in a determined voice. "The massa ain't gonna die."

For the next few weeks, Mammy and Desirée fought a desperate battle for Jason's life. His fever raged dangerously high as Mammy applied one poultice after another to the wound, and hardly a day went by that Moses didn't make a trip into the countryside for the herbs Mammy needed.

Desirée thanked God for O'Malley's dedicated help. Despite Jason's weakened condition, it was impossible for anyone but the burly Irishman to handle him when he was wild with delirium. Desirée was amazed at the sergeant's strength. After she and Mammy had bathed him, O'Malley would pick Jason up and hold him in his arms, as if he weighed no more than a baby, while the two women changed the sheets.

One day, when Jason was raging with fever and fighting Desirée and O'Malley to get out of bed, Jason looked straight into Desirée's eyes and asked, in what seemed to her a perfectly lucid voice, "Why are you doing this to me, Desirée? Why are you so determined to hurt me?"

Seeing Desirée pale at the question, O'Malley said, "Now, ma'am, don't you be payin' no attention to him. The major don't know what he's sayin'."

After Jason had again lost consciousness and O'Malley had left the room, Desirée sat by the bed, staring down at her husband, feeling overwhelmed with guilt. Jason's delirious accusation had brought new guilt to the surface.

If it hadn't been for me, Colonel Anders wouldn't have had any reason to hate Jason nor had him transferred to a field command, she thought bleakly. Then Jason would still be sitting in his office and not lying in this bed, fighting for his life. To make matters worse, I helped sneak supplies to the Confederacy, the same men who did this to him. If he dies, I helped to bring about his death.

For a long while, Desirée sat and brooded over these dark thoughts. Finally, she rose and stared down at Jason, whispering, "I'm not going to let you die. Do you hear me, Jason? I'm not!"

Chapter 19

Vicksburg surrendered on July 4, after its long, historic siege. General Pemberton's haggard, half-starved Confederate troops marched out of the city and stacked their rifles, ammunition, and flags before a hushed Union Army. And then, a cheer went up from General Grant's Army of Tennessee—not one of victory but a show of their respect for the courageous defenders of Vicksburg, whose lines had never broken.

Five days later, Port Hudson, where the Union had suffered such a terrible defeat only weeks before, surrendered. The Mississippi River was finally open. The South had been split in half. For the Confederacy, it was the beginning of the end.

When the war news arrived in New Orleans, Desirée paid little attention. She was still fighting her own battle to save Jason's life. He would rally, then fall back into a new bout of fever and delirium, over and over.

At the end of the summer, when Jason had finally gone two weeks without a relapse, Mammy pronounced him cured, a victorious grin on her chubby, black face.

The first time Jason saw his leg, he looked down in

horror at the gaping hole that had once been his thigh.

Seeing the expression on his face, Desirée quickly said, "Now, Jason, don't get upset."

"My, God, Desirée!" Jason choked out. "I'll never be able to walk again!"

"No, that's not true," Desirée said in a firm voice. "Mammy says if we massage it and exercise the leg, the muscles will regenerate."

"Muscles maybe. But not nerves. Christ! I can't even feel it! It's like it's not even a part of me." He shook his dark head. "No. Let's face it. I'm crippled. Hopelessly crippled."

"No, you're not!" Desirée said emphatically. "All you have to do is exercise it."

"How in the hell can I exercise it when I can't even move it?"

Desirée heard the despair in Jason's voice. "I'll do it for you. And I'll massage it, too. I'll do it three times a day, just like Mammy said."

"It won't do any good," Jason muttered in a defeated voice.

"Jason, we've got to at least try!" Desirée insisted.

Jason stared down at his thigh. The puckered mass of scar tissue repulsed him. He couldn't stand the thought of Desirée's touching that disgusting, ugly thing.

"Jason, will you let me try?" Desirée pleaded.

Jason desperately wanted to walk again, and he knew, to do so, that he would need Desirée's help. He struggled with his conflicting emotions, then spat, "All right! But keep the damned thing covered with a towel. I can't stand to look at it."

Two weeks later, when Desirée was massaging his leg, Jason looked at her thoughtfully and asked, "Why did you fight so hard to save my life?"

410

Desirée was stunned by his question. Had it been to assuage her guilt? or had some deeper emotion motivated her? Whichever, she couldn't admit either to Jason.

"Because you saved my life," she answered, refusing to look him in the eye. "Besides, I'm your wife. Naturally, I'd do everything in my power to keep you from dying."

For gratitude and duty? Jason thought and recoiled in horror. He had hoped she was beginning to love him.

The next few days, Desirée brooded over Jason's question. She couldn't get it off her mind. Was it guilt or something more that made her so desperate to save Jason's life? Yet, she couldn't—or wouldn't—delve deeper to find the answer.

Seeing how distracted she was, Jason wondered if Desirée was thinking of Beau. Did she still love him? Had she been secretly carrying him close to her heart all along? And does she regret marrying him? Particularly, now that he was a cripple, nothing but a burden to her.

The next morning, when Desirée returned from the kitchen with Jason's breakfast tray, Jason was awake. "Good morning," she said cheerfully, carrying the tray to the table by the window and setting it down.

When Jason failed to respond to her greeting, she turned and looked at him. He sat with his back resting on the headboard, staring out into space.

What in the world is wrong with him? She walked to the bed and said, "Are you ready to get up?"

"No. I'll eat in bed this morning," Jason replied, still staring out into space.

"But—but you've been walking to the table for your meals for the past week."

Jason's head snapped around. "Walking?" he

411

scoffed. "You call dragging my dead leg across the floor on a pair of crutches walking? No. I'm tired of that foolishness. I'll eat here in bed."

Desirée was stunned by Jason's bitter words. Deciding not to agitate him further, she brought the tray to him and placed it over his lap. She watched him from the corner of her eye as he listlessly shoved the food around in his plate.

When Jason said he was finished eating, Desirée removed the tray and walked to the dresser, picking up the towel lying on it. She turned, saying, "It's time to massage your leg and exercise it."

Jason glared at her. "No, we're not going to do that any more, either," he said in a hard, clipped voice.

"But why not?"

"Because it's hopeless, that's why! We've been doing it for weeks and nothing has happened."

"That's not true, Jason," Desirée objected. "I've felt movements in your leg."

"No! You just imagined them," Jason spat. An anguished expression came over his face. "It's dead! Don't you understand, Desirée? I'm crippled. I'm nothing but a useless cripple!" He looked away from her and stared out the window for a minute, then said in a low, bitter voice, "You should have let me die. I told you, I'd rather be dead than be a cripple the rest of my life."

Desirée didn't know why Jason was acting so strangely, but she did know she couldn't let him give up. She hadn't imagined the involuntary jerks in Jason's muscles. They had been real and growing stronger every day. And then, she remembered how hard she had worked to save his life. A slow anger filled her. She'd be damned if she'd let him give up!

She glared at him saying, "I thought I had come to know you well over the past year, but I never dreamed

412

you were a coward."

Jason's head snapped up. No one had ever called him a coward. "A coward?" he asked in disbelief.

Sparks flew from Desirée's black eyes. "Yes, a coward!" Desirée shrieked, so angry she was shaking. "You're afraid to go on. It's easier to sit back and say it's hopeless than to keep struggling, isn't it? Well, I'm ashamed of you. And I'll be damned if I'll coddle you or stand by and watch you wallowing in self-pity, either. If you're determined to be miserable, then you can be miserable by yourself!"

Desirée whirled and marched out of the bedroom, slamming the door behind her so hard the window-panes shook.

Jason stared at the door, feeling sick with self-disgust. She was right. He had been feeling sorry for himself. But he couldn't stand the thought of Desirée's feeling ashamed of him. If he couldn't have her love, he wanted her respect.

He struggled to sit up on the side of the bed, pushing his lifeless leg into a position he wanted, and reached for the crutches at the foot of the bed. It took all of his strength to pull himself up on them. Slowly, he walked, pulling his limp leg behind him, back and forth across the room, sweat beading his forehead from his efforts.

Desirée stood on the other side of the door, tears streaming down her face, her hand over her mouth to smother her sobs. She had deliberately goaded Jason by calling him a coward, and it pained her deeply to hurt him. But she had to do it. She couldn't let him give up.

Then, with sudden clarity, it came to her with such force it took her breath away. She loved him! That's why she had been so determined to save his life, and that's why it had hurt so much to hurt him. Her mind had told her not to fall in love with him, her heart had stubbornly rebelled and refused to listen. Now, she loved him with her whole heart and soul, with every fiber of her being, and strangely, that no longer frightened her.

She heard the scrape of Jason's crutch against the floor, and then, the sound of him dragging his leg. How had he gotten up on his crutches by himself? And he had never tried to walk without someone there to assist him. A second later, a terrible crash came from the bedroom, and Desirée heard Jason's grunt of pain as he hit the floor.

Desirée started to open the door, then hesitated, knowing that Jason would be humiliated for her to see he had fallen. But what if he hurt himself? She jerked open the door and rushed into the room, crying, "Did you hurt yourself?"

Jason sat on the floor, propped up on his elbows. His legs were sprawled out before him, one crutch over his lap, the other a few feet away. But instead of looking humiliated, as Desirée had feared, he was beaming.

Jason looked up at her, his misty-green eyes dancing with excitement. "Yes, I hurt myself!" he answered in an elated voice. He laughed, saying, "Isn't it wonderful?"

Desirée stared at him as if he'd lost his mind.

He struggled to sit up straight, asking, "Don't you understand? I hurt my bad leg. I felt pain! The nerves aren't dead after all. Mammy was right. I can walk again!"

Desirée was thrilled. She sank to her knees beside him, and they hugged each other, Jason laughing lustily with sheer joy and Desirée laughing and crying with relief.

From then on, Jason and Desirée worked even

harder at exercising his leg. While the return of the feeling in Jason's leg was a blessing, it was also a curse, for any movement of the leg caused him pain. Walking was especially painful for him, and Desirée had to fight back tears as she watched him clench his teeth and his forehead break out in cold sweat to keep from making any sound in front of her. She realized that Jason was showing her a special kind of courage, and her pride and love for him grew. By the end of October, Jason had graduated to a cane.

Throughout his long recovery, Jason never made any attempt to make love to Desirée. Even when the muscles and tendons had grown and his leg had returned to its normal size, he held back. To him, the scars on his thigh were horrible. He feared Desirée would be repulsed by them.

At first, Desirée attributed Jason's apparent lack of interest in making love to his weakened condition. As time passed, and he still made no romantic advances, she feared he no longer desired her. Then, she noticed the hungry gleam in his eyes when he looked at her but didn't think she was watching.

A new fear took hold of Desirée. What if Jason had suffered some injury she was unaware of and was incapable of making love? Had the exploding shell damaged him there? She had noticed no visible signs, but it had been almost two weeks after the battle before she had seen him naked. By then, if there had been swelling or discoloration, the outward signs of injury could have disappeared.

The new fear gnawed at her, but she was afraid to question Jason. She knew enough about men to know that, if it were true, Jason would never want to admit it to anyone. Even though it would make him no less a man in her eyes, he would feel humiliated; that his sexuality, his very essence was being questioned.

One night, when Desirée was sitting before her vanity and brushing her hair before the mirror, she saw Jason watching her, his look blatantly hungry. Her eyes drifted over his reflection and then came to a dead stop, seeing the telltale tending of the sheet over Jason's lap, a sheet that couldn't hide his erection.

Hardly believing her eyes, she turned. Jason rolled quickly to his side, placing his back to her and hiding the proof of his arousal. Desirée frowned, remembering other times Jason had hid nakedness from her. No longer did he walk about the room nude. As soon as he rose from bed each morning, he quickly pulled on his pants, always keeping his back to her. Nor would he allow her to wash his back as he had before his injury. He had even taken to bathing behind the screen. Why, he even insisted that a towel be placed over his leg before he would let her massage it.

Suddenly, it dawned on her. It was his scar he was hiding. Did he think she would be repulsed by it? But how ridiculous! She had seen his leg when it looked much worse. The scars didn't bother her in the least.

Should she just tell Jason his scars didn't bother her? No, he wouldn't believe her. She would have to show him, prove it to him. She smiled. Yes, she would have to seduce him—again. But if Jason feared she would be repulsed because of his scar, she would have to be much bolder. She would have to take the initiative all the way.

The next night, Desirée arranged for a bath. Instead of having the tub placed behind the screen, as she usually did, she had Benjie place it before the fireplace, using the excuse that the room was chilled and it would be warmer there. She deliberately dawdled while Jason undressed and quickly slipped under the covers.

Desirée undressed, but not hastily shedding her

416

clothing and scrambling into the tub as she usually did. Instead, her movements were slow and deliberately seductive. She didn't need to peek to know that Jason was watching her. She could feel his hot eyes on her.

And in spite of himself, Jason couldn't keep his eyes off her. He watched as she slowly stripped before him, her provocative movements playing havoc with his senses. He smothered a groan of frustration when she sank in the tub, and then, his hungry eyes devoured the sight of her ivory shoulders and the tantalizing swell of her breasts. When she stepped from the tub and dried off, he though he'd go crazy if she didn't stop giving him flashing, teasing glimpses of her rounded thighs and her rose-tipped breasts. And then, when she dropped the towel and stood before him totally naked, he sucked in his breath, his arousal at the point of pain.

He watched, mesmerized, as she walked across the floor, her hips swaying gracefully, a small, seductive smile on her face. His mouth turned dry and sweat popped out on his brow.

When she stood over him, Desirée said in a low, husky voice, "I'm going to make love to you, Jason."

A horrified look came over Jason's face. But before he could roll away, Desirée flipped back the sheet and threw herself half over him. For the life of him, Jason couldn't move away, not because Desirée's weight was holding him down but because the feel of her soft, satiny skin against his naked, feverish body made him feel suddenly weak. His mind commanded him to move but his body refused to obey. And then, as Desirée placed soft, feathery kisses over his face, then blazed a trail of fire across his neck, shoulders, and chest, her tongue darting and flicking over his male nipple, he groaned, his hands reaching to pull her

417

upward.

"No," Desirée whispered as he pulled her up. Her dark, passion-filled eyes gazed down at him. "I'm going to love *you*."

Before Jason could object, her head again lowered, nipping and tonguing his muscular shoulders, then across his broad chest, tracing each rib as she descended. Jason was powerless beneath her sensual assault. Every nerve in his body seemed to be tingling and burning, his muscles quivering. When she stopped to lazily circle his navel with her tongue, a deep moan rose in the back of his throat.

Then, as Desirée's head dipped lower, her lips brushing against his groin, Jason's mind finally surfaced from his passion-drugged senses. He stiffened, his fear overriding all. Frantically, he grabbed for her to pull her up. "No!" he choked out.

But it was too late. Desirée was already kissing the scars on his thigh and running her tongue over them. Jason was shocked by her surprising action, disbelief written all over his face. And then, even that was wiped out as Desirée ran her lips up the long, hot length of his manhood, her tongue dancing around him.

Jason was lost in sheer sensation as Desirée loved him with her mouth and tongue. A roaring filled his ears, and every muscle in his powerful body trembled. When he was so aroused he felt as if he would explode, he caught Desirée's head and pulled it up, whispering in a ragged, urgent voice, "Desirée! No more."

Desirée smiled down at him, elated at her victory over his fear. But when Jason tried to roll her to her back again, she whispered, "No, I'm moving you."

She straddled him, firmly locking her knees against his hips, and watched his face as she slowly lowered herself over him, inch by inch, stifling her own gasp of pleasure at the feel of his immense rigid maleness filling her.

Jason sucked in his breath as he felt Desirée's moist, velvety heat surrounding him. And then, as her muscles contracted greedily, feeling as if they would squeeze the very life from him, he clenched his teeth, girding himself against the exquisite feeling and struggling for control.

But Desirée was in no hurry. She wanted to delay this long awaited lovemaking, savor it to the fullest. Only when she felt Jason's tense muscles relax did she begin her movements: slow, languid movements that drove Jason wild. Even when his hands swept over her thighs and hips and rose to caress her breasts, sending a hot wave of fire to her loins, she refused to be rushed.

Jason caught her hips and thrust against her, trying to quicken her movements. Desirée shuttered at the delightful sensation, then withdrew, saying, "No, this is my loving."

Jason's eyes were filled with desperation. "*Cherie*, you're driving me crazy," he ground out. "I can't stand it anymore."

Desirée remembered all the times Jason had made her feel the same way with his lovemaking. So many times she had thought she would lose her mind if he didn't stop his delicious tormenting of her body and give her release from her agony. A new thrill ran over her, one of power. "Oh, yes, you can,".she whispered.

As Desirée again lowered herself over him, engulfing him in flame, Jason ground his teeth; a sheen of perspiration covered his body.

When Desirée felt his strength deep inside her, pulsating with a life of its own, her own need for release suddenly spiraled upward. This time she needed no urging. She rode him, fast and hard, pounding her hips against his. And then, as she felt herself hovering on that brink, she lowered her head and kissed him. Their tongues met and danced. Jason arched his hips, thrusting deeply, sending them over that quivering zenith. They climaxed in a sweet rush of intense ecstasy that hurled them into space and left them shuddering in its aftermath.

When the tremors had finally subsided, Desirée disengaged herself from Jason's embrace, rolled to her side and sat up. She looked down at Jason's leg.

Jason watched her warily, afraid she had been so caught up in her passion earlier that she hadn't realized what she had done. He steeled himself for her revulsion.

She bent and kissed his leg. Then she hovered over him, an intense look on her face. "Did you honestly think that your scar would bother me?"

Jason's eyes clouded. "It's—hideous." He turned his head away from her, muttering, "I'm ashamed of it."

Desirée framed his face in her hands and turned his head. Looking deeply into his eyes, she said in a firm voice, "*Non*, it's *not* ugly. And how dare you be ashamed of it! That scar is your badge of courage and *our* proof of the long, hard battle we fought against death, a battle we fought together—and won!"

Jason was stunned at her ferocity.

"Don't you ever try to hide it from me again. Do you hear?"

Jason nodded his head mutely.

Long after Desirée had fallen asleep, Jason lay awake, deeply touched by her actions and her words. But the battle isn't ended, he thought. Not until I can walk on my own two feet.

From then on, every night after Desirée had fallen

asleep, Jason slipped from bed and went to the library. There, he practiced walking without his cane, falling several times, determined that he would walk with no support.

That year, according to the Creole custom, they again celebrated New Years instead of Christmas. That night, when they were undressing for bed, Jason said, "I have another gift for you, Desirée."

Desirée looked up from where she was unbuttoning her bodice. "Another gift?"

"Yes," Jason replied with a secretive smile on his face. "It's a very personal gift. That's why I didn't give it to you earlier when everyone was around."

Desirée glanced around her. She couldn't see any package anywhere. "Where is it?"

"Right here, standing in front of you." A broad grin crossed his face as he tossed his cane to the side.

Desirée's breath caught, fearing he would fall. She started to rush to him, but Jason stopped her, saying, "No! Stay where you are." His green eyes sparkled with excitement. "Just watch."

Slowly and carefully, he walked toward her. He limped badly, but he was walking on his own two feet with no support. Desirée was so full of pride and love for him that she could hardly contain it.

She rushed to him, hugging him fiercely, saying, "Oh, Jason, you're the bravest, most wonderful man in the world. I—"

Desirée's eyes widened. *Mon Dieu*, she had almost blurted out her love. She ached to tell him, but she knew that she couldn't. She feared Jason would say the words back out of gratitude for saving his life and helping him to walk again or, worse yet, out of pity. No, as much as she longed to hear them, she could never bear that.

Jason held his breath, his heart racing in anticipation, hoping for the words. The minute that passed seemed a lifetime.

Finally, Desirée raised her head. Her dark eyes shimmered with unshed tears, tears that she hoped Jason would mistake for happiness. She smiled at him, saying in an emotion-choked voice, "I'm so proud of you."

Jason fought back his disappointment. When he had thrown away his cane and walked to her, he could have almost sworn he saw love in her eyes. To keep her from seeing his reaction to her words, he hugged her back, burying her head in his shoulder.

Resting his chin on the top of her head, he comforted himself. Well, he thought, at least I've gained her respect and pride. That's better than gratitude and duty. For the time being, I'll just have to be content with that.

Chapter 20

In the month of January, Jason's leg grew even stronger, his limp diminishing by the day. He also grew increasingly restless. At the end of the month, when he decided to rejoin the army, Desirée didn't object. She knew he needed something to keep him busy. Jason simply wasn't the type of man to sit around and do nothing. Nor was she concerned about his going back to war. She assumed, because of his leg, he would be given a desk job.

Desirée was in the salon the afternoon Jason returned from enlisting. She looked up as he stood in the doorway, admiring his new uniform and thinking that he was even more handsome than ever. His illness had left him with a few silver hairs over his temple, giving him a new maturity, a distinguished air. Even his slight limp added to, rather than detracted from, his powerful masculine aura, enhancing that hint of mystery about him.

Jason walked over to her. When he stood before her, he said, "Notice anything new?"

Desirée's eyes swept over him and then, seeing the embroidered spread eagle on his shoulder strap, she jumped to her feet, crying in an excited voice, "You're a colonel!"

Jason beamed proudly. "Yes."

Desirée couldn't believe it. "You mean Colonel Anders promoted you?"

Jason frowned at the name of his hated enemy. "No, believe me, he didn't have anything to do with it. It was my battalion that brought about this promotion. Every man in it signed a petition requesting I be promoted after the battle at Port Hudson."

"They promoted you at your men's request?"

"Yes, supported by several other officers who fought at Port Hudson," Once more, Jason beamed. Unlike his last promotion, he was proud of this one. He had earned it on the honorable field of battle, not as a spy. There was no hint of regret or betrayal to spoil this promotion for him.

Desirée was proud of him, too. She hugged and kissed him, then stood back, asking, "Now that you're a colonel, will you be in charge of the liaison officers?"

"No. They offered me that position, but I turned it down. I asked for a field command."

Desirée felt Jason's announcement like a physical blow. She sucked in her breath, and her legs turned weak. "But, Jason, you can't do that much walking on your bad leg," she objected.

"You're right. I can't," he said. His green eyes twinkled. At Desirée's puzzled expression, he laughed and pointed to his trousers, saying, "Didn't you notice my stripe? It's yellow, not blue. I joined the cavalry, not the infantry. I won't have to walk. I can ride. And you know what?" he asked with a hint of pride in his voice. "Half of my old battalion asked to transfer with me, even Sergeant O'Malley. He's going to be my aide again. But can you imagine O'Malley joining the cavalry? As much as he hates horses?"

Desirée wasn't surprised at O'Malley. She knew

he'd follow Jason to hell if necessary. And, for Sergeant O'Malley, with his poor riding skills, the cavalry would be just that—hell. But Desirée was upset with Jason for requesting a field command, her fear a tight knot in her belly. She looked up at him, intending to ask him to reconsider, to accept the position as head of the liaison officers, but seeing how pleased he was with himself and how happy he was, she couldn't do it.

"That's wonderful, Jason," she managed to say, knowing he was expecting some reaction from her.

In the weeks that passed, Desirée was still apprehensive. She prayed that Jason wouldn't have to go back into battle, hoping that the cavalry wasn't called out as often as the infantry.

One blustery March day, Jason walked in and calmly announced that his battalion had been called out and that they would leave the following morning for another attempt to take Shreveport and the Red River.

At his announcement, Desirée felt the room spin. Raw fear clutched her heart. Her terror brought on a surge of anger at Jason for placing himself in this danger.

She glared at him, lashing out at him angrily, saying "You just had to ask for a field command, didn't you? You could have had a safe office job, but no! You just had to go and endanger yourself!"

"Desirée," Jason said in a patient voice, "you know I hate office work."

"So what if you hate it!" she spat. "What about me? Did you ever stop to consider how I feel? Do you think I worked myself to death to save your life—only to have you go out and get yourself killed?"

"I'm a soldier. It's my duty to fight."

Tears glittered in Desirée's eyes. In desperation, she

threw her arms around him. She looked up at him, her eyes pleading. "You've done your part. You almost gave your life. Let someone else go this time. It's nor fair for you to have to go back."

Jason peeled Desirée's arms from around his neck and held her by her shoulders. "As long as I'm capable of fighting, it's never enough." His eyes pleaded, pleaded for understanding. "Fighting is my job. It's what I get paid to do. I've never shirked my duty, and I don't intend to start now." He shook his dark head. "No, *cherie*, I can't do it. Not even for you."

Desirée knew that there was nothing she could do or say that would change his mind. Her fear turned to fury; her dark eyes flashed. "All right, then! Go!" she shrieked. "Go out and get yourself killed—and see if I care!"

Jason watched as she ran from the room, a bleak look on his face.

That night, Desirée stood at the window in the guest room, staring out at the dark night. After her outburst that afternoon she had sequestered herself in this room, trying, in some way she didn't quite understand, to punish Jason, and yet she hoped he would come to her. But Jason didn't come, and Desirée knew that she couldn't let him go off to war with this between them. She was still terrified, but if anything happened to him, she'd never forgive herself.

She turned and walked from the room and down the hallway to their bedroom. She opened the door and saw him standing before the window, gazing out at the courtyard.

"Jason?" she said softly.

He turned, and Desirée saw the misery in his eyes. It tore at her heart. Fresh tears gathered in her eyes. "Oh, Jason," she sobbed, rushing to him.

Jason caught her in his strong arms and held her to him. "Desirée, don't send me away like this."

Desirée remembered another time before Jason had left for war. His words that night had been much the same. "I'm sorry," she mumbled against his broad chest. "I didn't mean those terrible things I said to you. It's just that I'm—I'm so afraid."

Jason felt the trembling in her body. "I know," he said, tenderly kissing the top of her head. He cupped her chin, lifted her head, and gazed down at her. "I'll come back, Desirée. I promise," he said in a soft but determined voice. "And in one piece this time." And then his warm mouth came down over hers in a deep, passionate kiss that obliterated all thought from Desirée's mind.

But Jason's promise only temporarily reassured Desirée. After he left, her terror returned, stronger than ever, a living, almost palpable thing that seemed to be smothering her. When the wounded from the new Red River campaign started arriving in New Orleans, Desirée haunted the port, afraid that she might see Jason among the men being carried from the hospital ships. Yet, she was unable to stay away.

Dorothy went with her every day, her heart going out to her friend. She watched as Desirée anxiously scanned the wounded being placed in the horse-drawn, wooden ambulances. She was relieved that her husband didn't have to go to war. She knew that waiting for men to return from war had always been the lot of women in wartime, a special hell designated to them since the beginning of time, but Dorothy was beginning to fear for her friend's health and sanity. There was a haggard look about Desirée, a wild look at her eyes that alarmed Dorothy.

Finally, Dorothy couldn't hide her deep concern any longer. "Desirée, you've got to stop coming down here to the docks and torturing yourself like this. If you don't get control of yourself, you'll have a nervous breakdown."

Desirée realized that she was letting her fear get the best of her. She hadn't had a decent night's sleep since Jason had left. "I know," she admitted. "But I just can't seem to help it." Tears glittered in her eyes. "Oh, Dorothy, if Jason should get killed, I don't think I could endure living without him," she said in an agonized voice, for the first time admitting the depths of her love.

"I know," Dorothy replied gently. "I feel the same way about Bob. But coming down here to the docks every day isn't going to change anything. It certainly isn't helping Jason, and it's not doing you any good, either. What you need is something to get it off your mind. Something to keep you so busy you won't have time to think about it."

"Like what?" Desirée asked.

"Well, you could come with me in the mornings and help roll bandages, like the rest of the officers' wives."

Roll bandages for the Union? Oh, no, she was still very southern at heart. She might not do anything against the Union because of her love for Jason, but she wasn't going to help them either. Then, she really would feel like a traitor to the South.

"No, I don't think so," Desirée answered. "I have things to do in the mornings."

The next day, Desirée didn't ask Dorothy to go to the docks with her, afraid Dorothy would admonish her again. She watched as the wounded were carried on litters down the gangplank. And then she noticed that some of the wounded were wearing tattered grey uniforms.

Desirée had never realized that the wounded prisoners of war were being brought back to New Orleans, too. She wondered how the Confederates were treated. Were they just left in a corner to die from neglect because the Union doctors and nurses were too busy tending to their own and didn't have time for them?

She remembered what Dorothy had said the day before. She needed something to do, something to keep her mind off of Jason. She could nurse the Confederate wounded. She certainly had enough experience nursing Jason back to health, and she wouldn't be aiding Jason's enemy either. Those men weren't soldiers anymore. They were prisoners of war. And since the North and the South had stopped exchanging prisoners, the war was over for them. None of them would go back and shoot at Jason, endanger his life.

For the first time since Jason had left, Desirée felt a sense of purpose filling her. She smiled and climbed back into the carriage, saying, "Take me to the St. Charles, Moses. I'm going to see if they'll let me nurse the southern wounded."

Moses grinned. It had been a long time since he'd seen that sparkle in Desirée's eyes. Not since the massa had left. "Yes, ma'am," he replied, whipping the horses' reins.

When they arrived at the hotel, Desirée rushed up the stairs to the ballroom that had been converted into a temporary hospital. She stood in the wide doorway and gazed about the huge, oval room but could see no grey uniforms on the men lying on the low cots that crowded the room. Had the prisoners of war been taken to one of the city's hospitals?

She stopped and orderly passing by, asking, "Do you know where the wounded prisoners of war are being taken? I'd like to offer my services to help nurse them."

"They're down the hall in one of the private dining

rooms, ma'am," the orderly answered before he rushed off.

Desirée turned and walked down the hall. When she reached the dining room, she stood and looked into it. Twenty or thirty cots were placed in the room, and milling all around them were women, many of them Creoles whom Desirée recognized. Apparently, she wasn't the only woman in New Orleans to get the idea of nursing the Confederate wounded, she thought. There must be three women for every injured man.

At that minute, one of the Creole women glanced up. Seeing Desirée and recognizing her, the woman glared at her with an accusing look on her face, as if daring Desirée, the wife of the hated enemy, to enter.

Desirée knew that she wasn't needed or wanted here. She turned and walked dejectedly down the hallway, tears stinging in her eyes. As she passed the ballroom, she heard someone pleading for a drink of water. She glanced into the crowded room and saw a soldier lying on a cot near the doorway. Within arm's length of the man was a bucket and dipper. But the soldier couldn't see it. His eyes were covered with a huge, blood-stained dressing.

Desirée came to an abrupt halt, wondering if she should give him a drink. She glanced about the room. The doctors and nurses were all rushing about; no one was paying any attention to the young soldier by the doorway.

"Please—water," the soldier begged between parched lips.

Desirée's moment of hesitation was past. She went to the soldier and knelt by his side. Then, lifting his head, she held the water dipper to his cracked lips. The man blindly groped and caught her wrists, drinking thirstily. When he was finished, Desirée gently lay his head back down.

"Mother? Is that you?" the soldier asked in a disbelieving voice.

"No," Desirée answered. "What made you think that?"

The soldier flushed. "Because—because you smell so good and your hands are so soft."

Desirée looked at the soft fuzz on the soldier's chin and realized that he was hardly more than a boy. It must be terrible to be locked in a world of sudden darkness, unable to see anything around you, she thought. And to be in pain, too, would make it even worse. Her heart went out to the young soldier.

She glanced at her hand. The youth was holding it tightly, as if he thought it was his last link to the world. "Would you like for me to sit here and hold your hand until you go back to sleep?" Desirée asked in a soft voice.

"Would you—would you do that, ma'am?" the boy asked in a choked voice.

"Yes, I'll stay," Desirée answered, fresh tears looming in her dark eyes, tears of pity for the boy.

A few minutes later, the boy's grip on her hand relaxed and his breathing became deep and regular. Desirée knew that he was asleep, but she hated to leave him. She looked about the crowded ballroom, observing how busy the doctors, nurses, and orderlies were, and how exhausted they all looked.

Suddenly, Desirée was ashamed of herself. She had come to nurse the Confederate wounded, not once giving a thought to the Union wounded. Now, looking over the scene before her, she realized that the wounded and dying wore no uniforms. They were simply human beings in pain. No, in this room another battle was being fought, one even more ancient than war: the age-old battle of man to prevail over suffering and death. And she wanted to be a part of it.

Desirée carefully lay the boy's hand down so as not to awaken him. She rose and walked to the same orderly she had questioned earlier.

The man looked up from the leg he was bandaging and frowned at her. "Didn't you find the prisoners of war?"

"Yes, but they don't need me." Desirée scanned the ballroom, saying, "I'd like to help in here, if I may."

The orderly's expression changed from one of annoyance to surprise. "In here?" he asked, as if disbelieving his ears.

"Yes. It looks like you could use some help and I have nursing experience."

The orderly came to his feet, saying, "We sure could use some help. But I'm afraid you have to get the commanding officer's permission, and he's in surgery right now."

"I'll wait."

"It might be a long time, ma'am," the orderly warned.

"I have nothing to do today." Desirée glanced around, then said. "I'll wait over on that bench by the wall. That way, I won't be in anyone's way."

"All right, ma'am. I'll tell the doctor you're waiting for him."

Desirée waited for hours, her eyes filled with compassion for men moaning and thrashing in pain on their cots. Then, concerned that Moses might be worrying about her, she hurried down to the carriage to tell him what was delaying her, suggesting he go home and come back later. The old man stubbornly refused to leave, saying he'd wait.

When darkness fell and the lamps were lit, Desirée began to think that the doctor had forgotten her. She rose, looking about the crowded room for the orderly to ask him if he had relayed her message.

"Are you the woman who had offered her help?" a male voice said from behind her.

Desirée turned to face the man. Then, seeing it was Colonel Bennett, the same doctor she had crossed swords with over Jason's leg in the field hospital outside of Baton Rouge, her heart fell. She felt sure he would never let her nurse his patients. A feeling of acute disappointment filled her.

And then, to her utter surprise, Dr. Bennett smiled broadly when he recognized her. "You're Desirée, Colonel Steele's wife, aren't you?"

"Yes, I am," Desirée answered, stunned by his reaction.

"Well, anyone who can do such a remarkable job of nursing as you did on your husband would be more than welcome here."

"You've seen Jason?"

"Yes, I was the doctor who gave him his physical examination when he reenlisted. And I must admit that I was absolutely amazed at his leg. I could have sworn it was gangrenous."

He looked over her head and gazed about the ballroom, a thoughtful look on his exhausted face. "I've wondered since then how many times we army doctors have amputated when it wasn't necessary. How many times we've simply cut off an arm or leg because we didn't have the time or the personnel to give every man the personal attention he needed."

Desirée was disturbed by the haunted look in the doctor's eyes and the regretful tone of his voice. "You couldn't possibly give your patients that kind of attention, doctor," Desirée said, hoping to ease some of his guilt and frustration. "There were three of us nursing Jason, night and day, and even then, he

433

almost died."

"Yes, he told me that," the doctor admitted. He looked back at Desirée, saying, "He also said your old mammy used poultices on the wound. Do you know what was in them?"

"No, but I can ask her."

Dr. Bennett smiled sheepishly, saying, "I'd like to try them. I don't care if the other doctors do laugh at me. If it could save one arm or leg, it would be worth it. Perhaps you could bring me the recipe." He laughed. "Or whatever she calls it—when you come back tomorrow morning to report for work."

"I can stay tonight if you need me."

"No, you get a good night's rest tonight." He looked around wearily. "You're going to need it."

Desirée threw herself into her work, going from dawn to dusk, too busy to worry about Jason during the daytime and too exhausted at night. It didn't take her long to get to know each soldier personally, and in each case, nursing him back to health became a personal challenge for her. The first patient she lost, she cried long and bitterly, feeling an acute sense of failure. She wondered how the nurses and doctors could stand taking such defeats over and over. And then, when new wounded arrived, she understood. There was no time for regrets or grief. The battle was still being waged.

As time passed, no more Confederate wounded arrived, but the northern wounded increased daily. One afternoon, when Desirée was changing the dressing on one of her patients, she looked up to see several of the New Orleans' women standing in the doorway. One of the women was the Creole woman who had glared at Desirée that first day.

Seeing the woman walking toward her, Desirée thought the woman meant to reprimand her for nursing the enemy. Desirée shot to her feet, her eyes flashing with defiance.

The Creole woman smiled weakly at Desirée, then said nervously, "Desirée, I have an apology to make to you for the way I treated you the day you came to offer your help." A flush crept up the woman's face. "And for the way I've treated you all along."

Desirée couldn't believe her ears. She stared mutely at the woman.

The woman's dark eyes swept over the ballroom. "With all this misery and suffering, that kind of hatred seems petty and childish now." Her eyes came back to rest on Desirée. "They moved our wounded to the prison at Fort St. Phillips a little while ago."

"I know," Desirée replied.

The woman's eyes once more scanned the wounded men lying about the ballroom. "Do you—do you think they would allow us to help in here?"

Desirée look at the Creole woman in surprise, then glanced at the other women standing in the doorway. Their eyes were filled with pity and compassion. She knew that, like her, they had passed over that boundary of hatred. Like her, they realized that it had no place here. This room held no enemy, only suffering human beings.

Desirée smiled warmly and said, "I'm sure they'd welcome your help. If you like, I'll ask Colonel Bennett for you."

The doctor was grateful for the women's offer, and as Desirée worked beside them, the barriers that the war and circumstances had put between them came tumbling down. In its place a mutual respect was born.

One day, when Desirée was changing her patient's bed linens, she was startled by a sharp, angry voice, crying out, "What in God's name is this woman doing here?"

Desirée turned and saw Colonel Anders glaring down at her, his face beet red. Desirée rose to face him, her body trembling with both fear and anger.

Colonel Bennett rushed up to them, saying in a demanding voice, "What is the meaning of this?"

Colonel Anders whirled around to him, saying, "I'm Colonel Anders and I want to know what this woman is doing here nursing our wounded. Don't you know she's a southerner?"

"Of course, I know she a southerner," Colonel Bennett retorted. "But I fail to see what that's got to do with it. I've several women from the city helping me here."

"My God!" Anders thundered. "Are you crazy? Why, they might be spies, hoping to get military information from these men while they're drugged or delirious. Or—or they might even be killing them, when your back is turned."

The doctor's face filled with rage. "You're a damned fool if you think that! These women aren't spies. They're only compassionate human beings. Something that a stupid idiot like you wouldn't understand." His eyes narrowed suspiciously. "Just what in the hell are you doing here, anyway?"

Colonel Anders stuck out his chin, saying in a haughty voice, "I'm making an inspection."

"An inspection? Why, you stupid jackass, you haven't got enough sense to inspect a pigsty. Now, you get the hell out of my hospital."

Colonel Anders glared at the doctor, saying in a threatening tone of voice, "Have you forgotten who you're talking to, colonel? As an officer of equal rank, you could be court-martialed for talking to me like this. When I tell General Banks how you treated me—"

Colonel Bennett stepped closer, his black eyes pinning Anders to the spot. "You're not going to tell General Banks anything," he interjected in a low, steely voice. "Because if you do, I might have to tell the general about some ugly rumors I've heard about a colonel who sent a certain major and his battalion on a suicide charge during the battle of Port Hudson."

Desirée head snapped up at this information. Her eyes darted to Colonel Anders. His face whitened.

"Don't threaten me with court-martial, Colonel Anders," the doctor continued angrily. "And you get the hell out of my hospital—before I have you thrown out!"

Anders shot Desirée a look of pure hatred and whirled, stomping down the aisle angrily.

Desirée watched as he stormed away. "Is it true?" she asked in a weak voice. "Did he send Jason and his battalion on a suicide charge?"

The doctor sighed deeply, saying, "I'm sorry, Desirée. I shouldn't have used such foul language in front of you, and I shouldn't have let that slip. Yes, it's rumored that Anders sent your husband on a suicide charge. And after meeting that slimy bastard today, I believe it."

Desirée remembered that O'Malley told her they had been sent on an impossible mission and how long they had to wait before they received reinforcements. But she had never realized that it had been Colonel Anders who was behind all this. She remembered Anders's threat and knew, without a shadow of a doubt, that he had deliberately ordered Jason to what he hoped was his death. She had known that he was evil all along, but she couldn't imagine any man would sink so low as to sacrifice a whole battalion of men just to get revenge on one man. Her hatred for Anders rose to new heights. She wished that she had known before he left. She would have gladly sunk a knife deep in his black heart.

A few days later, Desirée was tidying the medication room when an orderly stuck his head in, a wide grin on his face. "There's a man out here to see you, Mrs. Steele."

Before Desirée could ask who the man was, the orderly had rushed off. Frowning, she walked from the room, wondering who would be coming to see her at the hospital. And then, seeing Jason striding down the aisle with his slight limp and a broad smile on his face, she came to a complete halt. A feeling of unbelievable relief and happiness filled her. "Jason!" she cried out in sheer joy and ran to him.

Jason caught her with a laugh, Then, before she could open her mouth, he kissed her soundly. The soldiers all around them hooted and threw out good-natured jibes to Jason, egging him on.

But Desirée was totally unaware of the others. Jason was back. That was all that mattered.

When Jason broke the kiss, Desirée pushed him back, her eyes scanning him anxiously, her hands skimming over his broad shoulders and arms, asking, "You're all right? You weren't wounded or anything?"

"No, I'm fine," Jason replied absently, his eyes searching her face. She must love me, he thought. If she was that concerned about me and that happy to see me, she must feel some deep emotion for me.

A surge of elation ran through Jason. Suddenly, he couldn't keep his hands off her. He drew her to him again, this time kissing her deeply, passionately. As their tongues danced around each other, Desirée moaned, pressing herself closer to him. And then, through her dulled senses, she heard the soldiers hooting.

Flushing with embarrassment, she pushed away

from Jason. *Mon Dieu*, they must think her a wanton to kiss a man so passionately in public. Her face was beet red as she said, "Gentlemen, this is my husband, Colonel Jason Steele, newly returned from the war."

Several of the wounded called greetings to Jason, and he answered them back. Then one man asked, "How's the war coming along, colonel? Have we got those Johnny Rebs on the run yet?"

Jason's eyes swept over the wounded men, seeing the anxious look on their faces. "Sure have, soldier," Jason replied. "Got them running with their tails between their legs."

A cheer went up from the soldiers at this news, and Jason glanced at Desirée, wondering how she was taking the men's reaction to hearing the South was on the run. To his relief, she was smiling.

Colonel Bennett walked up, saying, "Welcome home, Jason," and shook his hand warmly.

"Thank you," Jason replied, his eyes flickering hungrily to Desirée.

Colonel Bennett chuckled to himself. He hadn't missed Jason's look. He turned to Desirée, saying, "Why don't you take the afternoon off? I know you and your husband want some time to yourselves."

Desirée wasn't about to object. She could hardly wait to be alone with Jason. His heated kiss had ignited a slow fire in her blood, one that was steadily growing just by being near him. She nodded eagerly and hastily untied her apron.

When she returned from hanging up her apron, Jason caught her around the waist, and as they walked to the door, Colonel Bennett joined them.

When they reached the door, the doctor asked in a low voice, "What *is* the war news, Jason?"

Jason turned, a surprised expression on his face. "You knew I was lying when I told those men we had the enemy on the run?"

"I suspected as much," the doctor admitted. I figured, with this many wounded, things couldn't be going too well. But I'm grateful to you for not telling them the truth. Bad news at this stage of their recovery could be detrimental to them."

"I thought as much." Jason admitted.

"Then the news isn't good?"

"No," Jason answered, "it isn't. General Mouton and his men led us on a merry chase, up one bayou and then another, always slipping away just when we thought we had him. Then, at Mansfield, he turned and fought. He defeated us—soundly. General Banks ordered a retreat, but we almost got trapped. The water in the Red River went down, just like it did last year. We had to build a dam across the river to get enough water in it to float our boats off the sandbars." Jason shook his head in disgust, saying, "No, the whole campaign was just another disaster."

"I heard General Canby has been sent to replace General Banks. Do you think he'll launch another campaign to take the Red River?" the doctor asked.

"No, I heard they were just going to blockade it," Jason answered.

"Blockade it?" Colonel Bennett asked in surprise. Then an angry look came over his face. "Then why in the hell didn't they do that in the first place? Before all of those men were killed and maimed?"

Jason couldn't answer. He didn't know the answer. It seemed the whole war had been nothing but mistakes, costly mistakes on both sides.

After Jason and Desirée had settled in the carriage, she snuggled into his arms and said, "So your Cajun hero, General Mouton, is still going strong."

Jason's face filled with sadness. "No, Desirée, General Mouton is dead."

440

"Dead?" Desirée asked in a shocked voice. "But you said he fought at Mansfield."

"He did. And he defeated us, too. He was shot from his horse by a Yankee sniper, after he had given his men the order to cease fire."

For a long while, Desirée and Jason sat in silence, mourning the brave man they had never met but had come to admire.

When they drove up to their house, several of their Creole neighbors came to the carriage to welcome Jason home. Desirée was pleased, knowing that he had earned their respect in both his treatment of them as liaison officer and in his valiant struggle for his life.

After they had left, Jason turned to Desirée, a surprised expression still on his face. "What happened to them?"

Desirée told him what had happened to her with the Creole women at the hospital and ended by saying, "I think they're beginning to put their petty hates and prejudices behind them. They've learned to judge people for themselves and not the color of their uniforms." She smiled. "Just as I learned."

Jason was astonished. He hoped it meant that the wounds of the war were beginning to heal, at least here in New Orleans.

That evening, Jason and Desirée could hardly sit still during their evening meal, each anxious for the lovemaking that they knew would follow. It if had not been for the fear of hurting Mammy's feelings by refusing to sit down to the special dinner she had prepared for Jason's homecoming, Desirée would have gladly skipped the meal, and from the warm looks Jason was sending her, she knew that he would, too. Finally, the long ordeal was over, and Jason and Desirée hastily said their good nights.

Jason didn't even wait until they were in the bedroom. As soon as they were in the hall, he whirled Desirée around in his arms and kissed her hungrily, his hand rushing over her back, hips, and thighs. Then, still locked in that fiery kiss, he swept her up in his arms and carried her to their room, slamming the door shut behind them with the heel of his boot. Unbearably excited, he rushed across the room, took a flying leap and landed hard on the bed.

There was a loud crack of wood, and the bed came crashing down on one side. Jason and Desirée slid to the floor with a loud thump. Sprawled there, they stared at each other in surprise and then broke out into laughter.

Jason sat up and pulled Desirée with him. He looked at the bed and grinned. "I guess I got a little carried away."

Desirée giggled. "I don't think we'll be sleeping there tonight."

Jason chuckled. "No, I guess not." His eyes swept the room. "But there's a nice, soft rug before the french doors."

Desirée glanced at the doors. They were open, and the moonlight was flooding in. "Yes, but blow out the candles. We don't need them."

Jason helped Desirée to her feet, turned, and blew out the candles. They walked to the french doors and gazed out at the moon-washed courtyard.

She turned to him and framed his face with her hands, saying, "Oh, Jason, I missed you so much."

Jason would have rather heard other words, but to him those were almost as good. Slowly, he undressed her, stopping to pay homage to each inch of skin he bared with his lips and leaving Desirée's skin tingling in his wake. By the time she stood nude before him, she was trembling all over.

And then, Desirée undressed him, once again mar-

442

veling at the feel of his smooth skin and powerful muscles under her fingertips. When she had finished, she stood back and looked at him, her breath catching in her throat at his magnificent male beauty. He looks like a god, standing there in the moonlight, she thought. Some proud, fierce, primeval god hewed in silver. Her god!

Suddenly, her need rose up in her, even more urgent than earlier. She looked up at his face and saw the desire smoldering in his eyes. "Jason," she cried in a half-strangled voice, "love me."

Then, she was in his arms, and he was drawing her to the rug with him. Their kisses were urgent and feverish one minute, deep and passionate the next. Hungrily, their hands sweep over each other, reexploring, rediscovering each other's secrets. The passion that had been smoldering ignited like a firestorm.

With a small growl, Jason rolled her to her back and plunged into her warm depths in one smooth, strong thrust, and Desirée felt as if a bolt of lightning had entered her, sending sparks racing to her brain. She cried out in sheer joy, arching her hips and bringing him even deeper. And that still wasn't enough. She clutched him frantically, desperately wishing she could take all of him into her and hold him there forever.

As Jason began his movements, his mouth crashed down on hers in a deep, searing kiss that seemed to suck her very soul from her, Desirée strained against him, meeting each masterful stroke with one of her own.

Their movements became frenzied, both knowing that this lovemaking was expressing more than just their need for physical fulfillment. To them, it was an affirmation that Jason had returned alive and whole, that life would go on, that there was a future. It was a celebration of their triumph over death.

Even after they had reached that quivering zenith and soared into a burst of exquisite ecstasy, Desirée crushed Jason to her. She gloried in the feel of his powerful chest rising and falling against hers, his heart pounding against hers, the muscles on his back rippling beneath her fingers.

"Jason," she whispered against the bronzed column of his neck.

Jason ducked his head and locked into her face, "Yes *cherie*?"

"Will you have to go back?"

Jason rolled from her, gently pushing a strand of damp chestnut hair from her forehead, and said, "No, I don't think so. As I told Colonel Bennett this afternoon, the campaign was a total failure. I don't think they'll try again." He kissed the mole by her mouth and then grinned at her. "I fear you're stuck with me, *cherie*. From the looks of things right now, the Army of the Gulf has seen its last campaign. My guess is we'll be strictly an occupational force from now on."

Tears of happiness glistened in Desirée's eyes. "I'm glad," she whispered, hugging him fiercely.

Desirée continued her work at the hospital, with Jason's blessing. Since the campaign to take the Red River had failed and the troops had returned to New Orleans, no new wounded arrived. When the men began to be discharged from the hospital, the other New Orleans women left, one by one. Then, the only wounded left were the more seriously injured and those who had been permanently handicapped: the amputees, the paralyzed, the blind.

A week later, Colonel Bennett called Desirée to his

office.

"We're moving the rest of the wounded to one of the regular hospitals tomorrow," he informed Desirée. "We won't be needing your help anymore, but I want to thank you personally for everything you've done."

Desirée felt a twinge of disappointment. "You're welcome, doctor, I'm glad I could be of service."

Desirée left to tell her patients good-bye. She was just saying farewell to the last man, when she saw Jason waiting for her at the doorway. Feeling a sense of sadness, she rose and walked to him.

And then, in a tribute to her, the Union soldiers began to sing "The Bonnie Blue Flag," and those who could stand came to their feet, many struggling up on their crutches. Desirée was deeply touched. She could hardly hold back her tears as she walked down the aisle. Jason, watching the scene from the doorway, was so proud of her he felt as if he would burst.

When the soldiers had finished the song, the boy Desirée had sat beside and comforted the first day stepped forward, his blind eyes staring at a point over Desirée's shoulder. "We just wanted to show our appreciation, Mrs. Steele," he said. "And say thank you."

Desirée blinked back tears and swallowed the hard knot in her throat. "But it's I who should thank *you*. Each and every one of you."

"Thank us?" the blind boy asked in a puzzled voice.

"Yes, thank you for allowing me to work with such brave men."

A soldier, standing on crutches, his pants' leg neatly pinned back over his amputated thigh, smiled sheepishly, saying, "No, ma'am. You got us all wrong. We ain't heroes or nothing."

"Oh, but you're wrong," Desirée objected in a firm

445

voice. "You men showed more courage in this room, fighting your own battles against death, than any man on any battlefield." She glanced at Jason. "Believe me, I know that takes a special courage." Her eyes drifted over the men's faces. "No, in my eyes you're all heroes, and I consider it a privilege to have been able to serve you."

The men were stunned at Desirée's words. They glanced at each other with disbelief.

Desirée turned and walked from the room. Then, before he turned and followed her, Jason gave the men his own tribute to their courage: a salute.

Chapter 21

As Jason had predicted, the war for the Army of the Gulf was virtually over. But not in the rest of the nation. The people of New Orleans sat back and watched as the war ground to its long, bloody end, only wanting the destruction, death, and suffering to end.

One day, when Dorothy came to visit, she could hardly contain her excitement. As soon as she and Desirée entered the salon she said, "Have you heard the news about Colonel Anders? He was murdered. They pulled his body from the river yesterday."

"Murdered?" Desirée said in a shocked voice. "By who?"

"They're not sure, but they suspect a prostitute killed him. The last time he was seen alive was when a carriage driver dropped him off outside one of the curbs on St. Charles Street."

"But that doesn't necessarily mean a prostitute killed him," Desirée objected. "He could have been robbed or anything."

"No, there's more. He was stabbed to death, but there weren't any holes in his uniform. They think he must have been naked when he was killed, then dressed in his uniform and thrown in the river. But

Bob says he doubts that they'll ever find the murderer. Everyone in the neighborhood is swearing they didn't see or hear anything. And between you and me, Bob doesn't think the provost marshal will push the investigating either."

"Why not?"

"Bob said they've suspected Anders of dealing in white slavery for a long time, but they could never prove anything against him. Many of the officers consider his death a good riddance."

Desirée felt absolutely no compassion for Anders. He had been an evil man and deserved his fate. But she did feel sorry for the woman he had apparently abused so badly that she was pushed into murdering him. She wondered if he had succeeding in forcing her to be his mistress. Would he have sold her into white slavery, too, when he had tired of her? A shudder ran through her at the thought. She thanked God for sending her Jason.

On one sunny August day, Jeanne Marie visited. Desirée was delighted to see her cousin. She hadn't seen her in over a year, not since Jeanne Marie had told Desirée that the garden at Terre Doux had produced so well that she had been able to sell a good deal of the surplus produce and no longer needed Desirée's financial help.

As soon as they were in the salon, Desirée admonished her cousin, saying, "Jeanne Marie, why haven't you visited sooner?"

"I'm sorry, Desirée, but I've been so busy. First, the garden kept me busy, and then, this past winter mother was ill with the flu for a long time, and then—"

"Then what?" Desirée asked, alarmed at the distraught expression on Jeanne Marie's face.

"And then Armond came back from the war. Oh

Desirée," Jeanne Marie wailed, "he lost his left arm, and he's been so despondent and depressed. Now, he says he's going to sell Terre Doux."

"Sell Terre Doux?" Desirée asked in a shocked voice. "*Mon Dieu*, I don't believe it. Why, he loves Terre Doux more than anything in this world."

"I know. But he seems to have just given up. That's why I came to you. I was hoping that maybe you could talk to him and make him change his mind."

"Of course, I'll talk to him, if you think it will do any good."

Jeanne Marie turned to Jason, who had been standing by the window and listening. "Would you come, too, Jason? Maybe if Armond sees how you've overcome your handicap, he won't give up so easily."

"I'm pleased that you asked me, Jeanne Marie," Jason answered, "but do you really think that would be a good idea? After all, I'm a Union officer, and Armond has just returned from war—returned without an arm. He's bound to hate me—his enemy."

"No, Jason. I told Armond how you helped us while he was gone, and he doesn't hate you. If anything, he's grateful to you."

"In that case, I'll be glad to come, too," Jason replied.

Jason and Desirée left for Terre Doux early the next morning. Since they didn't know how long they would be gone, Moses was left behind with the women, and Jason drove the carriage himself. As he drove through the countryside, Desirée saw several burned-out plantations, testimony to General Butler's greedy raids. But they still didn't prepare Desirée for what she saw when they reached Terre Doux. Everything—the storehouses, the slaves' quarters, the sugar factory, the out-buildings, was nothing but blackened shells. The sight made her sick at heart.

When she saw Armond, she was even more shocked, not just by his missing arm; she had prepared herself for that. No, it was the pale, drawn face and the look of defeat in his eyes that deeply disturbed her.

When they were all seated in the salon, Armond said, "I know why you've come, Desirée, but you can save your breath. I'm selling Terre Doux."

"But why?" Desirée demanded. "You love this land. It's a part of you. How *can* you sell it?"

Armond refused to answer her. He turned his head and gazed off into space.

Jeanne Marie shot Desirée a look, a look that said, see what I mean?

But Desirée wasn't about to be put off so easily. She hadn't let Jason give up, and she wasn't going to let Armond do so either. She rose from her chair and marched over to stand in front of him. She glared down at him, saying, "I'm ashamed of you. I never thought I'd see the day when you, my own flesh and blood, would give up. Do you think Jeanne Marie worked her fingers to the bone to hold this plantation for you, only to have you turn around and sell it? No, Armond, there aren't any cowards in this family. You're not going to give up!"

Armond's eyes clouded with pain. "I'm not giving up. I have to sell Terre Doux. I don't have any choice."

"Why not?"

"Because there isn't any money to pay the back taxes. If I don't sell, I'll lose it anyway."

Jeanne Marie gasped at his words. "Why didn't you tell *me* that?"

"Because I didn't want you to worry."

"That's no problem," Jason said, for the first time entering the conversation. "I can loan you the money to pay the back taxes."

"Yes," Desirée agreed, feeling an immense wave of relief washing over her.

"It's not just the taxes," Armond said, a bleak look on his face. "I don't have any money to start over. Didn't you see when you drove up. Everything is burnt to the ground and would have to be rebuilt. And that would take a lot of money, particularly the factory."

Jason's heart thudded so hard that he was afraid it would jump out of his chest. Whispering Oaks *could* be his and Desirée's, the consummation of his dream and the return of her heritage. He fought down the excitement and rose from his seat, saying, "Then why don't you sell Whispering Oaks and use the money from that sale to rebuild Terre Doux?"

Desirée was horrified at Jason's suggestion. *"Non!"* she cried out. "Armond, you promised you would never sell Whispering Oaks."

"Oui, I know," Armond said with a thoughtful look on his face. Then he smiled as a gleam came into his eyes. "I'll sell Terre Doux and keep Whispering Oaks."

Suddenly, Desirée was ashamed of herself. *"Non*, Armond, I can't let you do that. You love Terre Doux as much as I do Whispering Oaks. That was selfish of me."

Armond came to his feet with a rush. *"Non*, Desirée," he said in an excited voice. "Selling Terre Doux would be the most practical solution. Whispering Oaks wasn't damaged, because the Yankees never noticed it with the driveway being so overgrown with brush. The buildings are all still standing. Oh, I'm sure the machinery in the factory is rusted by now and would have to be replaced, but that's nothing compared to the cost of building a new one. *Oui*, it's the

451

perfect solution!"

"I'm afraid I'm not interested in buying Terre Doux," Jason said in a quiet firm voice. "I want Whispering Oaks."

Armond and Jeanne Marie turned to him in surprise. Desirée stared at him in shocked disbelief. She had always assumed they would move back north after the war and had been dreading leaving her beloved Louisiana.

"Do you mean we'd live here in Louisiana?" she asked, once she had recovered.

"I always planned to stay here, *cherie*." A smile flicked across his face. "And I've always wanted a sugar plantation. But don't get your hopes up yet. Armond hasn't given me his answer." He turned to Armond, saying, "Will you sell Whispering Oaks to me?"

Armond glanced at Desirée. Seeing the anxious, pleading look in her eyes, there was only one answer he could give. "*Oui*, I'll sell it to you." A teasing twinkle came to his eyes. "But only because I can do so and still keep my promise to Desirée to never sell it out of the family."

Desirée spirits soared, then suddenly plummeted. Disappointment filled her face as she said, "Oh, Jason, you don't have that kind of money. Plantations are every expensive, particularly sugar plantations."

Jason laughed, saying, "You're wrong, Desirée. I do have money. I inherited a sizable amount from my grandparents when they died and made good investments on it. I think Armond and I can come to an agreement. It might take everything, but I still want Whispering Oaks."

To Desirée, the thought of living at Whispering Oaks again seemed an impossible dream come true. Happiness welled up in her. She rushed to Jason, and he opened his arms to her.

"Oh, Jason, it's wonderful. I can hardly believe it," Desirée laughed and sobbed, hugging him.

Jason beamed with his own elation. He held her against him and looked over her head at Armond, saying, "I see no reason why we can't use the same factory at Whispering Oaks and share the expense of repairing it, do you?"

Armond brightened at the suggestion. Then a look of profound disappointment came over his face. "I'm afraid we've forgotten something. It takes a lot of men to plant and harvest sugarcane, and all but one of my fields have run off into the swamps."

"Yes, I know," Jason replied. "And I'm sure by now they're sick and tired of struggling to live out there. They'd probably be glad to get back to growing cane."

"*Oui,*" Armond said. "But we have no way of finding them to ask if they want to work for us."

"I can find them," Jason replied.

Armond looked at Jason as if he had lost his mind. Desirée laughed at his expression and said, "Jason is half Cajun, Armond. He grew up in the swamps and knows them like the back of his hand."

When Armond recovered from this surprising information, he said, "But even if they agreed to come back to work for us, it wouldn't do any good. We won't have anything left to pay them with. Repairing the factory at Whispering Oaks might easily take as much as forty thousand dollars."

Jason was stunned. "My God! How much does it take to build a brand new one?"

"Well over a hundred thousand dollars," Armond answered. Seeing the shocked look on Jason's face, he laughed and said, "Now you know why it's said you have to be a rich cotton planter before you can be a

453

poor sugar planter."

"Yes, Jason," Desirée said. "The outlay for growing sugar is much more than cotton, but sugar also brings the better prices. Why, with one good crop, a planter can pay off the entire cost of his investment and make a handsome profit, too."

Jason frowned. After he had paid Armond for Whispering Oaks, paid for his share of repairing the factory, and made repairs on the other buildings at Whispering Oaks, he wouldn't have much money left, certainly not enough to support his family until next fall *and* pay for laborers, too. He walked over to the fireplace and stared down at it, thinking the problem over.

Then he turned to Armond, saying, "I have an idea. Suppose we make an agreement with the ex-slaves to pay them a percentage of the profits on the first crop. That way, they would be sharing the gamble with us, but if we're successful, their profits would be much more than if we simply paid them monthly wages."

Armond thought Jason's proposition over, then said, "It might work. It depends upon how desperate those men in the swamps are for work. But let me warn you, Jason. It is a gamble. A flood or hurricane could wipe us out. And if we don't cut before the first frost, we could lose the whole crop."

Jason grinned. "I'll leave the floods and hurricanes in God's hand and the time to cut in yours, Armond."

"Is it too late to get a crop in this year?" Desirée asked.

Armond frowned. "I don't know, *petite*. The cane has to go in the ground before winter, and there's so much to do. The out-buildings have to be rebuilt, the fields cleared. The—"

"What if we put everything else aside but clearing

the fields and planting the cane?" Jason interjected. "We can do the rest of that stuff after the crop is in the ground."

"*Oui*, it might be possible," Armond admitted. "If we have the manpower and we work very hard."

"I'll get us the manpower," Jason assured him. "I'll go into the swamps next week and seek out the runaways."

"Can you leave just like that, Jason?" Armond asked with a frown. "Won't the army object?"

"I'll ask for a two months leave. I don't think I'll have any trouble getting it. I haven't had any since the beginning of the war, and there's nothing going on for the Army of the Gulf right now, certainly nothing that my executive officer can't handle for a few months."

"Two months? Do you think it will take that long to find those men in the swamps?"

"No, but I want some time off to help get us settled in at Whispering Oaks and get the cane in the field. I hope you don't mind if I lean on you for a while, Armond? Until I can learn the sugar business."

"*Non*, not at all. In fact, I owe you a great deal for helping my family while I was away."

"You don't owe me anything," Jason replied. "I'm part of the family now." He grinned and looked at Jeanne Marie with a teasing gleam in his eyes. "I'm just curious, Jeanne Marie. Did any of those supplies you were sneaking to the Confederates by any chance go to General Mouton's men?"

Desirée and Jeanne Marie were flabbergasted by Jason's question. "You knew all along?" Desirée gasped.

"Yes, I knew."

"Then why didn't you say anything?" Desirée asked. "Why didn't you stop us."

"Because, at the time, it was something you needed

to do."

"What are you talking about?" Armond asked.

Looking very shamefaced, Jeanne Marie nervously explained how she and Desirée had slipped supplies to the soldiers hiding out in the swamps.

Armond was furious with Jeanne Marie. "Is this how you repaid Jason's generosity, his kindness? By sneaking behind his back and buying supplies for his enemies—with *his* money?"

"No, Armond," Jason said in a firm voice. "Don't be angry with Jeanne Marie. If I had known it would upset you, I wouldn't have said anything. I never approved of starving an enemy out, and as I said, Desirée and Jeanne Marie both needed something to hit back at the enemy. Helping those soldiers in the swamps not only satisfied their need for revenge but helped them regain their self-esteem."

"But to use *your* money," Armond objected.

"I didn't mind the money," Jason assured him. "Believe me, what it did for their spirits was worth it." He turned to Jeanne Marie and again grinned, asking, "Well?"

"Yes, they went to General Mouton's men," Jeanne Marie admitted.

Desirée was deeply touched to know that Jason had been concerned about her emotional needs, even then. She wondered if a man who just desired a woman would really go to such lengths to make her happy. Had some deeper emotion motivated him? Her spirits soared. And then, she remembered that Jason was an unusually perceptive man, sensitive to everyone's needs. Hadn't he done as much for Jeanne Marie? Her hopes plummeted back to earth.

After Jason and Armond had signed the agreement for the sale of Whispering Oaks, Jason and Desirée stayed for dinner. All afternoon, Desirée had been very aware of *Tante* Josephine's absence, and when her aunt didn't show up for dinner, Desirée was left to assume Josephine was still snubbing her. Desirée was very disappointed. She had hoped that, after all this time, her aunt had forgiven her for her little transgression. After all that had happened over the years, her aunt's behavior seemed so petty.

When she and Jason were standing in the foyer and saying their good-byes to Armond and Jeanne Marie, Josephine stepped out of the library. Desirée was shocked when she saw her aunt. Her hair had turned completely grey, and her face was deeply wrinkled. Why, she looks like an old woman, Desirée thought.

"Desirée," Josephine said, "may I speak to you a moment—alone?"

It wasn't a demand. It was a request. And for that reason, Desirée answered, *"Oui,* if you like."

As soon as she had shut the library door behind them, Josephine said, "I didn't come to the table tonight because I was too ashamed to face you. But I can't live with it on my conscience any longer. I have something to confess to you, something that I have never admitted to anyone else." Josephine hesitated a minute, then said in a low voice, "I was in love with your father. I fell in love with him the minute I saw him. But he never even knew I existed. He only had eyes for your mother, and I hated her for it—with a passion. When she died, everytime I looked at you, I thought of her. You look exactly like her, you know—except for the color of your hair. I simply transferred my hate to you."

Desirée had always sensed that her aunt hated her, and now, she knew why. Strangely, Desirée couldn't hate her aunt for how she had treated her. The only emotion Desirée felt was pity for her aunt.

Josephine continued, saying, "What I did to you

was bad enough, but what I did to my husband was an even greater injustice. I married Paul, even though I didn't love him. Oh, I know the marriage was arranged by our families in Creole fashion, but I could have objected. I didn't because I knew marriage to Paul would give me an excuse to be around your father." A haunted look came over Josephine's face, and her voice took on an anguished tone. "I didn't realize until Paul was dead that I'd fallen in love with him. Before, I was too caught up in my hate. When I think of how much I must have hurt him, of how I cheated us both of years of happiness—" Josephine's slim control broke. She buried her face in her hands, saying, "And all because I was so stubborn, so blind."

Desirée understood. She remembered how long she had denied her love for Jason. Not until he had almost died had she finally admitted it, at least to herself. She took her aunt in her arms and held her while she cried. When Josephine's sobs finally subsided, Desirée said softly, "I forgive you, *Tante* Josephine. I understand."

Josephine dried her tears and replied, "Thank you, Desirée. Now, if I only knew Paul could forgive me, I could live out the rest of my life in peace."

Desirée watched as her aunt walked away, thinking that hate could be such a destructive emotion. Because of it, her aunt, a woman who should have been at the prime of her life, was a broken woman, aged far beyond her years.

When Jason and Desirée were driving away from Terre Doux, both of them on the driver's seat, Desirée asked, "Can we spend the night at Whispering Oaks?"

Jason looked down at her in surprise. "Have you forgotten that there's no furniture in the house?" He grinned. "Not even a rug, if I remember correctly."

458

Desirée smiled, remembering the night they had made love on the rug in front of the French doors because Jason had broken the bed in his enthusiasm. "I wasn't thinking of the house. We could sleep on the ground, like we did in the swamps, under the oak trees."

Jason's heart raced at the though of making love to Desirée at Whispering Oaks. To him, nothing could be more perfect. It would be the fulfillment of all his dreams.

He urged the horses to a faster speed, and they flew down the road, the full moon above them playing hide and seek through the towering trees hovering over the road. When they passed the swamp beside Whispering Oaks, Desirée didn't even glance at it. She never stopped to wonder why that strange lure that had always drawn her to it was no longer there. And even if she had wondered, she wouldn't have realized that the reason was because she had found what she had been seeking. He was sitting right beside her.

When they reached Whispering Oaks, Jason stopped the carriage on the main road before it and helped Desirée down. He opened the door to the carriage and raised one of the seats, where the lap blankets were stored. Taking them out, he stepped back down and led Desirée through the thick underbrush that had grown across the driveway. Not until they had almost reached the plantation house did the lush vegetation finally give way.

Desirée and Jason stood gazing at the towering mansion silently, both too full of emotion to speak. In the moonlight, its huge white pillars glowed with a life of their own, and standing out in the shadows all around it, the building seemed even more massive, even more beautiful and breathtaking than in the daylight.

Finally Desirée whispered, "Oh, Jason, tell me I'm not dreaming. Tell me I'm really going to live here again. Tell me it's really my home again."

It was hard for Jason to accept the reality of Whispering Oaks being his, considering how long he had dreamed of it. He brought her closer to his side, whispering, "It's true, *cherie*. It's ours. Now, and forever."

They walked beneath the huge, spreading oaks. The Spanish moss fluttered in the breeze, whispering and welcoming them back. A bat darted out from one of the branches of one tree and flew away, briefly silhouetted against the pale full moon before it disappeared in the darkness. Desirée didn't resent its presence. To her, it was as much a part of Whispering Oaks as the birds that nested in the thick branches above her.

Jason spread the blankets on a moonlit patch of ground, wanting to see Desirée as well as feel and taste her when he made love to her. Then he undressed he slowly, savoring the sight of each inch of her skin. When she stood before him totally nude, her ivory skin glowing in the moonlight, he quickly shed his own clothes and drew her to the blanket with him.

He nuzzled her throat, drinking deeply of the sweet scent of her skin and hair, before he nipped at the lobe of her shell-like ear. Desirée shivered and slipped her arms around his broad shoulders, lying back on the blanket and bringing him with her.

Her blood sang at the feel of his warm skin against hers and his hard, muscled body against her soft one. As he placed a trail of soft kisses up her throat, she drew him even closer, thrilling as she felt his powerful heart quicken against hers. Oh, how she loved him, she thought, her magnificent god, her strong, fierce warrior, her exciting, tender lover. And then, as Jason nibbled the mole on her chin and his tongue flicked at the corner of her mouth, all thought fled.

The tip of his tongue teased her lips, then brushed across her teeth, before plunging into her mouth, stroking, swirling, tasting the sweetness within. And Desirée answered him with her own sensuous strokes. Their breaths mingled as the kiss deepened, their tongues dancing wildly and igniting their passion, sending both of their senses reeling.

Desirée moaned in objection as Jason broke the kiss, then sighed in rapture as his lips glazed her shoulders before seeking the softness of her breasts. He buried his face in the valley between those twin mounds, once again savoring her intoxicating scent before he covered one breast with tiny kisses and nips, then laved it with his tongue. Desirée's breath caught at the exquisite feel of his tongue rolling and flicking the sensitive peak, then she moaned when he took it into his mouth.

She clung to him as Jason turned his attention to its twin, and she felt a fire smoldering in her loins. She drew his head closer, never wanting these wonderful sensations to end.

Jason's head descended, his tongue a fiery dart as he slowly traced each rib. His hands smoothed over the swelling hips, then stroked the insides of her thighs, slowly—ever so slowly—inching upward. Desirée sobbed, the anticipation almost unbearable, and then sighed when his fingers slid over the swollen lips and parted them to explore the damp depths of her femininity. As those skillful fingers moved upward and found the core of her womanhood, stroking and tantalizing, Desirée felt the sweet waves of pleasure rushing over her, her senses spinning, her toes curled.

She looked up to see Jason kneeling between her legs. A flicker of a smile crossed his lips before he lifted her hips. Desirée's heart pounded in anticipation as he lowered his head. And then, she gasped in surprise as he hooked her legs over his broad shoulder.

She stared at him in disbelief, a little shocked at the new, rather ignominious position—but only for a second. All reservations fled as Jason's lips and tongue worked their magic on her, swirling, flicking, nipping, tantalizing, then dipping deeper. Before, there had been sweet ripples of delight; now, there were wonderful undulations of ecstasy, shaking the very foundations of her soul. Jason brought her to that shuddering peak of rapture, over and over, until Desirée's breath came in ragged gasps. Her heart pounded in her chest as if it would leap out—until she feared she would die if he didn't stop.

Jason heard Desirée's pleas to stop, but he couldn't stop. The sweet-salty taste and exciting scent of her was driving him wild. He devoured her, his tongue probing even deeper to taste her honeyed nectar.

Desirée was weak and lifeless when Jason lowered her legs and hovered over her. She felt empty and totally drained. That she even had the strength left to breath seemed a small miracle.

His warm breath fanned her face as Jason whispered against her lips. "Taste your wine, *cherie*."

Jason placed his lips against hers. Then, as his tongue slid briefly into her mouth, she tasted herself. A surge of desire rose in her, surprising her with its suddenness and its intensity. She reached for him, wrapping her hand around his rigid length, once again amazed at the velvety texture of his skin. She stroked him, his moans of pleasure exciting her even more. She rolled him to his back, her mouth replacing her hand.

Jason cupped her head, exerting a gentle pressure as Desirée worked her magic on him. Her lips nibbled; her tongue danced, swirled, and tantalized, driving him up that peak of unbearable excitement until he felt he would explode.

With a strangled cry, he caught her head and jerked her up to face him, then rolled her to her back. His plunge was swift and true as he buried himself deep in her moist heat, and Desirée welcomed him with a cry of gladness. For a long minute, they lay perfectly still, savoring their joking, their hearts beating in unison. As he began his movements, he bent his head and kissed her long, deeply and lovingly. The kiss grew wilder, more and more passionate, as his thrusts became harder, deeper, swifter. They raced up those breathless heights and exploded in a blinding white light, their souls ripped from their bodies as they plunged into a deep, dark void.

When Desirée finally opened her eyes, she muttered in an awed voice, *"Mon Dieu! Petit de mort."*

Jason smiled against her throat, where his head was buried. "Yes, *cherie*," he whispered. "The little death. We both experienced it."

Jason rolled to his back, bringing Desirée with him. As she lay on his shoulder with his strong arms around her protectively, Desirée was filled with contentment and serenity. Once again, she knew it was something much more profound than coming home to Whispering Oaks that made her feel this way. She sensed that she had finally reached something she had sought, had strived for all her life. She had attained some profound goal that she had been directed toward since the beginning of her being. And furthermore, she sensed that Jason felt it, too.

The next morning, as they were preparing to leave Whispering Oaks, Desirée said, "I'd like to see the

463

baby's grave before we leave."

Silently, they walked to the family cemetery. If it had not been for the small wrought-iron fence that surrounded it, they might not have found it. The plot was choked with tall weeds and brush. Desirée glanced at the tall tombstones of her parents. She could barely see the stones because of the thick vines that covered them.

"Where did you bury him?" she asked.

"At your parents' feet."

Desirée's eyes dropped. Then she looked closer, seeing the small stone marker beneath the weeds. "When did you put up the tombstone?"

"A few weeks after I buried him."

"Why didn't you tell me?"

"I didn't want to upset you any more than you already were."

Desirée gazed down at the marker, wishing that she could see it better. "What did you have inscribed on it?"

"Michael Steele, beloved son of Desirée and Jason, and the date. I hope you don't mind that I named him without consulting you, and I felt he deserved a name."

Tears glistened in Desirée's eyes. She was glad that he had named the baby and deeply touched that he had named him after her father. "No, I don't mind, and I'm sure my father would be very pleased."

Desirée looked down at the grave of the baby she had loved but had never seen or held. An ache filled her, not just grief for her dead baby but for those she still wanted so badly.

There were only two things that kept Desirée from knowing sublime happiness. The first was her inability to conceive. She feared that her miscarriage had damaged her in some way and left her barren, that she would never be able to give Jason the child she so desperately wanted to give him.

The second thing that marred her happiness was the knowledge that Jason would never love her.

Both were burdens she held close to her heart.

Chapter 22

During the week between their visit to Terre Doux and Jason's departure for the swamps, Jason and Desirée packed up everything and moved to Whispering Oaks, taking everyone in their household with them, except Sergeant O'Malley.

When Jason asked the sergeant if he would like to move with them, O'Malley, replied, "Ah, colonel, would you mind if I didn't go with you? You see, I've found myself a pretty colleen down on the Irish Channel, and I'm thinking of marrying."

Jason's dark eyebrows rose at O'Malley's surprising announcement. Then he felt a twinge of disappointment. He was going to miss the tough sergeant, but not because of the duties O'Malley performed for him. He really didn't need an aide-de-camp. No, he would miss O'Malley as a friend and companion, for they had passed over the boundaries the army set up between officers and enlisted men long ago.

Jason suppressed his disappointment, saying, "No, I don't mind. Will you be asking for an assignment to another officer or regular duty?"

"Regular duty, I'm thinking. Until the end of the war." O'Malley's ruddy face turned a shade deeper red than normal. "You see, sir, after you, I couldn't be an aide to another officer. It wouldn't be fair to the man. I'm afraid I'd find myself comparing him to you and find him lacking."

Jason was touched by O'Malley's compliment. "Are you planning on staying in the army after the war?"

"No, sir. The lass wants to stay here in New Orleans."

"If you need a job, I could always use you at Whispering Oaks."

"Thank you for the offer, but I think not. Like I said, the lass doesn't want to leave the city." He grinned. "Besides, plantation work takes a bit of horseback riding, and you know how I feel about the blasted beasts."

Jason chuckled. "But you will come to visit?"

"Yes, sir. I'll keep in touch. You can be sure of that."

While Jason was gone to find the ex-slaves in the swamps, and Benjie and Moses were breaking the ground for the fall garden, the women set their energies to cleaning the huge mansion. Out went the dust and cobwebs. The windows and chandeliers were washed until they were sparkling clean, and the beautiful wooden floors waxed until they gleamed.

As they worked from room to room, Desirée decided how she would eventually refurnish the house, determined she would rectify the injustice done to it before. This time, the mansion's natural beauty would be enhanced, not hidden. Her only regret was that it would have to wait until after the first sugar crop was in and she had the money to do it.

Desirée's second project was to clear the family cemetery of the weeds and tangled vines that had overgrown it. She refused to accept any help from the others. For her, it wasn't a chore but an act of love she wanted to do alone.

One day, when she was walking back to the plantation house from the cemetery, she looked up and saw Jason walking from the swamp. With a cry of joy, she tossed the hoe aside and ran to him.

He caught her with a laugh and whirled her around, then kissed her soundly. She peeked around his broad shoulder and saw a score of darkies filing up from the swamp.

"Is that all you could find?" she asked in a disappointed voice.

"No, I found over a hundred or more, whole communities of them, but that's all who came back with me. I told the others if they wanted the job to be here by the end of the month."

During the next few days, the ex-slaves drifted in, until they numbered over two hundred. In typical fashion, the word had spread through the black grapevine. At the end of the month, Jason and Armond called a meeting with them.

At Jason's request, Armond acted as spokesman for both of them. Armond stood on a wagon on the front lawn of Whispering Oaks, the ex-slaves crowded around him so they could hear, and explained how he and Jason couldn't afford to pay them monthly wages but would give them a percentage of the profits when the sugar crop was in.

"What's that mean? That per—centage?" one darkie asked.

"It means that each of you will get a part of the money we make. The more successful the crop, the bigger your part will be," Armond answered.

"If you ain't gonna pay us, then how're we gonna eat until then?" another asked.

"We'll feed, clothe, and give you shelter, just as we

did before the war," Armond told him.

"And how do we know we can trust you to pay?" a beefy-looking man asked.

"I'm afraid you'll just have to take our word for it," Armond answered.

"Your word?" another asked in a surly tone of voice. "A white man's word?"

More than a few of the ex-slaves exchanged wary glances.

A tall, gangly man stepped forward, saying, "I worked for this man's papa before the war. His papa was a good man." He looked Armond in the eye and said, "I'll work for you."

But suspicion is a contagious emotion. The crowd of darkies began to whisper to each other, casting doubtful glances at Jason and Armond. A few at the back of the crowd turned and started walking back toward the swamp.

"How do we know they ain't trying to trick us?" the surly man called out to the crowd. "Trying to get us to work for nothing again?"

At these words, a score or more of the men turned and joined the others.

"Wait, don't leave!" Armond called.

But the blacks just kept walking, ignoring his plea.

Desirée felt sick with disappointment. All of their dreams for Terre Doux and Whispering Oaks seemed to be shattering.

Then, a huge black man vaulted to the top of the wagon, towering over Armond and dwarfing him with his immense size. Desirée gasped and Jason tensed at the angry look on the giant's face, both fearing he meant to do harm to Armond.

But then Desirée recognized him. It was Sam, the man who had helped Jeanne Marie take the supplies to the soldiers in the swamps. As Jason stepped forward to go to Armond's aid, Desirée caught his arm, saying, "No! That's Sam. He won't hurt Armond."

Sam called angrily to the men who were walking away. "You, there! Stop right where you are. You ain't going no place until I've had my say."

The ex-slaves turned. And then, seeing the giant, who looked even more awesome standing on the wagon, they all stood in their places. Sam's size alone commanded their respect. No one was willing to tangle with this huge, fierce-looking man.

"Do you know what you are?" Sam asked the crowd in an accusing voice. "A bunch of dumb niggers, that's what! You'd rather go back to the swamps and starve to death than trust a white man. Well, I'm gonna tell you something." He laid his huge hand on Armond's shoulder. "I've known this man since he was a boy. He's telling you the truth when he says he'll pay you when the sugar is in. I'm giving you *my* word on it. Now, if any of you want to call *me* a liar, you just step forward."

"What about him?" the surly man asked, pointing to Jason.

"I don't know about him," Sam admitted. "All I know is he's one of those Yankees."

Every eye in the crowd swiveled toward Jason. The expressions on their faces were even more distrustful than before.

"I can give my word for him," a voice called out.

Desirée turned and saw Moses stepping up the wagon. She smiled at the old man gratefully.

Moses's climb onto the wagon was in stark contrast to Sam's earlier ascent. The old, woolly-haired man climbed slowly and painfully up, waving back Sam's and Armond's hands when they offered to help him.

Finally, he stood on the wagon, forcing his stooped

shoulders back. His dark eyes swept over the crowd as he said, "I've been with Colonel Steele for three years now, and I've never known a better man. Ever since that Yankee president freed us black folks, he's been paying me to work for him. And he's been paying that old woman and that boy, too," Moses said, pointing to Mammy Lou and Benjie. "Now, I reckon if he's been paying two, worn-out old folks and a boy for doing next to nothing, he'll sure pay you big, strong men for working hard in his fields. Yes sir, when I say you can trust Colonel Steele, you sure better believe it's the gospel truth."

While Sam had commanded the crowd's respect with his size, it was Moses's sincerity that determined their decision. The ex-slaves who had started to leave began walking back to the wagon.

"I still don't trust them," the surly black eyes called out.

Sam looked down at the man, his black eyes boring into him. "I know who you are. You're that trouble-maker from that plantation up-river. You're one of those lazy niggers. Why, you don't know nothing about growing sugar. Only thing you know is making trouble. Now, you get out of here. We don't need the likes of you around here."

The man glanced around him nervously. Seeing the accusing looks the other blacks were sending him, he turned and slinked away through the crowd.

When Moses climbed down from the wagon, Jason said, "Thank you for your vote of confidence, Moses. I hope I don't let you down."

"Ain't no need for you to thank me," Moses answered. "I meant every word I said. And you won't let me down, either. You ain't never let nobody down."

Armond took command of the situation once more, saying, "If any of you have families back in the swamps, go and bring them back. But don't dally. You all know enough about raising sugar cane to know we've got a race on our hands. That cane has got to be in ground before the first frost."

The next day, the men began clearing the fields. To the blacks' amazement, Armond and Jason worked right beside them. The ex-slaves worked even harder, determined not to be shamed by being out-worked by two handicapped white men.

When the awesome chore was finally finished and the fields were plowed to loosen the packed dirt, the stalks of seed cane were cut into sections, and the pieces placed on their sides in the fertile ground, then covered with dirt. Each joint of the cane would become a new plant.

But even when the cane was safely in the ground, the work was far from done. The men began shoring up the levees on the bayous and repairing the quarters and out-buildings. Then everything, including the mansion itself, received a fresh coat of paint. Last, but not least, the repairs were made in the huge sugar factory.

That year, like every year since they had been married, Jason and Desirée celebrated New Years instead of Christmas, and even though money was tight, they decided to have the typical Creole plantation festivities.

That morning, Desirée awakened Jason with a quick kiss and an excited, *"Bonne Annee,"* and then, before he could even kiss her back, she was off to fill the stockings to be placed beneath the New Years tree, an undecorated young cypress that had been brought in from the swamps.

The ex-slaves filed in as Jason and Desirée handed out their gifts to the adults, while a black Papa Noel, dressed in a red and white suit, distributed the small

472

gifts and sweets to the excited children. After a huge breakfast, the blacks sang and danced, the tempo of the music reflecting their joy in living.

The afternoon of the big day was restricted to a more personal celebration as family and friends called and presents were exchanged. Besides Desirée's family, Dorothy and Bob came from New Orleans and, to Jason and Desirée's delight, Sergeant O'Malley and his new bride also arrived.

That night, Desirée stood in their bedroom absently undressing for bed, deep in thought. This had been the first New Years she had spent at Whispering Oaks since she had been a child, and even though she had known much more lavish celebrations, this was the happiest she had ever known.

When she was dressed in her gown and turning down the covers, Jason said, "I have something for you."

Desirée turned to see Jason holding a small package wrapped in bright calico and tied with a ribbon. "Oh Jason, we agreed not to exchange gifts, so we could spend the money on the darkies instead," Desirée admonished.

Jason smiled, saying, "I didn't cheat on you, *cherie*. I've been saving this gift for a long time."

Desirée looked down at the package in his hands, saying curiously, "What is it?"

Jason handed it to her, saying, "Open it and see."

Desirée hastily unwrapped the package and opened the box in it. Then, she gasped, her dark eyes staring down at the open box in disbelief. "My family jewels," she whispered.

Jason's smile widened at the look of pure joy that came over Desirée's face. He had convinced himself that Desirée must love him and had decided to give her the jewels.

473

Desirée picked up a fragile, filigree cross that had been her grandmothers. It was her favorite. "When did you buy them?"

"Shortly after we were married. I noticed you didn't have any jewels and suspected that you had pawned them. I asked Mammy where I could find them and bought them back."

Desirée knew why Jason hadn't given her the jewels then, to save her pride. She was deeply touched by both his gift and his sensitivity.

Tears shimmered in her eyes as she looked up into his beautiful misty-green eyes. For a long moment, they stared at each other, each holding their breath, each hoping to hear the words they had waited for so long. But neither spoke, both afraid to be the first, both still feeling too vulnerable.

Finally, Desirée couldn't stand the tension any longer. She tossed the box aside on the dresser and rushed to Jason, burying her face in the crisp, dark curls on his chest. She embraced him fiercely as tears streamed down her face and soul-tearing sobs shook her small body.

Jason held her, fighting down his disappointment—once again. Then he swept her up in his arms and carried her to the bed. There, he told her with his body what he hadn't been able to put into words.

Under the warm, spring sun, the cane sent up its tender shoots. Then the rain came—and came—and came. The bayous rose alarmingly, threatening to spill their waters into the field and drown the vulnerable new shoots. Everyone at Whispering Oaks and Terre Doux worked frantically filling up the gunnysacks with dirt and piling them on the levee to hold back the water. Even after the sun had come out, turning everything steamy, the flood waters rose. There was nothing more they could do but wait and see. The water came to within an inch of their man-made dam and then fell.

Later in the month, word arrived of Lee's surrender at Appomattox, and even though General Johnson and General Beaureguard had yet to surrender, everyone knew it was the end of the war.

Desirée felt no bitterness or even sadness at the news of the South's defeat. She had been expecting it for over a year. And even though Jason had fought for the Union, he felt no victorious elation. The only emotion they both felt was a relief that it was finally over, that the death and destruction were finished.

More shocking to Jason and Desirée was the news of Lincoln's assassination a week later. Even Jefferson Davis acknowledged that this was a blow to the South, saying when he heard the news, "We have just lost our best friend in the court of the enemy."

By the end of the month, Jason was a civilian again and happy to be able to throw all of his energies into Whispering Oaks. At the same time, the Confederate soldiers started returning from the war.

Many of the soldiers passed Whispering Oaks on their way home, and Desirée was shocked by what she saw. Their clothing was in tatters, many wearing part Confederate grey and part Union blue. Many of the men were barefoot and had rags tied around their feet to protect them. All were shockingly thin from starvation and dysentery. Some were supported on crutches made from tree limbs and some wore bloody bandages. But even more pitiful than their miserable physical condition was the look in their eyes, the hollow look of defeat.

Appalled by what they saw, Desirée and Jeanne Marie set up a way station on the front lawn of

Whispering Oaks. Here, they offered the battle-weary soldiers a place to rest and hot soup before they continued the rest of their journey home to western Louisiana or Texas.

One day, a new group of soldiers arrived, two of the men carrying a litter between them. The man on the litter moaned in pain and thrashed in delirium as his companions sat beside him, drinking the hot soup Desirée had offered them.

One haggard soldier looked around him, saying, "You sure have a nice place here, ma'am. It's a shame the major here can't see it. He has a plantation back home—a cotton plantation. Seeing yours sure would have raised his spirits."

Desirée looked down at the man lying on the stretcher. His chest was wrapped in a filthy, blood-stained dressing, and she knew, by the deep flush on his face, that the wound beneath it was dangerously infected.

"Where is home?" she asked.

"East Texas."

"Texas?" Desirée asked in a shocked voice. "You're going to carry this man all the way to Texas?"

"Yes, ma'am, we sure are."

"He'll never make it," Desirée objected. "That man is seriously ill. He'll die long before you reach Texas."

The weary soldier gazed at the man on the litter. His face filled with sadness. "Yes, ma'am, I don't reckon he will. But we promised him we'd try to get him back to Texas. Besides, we can't hardly go off and leave him in his condition."

Jeanne Marie stepped forward. "I don't see any reason why you can't."

"You mean you'd keep him here?" the soldier asked in surprise.

"No, not here," Jeanne Marie answered. "At Terre

476

Doux, my plantation down the road."

Jeanne Marie took the seriously ill Texan back to Terre Doux and nursed him back to health. As he recuperated, a romance blossomed, and no one was surprised when Jeanne Marie announced that as soon as the major was completely well, she would marry him and go back to Texas with him.

As the summer progressed, the returning soldiers dwindled, until there were no more to be seen wearily trudging down the road in front of Whispering Oaks. As the heat intensified, the can shot up, its green tassels waving in the gentle breeze and looking like a huge lake from the upper windows of the plantation house. Jason and Desirée watched the sky anxiously for any sign of a hurricane that could wipe out the cane and destroy the future of Whispering Oaks. August slipped into September, then October. When the air turned cooler, they both sighed in relief and thanked God.

The sugarcane took on a purplish tinge, and the stalks grew heavy with their juices. Then the second crop was planted between the rows of towering, ripening cane.

One day, toward the end of November, Jason watched Armond as he examined the stalks. "How much sugar will we actually get from one stalk?" he asked.

"About a tablespoon of refined sugar," Armond answered. "The cane never fully matures here in Louisiana. The growing season is too short." Armond looked up at the sky thoughtfully, then said, "I think it's time to cut, *mon ami*. After all of this, we can't risk losing it to a freeze."

"Whatever you say, Armond. I told you, I'd leave that decision up to you."

Then the real work began. For weeks, the men went

out into the fields with their long knives and hacked the cane down, stripped off the leaves, and loaded the stalks on wagons to be taken to the factory. At the big, brick factory, workmen fed the stalks into the grinders, and the juice ran in streams into a procession of kettles. Here, the juice was heated by a heavy furnace fed by wood collected from the swamps. The boiling juices sent up a cloud of steam, and the blacks' thick shoulders and backs glistened in the firelight. Soon, the air over Whispering Oaks was filled with black smoke, so thick it darkened the sky, and the smell of cooking sugar permeated everything.

At this point, Desirée had a sugar party, where her guests sampled the dish—a thick syrup almost at the point of crystalline. She fastened shelled pecans on strings and dipped them into the bubbling sugar to make candy. Then they drank a smoking syrup drink, a punch well fortified with whiskey.

The cooling sweet mass was ladled into containers and transferred to another room, where it was poured into tanks. Gradually, the molasses separated, and from it evolved the crystals, tinged with brown, imperfect and yet to be refined.

When it was all over, the workers were rewarded with a huge feast. Well into the night they danced and sang, as excited about the success of the crop as were Desirée and Jason.

That night, Desirée lay in bed, listening to the blacks celebrating under the huge oak trees below her. Jason lay beside her, sleeping in utter exhaustion after the strenuous weeks of harvesting the cane and refining the sugar. She smiled. A feeling of joy filled her. They had gambled and won.

Chapter 23

Desirée stretched, catlike, and smothered a yawn with her hand. Then she turned to her side and, for a minute, luxuriated in Jason's lingering scent on the bed linens beside her. A wide contented smile spread across her face, a smile that had nothing to do with her happiness over the success of the sugar crop, as it had been the night before.

Her hands cupped her lower abdomen proudly. A thrill of sheer elation ran through her. She was pregnant! After all these years, after she had given up all hope, it had finally happened.

She had put off telling Jason. First, she wanted to be sure this baby was firmly embedded in her, and then she waited for all the excitement and activity of the harvest to calm down. Tonight, she planned to have a quiet dinner for just the two of them. Then she would tell Jason her very special news.

That afternoon, Desirée saw Armond riding up the circular driveway to the plantation house. She walked up on the gallery to meet him.

When he had dismounted and walked up the steps to her, Desirée said, "Good afternoon, Armond. I think Jason is at the factory, overseeing the clean up."

"I didn't come to see Jason, Desirée. I came to see

you."

"Me? Whatever for?"

Armond glanced around him. Seeing a woman sweeping the gallery a few yards from them, he said, "Come inside. I want to talk to you privately."

As soon as they were in the salon, Desirée turned to him, saying, "What in the world are you acting so secretive about?"

Armond took a deep breath, as if steeling himself for something unpleasant, then said, "Beau is back. He wants to see you."

Beau? Why, she hadn't thought of him in years. She tried to summon a mental picture of him, but all she could manage was a vision of him as a child. "Doesn't he know I'm married?"

"Yes, he knows all about Jason. But he still wants to see you."

"Then why doesn't he just come to Whispering Oaks?"

"Because he doesn't want to risk running into Jason. He wants to see you alone."

If he wanted to see her, that must mean he still cared for her, Desirée thought. And he must be bitter. She *had* promised to wait for him. She wondered why it had taken him so long to return to Louisiana. Had he been in a Union prison or so badly wounded it had taken him longer to get back than the others? She imagined him like the other Confederate soldiers she had seen: half starved, broken in body and spirit.

Armond watched Desirée as she mulled over these thoughts, his eyes searching her face for some clue of what she was thinking. He didn't like being put in the position of passing Beau's message to Desirée. He felt like he was betraying Jason, a much better friend to him than Beau had ever been. "Do you still love him?" he finally asked.

480

"Who? Beau?" Desirée asked in disbelief.

"Yes, Beau."

"No, Armond. The only feelings I have for Beau are those of an old friend, one I shared my childhood with. For that reason, I feel I owe him some explanation. I did promise to wait for him."

"Then you'll see him?"

"Yes."

"Where shall I tell Beau you'll meet him?"

Desirée thought for a minute, then said, "Tell Beau I'll meet him on the old wagon road between Terre Doux and Whispering Oaks at four o'clock. By that big oak tree we used to picnic under when we were children. Jason never rides in that direction. I don't think he even knows it's there."

Unknown to either Desirée or Armond, Jason walked past the salon just as Armond was asking Desirée where she'd meet with Beau. The name of Desirée's old betrothed caught Jason's attention and he stopped in mid-stride. Then, hearing Desirée's answer, he was shocked. To him, there was only one plausible reason why Desirée would be arranging a secret rendezvous with her old betrothed: She still loved Beau.

As Armond walked out of the salon, Jason quickly stepped out of sight, so Armond wouldn't see him. There, he stood, stunned and shaken to the very depths of his soul, his whole world crumbling around him.

When Jason finally summoned the courage to walk into the salon and face Desirée, she was gazing out the window with her back to him. Already, she had forgotten Beau, caught up in daydreams of how she was going to tell Jason about their baby. She hugged herself, so full of happiness she felt as if she were going to burst.

Then, hearing Jason's step, she turned, a radiant glow on her face. Jason was stunned by the look of happiness on Desirée's face. Nothing *he* had ever done or said had made her look that happy. Deeply hurt, a bitterness filled him.

"So, the golden boy is back?" he asked in a hard voice.

Jason's question puzzled Desirée, not so much because he knew Beau was back but that he knew what Beau looked like. She had no pictures of Beau. Nor could she remember ever telling Jason that he was blond-headed.

"You're going to see him?" Jason asked.

Realizing Jason must have overheard the conversation, she answered, "Yes, I—"

Before Desirée could offer him an explanation, Jason said in a low, anguished voice, "I think—deep in my heart—I always knew that you still loved Beau. All this time, I've been deceiving myself, thinking that you had come to love me." A bitterness entered his voice. "I should have known that dreams don't come true."

"What are you talking about?"

"When I was a boy, I used to come to Whispering Oaks and stand for hours looking at it, admiring it and promising myself someday I'd own a plantation just like it."

Desirée remembered Jason telling her he had always wanted to own a plantation. "That was your dream?"

"That and more—much more. There was a girl who rode over its grounds, her long chestnut hair trailing behind her. She was my fairy princess. I think I loved her even then—maybe since the beginning of time. I wanted her so badly that I convinced myself we were destined for each other. I should have known it was just a silly dream of a swamp rat."

At the words, "swamp rat," Desirée's head snapped up. That little glimmer teased in the back of her head. She looked deeply into Jason's eyes, eyes that were the same color as the morning mist that rose from the swamps. Then, the recollection that her subconscious had fiercely guarded for so long came bursting through. Jason had been the boy on that fateful day! Many times after that, she had gone back to the edge of the swamp, looking for him, but she had never seen him again. As time passed, she forgot him, the memory locked deep inside her. That was what had drawn her to the swamp. She had been looking for Jason. They *were* destined for each other. And he said he loved her, had always loved her!

Jason totally misinterpreted the shocked look on Desirée's face. He thought she believed that he had deliberately arranged everything to make his dream come true, that he had trapped her into marrying her. Unable to face the anger and hate that he thought she would feel, he turned and walked rapidly from the room.

By the time Desirée recovered from her shock and regained her senses, Jason was gone. She ran into the hall, calling him. Then she searched everywhere in the house, wanting to tell him of *her* love, but she couldn't find him anywhere. Finally, she ran across the plantation lawn to the stables.

Seeing Moses, she called, "Moses, have you seen Jason?"

Moses watched as Desirée hurried up to him, wondering what was going on. First, the massa comes tearing out of the house, looking like death itself and riding off like all the demons in hell were after him, and now Desirée, coming after the massa, looking so apprehensive. "Yes, Miss Desirée, I've seen him. He took his horse and rode off."

"Do you have any idea where he may have gone?"

"No, ma'am."

Desirée glanced down at the watch pinned on her bodice and saw that it was almost time to meet Beau. She really didn't want to go, particularly after everything that had happened. But apparently, Jason had some crazy idea in his head that she still loved Beau. Perhaps, it would be best to go after all. Until she sent Beau firmly on his way, Jason would always wonder and worry.

Making her decision, Desirée said, "Please saddle my horse for me, Moses."

A few minutes later, Desirée galloped her horse down the road, then turned down the rutted old wagon trail, deep in thought. Why had she and Jason waited so long to admit their love to one another? Why had the words been so hard to say? She knew the answer. Pride. No wonder the priests called it one of the cardinal sins. What a destructive emotion it could be. Just look at all the pain it had caused. But then, why had she even needed the words? Jason had shown his love for her everyday, in so many ways. How could she have been so blind and foolish?

Desirée!"

Desirée's head jerked up. She had been so deep in thought that she hadn't even realized she had reached the big oak. She saw Beau standing under the tree, as handsome as he had ever been.

She was shocked by his appearance. He certainly didn't look anything like she had imagined he would. He hadn't lost an ounce of weight, and there wasn't a grey hair in his head or a new line on his face. How had he managed to survive the ravages of war that the rest of them had suffered?

Beau walked up to her and looked up, his blue eyes

dancing. Then he gave her his dazzling smile. As he helped her to dismount, Desirée wondered why that smile had disturbed her. Then she knew. There had been a certain smugness about it.

When Desirée's feet were firmly on the ground, Beau drew her to him and bent his head to kiss her. The thought of any man but Jason kissing her repulsed Desirée. Quickly, she stepped away, asking, "How are you, Beau? Was the war hard on you?"

Beau scowled at Desirée's rejection of his kiss before he answered, "If you mean did I see a lot of fighting, the answer is no. I was an aide to President Davis during the war."

"When did that happen?" Desirée asked in surprise. "You left with Thad."

"Thad and I separated before the battle of Shilo. My father had connections in Richmond and got the position with the president for me."

No wonder he looked the same, Desirée thought. Why, he sat in a safe office the entire war, a position that he wasn't assigned to because of his capabilities, like Jason, but manipulated by his father. And he had come out of the war totally unscathed, while Armond and Jason had been left handicapped with horrible scars. A resentment rose up in her.

But what took him so long to get back? Had he been a part of the military escort taking President Davis to Mexico? Had he been captured in Georgia along with the president and sent to prison with Jefferson Davis? "What took you so long to get back to Louisiana?"

"I've been in Mexico, looking things over," Beau answered. An excited look came over his handsome face. "I'm going to move down there with a group General Jo Shelby is getting together. Maximillian and Napoleon are welcoming us with open arms."

"You'd leave the South?" Desirée asked in a shocked voice.

"The South is dead!" Beau spat. Then he smiled, saying, "We're going to build a new one in Mexico."

Beau's words infuriated Desirée. No, she thought hotly, the South isn't dead! She's just badly wounded and, to recover, she needed all of her loyal people. And Beau, who had claimed to love her so much, was deserting her. Why, he was nothing but a coward. First, hiding behind a desk, and now, running from his responsibilities to his native land. She wondered what she ever saw in him. Why, she didn't even like him!

"Desirée, I want you to go to Mexico with me," Beau said. "I still love you. We'll be married there."

"Married?" Desirée asked in disbelief. "Have you forgotten? I'm already married."

"You were forced into marriage by circumstances beyond your control," Beau replied calmly. "You can get an annulment on grounds of coercion. I'm sure you won't have any trouble getting one, particularly if my friend, Maximillian, puts his weight behind it. He does have considerable influence with the pope, you know."

Beau turned and paced beneath the huge, spread oak, impatiently pushing the long festoons of Spanish moss out of his way as he told her of his plans for them when they reached Mexico.

But Desirée wasn't listening to him. She remembered what Jason had said about Napoleon's having designs on the South, that he feared Louisiana, with its large French population, might even encourage the rest of the South to join up with the French emperor. At the time, she had thought Jason was insane. But Beau had said Napoleon and Maximillian were welcoming the defeated southerners with open arms. She wondered if the South *had* won the war, would Beau have been one of the ones who would encourage it to join up with Napoleon? And then, when the rest of the South balked, would he have rebelled again, like a spoiled child, thinking only of his own selfish needs, instead of the whole? Suddenly, Desirée realized what Jason had been trying to tell her. He fought for the whole, North and South alike, not for the selfish interest of one part of the country.

"Desirée? Are you listening to me?" Beau asked in an impatient voice.

"No, I'm not," Desirée replied calmly.

An angry look came over Beau's face. "What's wrong with you? You don't even act like you're thinking straight."

"No, you're wrong, Beau. I'm thinking straight for the first time in my life." Suddenly, Desirée had to get back to Jason. She had so many things to tell him. She whirled and started walking to her horse.

"Where are you going?" Beau demanded.

Desirée turned, saying, "To my husband."

"Why?" Beau asked in disbelief. Then a sudden thought occurred to him. "Are you going to have his baby? Is that why you're going back to him? I don't care, Desirée. I still want you. I'll raise the child just like it was my own."

The thought of Beau's raising her child disgusted Desirée. "*Non*, Beau, I'm not going *back* to Jason, because I never left him. I'd never leave him, not for anything or anyone. I love him too much."

"How can you love him?" Beau asked angrily. "He's a Yankee! Your enemy!"

"*Non*, Jason was never my enemy, or the South's either, for that matter. And Jason isn't a Yankee. He's a man, a strong, wonderful man. I don't deserve him, but I'll be damned if I'm going to lose him."

Beau looked at her with a mixture of disbelief and disgust. "You're not the same girl I knew," he said stiffly.

Desirée laughed. "*Non*, I'm not—and thank God for that! I've been such a silly, little child. So foolish. I don't know how Jason managed to put up with me all those years."

Desirée turned and walked to her horse. She led the animal to a big rock and mounted. Then, without a backward glance at the astonished man watching her, she rode off, whipping her horse in her excitement to get back to Jason.

Jason had been standing behind a large bush by the driveway when Desirée rode off to meet Beau. Long after she had left, he had stood there, brooding. He had married her knowing that she didn't love him, but now, believing that she thought he had deliberately tricked her into marrying him, he couldn't bear the thought of living with her hatred the rest of his life. He decided he'd offer her an annulment. Since she hadn't entered the marriage of her own free will, and there were no children involved, he felt sure the church would grant them one. Then she could marry Beau, the man she had always loved. She'd be happy.

Jason's decision offered him no comfort, even if it would bring Desirée happiness, something that had always been foremost in his mind. He felt as if his life were seeping from him. Without Desirée, there was no future, no reason for living, no nothing.

Finally, Jason stepped from behind the bush and walked up the driveway, leading his horse behind him. With his shoulders slumped in defeat and his limp more pronounced than it had been in years, he looked the picture of utter despair. Then, hearing the sound of a horse galloping, he turned.

Seeing Desirée ride up, he stared at her, thinking

that she couldn't have returned from her meeting with her beloved so soon. Riding across Whispering Oak's spacious lawn, with her long, chestnut hair trailing behind her, he decided that his dream had come back to haunt him once again. He watched silently, grimly, as she jumped off her horse and ran to him, still thinking she was a vision his mind had conjured up to torture him.

Desirée raced up to Jason and stopped before him, her dark eyes dancing with excitement. "He's gone, Jason. I sent Beau on his way for good. I never loved him. Why, I don't even like him."

Jason stared at her, finding it hard to believe she was real.

"I love you, Jason," Desirée said, wondering why he was looking at her so strangely. Didn't he want her anymore? "Do you—do you still want me?" she asked in a hesitant voice.

Jason had waited all his life to hear those words of love from Desirée. He was too choked up with emotion to answer. He simply opened his arms to her.

Desirée rushed into Jason's strong arms, her own special haven. Tears of relief and happiness streamed down her face. She looked up into his misty-green eyes, shimmering with their own tears. "I remembered everything when you said swamp rat. I knew that day we were destined for each other. I looked for you everyday after that, but I never saw you again. Why didn't you come back?"

"My mother died, and my father and I moved away."

Desirée nodded, then said, "Over the years, I forgot. Or at least, a part of me forgot. But something kept drawing me to that swamp. I didn't realize it, but I was still looking for you." And then, in a rush of words, she said, "Oh, Jason, I've been so wrong about so many things. I understand now why you fought for the union. You were—"

Jason placed his fingers over her lips, saying softly, "Sssh, it's not important now. All that matters is that you're here in my arms and that we love each other."

He pulled her closer, and Desirée slipped her arms about his waist. For awhile, they stood that way, content just to hold each other.

They turned and walked across the lawn of Whispering Oaks, his arm about her waist and her head resting on his shoulder. The long, grey Spanish moss fluttered in the breeze.

Desirée looked up at the ancient oak trees, their thick, spreading branches hovering over them protectively. "Listen, Jason," she said in a soft voice. "They're whispering to us. What do you think they're saying?"

Jason cocked his head and listened. Then he smiled, saying, "No, *cherie*, I don't think it's the oaks talking to us this time. I think it's some old friends of mine—the gods of fate—laughing at me and saying, 'See how stupid you mortals are? Didn't we promise you? And all the time you thought we didn't know what we were doing, that we were only playing games.' "

"What in earth are you talking about?"

"I'll tell you some other time. All I want to do right now is hold you and show you how much I love you."

His dark head dipped, and Desirée lifted hers to meet him. Their lips locked in a kiss that transcended the physical and reached into the spiritual planes. It was more than just the union of two souls. It was a fusing—the final, ultimate consummation.

The god of fate smiled down on them, proud of their work. They knew that nothing good came from hasty labor. Perfection took time. Patiently and diligently, they had built this link between two souls, molding it and shaping it, forging it with trials and tribulations, tempering it with pain and anguish, until it was a link so strong and powerful that nothing in heaven, hell—or anything in between—could ever break it.

The gods of fate weren't the only ones watching Desirée and Jason as they kissed. Moses and Mammy Lou stood in the front doorway of the plantation house, tears streaming down the old woman's face.

Moses looked down at her and frowned, asking, "What're you crying about, old woman?"

Mammy lifted her head. The tears glistened on her black, chubby cheeks. "I'm crying because I'm so happy." Her big bosom swelled with pride, and a broad smile spread across her face. "My baby has finally grown up."

Epilogue

The South lay ravaged after the long, bloody, bitter war. Many of the great plantations, the symbol of the South itself, were destroyed forever. More would fall during the difficult years of Reconstruction. But some would rise again—a few literally from the ashes. Although they would never be the big business that they once were, and their families would never know the grand style of living they had known before the war, these valiant survivors would go on into the next generation—and the next—carrying their proud heritage with them.

The next spring, Desirée gave birth to a lusty son, the exact replica of Jason. Another son was born two years later, followed by two beautiful, spirited daughters.

During the succeeding years, Whispering Oaks continued to grow and prosper, eventually becoming one of the most beautiful showplaces of the South. And in the golden years of their lives, Desirée and Jason sat beneath the huge, spreading oaks, watching their great-grandchildren play and listening to the whispering of the Spanish moss. Occasionally, their eyes would meet and they would smile at each other, knowing that their destiny had been fulfilled.

CONTEMPORARY ROMANCE
FROM ZEBRA

THE BEST IN REGENCIES FROM ZEBRA

PASSION'S LADY   (1545, $2.95)
by Sara Blayne

She was a charming rogue, an impish child—and a maddeningly alluring woman. If the Earl of Shayle knew little else about her, he knew she was going to marry him. As a bride, Marie found a temporary hiding place from her past, but could not escape from the Earl's shrewd questions—or the spark of passion in his eyes.

WAGER ON LOVE   (1577, $2.50)
by Prudence Martin

Only a cynical rogue like Nicholas Ruxart would choose a bride on the basis of a careless wager, and then fall in love with her grey-eyed sister Jane. It was easy for Jane to ignore the advances of this cold gambler, but she found denying her tender yearnings for him to be much harder.

RECKLESS HEART   (1679, $2.50)
by Lois Arvin Walker

Rebecca had met her match in the notorious Earl of Compton. Not only did he decline the invitation to her soiree, but he found it amusing when her horse landed her in the middle of Compton Creek. If this was another female scheme to lure him into marriage the Earl swore Rebecca would soon learn she had the wrong man, a man with a blackened reputation.

DANCE OF DESIRE   (1757, $2.95)
by Sarah Fairchilde

Lord Sherbourne almost ran Virginia down on horseback, then he silenced her indignation with a most ungentlemanly kiss. Seething with outrage, the lovely heiress decided the insufferable lord was in need of a royal setdown. And she knew the way to go about it . . .

Available wherever paperbacks are sold, or order direct from the Publisher. Send cover price plus 50¢ per copy for mailing and handling to Zebra Books, Dept. 1802, 475 Park Avenue South, New York, N.Y. 10016. DO NOT SEND CASH.